MOSCOW
STING

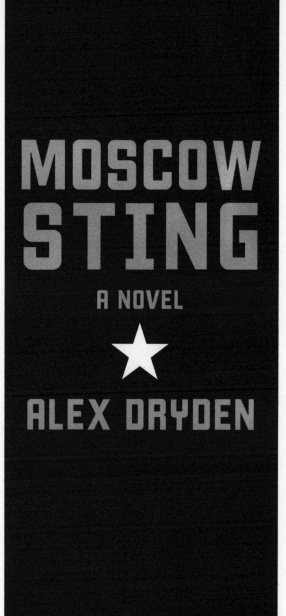

MOSCOW STING

A NOVEL

ALEX DRYDEN

ecco

An Imprint of HarperCollinsPublishers

HarperCollins books may be purchased for educational, business, or sales promotional use. For information, please write: Special Markets Department, HarperCollins Publishers, 10 East 53rd Street, New York, NY 10022.

FIRST EDITION

Designed by Suet Chong

Library of Congress Cataloging-in-Publication Data has been applied for.

ISBN: 978-0-06-196684-2

10 11 12 13 14   ID/RRD   10 9 8 7 6 5 4 3 2 1

ACKNOWLEDGMENTS

There are many individuals I have to thank for providing me with insight into the rise of America's private intelligence companies since the 1990s. They work both in national intelligence agencies and in the private companies themselves. I am grateful for their help and for the insight they have given me into the unintended consequences of private intelligence replacing national intelligence agencies.

MOSCOW
STING

—————— PROLOGUE ——————

JANUARY 2008

A DRIAN CAREW GLARED THROUGH the rain-streaked window of a British intelligence pool Vauxhall Carlton as if the application of his undoubtedly impressive willpower could unsnarl the traffic. Cars were bumper to bumper going west out of London, and the weather was only making things worse.

His driver, Ray, with fifteen years of service and an almost Zen calm by comparison with his boss, half turned towards the rear seat.

"We'll be through this in a minute or two, sir." His words barely made their way through the noise of the rain drumming on the roof of the car.

With his usual expression of muscular irritation in place—teeth clamped, jaw muscles twitching—Adrian coldly addressed his reply to the side window.

"Never mind."

At sixty-three years old, the former SAS hero, military intelligence wizard, and later chief of MI6 Moscow Station, had earlier in the day gleaned from one of his eyes and ears at Joint Intelligence that he had been elevated to the informal short list for the top position at MI6; Spymaster in Chief, the media called it.

He should be out celebrating, he thought, not trotting off abroad like some messenger boy—and to bloody Finland, of all places. But the Russians had insisted that they would see him, and him alone.

Dimly now through the fogged-up window, Adrian eyed the scene and piled on his choleric distaste for the mass of humanity that was getting in his way. As the car headed westwards, he noted the decline of London's grandeur into ever greater human shabbiness with every mile they left the centre behind them. The city's clean cut-stone heart at Whitehall degenerated, first to the redbrick postwar semis of Shepherd's Bush and then on past the shades-of-grey plastic shop fronts at London's ragged edges, whose bleakness and grime seemed to leach into the countryside.

Adrian came this way at weekends, but only after dark on a Friday night, when he was going down to the country house in Hampshire where his wife, Penny, now spent most of her time. During the week he remained in London, with its gentleman's clubs for male ritual and his discreet mistress, Hazel from the Far Eastern Desk, for female diversion.

He wiped the window with the back of his hand. The sky was thick with angry black clouds. It would be a bumpy flight, he thought without concern, and a noisy one. The vintage RAF transport plane that had been press-ganged into giving him a last-minute lift on a routine flight to Helsinki was hardly five star.

Adrian listened to the swish of the steady, incessant rain turning to dirty brown spray under the car's wheels. It was a downpour; the heavens were throwing it at the tarmac so hard the rain was bouncing up again. The wipers cleared gushing waterfalls of rain from the windscreen every few seconds. The violent weather had broken up what was otherwise a typically monotonous January afternoon.

"We're going to be a few minutes late, I'm afraid, sir," Ray informed him.

"They'll wait," Adrian snapped from the back seat.

The whole affair, this journey to Brize Norton's military airport included, was suddenly reminding him of the days of the Cold War, and the thought briefly buoyed his spirits.

Short in stature, with a flop of slightly greasy brown hair over his forehead, Adrian possessed a stocky, muscular frame maintained through regular games of squash. His tried and trusted modus operandi, from his days in the jungles of Borneo to the present-day jungles of Whitehall, was to storm through the world sucking the air from everyone in his way. He was the embodiment of preemptive attack, one colleague had observed. Others offered their amateur psychological diagnosis that Adrian behaved as if the planet had done him some grievous disservice.

His physical deportment and mental attitude was one of pugnacious defensiveness. Under the good-life flab that now showed signs of mushrooming around his waist, his wired-up muscles were ready to spring, his fists regularly clenched, and the dark eyes in his livid red face rarely rested.

Adrian was never as meticulous about anything as he was in matters of revenge, and that was the purpose of his trip this evening.

It was revenge against a broken home that had driven him to excel in the military, some said, and revenge against his small stature that drove him to graduate from SAS headquarters at Hereford in the 1960s ahead of all his contemporaries. Others pointed to a sort of muddled revenge against the Establishment while all the time wanting to be deep inside it. This, they said, was what had propelled him upwards in MI6, now almost to the top. But it was a particular revenge that had brought him out of his lair today.

It had taken Adrian fourteen months just to get to this point, but at last here he was, at first base. He was now in possession of an identity; the identity of an assassin, with a name, address, phone number, and probably an inside length measurement, given the heightened efforts of the office researchers on this particular assignment.

For this assassin, a Russian hood by the name of Grigory Bykov, had terminated the life of one of the Secret Intelligence Service's own officers; and one of a select few Adrian liked to call his "best boys."

Diligent researchers on the third floor had gladly embraced overtime without pay. Finn had been family, popular too—even loved. Interdepartmental cooperation had been unusually fluid, and the focused urgency of revenge for Finn's murder had driven everyone on, Adrian included, until the task was done.

Drip-fed leads from sources as diverse as a disaffected KGB officer in Azerbaijan, to the owner of a steam bath and brothel in the Siberian city of Irkutsk, had led conclusively to Grigory Bykov.

Finally the researchers had drawn up Bykov's biography with meticulous care. In short, Bykov was a petty criminal and south Moscow mafioso, coached to KGB standards and then inducted into the Russian foreign intelligence service east of Moscow, known as the Forest. There they had primed him for this single murder. After all this expert training, Grigory Bykov had finally tracked down Finn in Paris, then killed him with a deadly nerve agent—type unknown—that he'd smeared on the steering wheel of Finn's rental car.

That was the Russian side of things.

The British side was more complex. Finn had once been one of Adrian's "best boys"—that was the truth of it. Adrian had recruited Finn personally at Cambridge, back in 1985, back in Gorbachev's time. And no matter that Finn had turned his back on the Secret Intelligence Service in later years; Finn was still Adrian's property, in death as well as in life. Nobody—Vladimir Putin included—was going to get away with ordering the death of one of Adrian's best boys.

In his grey silk suit and expensive Oxford blue cashmere overcoat, both of which were courtesy of Penny's private fortune rather than his SIS pay, Adrian might look like a toothless catwalk panther, but underneath it all the animal core was still the same one that had driven him through Far Eastern jungles forty years before, where he'd shot or cut the throats of Commie insurgents, and saved the world from Putin's KGB predecessors.

Adrian began to stoke his own righteous anger now, in preparation for the meeting with Sergei Limov, Putin's go-between for this evening. More than three days it had taken Finn to die, thanks to Bykov, in the trunk of a car somewhere in Germany, it was said, though Finn's body had been delivered anonymously to the British embassy in Berlin.

There'd been a note attached to Finn's body, laid out respectfully on the back seat of a Cherokee Jeep, which was abandoned outside the embassy. The note was addressed to Adrian personally. "You betrayed him in life," it said. "Honour him in death."

Who would deliver a body, let alone one as hot as that one? And who was it, with Finn's corpse on their hands, who dared express such anger—and such accuracy—at the steps of the British embassy? The note pointed him towards two people.

Adrian's mind turned once again to Finn's woman, Colonel Anna Resnikov. Was it she, Anna, formerly the youngest female colonel in the KGB, who had first betrayed her country, then run away with Finn and married him? Had she in cold fury delivered the dead body of her lover and, later, her husband? Trained to the highest degree you could reach in Russia's foreign intelligence service, the SVR, she was more than capable of it—she possessed all the cunning and subterfuge needed to pull off a feat like that.

Or, more interestingly perhaps, Adrian wondered, was it Mikhail who had slyly delivered Finn's body?

Over the previous Friday afternoon, before he went down to Penny's country house for the weekend, for another boring Saturday-night dinner party with her friends, Adrian had read through Mikhail's file once again, even though he knew it almost by heart.

Code name Mikhail had approached Finn in February 1995 in

Moscow, where Finn was using the cover of the British second secretary for trade and investment at the embassy. Right from the start, Mikhail would talk only to Finn. That was the deal. From day one, code name Mikhail was adamant that he would communicate with—and be known to—nobody else, and so Finn's strategic importance had rocketed.

For the next five years, Mikhail had fed the highest quality intelligence to the British, via Finn. It was so good that it had kept the British right up there, sitting at the high table with the Americans, for a while.

And then, in 2000, Vladimir Putin ascended to power in a well-planned KGB coup. Mikhail was so close to Putin that—as Finn put it—"he practically shits in Putin's bathroom." Mikhail was one of the tiny group of so-called Patriots deep within Putin's innermost circle. The quality, the importance, of his information was greater than ever.

But at that moment, politics back home intervened. The prime minister insisted that Vladimir Putin was a man he could do business with. The American president George W. Bush added the honorarium that he had "looked into Putin's soul" and liked what he saw.

Suddenly Mikhail's warnings about Putin's Russia were off-message. The politicians didn't want to hear what he had to say. Under orders from Downing Street, the SIS was told that Mikhail must be dropped—exposed as a fraud, was the method the politicians suggested. And so Adrian—promotion and a knighthood at the front of his mind—followed orders. Mikhail was excised.

But Finn hadn't followed orders. He left the SIS, rather than see his priceless source trashed for reasons of political expediency. And Anna defected from Russia, just for him, not for some cause, and they married. A love story, Adrian supposed, if such a thing existed.

For the next six years, the two of them and a team Finn put together, financed from Russian exiles' money, independently pursued Mikhail's leads, which the British refused to touch. And Mikhail's material was as good as it had ever been. It was so hot, in fact, that Finn had been murdered for it.

The British government's craving to be on friendly terms with Vladimir Putin had cost Britain and the West five years of high-level intelligence. But it had cost Finn his life.

Now, there was a new twist. The wheel had turned full circle. At the dawn of 2008 politics intervened for a second time, and the attitude to Putin's regime had gone into reverse. It turned out you couldn't do business with Putin, after all, and there was apparently nothing very nice to be seen in his soul, if indeed he had one. Orders went out that Mikhail was to be rehabilitated. "Find Mikhail" was the cry.

But with Finn dead, and former colonel Anna Resnikov disappeared, nobody knew how to contact Mikhail.

One of the many reasons for the new policy towards Russia was Finn's assassination and its aftermath. Grigory Bykov's reward for the murder of a British intelligence officer was the title of Hero of the Russian Federation—Russia's highest award—and a seat in Russia's parliament, the Duma. These days, the Russians made their killers MPs.

Adrian looked at the road ahead and broke away from his thoughts for a moment.

"Foot down, Ray," he demanded. They were on the motorway, and the traffic had stretched itself apart.

"There's a weather speed limit, sir," Ray objected.

"Never mind the bloody speed limit."

Adrian settled back in his seat. Something else—now it was the damn speed limit—was getting in his way.

Adrian was not planning to be as generous to Grigory Bykov as the Kremlin had been. He hadn't spent fourteen months finding Bykov, in order to have a British diplomatic rap over the knuckles administered to the Russian ambassador.

At a claret-fuelled encounter with the Perrier-drinking Teddy Parkinson, the Joint Intelligence chief, at the Special Forces Club in Knightsbridge, Adrian had demanded Bykov's life. "An eye for an eye . . . just as it should be, always has been, and always shall be, Teddy."

To return murder for murder was, after all, the standard procedure. An intelligence officer had been the victim, and MI6, Adrian's Secret Intelligence Service, was not to be viewed as a patsy. That would be tantamount to inviting future acts of murder against SIS officers, not to mention a savage blow to the morale of Finn's colleagues.

Nevertheless Adrian had known that he would need to lobby Teddy Parkinson hard and cleverly to obtain this natural justice. A British government that could blithely march its armies to slaughter in Iraq—against an abstract enemy and on the basis of false information, to boot—was surprisingly squeamish when it came to dealing death to an actual person; a person with a name and an identity. No matter that the evidence against Bykov was overwhelmingly clear. Without a doubt, the state-sponsored, state-trained, and state-armed Russian hood had murdered Finn, a British intelligence officer.

And so Adrian had entertained Teddy on his own ground at the Special Forces Club, where the beneficial results of force were everywhere in evidence; in the photographs of heroes on its walls, in the letters written in the blood of Gestapo torture victims who had died rather than give up British secrets. The club was a place where bureaucrats like Teddy were viewed with, at best, suspicion.

Adrian, florid of face and with a pugnacious tenacity to match, wanted to show his superior what intelligence work at the sharp end was really about. Unlike himself, Teddy had never been in the armed forces, and dealing with Grigory Bykov was going to be brute work. In his own take-no-prisoners diplomatic style, Adrian had wanted to remind Teddy of both of these facts.

"But he's a Russian MP, Adrian," Teddy had pointed out with exasperation, when Adrian, displeased at not getting his demands immediately met, was rounding off lunch with a serviceable cognac. "It makes things complicated," Parkinson reasoned.

"That's why they made him an MP, isn't it? So we would back off," Adrian insisted, leaning right in across the table so that Parkinson almost flinched. "Are we going to let rogue states go around assassinating our officers just because the KGB turns its murderers into MPs?"

"Russia is not a rogue state, Adrian," Parkinson said mildly.

"It just smells like one, looks like one, and acts like one," Adrian said. "What if it had been Syrian intelligence who had murdered Finn? Would we be pussyfooting off to the Middle East requesting a fair trial?"

Parkinson had dutifully delivered to Adrian the message from the prime minister's office. First, before extreme measures were even contemplated, they were to demand Bykov's extradition at intelligence level, away from the media. That way the Russians had the opportunity to ditch Bykov without losing face.

But Adrian was well aware that these new Russians were never going to give Bykov up. Putin's Russia had made it clear a dozen times in the past eight years that they would flaunt their old-style power and arrogance with complete immunity.

And so, sitting in the car now, he knew this was first base only; a winter evening flight to Helsinki; a meeting with one of Putin's stooges, followed by the Russians' inevitable rejection of the prime minister's ponderous and deliberately indecisive plan.

Make a reasonable request for the hood Grigory Bykov's extradition? There was nobody reasonable left in power in Russia.

Outside the window of the car, the rain was backing off a little. The day was heading into night without ever having put in a real appearance. The SIS car turned off the main road and ran the few miles to the airport along country lanes clogged with mud and excrement left by a herd of cows being moved to a new field.

High winds battered and shoved the twin-engine converted reconnaissance plane across the North Sea as the temperature outside plummeted. Adrian rubbed his hands, more from nostalgia for the old days than from the cold. It was good to feel he was on a mission, even a mission he had little respect for, rather than sitting behind a desk. As they descended onto Helsinki's military airfield, the snow was driving down hard, and he spotted the lights of the snowploughs at the end of the runway. An embassy car met him, and he sped away without formalities.

The meeting was to take place in a rooftop conference room at the Heikinen Hotel. The high windows in the long room framed a fine view of Helsinki's marketplace and the twinkling lights of the waterfront beyond, through the driving snow. Distant sounds of splashing and shouts from a hot tub permeated the otherwise silent venue. A party of loud, naked Finns were disporting themselves, then rolling in the rooftop snow, exiting to a sauna, and finally coming back for more—all lubricated with several bottles of vodka.

The Russian, Sergei Limov, had refused to come to the British embassy, and Adrian had rejected the Russian offer of "hospitality," for obvious reasons. The Heikinen conference room was hastily swept for bugs by both sides.

Now Adrian sat opposite the huge figure of Sergei Limov. The heavy-lipped, frowning multibillionaire owner of oil transportation and shipping companies was a trusted servant of Vladimir Putin from the old days, and KGB to the core. In the Soviet 1980s, Adrian recalled, Limov had been the chief Soviet trade representative in western Europe. But he had morphed since those days of Russia's atrophied economic policies to become one of the world's richest men, due partly to his own cunning, but mainly to his KGB and Mafia sponsors.

There were two bottles of Finnish mineral water and a bottle of Finnish vodka, neither of which they had touched so far, on the table.

Briefly, Adrian presented the case against Bykov and thrust a file of backup documents across the table, which Limov ignored and looked as if he planned to continue ignoring. Now Adrian waited for the ritual slap in the face, but his anger was directed more at Teddy Parkinson than at the Russians. The request itself, his own presence, and the cap-in-hand nature of British policy in general towards the Russians seemed designed to humiliate him.

"What have you got for us in return for Bykov?" Limov said at last, leaning back in the seat that was too small for him, and fiddling with the diamond-encrusted gold Rolex watch on his right wrist as if he had more important things to do. Adrian noted all this with growing fury.

So they wanted a trade. What did Limov—or Putin—want? Adrian wondered. Did they expect the Russian assets of British Petroleum to be handed over to the Kremlin on a plate? The Houses of bloody Parliament, perhaps?

"It's not a deal, Sergei," Adrian replied smoothly. "It's a matter of international law. The one you're signed up to. A Russian citizen has murdered a British citizen."

"Ah, justice," Limov said, as if it were something stuck to the sole of his shoe.

"Call it what you like," Adrian said generously. "As I say, it's a matter of international law. Either Russia obeys what it's signed up for, or it doesn't."

He could see Limov blanch at the word *obey*, just as he'd intended.

Limov leaned across the table and picked up the bottle of vodka and two glasses with one huge hand. He poured Adrian a glass and then one for himself.

But Adrian withdrew a silver flask from the inside pocket of his silk suit and poured himself a nip of Scotch into the silver cup that served as a lid. He raised it towards Limov.

"You can't be too careful these days," he said, and drank it.

"What are we drinking to?" Limov said, as Adrian helped himself to another shot.

"Why don't you choose, Sergei?" he said.

"To justice," Limov replied, and roared with laughter. He drank the vodka in one gulp, placed the glass on the table as if making a winning chess move, and leaned in.

"What we want is Resnikov," he said. "That's the deal."

So. That was the quid pro quo, Adrian thought. They wanted Finn's woman, Colonel Anna, their beautiful but vanished KGB defector who had given the Russians, the British, and all the rest of them the slip.

"As far as I know," Adrian said with icy calmness, "she hasn't murdered anyone."

"Worse. A lot worse," Limov replied.

"So this is a refusal to give us Bykov to face a trial," Adrian stated, and he realised that this was what he'd hoped for all along. He wanted Bykov dead, on his orders, not in court.

"We want her," Limov replied simply, without being drawn into Adrian's refusal scenario. "Then you can have your justice."

"I'll convey the Kremlin's thoughts to London, in that case."

"When we have the woman, we can give you Bykov," the Russian said. "With pleasure," he added.

In the car that drove him through the now softly falling snow back to the embassy where he was staying overnight, Adrian thought of two things. The first was that the Kremlin would happily give up a Hero of Russia in return for what they wanted. Their cynicism was boundless. It outstripped even his own.

But the second, unexpected piece of information was that the Russians didn't have her. Colonel Anna was still free; she was still out there somewhere, an asset to be won by whoever got there first. And with her would surely come the main prize itself, the source he had been instructed to reinstate: code name Mikhail.

PART
ONE

---- 1 ----

LOGAN HALLORAN IDLED ALONG the narrow pavement in the Marais district of Paris, glancing in the shop windows. Stopping in a shaded doorway, he noticed in the reflection that he had shaved. He didn't shave regularly. He did nothing, in fact, with regularity. He was, it occurred to him, an "irregular" in every way and had always been, even when he'd had what people called a proper job.

At thirty-six years old, he'd been described as having a face with a "lived-in quality," a little more than his age justified. But his reflection in the windows ironed out these details, showing an athletic, rangy figure, encased loosely in an old off-white linen suit. The reflection didn't show his rich tan, or his intense deep blue eyes, or the faded scar on his forehead. Neither did it show his natural expression of amused interest in the world around him.

Logan checked his watch. He was early.

He looked into the shop with a kind of admiration that never decreased, no matter how many times he visited Paris. The French knew about commerce; small, specialised commerce, quality, not quantity. Finely complex chocolate sculptures seduced his eyes through the window of the *chocolaterie*. As he walked farther along, the rich smell of tobacco filled his nostrils from a *tabac* next door. There were fox-hunting clothes on mannequins in the shop after that; its windows looked as if they hadn't been cleaned since Louis XVI hunted the fields of Versailles.

It was a street of variegated delights, he observed, not a mall, not a grey mush of globalised names. Each had its own identity.

He stepped off the narrow pavement to allow two laughing women to pass. They were in their early twenties, Logan guessed; his own kind, Americans—and tourists, a rarer sight in Europe in the past few years. Logan recognised the accent of his home state of Pennsylvania.

The women's eyes lingered slightly longer than necessary on the man who'd moved aside for them. Logan was smiling easily at them, apparently to encourage their laughter.

They returned his smile with a lack of constraint that, if he hadn't been on his way somewhere, might have encouraged him to say something that backed up the invitation of his smile.

But he walked on.

The street was full of tourists. Paris was emptied of Parisians now that it was August, and replenished with visitors. The older, established restaurants were closed for the French vacation, and the waiters left behind to serve the visitors in pavement cafés—as a punishment, they seemed to think—were surlier than usual, the heavy heat sweating out tempers that were short enough at the best of times.

Identity hung for a moment in Logan's thoughts. Perhaps it was triggered by the individual nature of the shops he was passing. But introspection never troubled Logan for long. He was a watcher, a listener, a man who looked outwards rather than in; a highly trained expert in visual observation who could spot the faintest movement of an enemy on a distant hillside.

Logan could also analyse the mood and even the intentions of friend or enemy in seconds. He possessed the knack of ruthlessly forming in his mind a usually accurate critique of others. He knew how to elicit the responses he wanted from people—like the women he'd just passed.

Logan's start in life—born into a wealthy family who'd lived three generations in southern Pennsylvania—and his own natural talents had promised great things. If anything, his many advantages—on the sports field, in the classroom, in social circles, and particularly with women—had threatened to be so diverse and successful that they could have led, as his father had warned, to his being spoiled for choice. But he had somehow kept all the balls in the air and progressed smoothly to Harvard, where, in the course of earning a summa cum laude law degree, he had been approached by the CIA, in the person of his recruiter, Burt Miller.

For Logan, it was an offer he couldn't refuse. Everything had come so easily for him that all that piqued his interest were new challenges. Burt Miller's huge personality and Logan's own lack of direction had made the decision for him.

Was that his identity? he wondered now on this Paris street in this late, bright August afternoon. One that was laid over him by Burt Miller and the many other gurulike figures in his childhood—not to mention the numerous women of his adult years? Other people thought Logan had a superb mind—and they were right—but they didn't see this unwillingness to look inside himself. There was an unexplored place there.

He continued up the street, weaving past the carefree tourists.

For nearly ten years now he'd been walking streets like this. They may not have had the style, the panache, of this one, but still the weariness of the footpad, the watcher, now welled up in Logan. In his old haunts in Bratislava, Belgrade, Sarajevo, Zagreb, Podgorica, with occasional visits to London, Paris, or New York, he had paced and apparently idled while what he was really doing was waiting and observing; the man on the outside looking in, the man who went to others, not they to him.

Since his disgrace—and subsequent exit from CIA employment—Logan's lot had been that of the freelancer, but not to create newspaper stories. Logan was a freelancer of secrets.

For a moment he looked up at the faded red shop front of a fabrics atelier and imagined, in gold lettering, the words "Logan Halloran—Purveyor of Secrets" written on the cross beam. It would be a perfect fit in this street of specialists.

He turned off the rue du Temple toward the place where he would meet his contact, deciding to walk rather than take a taxi. It was hot, the sun still blazing at six in the evening, but in the narrow streets he could pick the shady side when the heat became oppressive.

The man he was to meet in half an hour was a former and potential source for him and, like him, a denizen of the secret world.

Thomas Plismy had spent most of his working life inside the French foreign intelligence service, the DGSE. Plismy had been a contact of Logan's ever since the glory days when Logan was an agent under the guiding hand of the CIA station in Belgrade, the days when he was known by colleagues as "Lucky Logan." But that had all gone wrong, and now, unlike Logan, Thomas still had the security of a government job. Logan's thoughts were at once pricked by the long bitterness that memory contained.

Some once called Logan the best intelligence officer the CIA had in Europe's southeastern sector, the "Balkan beat," as the British called it. But then a deskman somewhere in Washington or Virginia had saved his own skin by flaying Logan's, and he became the fall guy for someone else's mistake in the Serbian war.

And so, at thirty-six years old, Logan had nearly a decade behind him doing what he was doing this evening, meeting contacts like Plismy, looking for a niche, an entry point, like a lone mountaineer on a sheer rock face. Logan was searching for a handhold of a different sort—some piece of information he could develop and add value to. And then sell.

Since his fall from grace, he'd sold secrets to anyone; to his former masters in America first of all, then to anyone else who had the cash. He often sold the same secrets more than once, to opposing sides in the world's many secret intelligence wars.

Logan wondered, as he often did these days, how much longer he could go on chasing shadows. As so often, when this loneliness began to take him over, he thought of the life that he might have had, of his daughter Angelica and her mother, who he'd married when he was twenty-two years old. She had gone on to marry another man, a lawyer as it happened, and he hadn't seen his daughter in six years.

But this evening was going to be different. Plismy was a kind of friend, he supposed. Logan vaguely thought he liked him better than most he dealt with. They would drink first, then dine somewhere Plismy knew that soared in quality above the tourist miasma—such places could be found, even in the dog days of August. Then they would go to a club, looking for paid girls. Plismy knew a lot of good places for that, Logan remembered.

But even though the meeting was more social than usual, Logan was working just the same. He was always working, he thought. That was the lot of the freelancer. No hours, no boss, no routine—it all sounded good until "no hours" turned into "all hours" and "no boss" into "no structure" and "no routine" into "chaos"; until work became life and vice versa.

The basic skill he deployed in all his meetings was to delude his contacts into believing that he was there simply to enjoy their company. Quite simply, he fielded what was perhaps his greatest skill and curse—his charm. Logan was everybody's friend, and nobody's. By this artifice Logan made people like Plismy freer in their speech, more indiscreet with him than they would otherwise be. Plismy, in particular, was always good for gossip.

Logan loped up past the Pompidou Centre and down the rue de Rivoli, into an office district a walk away from the Tuileries. The tourists were absent here; there were no shops, just hidden courtyards with ancient paving behind huge old wooden doors that abutted the modern office fronts slapped onto the same old stone.

Down one of these silent streets, he saw the bar sign, L'Algérien, a hundred yards away.

He stepped into the gloom of the small, neat establishment, which sold beer and wine. Simple wooden chairs and round tables with plastic cloths dotted a chipped Islamic tiled floor in faded green. The bar counter was made of polished, gleaming zinc, in the old-fashioned French style.

He saw Plismy sitting at the far end of the counter, sipping a *coupe de vin.*

It was an odd choice of Plismy's, this bar, Logan thought. Forty years before, Plismy had been yanking out the fingernails of Algerians like the one who served behind the zinc counter. He'd fought France's secret war on the ground and in the torture chambers of Algiers against the country's independence. Yet this was his favourite bar in Paris, he'd once told Logan.

Did he come to gloat? France had lost the war. No, he thought. Plismy took a sadistic glee being in such close proximity to a man like those he'd tormented and who now had to serve him.

But it was a good bar too, he thought, an old bar of the type you could find everywhere back in the days of the Fourth Republic. Maybe a more decent nostalgia for those days played a part too, who knew?

Plismy was a large man with a pitted face like a cactus with the thorns extracted. That was his nickname at the DGSE. Cactus. The Frenchman's oily face gleamed, and his thinned hair was flattened to his skull by sweat. His dark southern eyes bored into you. The vinous paunch that took decades to create, unlike a beer drinker's, rested comfortably—naturally, Logan thought—on a black leather briefcase worn bare in numerous places, trapping it in its fold. With his thick neck, thick hands, and thick thighs that filled ample light grey trousers, Plismy was like a French rugby prop who'd seen better days.

Logan watched the Frenchman look to his right, toward a wall mirror with a lime green frame, so that he could see Logan approaching from his left. When he was sure it was Logan, Plismy turned to face him.

"Good. Now we can get a bottle," Plismy said, grateful for his companion's arrival. "You're still allowed to drink in America, I suppose?"

He grinned and showed a set of smoker's teeth that turned darker brown the closer they approached the gums.

"In the privacy of your own Dumpster," Logan replied.

Plismy laughed. It was a staccato noise that contained no humour. Then, as he nodded abruptly to the Algerian, his smile evaporated, replaced by a scowl. The stooped Algerian barman didn't need to be told, Logan noticed. He was used to Plismy treating him like a dumb animal, knew what he wanted, and didn't expect any courtesy.

"I didn't expect to find you," Logan said. "What are you doing in Paris, Thomas?" He took the high stool next to Plismy. "Why aren't you on the Côte d'Azur? Getting a tan."

"The Anglo-Saxons destroyed it years ago, that's why. And now the Slavs are scoffing up the leftovers like the dogs they are."

"Jews and blacks are off the hook this time, then," Logan replied.

"This time." Plismy laughed. "I'm an uncomplicated man, Logan."

"Some might call it 'Neanderthal.'"

Plismy's face darkened, then broke into a smile. Logan knew how to play Plismy. Plismy was another sadistic bully who fell for the masochism of being bullied himself.

A bottle was set on the counter, and the Algerian opened it swiftly and poured a measure into two glasses, a new glass for Plismy.

"A good burgundy," Plismy said, raising his glass. "You'll see. Santé."

"Santé," Logan responded. It was a very good burgundy indeed, he thought, and Plismy saw his reaction.

"I've been promoted!" the Frenchman said, unable to contain the good news. "My superior died in an air crash in the Côte d'Ivoire."

"Congratulations, Thomas," Logan replied, and raised his glass again. "To dead men's shoes," he toasted him.

Plismy laughed again, the short, staccato sound. "You have a taste-less humour I find so sadly lacking in your compatriots," he said, and drank thirstily.

They drank the bottle steadily, like two professional drinkers rather than connoisseurs. The talk ranged from the forthcoming presidential elections in America—who did Logan think was going to win?—to the Russian invasion of Georgia; from the stock markets to the Olym-pic Games in Beijing. By the time they'd finished the bottle, like true drinkers they were beginning to comprehend the state of the world in all its futility. But unlike Plismy, Logan remained clearheaded, as he usually did unless he'd decided to drink alone, for a lonely reason. He saw that Plismy had already been drinking, probably celebrating at the office before they met.

Good, he thought. A loose tongue in a euphoric head was a most reliable recipe for the one-way exchange of confidences.

When they'd finished the bottle, they took a taxi to a place Plismy knew—and that knew him. Located near the Gare de Lyon, it was a small, family-run restaurant, with excellent Alsatian cuisine. Plismy talked all the way through the depleted August traffic about his new responsibilities, his new salary, and the new perks that came with the job.

Logan might have been more envious of Plismy's secure employ-ment position had he not been entirely focused on how, this evening, he could exploit Plismy's garrulous desire to impress him. Lead him on, Logan, he told himself. That's all it takes.

The waitress, a daughter, Logan assumed, brought two plates of something concealed beneath a rich-looking cream-coloured sauce.

Plismy had insisted on ordering for both of them. He knew every-thing tonight; he was completely full of himself, Logan was pleased to see.

"Surely you must have been thinking about retirement?" Logan inquired. "Before the promotion, I mean. Haven't you had your fill of the world's secrets?" Plismy was twenty-five years older than him, at least.

"Before my promotion? Maybe, yes. A little." Plismy beamed with pleasure. "But now, why should I retire? I have even greater power, Logan. Access. The secrets behind the lies, the lies behind the secrets. Something you and I know all about. And also I have bigger allow-ances, a higher pension, and a new car," he boasted.

A fat pension sounded nice. But it was an equation that had never quite convinced him. The longer you worked, the bigger the pension, the less life you had to freely spend it. Illogically, having a cut-price pension suddenly made him feel better.

Logan wasn't sure whether Plismy knew about his fall from grace back in the 1990s. They'd both worked out in the East, Plismy in Russia, Logan in the Balkans. They'd met during the western standoff with Russia over the Serbian war. But if Plismy did know, he'd never mentioned it. Plismy didn't think a great deal about other people, however. Whether he knew or not, Logan wasn't going to supply the information.

"Don't you get trapped by it, though?" Logan persisted. "I some-times feel I do. There are so few people to talk to about what the world isn't supposed to know. You've been at this game for—"

"Thirty-three years," Plismy said expansively. "And counting. I've seen a lot, believe me. And now? Now things are just getting more interesting."

Get him onto Russia, Logan told himself. That's his speciality. That's where the game has squarely shifted once again.

"What happens to your old desk, then?" Logan said. "Some young Russian expert taking it on?"

"Nobody has my experience," Plismy said grandly. "I've been there through it all. Before the Wall, when the Wall came down, and after the Wall. You know I was in Moscow through the whole period, almost. And when I wasn't, I was running agents from here." He paused. "No, I'll keep my interest in the Russian desk. In fact, I've recently returned from a very interesting trip out East."

"Chasing hookers round the nightclubs of Samara?" Logan asked. "Isn't that where you tell me the real beauties come from?"

Plismy looked torn between telling Logan some hooker story for a laugh, or demonstrating his own importance in the thick of things, at the centre of power. He chose the latter.

Leaning across the table to indicate a confidence was about to take place, he said, "Do you know that we are going to take all the lovely Russian oil from the British and the Americans?"

"What? You and me, Thomas?"

Plismy pulled away sharply, cross that Logan wasn't taking his confidential leak more seriously. He poked his fork across the table at the young American.

"I was there," he said, mysteriously, and then filled the fork and put it decisively in his mouth. For a while he chewed his food thoughtfully, and Logan made no attempt to prompt him.

"The French have always known how to handle the Russians. With subtlety," Plismy explained, when there was room in his mouth to speak.

"Like when they burned Moscow to the ground?" Logan said.

"Particularly then." Plismy smiled. "Napoleon knew how to deal with the Russians."

"And the Russians, I seem to remember, subsequently knew how to deal with him," Logan said, with too much acidity in his voice.

But Plismy just laughed. He glowed at the memory of Napoleon's two-hundred-year-old victories and forgot the defeats.

"So the French are taking lots of Russian oil?" Logan prompted this time. "Good luck to you."

"Oil fields. New ones. The biggest. I tell you, I was there. In Sochi, down on the Black Sea, three weeks ago. Then in Moscow. Putin, Medvedev, Ivanov—we met them all. I was one of the team out there with 'one of France's major oil companies.'" Plismy winked coyly at the anonymity. "And we all sat around the same table with the men of power, the *siloviki*. Cover name, of course, cover position in the company. Usual rules."

Plismy threw his head back like a horse and then dipped in towards Logan again.

"The Russians are going to hand us—France—the big Siberian oil fields, take them away from the Americans and anybody else. The biggest fields, Logan. The Sakhalin fields in particular, the biggest prize of all."

"Sounds like a good day's work," Logan replied.

"It was a couple of days, actually," Plismy said, blithely unaware of the foolishness of his own self-importance.

Logan now saw that Plismy didn't know about his fall from grace. He was taunting him with what French aplomb and acumen could do, as opposed to American ham-fistedness—as Plismy saw it, anyway. Plismy thought he was still CIA.

"Look, Thomas, dinner's on me," Logan said suddenly, and smiled openly. "I want to be the first outside your office to congratulate you on the new job."

"Well. That's good of you," the newly enriched Plismy replied. It was this sort of respect that a man like him, in his new position, could only expect.

They took a taxi back into the centre when they'd finished dinner. Plismy knew a place, which he and similarly ranked Parisians from different professions attended for what he called "late evening delights." It was off the Faubourg Saint-Honoré, at the smart end, Plismy noted.

"It is where the French elite from the *grandes écoles* go for discretion," Plismy said—though he was not, Logan knew, one of them.

He'd come up from the rough *banlieues* of Marseille, where he'd learned his hatred of other, "lesser" races.

In the taxi Plismy returned to the Russian theme. Russia had been on everybody's minds since the Kremlin's show of aggression in Georgia. Putin had been photographed with the invading troops, openly displaying his power over the nominal president, Dmitry Medvedev.

"Top secret," Plismy said. "The Russians captured some American special forces troops fighting with the Georgians. They told me that in Moscow. Very embarrassing for your people, I'd have thought."

"I know nothing about it." Logan grinned, in order to give the impression he knew exactly what Plismy was referring to.

But Plismy went off on another self-congratulatory tack, around the role he'd played in Moscow for many years, which now seemed to be bearing such rich fruit.

"The Americans, the British, they took the early, easy pickings in Russia," Plismy said pompously, as if he were giving a lecture at the Hautes Etudes Commerciales. "But the French are the ones the Russians trust now. Perhaps for that reason. We weren't in there like you, stripping the place in the nineties. But now France is coming up, just as Russian power expands. It couldn't be a better moment. It will be a good few years, Logan, believe me, a profitable few years ahead. And don't think our oil company doesn't appreciate my own role in their giant strides in Russia," he added, and winked across the seat of the taxi.

By which he meant, Logan knew, that Plismy was getting a slice of the action on the side.

"Look at what's happened over Georgia," Plismy continued. "The Russians march in—provoked by that madman Georgian president. The Americans do a lot of huffing and puffing. But it's Sarkozy, our leader, who goes in and does the deal with Putin."

"You mean Medvedev."

"Medvedev may be president, but Putin pulls all the strings. Him and his cronies have it all sewn up. I'll tell you a story."

Plismy sat back in his seat and opened the window a little wider.

"Go on, tell me, Thomas—as long as it doesn't reflect well on you, you old bastard."

Plismy laughed and punched Logan's arm. He was quite drunk, Logan noted.

"Up in Moscow, on this deal, I spoke with a very beautiful woman," he said. "She's in the Russian parliament, the Duma. Ex ice-skater. She was very attentive to me."

I'll bet she was, Logan thought. And I bet ice-skating skated over her real reason for giving you the time of day.

"She told me," Plismy continued, "that the president of Uzbekistan came up to meet Medvedev in the Kremlin. In the course of much discussion, about many things, Medvedev asked why the political opposition in Uzbekistan disliked Russia so much. The president replied that they didn't dislike Russia, they disliked Putin. Medvedev leaned back in his chair and sighed. 'I know how they feel,' he said."

Plismy clapped his hands with delight at the story, but mainly, Logan observed, because he knew it. He knew an insider's tale of a conversation between the president of Russia and another national leader that had taken place in private, in the heart of the Kremlin, the heart of power.

"I know how he feels!" repeated Plismy, way off his usual vocal register. "The president of Russia is terrified of Putin. Medvedev's just Putin's poodle, you know I'm right about that. But don't think we're in Russia's pocket for a second," Plismy cautioned, as if Logan had been thinking such a thing. "We're not like the Germans, handing out pipeline contracts that the Russians alone will benefit from. No. France is going to reap a rich harvest from these oil fields, but we've kept our independence intact. We play both sides with the Russians, Logan. We carry a stick, and we dangle a carrot. We have plenty up our sleeve in France, if the Russians ever get nasty."

"And they will, believe it," Logan said, to Plismy's irritation.

Plismy leaned in towards Logan so that the taxi driver wouldn't overhear. Logan could smell the hours of alcohol on his breath.

"We have some very important, very senior anti–Putin officers from the KGB under our protection. Here. In France," he said. "We keep them up our sleeve, so to speak, for a rainy day. They have a great deal of compromising information about Comrade Vladimir. Bank accounts in Switzerland and so on. We keep our own *kompromat* against the Russians, just as they do against each other. We are well prepared."

"Really? How senior?" Logan said. He knew they were approaching their destination, and it tempted him to take a leap.

But just as Logan thought Plismy was about to unburden himself a little more, the taxi drew up at the kerb.

"Oh, yes, France is looking after herself," Plismy said importantly. And as he opened the taxi door, he veered off the subject completely, possibly recalling an earlier motif. "And the damn Jews in London and New York deserve everything they get," he said randomly.

Two and a half hours later, after Plismy had been sated by a bottle of 1986 Krug champagne and the "most beautiful eighteen-year-old philosophy student you ever saw," Logan found himself in another taxi with the Frenchman, on the way to another bar.

"So," the Frenchman breathed, heavily and too close to Logan's face. "What have you got for me, Logan? What's the meaning of our meeting?"

It had taken Plismy nearly five hours to reach this point. He really believed that Logan enjoyed his company, Logan realised. Just like all the others. But Logan saw too that the cunning in Plismy's eyes, even through the hours of drinking, was still engaged.

"You may need to use some of these KGB defectors you have up your sleeve here, Thomas," he said.

"Oh, yes? And why is that?"

Logan decided on telling the background from truth, and then adding the big lie under this camouflage to hook in Plismy.

"It's from our station in Vienna," he said.

He saw Plismy watching him avidly.

"As you know, the Russians have increased their operations there tenfold," Logan said. "It's back to Cold War levels."

"It's true, they're trying to march across Europe again," Plismy agreed. "Money is no object for them now."

And now Logan embarked on the embroidered story he had prepared for the Frenchman.

"Last week," Logan continued, "a man was abducted in Vienna, in the trunk of a car hired by a KGB sleeper who works in an Austrian bank. He was taken to the outskirts of the city, roughed up by a couple of KGB hoods, threatened with worse, and ordered to do a job for the Russians."

"What job?" Plismy asked.

"To cause a run on one of your biggest banks," Logan said. "To crash it, effectively."

"So the man abducted is a banker."

"Yes. A very influential foreign banker."

Plismy whistled softly. "They haven't abducted people like that since before Gorbachev came to power," he said. "Since the early eighties."

"Right. They're turning to the attack."

The taxi drew up at yet another bar, in the seedy district below the Sacré-Coeur. It was after one o'clock in the morning, and Plismy now needed a little help getting to his feet. Logan led the way into the bar and ordered a coffee to clear his head. Plismy had a cognac. They withdrew to the farthest table, though the bar was almost empty.

Plismy wasn't going to ask which French bank, or which influential banker had been abducted, Logan noted. Not yet. He would know there was a trade involved.

As the time wore on towards one thirty and Plismy's roaming conversation was broken up by numerous interruptions, it turned out that the French did have some very senior KGB officers on the run from

Putin's regime. There were two or three, perhaps, Logan guessed, correctly assessing Plismy's propensity for exaggeration.

Plismy was talking about women in general—a subject he constantly returned to—and then about one woman in particular.

"You should see her!" the Frenchman said, apropos of nothing. "Every inch a Russian princess. They say Gosfilm in Moscow was always trying to get her into the movies. But she was already taken for greater things. KGB father, uncle inside the Kremlin. She trained at Yasenevo for the SVR, right in the heart of the Russian foreign intelligence operations. Department S. She's a gold mine, believe me."

"You didn't get her into bed, did you?" Logan said with a fabricated leer.

"No, no. Not yet, anyway. She's still grieving the loss of her husband. British. Very peculiar. One of our kind, he was, Logan. SIS. I'm hands-off with her for now. But who knows? One day maybe. One day when she needs a favour, she'll have to come through me."

"You mean her Brit husband walked off?" Logan said, feeling a heat rising inside him, an instinctive feeling that he was close to something very important.

"He didn't walk off!" Plismy scoffed, as if he'd already told Logan all about the woman, a fact that Logan noted. "He was killed. Here in Paris. By the Russians, of course." He leaned in at the small table by the window. "Nerve agent," he muttered. "On the steering wheel of his car. All hushed up from the press, of course."

"No wonder she needs protecting," Logan said. "They must be after her too. She defected to you, to the French, did she?"

"The Russians are after her, and yes, she should be very grateful to us."

"Why didn't she go to the British?" Logan said.

"Because her husband had, let's say, blotted his copybook with London. Gone out on his own. But we have her safe and sound, tucked up under our wing now. Not far from where I grew up, actually."

Plismy was from Marseille.

"You won't hide her from the KGB for long," Logan said.

"Oh, but we will. It's a very out-of-the-way spot in the *garrigue*. In the 'Midi *moins le quart.*'"

The *garrigue*, Logan knew, was a local expression for the aromatic scrubland covering the limestone plateau on the far side of the Rhone from Marseille; people there jokingly called the area north of Nîmes and west of Avignon the Midi *moins le quart*.

"We should pay her a visit, by the sound of it," Logan said. "She sounds fabulous."

Plismy took on the look of exaggerated surprise that only a man who's drunk too much can manage.

"To the village," Logan prompted. "Where you have her."

Logan saw Plismy putting up his guard. No matter how much Plismy drank, he had a line over which he never stepped.

It was another half hour before Logan could lead him back to where they'd been. It was a rambling story, with many discursions about the beauty of the Russian colonel. But finally there she was again, as if emerging from a mist; a KGB colonel, a woman. She was a figure "everybody wants," according to Plismy. "You, the British, and, most of all of course, the Russians," Plismy stated. The French had given her a new name, a new identity. She was very valuable, very key to something-or-other, which Plismy had been vague about and clearly didn't know, Logan thought.

Then Plismy had dropped a name—Fougieres—before Logan saw him mentally retrace his steps.

"That's her cover name," Plismy said.

"You'll have to kill me now you've told me that," Logan joked, and Plismy forgot his reticence and laughed until tears poured down his cheeks.

Logan then deftly guided Plismy away from the subject of the Russian colonel, but the talking soon died off. It was the natural end to the evening. Plismy was exhausted from the effort of projecting his own importance and from the drink.

Logan helped him into a taxi and threw his briefcase in after him. He hadn't even needed to follow up his lie about the French bank. Then he returned to the bar and ordered another coffee.

He sat and thought for a long time before returning to his hotel in the Marais. There he used the hotel's computer to check for the first flight south to Nîmes in the morning—a Saturday. There was one leaving in just over five hours' time.

Then he asked the night porter for an atlas of France, and one was finally found with an index of place names at the back. Logan drew his finger down the page until he found it. Fougieres. It was a place name, not a code name. Fougieres was a small village about an hour's drive north of Nîmes.

That was what he'd detected in Plismy's voice, and in his withdrawal from the subject altogether after he'd spoken the name; a cover-up. It was a smooth cover-up of a mistake, one that would have gone unnoticed by anyone without Logan's antennae. An inflection in Plismy's voice, a little too much haste in the explanation, perhaps. But that was the answer. Fougieres was a place, not the code name for the woman.

Logan felt the heat rise again. Unless Thomas Plismy, newly elevated, drunk, sexually satisfied, and heady with new opportunities, was lying better than Logan had ever seen anyone lie, then Logan had gained a handhold from the evening. The French oil company was a story to cover his expenses, perhaps.

But the woman, the KGB colonel "everyone wants," might be the nugget of gold he was such an expert at seeing through the dirt. That was a handhold that might help him to reach much higher up the mountain.

2

THERE WAS NO WIND down at the foot of the tower block, just the hot stillness, as if the air itself had died.

But that didn't mean there wouldn't be a wind thirty-three floors up—a crosswind, perhaps, strong enough to affect his aim. He couldn't say until he was up there. And it would make all the difference.

Thick clouds, dirty grey around the edges, hung low over London and smothered the already breathless city. The stationary air was sultry with trapped August heat, and combined with the city's usual palpitating energy, it had forced the temperature into the eighties.

The man calling himself Lars shrugged. There was nothing he could do about it. There was no way he would know if it was going to work—if the stillness down here prevailed up there in the sky—until he reached the top of the tower block.

He slung the tattered holdall, stained with cement powder, grease, working stains of various kinds, back over his shoulder and studied the area around the bottom of the tower.

There was a listless park playground with bare earth where grass had grown earlier in the summer. Some broken swings and a few huge cracked concrete hoops and dugouts for skateboarders had been laid out once for children's entertainment, but were now the repositories for syringes, condoms, litter. A sculpture—at least he thought it was a sculpture—of intertwining metal in primary colours was stuck into another concrete platform. Empty bottles and food wrappings were scattered in every direction.

The prefabricated concrete pathways, splintered in places where the weeds had forced their way through, mirrored the decaying, weather-stained 1960s concrete edifice that soared grimly above them.

He had studied it half a dozen times already and knew the tower block and its surrounding area inside and out. He'd traced the routes in, the exit points, he'd watched the local characters for anyone who might cause trouble. Drunks who didn't understand the danger he posed were the worst. He'd ridden the elevator to the top of the tower block many times and now recalled the stink of piss inside it. The English were pigs.

He'd also ridden the service elevator on several occasions, just to make sure.

Putting his hand in his pocket, he jangled the keys to the steel door that accessed the service part of the tower block, accessible only to firemen, utility workers, and council employees. It hadn't taken him long, three weeks ago now, to take a mould of the locks and then have the keys cut. It reassured him that they were there in his pocket. He didn't like to rely on just one exit.

It was a Saturday, and that was in his favour. Apart from a few teenagers kicking a ball around in the "park," their baseball hats worn back to front and their faces sprouting adolescent hair in defiance of any style but their own uncertain manliness, there were few of the tower's occupants in view. Maybe they were shopping or doing some other weekend business. Maybe some of them, at least, were already on their way to the football match; the first match of the season, the

Charity Shield between the winners of the FA Cup and the Premier League.

Hopefully, this year the season would begin with a bang, he thought. But Lars didn't even offer himself a sardonic inward grin at his little joke. He was as grim-faced as the tower itself, as expressionless as the sky and the city that slunk febrile beneath it.

He didn't look up in anybody's direction or catch anyone's eye. He just traipsed across the battered concrete paving to the steel door the way a man called out on a Saturday for maintenance work might: grumpy, uncommunicative. He called himself Lars, in case anybody challenged him, and then he could retreat into an ignorance of the English language that he could speak perfectly well. Just another foreigner working for the council.

He would go up that way, he thought, up in the service elevator, and choose afterwards which of the two elevators to descend by.

There was nobody in view of the steel door, buried as it was along a trash-filled concrete corridor at the foot of the tower block. Even if there were, he was dressed for it: a plastic yellow jerkin with the council logo, overalls, and, pulled roughly over them, worker's boots. The well-used holdall, packed with what he needed, weighed exactly thirty-two and a half pounds, and was slung over his shoulder. But he pulled his cap a little farther over his eyes, just in case.

The steel door opened easily to his forged keys, as it had done several times before. He locked it behind him, tested it with a push to be sure, and pressed the code for the elevator. It was already at ground level, so that meant there was nobody up there. Then he stepped inside for the swift ride to the top.

A steel ladder greeted him, as he knew it would, when he stepped out above the accommodation on the thirty-third floor. But before climbing the ladder, he inserted a key into the elevator mechanism that sent it to the bottom again. Then he connected a cord to the mechanism and carried the other end with him.

Then he climbed the ladder, unlocked a padlock that kept a steel trapdoor shut, and pushed it open all the way. He walked up the remaining four steps and out onto the flat, pink-gravelled roof where the lungs of the tower block—the heat vents and other apparatus—clawed their extremities into the sky. He laid the cord down on the roof, close to where he was going to set up, so he would see the cord move if the elevator was used, and propped the trapdoor open with a small pebble.

The first thing he did when he stood up, without thinking, was sniff the air, test its eddies and currents. There was marginally more movement in it than there had been at the bottom of the tower block. He would have to measure it. There was an anemometer, of course, among the other necessities in the holdall. Over the distance he was planning to fire, even the heavy .50-calibre shell would form an arc of up to a hundred feet vertically and, depending on the wind, might err fifty feet to right or left. He knew that even he couldn't cope with anything like a crosswind, not at this distance.

But in any case, there were still two hours before the match began, and anything might happen meteorologically in that time. He knew he'd be measuring the wind in the final minutes to be certain of the best information. It was a fine enough piece of work he had to do, even without a single breath of air to intervene.

He didn't set up his equipment immediately, but laid the holdall carefully on the gravel roof unopened. There was a fine view. If you ignored the fact you were standing on a decaying glass-and-concrete rectangle, you could imagine it had been put here for the view, he thought. There were few high buildings around him, just three other similar blocks, slightly lower than this one, and London wasn't a high city anyway. He could see all the way, unobstructed, the eight miles across town to the highest buildings that housed the banks and office blocks in the City and Canary Wharf.

The nearly one and a half miles between him and the football stadium was clear of anything high. Atop the tower block, he was far above anything in his line of fire.

But it wasn't as easy as that. The distance was huge for the best sniper shot—close to record-breaking, he knew. And the stadium itself had a roof that curved up and then down, so that all inside it was obscured apart from one small corner of the pitch and one half of the eastern stand. That was fortunate, at least. If the director's box had been on the western side, there'd be no shot.

Removing the fluorescent yellow council jerkin, he turned it inside out so that a grey lining he'd sewn in himself was all that could be seen. Then he unrolled some grey parachute silk from around his waist and spread it on the roof. He fitted snap-on aluminium struts from regular camping equipment into sleeves in the material that he'd also made and set up this rigid, flat canopy, two feet high, under which he could stretch full length, concealed. Though it was unlikely they would be looking for anything at this distance from the stadium, the police helicopters that monitored the match crowd would see nothing moving on the roof, no human figure.

He settled down under the canopy for the ninety-five-minute wait, and that was just for the match to start. It would require a goal from the home side to be able to make the shot at all. Otherwise the seated figure—his target—was half obscured by a wall. But a goal would undoubtedly bring the target to his feet, and that was the moment—"the moment of truth," as the bullfighters called it. The *mise à mort*. He imagined the blade descending through the muscles of the bull's neck, its shoulder blades opened by the lowered, charging head, a way to the heart exposed. He too would go for a heart shot.

London shimmered, but not with sunlight, just the heavy heat. Thank God the sun was behind clouds. Under the silk on the roof it would have been unbearable with the August sun beating down.

He listened to the faint sound of traffic down below. A seagull perched briefly on one of the heating vents, then flew off again.

Unzipping the holdall, he took out the gun stock first. He stroked it with his right hand; a precision piece, custom-made and then adapted for a left-hander. Left-handed Lars. It was very light, thirty-one pounds without the sight. The semiautomatic could be disassembled and assembled in three minutes with the right tools. It was a long-range rifle used by U.S. Navy Seals, among others.

It had been a difficult choice whether to go for the semiautomatic, with five rapid shots, or the simpler, maybe more accurate single-shot rifle. At this range he might easily need a second shot if there was an opportunity, and reloading would be slow. But he'd had to weigh taking a second or even a third shot against the marginally less accurate nature of the semiautomatic. Either way, there was a risk. The free-floating barrel gave less recoil than a bolt-action rifle, and that was also a consideration. Its accuracy was proven to a range of more than a mile. After that, it was entirely down to the hair's-breadth expertise of the sniper himself.

He assembled the barrel into the steel receiver and fished out the Bender optical sights from the holdall; three screws either side, tightened with a key. You could take the sight off and fit it back on without it losing the zero. Then he fitted a forward bipod and rear bipod for maximum steadiness. He carefully placed the belt with its five shots, five individual opportunities if there was time, next to the mounted rifle. Then he turned over onto his front and set himself up in a firing position, legs splayed, the right one slightly cocked.

He looked through the sight at the directors' box thirty streets away and read off the distance on its red digital rangefinder: 2,380 yards. It was a huge shot, but not impossible, not a record after all. The record was held by a Canadian corporal serving in Afghanistan, who'd killed an enemy over nearly a mile and half, and then immediately killed a second at eight hundred yards. Good shooting.

He zeroed in the rifle at a seat in the centre of the box, half obscured though it was. Then he rolled over and stretched his limbs and crawled out from under the parachute silk to spend the next half hour relaxing against a heating vent and watching and listening for the sound of helicopters, glancing at the still cord that disappeared through the trapdoor, and composing himself mentally for the task.

It came as a low hum at first, and he sat up, alert, before realising the sound was the crowd in the stadium, its collective 35,000-strong murmur rising above the stadium roof and wafting across the distance to the tower block. Crawling back under the parachute silk, he lay and waited.

The sound of the stadium's speaker system sent announcements and rock music through the air. They were cranking up the crowd for the spectacle ahead. He looked down the sight and saw the directors' box filling up. They were the last to arrive—greetings, hand-shakes. They were mostly Russians, flown in on private jets from Moscow that morning to watch the first big game amid the high hopes their man's team carried for the forthcoming season in England and Europe.

He watched the target, standing, clapping one man on the back, shaking another's hand. At 2,380 yards he could see the gold signet ring on his finger, the stubble on his chin, the colour of his wife's ear-rings. But there was no clear shot. Then he watched them take their seats, and a roar went up for the kickoff in the centre of the pitch, which he couldn't see.

The match coursed to and fro, he guessed, judging from the noises of the crowd, the partisan songs of rival supporters. Occasionally he saw action, down in the corner of the pitch on the eastern side that was visible to him; a corner kick, a long ball followed by an attacking player who trapped it and was then wedged in by defenders to prevent the cross. The target's side was attacking against the goal mouth at that end, a goal he couldn't see.

Once, there was a roar from the crowd behind that goal mouth, and the target came to his feet, beginning to clap his hands, only to stop and sit back down, an opportunity missed, both down there in the stadium and up here on the roof of the tower block.

The game had been playing for just over thirty-five minutes, and Lars was getting stiff with waiting, when a huge roar confirmed the goal he and the target had been waiting for. The target jumped to his feet, clapping, then raising his hands above his head in triumph in a sustained celebration of a goal.

Everything stopped. Five minutes before, the reading on the anemometer had been negligible.

Lars took his aim through the sight, marked up three bars above the zero to account for drop. The target remained in position, once turning to hug a man to his left. The celebration was sustained. Lars was still, his breathing utterly stopped. No muscle moved, except the one on his trigger finger. He pulled just enough to feel the resistance. He was composed; the target was in full sight.

He hardly felt the recoil. But he lay still, exactly as he had been to take the shot. Through the sight, he saw the Russian appear to explode. A .50-calibre shell would penetrate two sheets of metal six feet apart; the target didn't have a chance.

Within four minutes, Lars was off the roof, rifle and parachute silk packed away, the cord rewound, the pebble kicked from under the trapdoor. He took the service elevator back down. It seemed the lucky way. And as he descended, he thought of the shock, the incomprehension, followed by the mayhem and panic that would start in the director's box and slowly spread through the stadium as it sank in.

The Russian was dead, of that he was certain. And tied up with him were $30 billion worth of assets, as well as his tight, close relations with the Kremlin, and with a business empire that stretched across the world. But that was the aftermath, he thought. That was nothing to do with him. That was effect; he was cause.

He locked the steel door at the foot of the tower block, checked the entrance to the concrete corridor, and stepped out across the playground, slowly, until he reached a white van parked in a street around the corner. The wind puffed suddenly. A front was coming in, and the wind would precede it.

3

L OGAN RENTED A CAR at the Nîmes airport, 350 miles south of Paris. It was seven and a half hours after he'd put Plismy in a taxi. He hadn't slept.

It was a Saturday; the air was clear and blue in the south, and the country as he drove north of the city was parched. When he crossed the bridge at Sainte-Maxime, he saw that the river was reduced to a trickle.

He wanted to be at Alès before lunchtime to set the first stage of his plan, and he drove the Peugeot into the old coal-mining town at the edge of the Cévennes just before midday. Removing all signs of the rental company, he threw them in a municipal dump at the edge of town and drove into a small mechanic's shop situated up a dusty side street, which the Michelin guide said was open on a Saturday.

The shifty-eyed owner in this one-man operation had just withdrawn on a wheeled trolley from beneath a car and was cleaning his hands on a rag before returning home to lunch. He waved Logan away, but the American persisted.

The clutch was giving him trouble, he said, and he couldn't go any farther. Without examining anything, the man shook his head, telling him he was shut, and nothing was possible until Monday. Logan asked whether he could leave the Peugeot there until Monday, then, and whether the man had another car he could hire for the weekend. He had money, he explained. It was urgent; he was desperate. This arrangement finally suited the man, and Logan headed eastwards in an old red Renault van with the side panel advertising a local baker's shop in chipped and fading cream lettering.

He parked at the edge of the market town of Uzès, on a piece of waste ground that doubled as a car park on Saturday market day, and walked into the medieval square for a beer and a ham and cheese baguette. He watched the stalls being dismantled and the crowds of shoppers thinning away. After lunch, he strolled around the outside of the square and found a digital electronic announcement board near the main entrance to the square, which had no announcements written in its dotted yellow writing, other than "Samedi, 16 août 2008."

He bought a local map and found Fougieres a little to the north of town, up on the high plateau of the *garrigue*.

When he felt relaxed and ready, he walked back to the van and checked his camera and film for the second or third time that morning. Then he headed out of town along a plane-tree-lined road that climbed up onto the plateau in a series of curves and switchbacks. He smelled the wild rosemary growing along the side of the road and saw the scrawny vines of the region that produced much of France's undrinkable—and heavily subsidized—wine.

The little village was very ancient and partly walled—where the stones hadn't been dismantled for building houses. A small square at the centre contained the mayor's office, with a tricolour above the entrance, hanging flatly in the windless air. A manor house that had seen better days and was now a bed and breakfast stood opposite the mayor's office, and various other less seigneurial habitations with wrought iron gates, with views that stretched for fifty miles to the high mountains of the Cévennes, randomly dotted the open space.

Logan parked behind a stone barn, which housed the office and weighbridge used for the grape harvest. It was after three o'clock in the afternoon, and there was a sleepiness about the village that perhaps, he thought, never left it.

He walked back up into the square. He caught the sound of splashing and noticed the unnatural blue of a swimming pool behind the hedge of the bed-and-breakfast manor house. He would ask there.

There were two men sunbathing beside the pool, and the door to the house was wide open. He walked up the path between shocking pink bougainvilleas and called down a dark, flagstoned corridor until a man wearing an unconvincing wig appeared.

He was a visitor, Logan explained, come to see the new resident in the village, the foreign lady.

"Avec l'enfant?" the man enquired.

Yes, the one with a child, he agreed, though Plismy hadn't mentioned that.

The man with the wig gestured generally up a small lane and mentioned a house with a palm tree in the garden, before dismissing Logan by turning his back and walking away. He was busy with something. That was good. It might mean he would forget their encounter.

Logan didn't walk straight up the lane, however, but took a more circuitous route, through a horse's meadow and past a tumbledown wood barn with a portable sawmill outside. The palm tree was visible, higher than the surrounding houses.

He crossed the lane. Heavy iron gates barred the entrance to the house—electrically operated, he noticed. That kind of security was nowhere else to be seen in the village. Through a crack in the join of the gates, he saw a light blue Mercedes parked in a dusty yard. That was what he needed.

Turning swiftly away, he walked round the other end of the village, away from the horse's field and away from the bed and breakfast where the man had given him the directions. Behind the barn the red van was cooking in the sun where he had left it.

Now was the time to wait. He turned the van around, still concealed behind the barn, and pointed it towards the route down the winding hill to Uzès.

At six thirty, after nearly three hours in the sweltering car, with brief walks down into the vineyards to cool himself a little, he saw the blue Mercedes begin its descent to the flatter ground below the plateau and onto the straight road with the plane trees. Switching on the engine of the van, he began to follow it from a distance of about half a mile.

It was twenty-four hours since he'd met Plismy in Paris, and he felt the eagerness of the chase, the excitement of new momentum.

When they reached Uzès, he drove slowly around the road that circled and concealed the square behind old, high stone buildings. He finally caught sight of the blue Mercedes, parked at the side of the street. Its two occupants, he now saw, were a woman in a baseball cap and a small boy. They were going through the process of preparing to get out, the boy strapped in, the woman forgetting it, then the boy urgently needing some small toy from the floor of the car.

When they finally climbed out, the woman pressed the key fob for the car alarm as Logan passed without looking at them. He glimpsed through the corner of his eye the woman taking the boy's hand on the pavement.

Logan kept going in the direction the two were walking until he was out of sight. He pulled the van into a parking space on the same side of the road, jumped out, and made for a café whose pavement tables led into a darker interior. He hoped they wouldn't turn off before the café. They didn't.

A few minutes later, he watched from the interior of the café as they drew level. The boy had stopped and was tugging the woman's arm. He had dropped his plastic toy, and she turned back to pick it up. Logan saw them illuminated in the sunlight from the darkness of the bar.

She was in her mid- to late thirties, he guessed, and wore tight jeans and a green T-shirt. Her hair, which had been tucked under the cap, was now free and came halfway down her back. It was a rich brown and gold colour. Her face, as far he could tell in the bright sun, and in the brief moment he caught sight of it, had high cheekbones, smooth-skinned.

It was a face that startled him—a beautiful face. But then she stooped, picked up the toy, and gave it to the boy.

Logan left a few euros on the counter and took his coffee to a pavement seat, where he sat and watched their backs slowly retreating. The boy seemed to be constantly stopping and pointing, asking questions, trying to pick some object of interest up from the pavement, tugging his mother's hand continually. And she was patient with him. They made slow progress.

A hundred yards ahead of them, Logan noted, if they stayed on the same path, was the electronic sign with the day's date written on it.

He finished his coffee, picked up the map, and unfolded it, leaving it half open, as if he'd just been studying it. Then he crossed the street, twenty or thirty yards behind them, and walked along the far side, his camera slung over his shoulder and the map carried loosely by his side. He overtook them easily.

The two of them, he saw, as he flicked through a revolving post-card stand, were still making slow progress. She seemed in no hurry, and the relaxed fluidity of her movements, for a moment, mesmerised Logan. She seemed to him to walk like a dancer.

He checked the position of the electronic sign. Then he saw an alley with another café, its white plastic tables and chairs shaded by the buildings. Taking a seat, Logan produced the camera from its case and tested the light and the distance to the sign.

They arrived in stops and starts; the boy seemed to be singing absently and was now waving a twig with some wan leaves attached to it that he must have picked up from one of the trees that shaded the road.

As they drew level with the electronic sign, the woman seemed distracted. She was leaning down at the boy and saying something. The boy responded crossly. She gave him the baseball cap, and he seemed satisfied. Then she stood up, and as she did so, Logan pressed the shutter.

He developed the film later that night in a hotel room in Marseille. He didn't know if the woman was a KGB colonel, an expat British divorcée, or the Queen of Sheba for that matter. But the photograph, he was relieved to see, gave a clear picture of her face, and those who wanted her would know. He made four copies of the picture, including one for himself. The other three were for his intended customers.

Then he fell asleep, exhausted, and dreamed of a terrified Plismy, surrounded by all the people he hated in the world, like some Benetton or Coca-Cola poster, but with the reverse message—a congregation of all the ethnic groups and religions in existence, closing in on the source of their persecution.

At eleven thirty the following morning, Logan mailed two copies of the picture, the first to the CIA station in Paris, the second to the SIS in London. He put a price on each picture of half a million dollars—in return for which he would reveal the location of its subject.

It was a high price. But if Plismy was right—and Logan sensed he was—then information about the woman was worth a lot of money.

Then he boarded an afternoon flight to Belgrade, to meet his third potential customer. As he took his seat on the plane, he opened up the Sunday edition of *Midi Libre* and read the headline: "Magnate Russe assassiné à Londres."

He fell asleep, not waking until they touched down in Belgrade two and a half hours later.

4

ADRIAN CAREW STEPPED INTO the chauffeured car outside his London apartment on Chelsea Green. It was a Sunday morning, and he usually only stayed here during the week.

He wished his driver Ray good morning in a way that suggested it wasn't, and his demeanour dissuaded further conversation. Rarely in London at any time over a weekend, let alone on a Sunday, he was very irritable that he'd been called back from Hampshire.

At weekends, Adrian liked to be at his and Penny's country home—or the Wine Cellar, as office wits referred to it—on the duke of Wellington's estate in Hampshire. Only a crisis brought him back to London. But during the week he lived here, in Chelsea Green near the Barracks. It was an area of multimillion-pound homes and, like the country house, his apartment was courtesy of Penny's private fortune. But this wealthy corner of London had been tiresomely invaded in the nineteenth century by a development for the homeless, put there by a do-gooder charity foundation. Adrian wasn't a person who admired the efforts of other human beings to haul their way out of predicaments he didn't share. Without giving it a great deal of thought, he instinctively condemned them—the alcoholics, the homeless, a wide range of such groups—for being in that position in the first place.

And now, as the black Mercedes pulled out of the side street, he noted with distaste the idling group of alcoholics who stood smoking cigarettes in the thin sunlight outside the housing project across the road. Normally he saw them on a Monday morning, for their meeting at seven thirty, he supposed. He now assumed they must also meet on Sundays at the same god-awful hour.

"JIC, Ray," he said. His chauffeur had been sufficiently sympathetic to his mood not to ask where they were going.

A special session of the Joint Intelligence Committee was just what he didn't need, not this weekend, not any weekend. The Russian Anatoly Semyonovich was dead, but why did they need to have a bloody Joint Intelligence meeting about it? It was first of all a job for Scotland Yard and the National Criminal Intelligence Service— maybe MI5 at a pinch—but not a matter for MI6, to which he had recently been appointed head, with a knighthood to match. Not at this stage anyway.

As he willed himself over the effects of too much excellent claret the night before, he vaguely supposed they wanted to pick his brains about Semyonovich the billionaire; Semyonovich the asset predator; Semyonovich the Kremlin stooge.

They would want his special knowledge of the Russian's connections both inside and outside Britain, which Adrian had on a few occasions discussed with his opposite number at MI5. He would explain the web of obscure and secret shell companies of which the Russian's business apparatus largely consisted. But mainly Adrian's role would be to reveal Semyonovich's closeness to those who ruled in the Kremlin.

Find the killer, that was Adrian's prerequisite for delving into the whole bad business.

And then his mind turned to what really preoccupied him.

While his son had been at the game yesterday afternoon, Saturday, in a friend's merchant banker father's private box ("Enjoy it," Adrian had told him, "the bloody bankers won't be able to afford boxes for much longer"), the Russians had finally made it clear, through their London ambassador, that they wouldn't be extraditing Grigory Bykov for Finn's murder, not under any circumstances.

So now Adrian was going to insist that his original plan, to take Bykov down in retaliation for the assassination, must go ahead. The time for negotiating was over. They had nothing to exchange for Bykov. The KGB colonel Anna's whereabouts were still unknown, even if she was a bargaining chip, which it seemed she wasn't any longer. An impasse had been reached. Now Adrian wanted Bykov's head. That was the way of the secret world, and the Russians knew it.

But first he was going to have to deal with the party now being gathered at the JIC. Only afterwards would he be able to collar Teddy Parkinson, its head, to make this special request.

As the black Mercedes cruised down through Victoria and onto Parliament Square, Adrian decided to have a cigarette, in his government-issue car, and damn the rules.

Adrian's son had returned home eight hours after the end of the match the previous evening. That was how long it took for the police to sift through the football crowd at the exit turnstiles, and search all 35,000 of them. And of course they'd found nothing. That should have been obvious, Adrian thought. Nobody would risk trying to kill Semyonovich with a sniper shot from inside the ground. It took a real pro to kill a man like Semyonovich—he had thirty-five regular bodyguards, all ex special forces and many from Adrian's old regiment, plus eight armour-plated vehicles—and that was just for his London encampment.

Then there were the other 35,000 people in the ground, who might just have noticed if a man with an assault rifle took careful aim from the seat beside them.

The Mercedes entered Whitehall and pulled up outside the building with the JIC operations room in the basement. Adrian, ostentatiously smoking as he stepped out of the car, told Ray not to wait. He was going on to lunch after the meeting, with Teddy Parkinson at his country home. That, he told himself, not this meeting, was the point of the day, and he cheered up a little.

There were six of them around the long table. Teddy Parkinson (Sir), the head of Joint Intelligence, sat at the head; then there was Foster from the Yard and Evans (Sir) from MI5, on either side; Crudwell (Commander) from NCIS and Adrian himself (newly Sir) at the opposite end of the table; and finally Trevor Lewis, the prime minister's private secretary (Scum of the Earth).

They'd finished discussing the method of the killing by nine o'clock. The type of weapon used for the kill seemed to have been narrowed down to about half a dozen, all sniper weapons known to Adrian and used by various national special forces. But they were readily available if you knew where to look. The distance was enormous—up to a mile and a half, forensics reckoned, beyond even what Adrian had assumed.

It was all he could do not to say, "Bloody good shot."

The identity of the assassin was anyone's guess; which left the motive and the fallout—the implications. Adrian's time to contribute.

"Adrian," Teddy Parkinson, the JIC head, addressed him at last. The ponderous preamble that looked into the nooks and crannies of events on the ground had finally been wound up. "The prime minister received a call from President Medvedev last night, a few hours after the killing. The Russian president was expressing concern."

So that was why they'd been called together this morning for this emergency meeting, Adrian thought. Jump to it for the Russians.

Lewis the private secretary nodded overenthusiastically. Nobody had yet asked for his opinion about anything.

"Why, Adrian?" Teddy Parkinson followed up. "Why a call from the Russian president?"

"Semyonovich was very close to the Kremlin," Adrian replied. "He helped put Putin into power at the end of the nineties. He's worth around thirty billion dollars, but worth a lot more to the Kremlin. He was spearheading the Kremlin's policy of acquiring strategic foreign assets—energy companies in the West, metals combines, you name it. All over the world, but particularly our world."

"So he had a lot of money that the Kremlin used as if it were its own?"

"That's about it. All those Russian multibillionaire tycoons are now arms of the state—covert ambassadors with bottomless pockets. That's why Medvedev called; Semyonovich was like an undercover representative of the Kremlin. The deal is, men like Semyonovich get to keep their private wealth, as long as they put it into the service of the Kremlin and its cronies."

Adrian knew that Teddy Parkinson was perfectly aware of all this. He was just explaining for the benefit of the others.

"What else? Anything we should know about?"

"We have good intelligence that Semyonovich was caretaking bank accounts on behalf of Putin and other *siloviki* types; Ivanov, Sechin—"

"Siloviki?" Lewis the private secretary interrupted.

"Men of power," Adrian said. "In Russian," he added caustically.

"So . . . but a call from President Medvedev would rather high-light that, wouldn't it?" Lewis leaped into the gap he'd been waiting nearly an hour to fill. "It would draw attention to the Kremlin's unhealthy—covert interest, you called it—in Semyonovich. Surely they wouldn't want to do that."

"The Kremlin," Adrian said carefully, though without disguising his distaste at being even on the same planet as Lewis, ". . . the Kremlin doesn't care what the world thinks. In fact, it has taken a delight in recent years in demonstrating openly that it couldn't give a shit. You may have noticed that it invaded Georgia last month. And since then it's not taken a blind bit of notice what the rest of the world says or thinks."

"Diplomatic channels are working with the Russians on that," Lewis said confidently. "The EU—"

"But they haven't got anywhere, have they?" Adrian interrupted with icy patience. "That's the point."

"This is another matter," Teddy broke in smoothly. He knew from old that Adrian was spoiling for a fight. "Who would want Semyonovich dead?" he asked baldly.

"There's a long list." Adrian shrugged. "Some individual, or clan, from the Kremlin itself, perhaps. The internecine power struggles in the Kremlin don't exactly represent one voice. Then there's a string of businessmen whose toes and other vital extremities Semyonovich has crushed over the years; there are Chechen bandits and other ne'er-do-wells with a grudge. Not to mention the owner of Manchester United," he added facetiously.

"Why the Kremlin? Why would they murder one of their own? If he looked after their cash?" Lewis demanded.

"As I tried to explain, the Kremlin isn't one entity, one single interest. It's a snake's nest of competing interests, with Putin prefering to keep it that way. Divide and rule, it's called. That's why Medvedev, the nominal president, is just a Putin clone, running the place on behalf of Putin's clan, which happens, at this moment, to be in the ascendant. We don't know why anyone in the Kremlin might want Semyonovich dead, but certain interests there, which want to damage Putin's clan, might well use the murder of Semyonovich as a lever to exert their power."

Adrian relaxed into his exposition.

"Alternatively, maybe Semyonovich had outlived his usefulness with his actual supporters there, Putin included. Maybe he'd got too big for his boots. Maybe he was bucking orders from Moscow. Maybe it's *pour encourager les autres*. There's a lot of possibilities. We don't know. And that's just the possible Kremlin involvement. There's a bloody long list of people with motive outside the Kremlin, that's what we do know."

"Here in Britain?" Lewis demanded.

"Everywhere," Adrian said.

"And the repercussions," Teddy said, "from Moscow—assuming he was still on the inside over there?"

"They'll be very angry indeed," Adrian acknowledged. "They'll look for someone to blame. They'll reel off a whole lot of guff about 'lawless Britain.' The usual hypocritical crap. Who knows, they might even try to blame us."

"Us?" Lewis repeated.

"The Kremlin will see what damage it can cause, and then try to cause it," Adrian replied.

"If we assume for a second that it's not a Kremlin hit, what's their reaction?" Parkinson said.

"If it's not a Kremlin hit, I should think it will worry them a great deal," Adrian said, suddenly thinking about this aspect for the first time. Yes, it was, in its way, a momentous murder. It could have very far-reaching implications. "Anatoly Semyonovich had an extremely complex business empire," he continued. "It has a real reach. It's very important to the Kremlin's foreign economic policy. And the way the Russians do things, Semyonovich would be the only figure who really knew what was going on inside it. It's not like a Western business model, where the head drops off—in this case Semyonovich's—and things carry on as before. In the West, there'd be plenty of people, competent boards of directors and so on, who know exactly what the company consists of. If the boss drops off his perch, it all goes on more or less uninterrupted. But that's not the Russian way. The Russians have an imperial attitude to business, with a single godhead who is all-seeing, all-knowing."

He looked up at Teddy. "There'll be chaos, I should think. The stock prices of his companies are going to take a real hit. He, personally, was very much identified with the success or otherwise of his assets. The value of Semyonovich Inc. will plummet when the markets open tomorrow, you'll see. And that will directly harm the Kremlin."

Adrian looked around the room, warming now to this theme.

"But that's just for starters," he said. "We don't know exactly what secret partnerships are woven into Semyonovich's business empire—outside the stuff on his company nameplates, I mean. What else was he doing for his masters in Russia? We think he may have been running arms on the Kremlin's behalf to Caucasian separatists, for example. Disrupting little pro-West republics like Georgia. Maybe he was funding East European, pro-Kremlin opposition groups? Particularly in Ukraine. That's a possibility. But we'll find out, you can be sure of that."

"There'll be a lot of collateral damage," Teddy said.

"That's about it," Adrian agreed. "Semyonovich was a key figure for the Kremlin. He was in many ways a bellwether for their commercial expansion in the West. We'll need to watch the Kremlin's reaction in the coming weeks, as well as seeing what unravels elsewhere from Semyonovich's death."

After the meeting had broken up, Teddy Parkinson unnecessarily repeated his offer to Adrian to come for lunch at his country home in Surrey, as if he'd just thought it up.

Never mind the assassination of Semyonovich, Adrian was caressing the idea of an assassination of his own, and he needed Parkinson's support. With the Russian refusal to extradite Bykov, there were no other options.

He thought of the note addressed to him and pinned to Finn's dead body outside the embassy in Berlin two years before.

"Honour him in death," it had ended. No matter how things had been left with Finn before he met his end, the SIS wasn't going to let him down after it. Adrian would see that he got his revenge.

5

LOGAN WALKED SLOWLY BETWEEN the rows of plastic reclining chairs planted twenty deep along the beach. They were all either occupied or claimed by towels, magazines, half-empty bottles of wine, picnic baskets—all the detritus of the summer tourists.

He'd taken a taxi from the industrial capital Podgorica, after his connection there from Belgrade and Marseille, down along Montenegro's Adriatic coastline.

Halfway to his destination, he'd paid off the taxi and taken a bus for the remaining twenty-five miles or so. It made slow progress along a winding road that traced the rocky shore broken with bays of fine curved beaches and dotted with islands where yachts were moored— some the second or even third vessel belonging to the Russian industrial barons.

It was ten years since he'd last made this journey. The country was very different now from the time he'd been stationed in the Balkans. Prosperity had arrived in Montenegro, in the form of Russian money. Billions of Russian dollars had first sucked up the local production enterprises of any value to the Kremlin, then turned to tourist development.

While the West was aiding the breakup of the former Yugoslavia, of which the tiny state of Montenegro was part, and notionally shoving it towards democracy, it was Russia that had then stepped in, first with its state-backed industrial giants who'd taken over the profitable parts of Montenegro's industry, and then with its real estate developers who bought most of the country's two-hundred-mile coastline.

The Kremlin was advancing into western Europe through the back door of the Balkans, its historic hunger for warm-water ports, backed with its huge new wealth, bringing it closer than it had ever managed under communism. A fledgling new country like Montenegro, barely able to fly, had been swiftly gobbled up by Russian cash.

Logan was looking away from the sea now, up at the cafés along the waterfront. He finally found the one he was looking for. It was called Slovenskja, named for the Slovenians who had made this little medieval Montenegrin town a popular resort in the 1920s.

It was a Sunday, and all the locals had joined the tourists on the beach to create one complex, almost geometric puzzle of oiled, heaving, semi-naked humanity, beneath which "one of the world's ten most beautiful beaches" was invisible.

That it was a Sunday was of some importance to Logan. The man he was to contact would be stretched for backup. The day after he'd developed the photographs in Marseille, Logan was going to make the third and final delivery of the woman's picture to the most dangerous and unpredictable of his freelance connections.

Stefan Stavroisky, SVR chief in Montenegro and protégé of Putin's from the days when he was deputy mayor of Saint Petersburg, had been stationed in Belgrade during the Serbian war. And that's where Logan had originally made contact with him. In the thaw between the West and Russia, the KGB and the CIA had fraternised, at least on a personal level. When Boris Yeltsin was Russia's president, both sides had been keen that the Balkan wars didn't develop into an American confrontation with Russia.

Logan had known Stavroisky well back then, in the late 1990s. NATO forces were pressurising the Serbs at the end of the war, and Yeltsin's Russia made protests on the Serbs' behalf that weren't backed up by any serious threat of Russian military involvement. But the war had remained a deeply humiliating snub for Russia, and later, under Putin, the resentment it caused had aided Putin's call to nationalism—the protection of fellow Slavs—when he'd become president in 2000.

Logan and Stavroisky had worked, sometimes together, sometimes in opposition, during those times. There had been some cooperation between the KGB and the CIA, both to limit the damage and to pursue a closer relationship after the war ended. When NATO had accidentally bombed the Chinese embassy in Belgrade in 1999, Stavroisky was one of those who had silently worked to calm the situation, and the Americans had been grudgingly grateful.

Stavroisky was Logan's age and had attached himself to Putin's cause early on in Putin's rise to power. He'd made the right choice, and had swiftly advanced through the ranks of Russia's foreign service.

Stavroisky was also meticulous in the cause of his own advancement. Like Putin, he was a fitness fanatic and took care to enjoy the sports Putin enjoyed. He was a keen fisherman and a judo black belt. He had played for the KGB's volleyball team, Logan remembered.

"What's the transfer market like?" Logan had joked to him one evening over a drink. But Stavroisky drew the line at jokes about the KGB.

Logan and Stavroisky had struck up a form of friendship, had met on maybe a dozen occasions, drunk together, whored together, and until Logan's recall and dismissal, it might have seemed they were even working together during those times.

Now, Logan heard, there was no fraternisation between the CIA and the KGB anywhere, let alone here. The Balkans were a new frontline of sorts. It had all reverted to the status quo ante 1989.

It being a Sunday, Logan figured that Stavroisky would have fewer resources to call on; August weekends would draw out significant numbers of his operatives to the beach, to yachts, to bars and restaurants, their mobile phones out of range or quietly switched off to evade his summons.

And he had given Stavroisky just an hour and a half's warning to be at the café, against the Russian's protests that it wasn't possible to get there in time.

"I have something with me that will make your masters very happy," Logan had told him. "It's a once-in-a-lifetime opportunity, Stefan," he'd said. "Promotion for you, maybe one of your Russian awards, certainly money," he'd said. "Certainly, lots and lots of money for you."

"Tell me on the phone," Stavroisky had told him. "I'm busy."

"It's a photograph," Logan had said. "Somebody your side wants very badly. I'll need payment within twenty-four hours. Be there by four, at the café Slovenskja, or I'll take it elsewhere."

The Russian would know that by "elsewhere" he meant the Americans, or maybe a European intelligence service, and maybe guess that Logan would do that anyway. Speed was essential.

"I can't make it in that time," Stavroisky protested. "I'm over sixty miles away."

"You're the head of the SVR in Montenegro, Stefan," Logan replied. "If anyone can make it, you can."

Logan decided he'd give Stavroisky until four thirty anyway.

"And make sure you're alone, Stefan," he'd added. "I'll be watching. Any sign of company, you can forget it."

Now, Logan looked away from the café and out to sea. Even with depleted Sunday resources, he knew that Stavroisky would not come alone if he could avoid it. He knew, fairly certainly anyway, that the SVR chief's backup would come from the sea, where it was less easy to detect a presence. There were dozens of small boats coming in and out, to and from the beach. Anyone in them could be at the café in a few minutes, if Stavroisky gave the signal.

Logan took out the photograph, wrapped up in its waterproof plastic cover, from inside his jacket and rolled it into a tube, tying it finally with a rubber band. Then he found a wastebin, behind a toilet cubicle and out of sight. It was thirty or forty yards from the Slovenskja. He thrust the rolled package deep inside the bin until he felt the bottom underneath the cans and paper cups that were overflowing from its upper edges.

Satisfied it was safely concealed, he walked up the beach towards the town. Just behind the beach, he turned away from the town and climbed past the medieval houses up towards a cliff, where there was another café, with a telescope for tourists.

But rather than the ancient monastery on the island in the bay, or simply out over the placid turquoise sea, the telescope also offered him a fine view of the Slovenskja café and the surrounding area. He settled in for the wait.

At 4:48, he saw Stavroisky approach the café in too much of a hurry for an experienced operative.

Stefan Stavroisky was a tall, fit man with thick black hair cut short. He had the manicured look and the consciously honed figure of a vain man suddenly aware that his age was beginning to tell. Logan watched him closely. The Russian was wearing a grey suit, the jacket slung over his shoulder, and black leather shoes. He looked incongruous—and very visible—next to the semi-naked bodies on the beach.

Through the magnification of the telescope, Logan saw that the Russian was in an agitated state. Swivelling the telescope, he studied the bay. There were too many boats to be certain, but he detected three or four that seemed to be approaching in time with Stavroisky. It could be any one of them—or none at all.

But the SVR chief had at least arrived at the café alone. Logan had watched him from the moment his BMW drew up by the café, and he'd parked in a handicapped space. No other cars seemed to be trailing him. If Stavroisky had only just managed to get here himself, then there was a good chance he would have no backup—at least for a while.

Logan dialled the number and watched Stavroisky open his hand and flick open the cell phone clenched inside it. "Where the hell are you, Logan?" the Russian demanded.

"Leave the café. Walk right, out of the entrance on the sea side, along the beach for around thirty-five yards. There's a blue-and-yellow sun awning. Behind that there's a toilet. And behind that there's a wastebin. At the bottom of the bin you'll find a black plastic waterproof package. You'll need to dig a bit. It's dirty work, Stefan."

"Where are you?" But the line had gone dead.

Logan watched Stavroisky looking around the beach, then up into the town and finally out to the water and the sea. He looked angry. But then he stepped out and began to walk in the direction Logan had indicated, an irritable figure whose office attire drew one or two catcalls from the sun worshippers.

Logan saw him stop at the blue-and-yellow awning and then go to the right, as if to the cubicle, but he disappeared behind it at the last minute. He was out of a sight for a minute or so, but reemerged holding the plastic package. He didn't look up, and Logan took that as a sign that he wasn't making contact with anybody.

Then, from the corner of his vision, Logan saw a black van moving slowly along the beachfront. It looked too commercial to have any business in the town on a Sunday, and it was moving too slowly for his liking.

He observed it for a whole minute. It was not stopping, either outside the Slovenskja or anywhere else, just trawling along as if watching or waiting for an instruction or—more likely—trying to pinpoint his cell phone transmission.

At that moment, his phone rang and he swivelled the telescope back to the café. There was Stavroisky, apparently calling for a drink and with his phone to his ear. He carried the package carelessly in his hand, unopened.

"The photograph is of a woman," Logan said. "A KGB colonel. If you want to know where she is, I'll need the money deposited before Tuesday morning."

Then Logan switched off the phone, watching the screen die. Then he tossed it in the palm of his hand a couple of times and finally lobbed it over the cliff and watched it fall onto the rocks below.

He returned to the telescope. He'd given Stavroisky instructions for payment, inside the packet with the photograph. But the photograph was useless without the location. There was no room for discussion. Either Stavroisky paid within forty-eight hours, and received the location of the woman, or he didn't.

Logan walked swiftly down the steep path from the promontory and looked back down at the black van a quarter of a mile away. It had stopped now at the edge of the road, roughly in the middle of the beach. There was an antenna rising from the centre of the van now—vainly trying, he assumed, to pick up his signal. But the van had arrived too late.

He took a taxi from the centre of the town to Bar, farther down the coast, and caught the night ferry to the Italian port of Bari.

6

TEDDY PARKINSON'S "COUNTRY HOME" was, in Adrian's eyes at least, a modest, modern three-bedroom brick house on the high street of an undistinguished Surrey village. Adrian considered that it cried "modesty" to an unnecessarily excessive degree.

But Parkinson had always been known for his low-profile tastes, and he hadn't, as Adrian had, married into money.

Teddy Parkinson was a safe pair of hands, which was why he'd been given the politically adroit position of head of the Joint Intelligence Committee. He was a man with reasonable horizons, who deferred to authority and had always kept his political masters' self-confidence buoyant.

He holidayed once a year in England—another example, in Adrian's opinion, of an almost sackcloth approach to personal enjoyment.

Adrian considered him a perfectly behaved, grammar-school-educated civil servant who knew his place, and whose main fault was in not aspiring to be more than that. But for precisely this reason, Adrian often needed him. Teddy's support was valuable in anything that might be considered by Downing Street to be too risqué.

Adrian, by contrast, had from the start brought a flamboyance to MI6, which had almost cost him the top job. It was only his own political adroitness, and this solely in the field of internal politics, that had beaten two other, more Parkinson-like candidates out of the running.

To some at the Service, this new style at the top was welcome. To others—in particular those whose feet Adrian had trampled over to reach the top—he was unsuitable, even dangerous. Teddy was a useful, a necessary ally for Adrian, therefore, when he needed something that required the imprimatur of a man with a reputation for safety first.

After lunch cooked by Teddy's wife, Elizabeth, a self-described "English rose," the two men decided to walk across the fields at the rear of the house and up to a small hill that looked towards the South Downs.

But Teddy knew that Adrian hadn't come for the lunch. Despite Adrian's scornful, snobbish opinion of him, he was well aware of Adrian's need—and Adrian's own faults that propelled that need. The two were not friends, and Teddy wasn't fooled by any pretence that they were. They'd never socialised together outside work.

He assumed it was further information about Semyonovich Adrian wished to impart, in private, but in this at least he was to be surprised. The matter Adrian wished to discuss was nothing to do with the murdered Russian.

"The Semyonovich business has overshadowed another development over the weekend, Teddy," Adrian began as they left the cultivated field at the rear of Parkinson's house and walked uphill across a rough, sun-scorched meadow. "Grigory Bykov. Remember him? The Russians have finally declared that they won't extradite him. It's taken them six months from my meeting in Helsinki. This is a matter that concerns us much more than the assassination of Semyonovich. It's one of my boys that got killed, our boys."

"Oh, yes?" Teddy replied.

"Yes. You remember Finn?"

Parkinson let the name hang in the still afternoon air and continued to tramp up the field.

"He'd left the Secret Intelligence Service, hadn't he, Adrian?" he said finally. "By the time he was killed, he hadn't been with us for . . . how long? Five, six years? Still on first-name terms with someone who deserted the SIS?"

"He's dead now, Teddy. And as you know, Finn was always my boy. When he was onside, he was one of the best officers I ever had."

This was a new argument of Teddy's, he saw, different from the one he'd used back in January. Parkinson was now distancing Finn from the protection of the SIS. The politicians were moving the target as usual. It was an argument Parkinson certainly hadn't used over their lunch at the Special Forces Club. Then, it was all about making an effort at quiet extradition first. Adrian gritted his teeth.

"But he'd given the SIS the push," Parkinson said. "Or we gave him the push. Both, perhaps. Either way, what do we owe him? Isn't that the question?"

"He turned his back on us, yes. In a way," Adrian agreed. "He became a liability, and we had to lose him. That was back in 2000. But . . ." He paused, for a rare moment uncertain how to continue.

They'd reached the top of the meadow, where a small copse was maintained for pheasant shooting in the winter. Wire netting and metal bird feeders were ready for the new young chicks to be reared. It was a beautifully clear day, and the view began to unfold as they breasted the hill.

Adrian didn't like to say what he was going to say. He rarely, if ever, admitted he was culpable. However, in this case . . .

"It's true, Teddy. Finn did leave us, in the sense that he rejected government policy back then. He suddenly got all hot about what was right and wrong, and so on. It became impossible for him to work any longer in the role he'd performed so brilliantly for many years in Moscow. But he left us for a reason, and that reason has come home to roost. The reason he left was that HM government was cosying up, as he saw it, to Vladimir Putin. He believed it was against the UK's national interest. Finn's view was out of whack back then, but now it's become government policy. Now Putin is out in the cold with our government, as Finn always said he should be."

"Policies change, Adrian. It's not our job, let alone the job of our officers, to interpret political necessities."

"Okay. Agreed. It wasn't right for Finn to take matters into his own hands. The awkward fact, however, is that he was right."

"So?"

"Finn was murdered by a KGB assassin for following up lines of enquiry we'd told him to drop. To drop for political reasons. Now, today, these are exactly the lines of enquiry we are pursuing. Again, for changing political reasons. He got murdered for it. And we were wrong," he added, including Parkinson in the assessment. "In January you told me to meet with the Russians. Give them an opportunity to hand Bykov over without losing face. That's all happened. I met Sergei Limov, as you know, seven months ago now. This weekend we learn the Russians aren't going to hand Bykov over. That leaves us with only one option, according to SIS procedure. We take out anyone who assassinates one of ours."

"One of ours, yes," Parkinson said, with heavy emphasis on "ours."

"To the Russians he always was one of ours. They never knew he'd left MI6. They murdered someone they believed to be a fully paid-up member of SIS. We can't allow that."

"Intelligence officers aren't paid to have political opinions," Teddy Parkinson said, returning to his earlier theme. He sounded hard-edged now, and ignored what Adrian perceived to have been his winning throw. He was better at dealing with Adrian than Adrian knew. "They're paid to put into play whatever they're told by HMG and by us."

"Finn was disobedient. I agree with you entirely, Teddy. But although he was no longer officially on our books, he was one of us. And the Russians thought so, that's the real point," Adrian repeated.

He was uncomfortably conscious that he was being far more supportive of Finn now than he'd been in the last years of Finn's life. *Honour him in death.*

"We don't allow people to kill our officers and get away with it," Adrian said. "It's part of the highest ethics of the SIS."

"So. You want to take action."

"Now that the Russians have refused extradition, yes. That was your condition, Teddy, not mine. We've done everything the prime minister asked us to do. Foreign agents don't murder our people with impunity. If we don't make the point, they'll just be encouraged, maybe to do a similar hit on another, acting SIS officer in the future."

Parkinson looked across the rolling hills that stretched into the haze of distance. He'd picked up a stick, Adrian noticed, and was flicking it in the air, like a headmaster wielding a cane.

"I share your concern," he said, without looking at Adrian.

"Thank you, Teddy. So I have your support?"

"So far as it goes," Parkinson said.

Parkinson observed Adrian standing impatiently on the hill beside him. Carew looked very out of place in this ordinary, unkempt, though to him spectacular countryside, he thought. He imagined that Adrian's country estate in Hampshire, with its tailored buildings and lawns, would accommodate Adrian rather better. The man's face had a city pallor, which accentuated the red parts of his face, but it wasn't the ruddiness of the open air. Maybe the pallor was also the smoking, Parkinson thought.

He noted Adrian's blue suit and black shoes—Parkinson had changed into his gardening clothes as soon as they'd arrived. Adrian's very stance as he stood on the top of the hill suggested to him someone deeply uncomfortable with the relentless ordinariness of nature. He was someone who needed action, for which the city was an illusory substitute, in his opinion.

Adrian now leaned down and picked up a smooth stone from the grass, though not from any admiration for the fossil that Parkinson saw in it. It was a tool, something to play with, an accessory to Adrian's central purpose. Adrian handled its smoothness, turning it in his palm.

"There is an additional factor," Adrian said suddenly.

"Let's walk down here and come back through the village," Parkinson said, ignoring the remark. "There's a very ancient Saxon monument I'd like to show you."

He could see the impatience flash across Adrian's eyes as the other man said brusquely, "As you know, Teddy, Bykov has actually been rewarded for killing our officer. With a seat in Russia's parliament. They're laughing in our face."

"Well, I know, I know," Parkinson said. "But killing MPs isn't exactly our beat, Adrian."

"They don't play by the rules, why should we?"

"What if they retaliate?" Parkinson said. "Suppose they suddenly decide it's open season on our MPs for instance? I say this just for the sake of argument, you understand."

"I'm not sure that would be such a bad thing, would it?" Adrian replied.

"Adrian, Adrian . . ."

Adrian smiled without apology.

"The point I'm making is that if the Kremlin can come here and murder our people, they shouldn't be allowed to get away with it just because they turn their killers into MPs."

"All right, I take the point. You made the same one in January, I remember."

They'd reached the bottom of the hill, on the other side from where they'd walked up.

A man and a woman were walking a pair of identical dogs. Parkinson hailed them. It was his way of saying to Adrian that they were back in the real world, a world where spies being murdered wasn't really of much relevance to anyone.

"We'll have to see how this might play with the PM," he said, when the couple had passed. They stood in front of a stile, the crossing of which, Adrian knew, signalled the end of the conversation. "Politicians, Adrian, don't like other politicians getting murdered, even their direst enemies. And certainly not on their orders. It sets a precedent. Leaves them feeling exposed." He tapped his stick on the stile. "And they don't like other politicians getting murdered even if they're fake politicians," he added.

"They're all bloody fake," Adrian said.

Parkinson chose to ignore another of Adrian's explosive verbal devices—EVDs, as they were known at SIS headquarters.

"Do we have to include them in the decision, then?" Adrian persisted. "The politicians? Shouldn't it just be an SIS matter?"

"I don't know. I'll have to have a think about that."

Parkinson looked down the lane and pointed. "See that stone there? Saxon monument with a Celtic cross on it. See it? Very strange," he said.

"I'd appreciate it very much, Teddy," Adrian said, ignoring the monument, "if you could back me on this."

Parkinson showed no sign yet of stepping over the stile.

"Any contact with Finn's old source in Moscow?" he suddenly said instead, looking almost in the opposite direction to Adrian, back up the hill. "High-placed, inside Putin's coterie, wasn't he. Someone we could do with now, I'd have thought. Mikhail, wasn't that it?"

It was a question Adrian would have preferred not to be asked, and Parkinson's archly vague memory of the most important source Britain had had in living memory irritated him still further.

"Not since Finn was murdered," he replied. "As you know, Source Mikhail only ever communicated through Finn. That was why Finn was murdered."

"Pity we didn't get through to him before Finn's death," Parkinson demurred.

Adrian detected the criticism, as he was intended to, he realised.

"That wasn't our brief, Teddy," he countered. "In fact, the opposite was the case. Back then we were told that Mikhail was discredited. Told by the politicians, if you remember."

"But he isn't discredited now," Parkinson said.

"We know that, yes. Now. Come on, Teddy, you were there back then. You know we were told to lay off the information from Finn's source as it was deemed anti-Putin. That's why Finn left the SIS, walked out on us. He was disgusted. And he was right."

"You didn't defend Finn then, I seem to remember."

"Nobody did. But I am now."

For a moment, Adrian uncomfortably recalled his last conversation with Finn, under a tree in St. James' Park in an autumn downpour. It had been a cold, wet October day. Back then, almost three years ago now, he'd practically told Finn he was dead meat, not for leaving the SIS, but for carrying on his investigations solo. And, worse than that, he'd threatened Finn's woman, the KGB colonel.

As if picking up his thoughts, Parkinson said, "And the woman—his wife, wasn't she?"

"They married, yes," Adrian said patiently. "After she defected from Russia."

"Well?"

"Not a word, not even a whisper. She's disappeared."

"Any ideas?"

"We think the French have her."

"And they're not talking."

"No."

Teddy Parkinson let the silence grow. Eventually he said, "With Finn dead, she's the last possible hope we have of ever reviving Mikhail." He looked steadily at Adrian. "We need that source now. Mikhail, Adrian. We really do need him now."

"I know that, Teddy."

Parkinson put his hand on Adrian's shoulder, but it was not a gesture of friendship.

"Find her, Adrian. And when you have, I'll do all I can to make sure you have free rein with this Bykov. But not until you've found the woman. Bargain?"

Adrian gritted his teeth in frustration.

It was the same instruction he'd received from the damn Russian, Sergei Limov, back in Helsinki in January. Find the Russian colonel. But the bitch had disappeared.

"Thank you," he managed to say. "I appreciate it."

"Now let me show you this monument," Parkinson said. "It really is very intriguing." He stepped with surprising agility over the stile.

7

ANNA RESNIKOV WALKED DOWN the slight hill from the house, holding her son's hand. They paused outside the wrought iron fence at the rear of the house, behind which the tall palm tree in the garden dropped its dead fronds into the road. The boy stooped to look at something on the ground. A trail of ants were crawling up into a hole in the wall like a party of sherpas.

They often stopped here on the two–hundred–yard journey to the square, where the boy's crèche was situated. The place held some magic, some child's attraction that was important to him. She let go of his hand and watched him as he squatted and stared at something in the road. Sometimes he picked up a bug that crawled slowly across their path, or just watched the ants that lived under the holm oak that had split its way up through the tarmac. She liked his curiosity. It echoed her own and his father Finn's. And it made her even more watchful herself.

It was her birthday. She was thirty–eight. Finn would have been fifty, she thought, and she smiled at the memory of her grandmother once chiding her to find a man her own age.

She saw her life thus far as being one of continual adaptation—most of it forced on her by external circumstances. First there'd been adapting to the lies of the Soviet state, before the Wall fell in 1989, when she was nineteen years old. Then there'd been her long efforts to fit in with her father's demands. A senior SVR officer, he had run the Russians' Syrian station in Damascus until his retirement. He'd wanted her to be like her mother, a quiet, compliant wife to a KGB careerist.

But rather than obey him, she had decided to outdo him; to beat him at his own game. And she'd succeeded in that. Only to discover that she'd become a successful SVR officer for the wrong reasons—with an eye to her father's approval, that was all. That was part of life's trickery.

And then there'd been Finn himself, the greatest act of adaptation of them all. First she was sent to spy on him. She'd first informed on him, then attempted to undermine his reasons for being in Moscow. Then, in the cause of Russia, she'd seduced him. And finally she'd fallen in love with him. Another of life's humourous twists.

But at the same moment as her professional liaison with Finn had developed into a personal one, she'd discovered that the man she'd once tried to impress, her father, was procuring girls as young as eight years old for the KGB, to be drugged and used as sexual favours for the entrapment of a Swiss banker. That was the truth about her father and about the organisation for which they both worked.

Finn had been her way out, as well as her lover. So she'd adapted to exile—and to constant fear of the KGB, which would never forget her treason.

And now she and her son had been in the village for just over a year, under false identities supplied by the French. She was becoming happy, she realised. She was finally beginning to feel that this little village was their home. And she knew she was dropping her guard, bit by bit.

At first, French security personnel had taken a house in the village too, while her safety was established. The villagers said nothing—they rarely commented outside their homes on the affairs of others. But she was aware that they connected her arrival with the two men and a woman from Paris. Her three guardians were unmistakably police or security officers. The mayor, at least, would have been told of the reason for their presence, and he was a drinker and a gossip.

Anna might now have a French name, and she spoke the language well, but she was clearly a foreigner, and to the villagers, she was someone special.

She felt lighthearted this morning, as she had done, she suddenly realised, for weeks now. The weight of the past was beginning to lift, and her grief at Finn's death was more of a numbing sensation than the all-consuming pain it had once been. She felt free to expand again—in herself and from this place of safety—more free than she had felt for a long while.

When her French guardians had finally packed up and gone, assuring her that she and the boy were now safe, they had left her with emergency numbers. Then someone from the DGSE in Paris would come to visit once a month. There was always competition for the job, for a trip to the south certainly, but mainly to spend time in her company. She was highly regarded for her expertise and experience in matters of espionage, but she was also admired by her French handlers for her cool beauty and her bravery.

Her controllers in Paris—and now she herself—believed that the secret of her identity and location was solid, and for her the monthly meeting had developed into a formality that became an irksome reminder that all was not right and never would be.

It was true, there had been one or two bad moments, like the incident at the village fete the summer before, just after they'd arrived. It was the only time of year when the village filled up with outsiders. A fairground had been set up in the square, and much was drunk late into the night. There was dancing, and two men had approached her, first flirtatiously, then aggressively, finally insisting she dance with them. But they were drunk, and when they ignored her refusals and began to manhandle her, she had instinctively laid them out on the grass, one with a blow to the side of the head, the other with a broken arm and leg.

The villagers had looked at her with new eyes after that. She became respected, but also an object of greater suspicion. She had made a few friends that night, but others wondered, Who was this foreign woman who could overcome two men and knock them cold? It was also noted that the police who arrived to arrest the men were over-respectful towards her.

But in general it had been an increasingly peaceful year. She felt stronger and more ready to take whatever steps life held in store for her now. She was beginning to understand that, in order to control her life, she needed to stop trying to control it, as she always had.

Her life was small, with the days centred around her son. She had named him Finn, Little Finn, as she and Willy referred to him. The villagers noted that she spent a great deal of time with him, that she never had visitors, except for the older man she called Willy, and that she was as independent and capable of fending for herself as anyone. A quiet admiration for her grew in the village. She never asked anyone for anything, never intruded into their lives, and slowly, her quiet, dignified calm drew the people of Fougieres out of their natural reticence with strangers to the extent that they greeted her and Little Finn in the street. She hadn't been invited inside their homes, but as another exile like herself—the gay owner of the village's bed and breakfast—had told her, it took at least a quarter of a century to become a local here.

She and Little Finn continued on their way, past the wrought iron fence and down the lane.

The French children were not yet back at the village school at the end of August, but the crèche was hardly a school and stayed open irregularly. Today it was open, however, and its rules were negligible. It didn't matter how late they were, or if Little Finn went at all. But today Anna was going to meet Willy for lunch on her birthday. Willy had been her only regular contact in the two years since Finn's death, apart from the sporadic meetings with the officers from French security. But today she needed to speak to him alone, with her head clear of her son's needs.

Anna and Little Finn walked on, past the head-high shutters of the old, huddled homes, closed as usual against the heat, but more, she believed, against prying eyes, and so that those inside could pry without being seen. These rural French were private, she thought, almost like the Sicilians; friendly enough in a monosyllabic sort of way when you encountered them, but unforthcoming, at any rate to anyone outside their own history.

The village was empty as usual. It was only ever full during the fetes, or when the grapes were being brought in, which would be soon. There were few visitors except for the occasional car full of tourists who had taken a blind diversion to see something they would otherwise have missed on the main roads. There was also the infrequent visitor to the gay bed and breakfast establishment at the manor house, where Jonny, the other exile, and his French boyfriend ran an Internet-only lodging. The two of them had become as close friends as she had anywhere. Everything—life, family, work, and friends— was either dead or left behind in Russia.

She recalled that in the years leading up to her defection, her chief worry had been that Finn would leave her as soon as she committed herself to coming over. It had never occurred to her that he would die. That wasn't something people in life-threatening occupations gave much thought to.

They stopped outside the bed and breakfast, and she saw Jonny and his boyfriend dipping in and out of the pool. "Come and have a glass of wine," Jonny shouted when he spotted her.

"It's eleven o'clock in the morning," she retorted, laughing.

"Exactly," he said.

She smiled without replying. They were unlikely friends, she thought, but she trusted them after a year. They were outsiders in the village like her, and with a cosmopolitan flair. It was the only house other than her own that she had entered in the village. They accepted her and Little Finn without asking questions.

"No visitors this week?" she called. It was a routine question.

"Two Danish lesbians just booked in for tonight." Jonny relished shouting the information across the village square.

She and Little Finn walked on.

It was a good place to be hidden, she thought. It was a good place, end of story. But most importantly, anyone new—and any strange car—would be noted down by someone. She felt the safety of being watched by the eyes of the village. And little from outside disturbed the slow torpor, apart from the library van on a Thursday and the baker's van on a Friday.

Even the hunters who visited in the winter months and surrounded the village on misty mornings all came from the surrounding villages, and she'd learned to identify them all in their first winter. They met at 5:00 a.m. in the "bar," a room owned by the mayor that was a bar only in name. Then they dispersed into the fog after a few *coupes de vin*, before it was light, and returned late in the afternoon, often with the carcass of a boar, which was butchered in the village and shared out. And then the bar was full until they all drove home with varying degrees of recklessness across the fields.

Anna and Little Finn reached the *mairie*, which was where the crèche had its home. She led him inside under the drooping tricolour at the entrance to find a room full of children on the floor, drawing, talking, shouting. The two women who ran the crèche were from the city, Marseille, and they were happier than the children to be living in this rural paradise.

"Madame Paulin," she was greeted by the younger of the two teachers. "Bonjour, Charlot." She smiled at Finn.

Finn didn't yet know there were two languages, only that he spoke different words for the same things at home and at school; and that sometimes his mother called him Charlot and sometimes Finn. He didn't seem to mind.

"A quinze heures, c'est bon?" the teacher said to Anna.

"Oui. Et merci." Three o'clock would be fine. She'd be back long before then.

"De rien," the teacher said, and smiled. "Bonne journée."

Anna let go of the boy's hand. He didn't look back, safe in the company of the women and his friends.

She returned to the house around the path through the fields. M. Barry was cranking the portable sawmill on the other side of the street from her house. There was a pile of tree limbs and bits of broken fencing, ready to be cut.

She'd learned that M. Barry, like the others, prepared long in advance for the winter. It was cold up here, not like in Russia, but a damp, chilling cold that entered the bones.

She wished him good morning, and he raised his cap; same clothes, same cap, summer and winter. He was a handsome man in his sixties, with a wife who suffered from Parkinson's disease. He'd told Anna once that he had never been beyond Uzès, seven miles away, in his entire life. In a year, she had come to enjoy her fleeting conversations with him out by the sawmill, conversations that went beyond the natural reserve of the other villagers. He had quietly assumed a paternalistic role of looking out for her.

"You need anything?" he enquired. "I'll have some wood soon, but anything else?"

"I don't think so. Thank you for asking."

He was kind to her and her son. He gave them homemade cheese sometimes, or sausage he made himself from one of the wild boars shot in winter.

"It's hot now, but soon it will be autumn," he said, as if to explain the woodpile. But she thought he looked awkward, more so than usual.

He paused, raised his cap, and scratched his head. He seemed to be thinking of what to say, not like his normal, relaxed manner at all.

"You are not too lonely?" he suddenly asked.

This was out of character—too intimate, she felt. But there was something about his face that told her he was serious.

"No, not lonely," she replied and smiled.

"Never any visitors," he remarked, again pricking her into wariness. It was not the type of conversation they had. There was never anything personal. Not like this at all. But equally she felt drawn to reply honestly, without fear.

"No. Never any visitors," she replied. "Apart from Willy."

Willy and M. Barry had struck up a joint friendship, in the unspoken cause of her protection.

M. Barry paused and lifted his cap again and wiped the sweat from his head with the back of the same hand. Then he took out a tobacco pouch and began to roll a cigarette. As he did so, he spoke, as if he needed something to do in order to say what he was going to say.

"Not the man on Saturday, then," he said.

She immediately froze. "Saturday?"

"He came to your gates. No farther. I thought you must be out walking."

"Did he ring the bell, then?

"No. No, he didn't."

He put the cigarette in his mouth, lit it, and picked up the crank handle for the sawmill.

She was silent, her mind racing through the events of Saturday, looking for something out of the ordinary.

"What did he look like?" she asked.

"He was slim, about your age I should think. White jacket. I didn't see him close to. He looked like an athlete, perhaps."

"A car? Did he have a car?"

"Not that I saw."

"Thank you," she said. "Thank you, Monsieur Barry. I appreciate it."

He tipped his cap and gave her a broad, confident smile.

"I'll have plenty of wood for you when winter comes, don't you worry," he said, and began to crank the handle again.

She walked around to the side of the house. She had the numbers to call in an emergency, but what could she say?

A man had come to the house. White jacket.

She paused and seemed to remember a man in Uzès on Saturday. He wore a white jacket, she remembered. It was certainly enough of a reason to call Paris, but she was reluctant. She didn't want to shatter the illusion she'd enjoyed moments before that her life had become safe. She decided to mention it to Willy first.

On entering the house, she took a gun from the locked drawer in the kitchen. It was a Thompson Contender pistol, a handgun that was unique for its range. With just a twelve-inch barrel, it could hit a target at over two hundred yards if you were good enough. And she was good enough. She realised she hadn't taken it out of the drawer for over a month.

She put her cell phone in the pocket of a jacket and took the car keys from the table by the door. She looked around finally, expecting to see something out of the ordinary, but the old farmhouse seemed calm. It had been built in the year of the French Revolution. There was a stone engraved with the date by the front gate. Maybe down here, in the small places, even great events like revolutions went unnoticed.

Locking the door behind her, she opened the big metal gates and drove the Mercedes out. She placed the gun under the driver's seat. Then she closed the gates behind her.

There was a pile of sand by the wall of the next house, left there after some building job had been completed. She was suddenly alert, her trained instincts activated. She stepped out of the car and sprinkled a little sand around the gates, not so much as would be noticed, but enough if you were looking for the faintest sign of a footprint later.

8

LARS SHADED HIS EYES against the high sun. Then he cast his gaze down again towards the monastery. It was tucked away in a grove of cypresses and pines, across an isthmus on a flat, man-made island out in the bay. Flipping the pages of a tourist guide, he pretended to study what he already knew. The monastery had been built in the eleventh century as a sanctuary for Orthodox Christians fleeing the Turkish invasion of Serbia. Inside its weathered, arched dark wood gates was a courtyard of rough flagstones in the cypress shade, and then a tiny church dedicated to Saint Sava of Serbia.

A few yards beyond the little white church was the monastery, built a few centuries later.

He looked up from the guidebook. It had been a month since his first visit, and he knew the layout from memory. The key element for his second visit was the tall bell tower that protruded above the monastery on the side of the island facing the open sea. Once again, he studied the height and position of the tower carefully. The tower had once doubled as a lighthouse for sailors from Venetian trading fleets,

Levantine merchant vessels, Arab dhows, and Turkish *gulets*, sent out to engage the West in commerce, when there was no war, from the Port of the Sultan. It had been built for the view.

Lars waited in the hot sun at the edge of the group of tourists.

There was an American couple, the woman with frizzy hair and a pinched, nervous face, the man taller by a head, with a flabby grin. He looked bulky in huge shorts and an open shirt. The others were local, Montenegrins or citizens from the surrounding Balkan countries; an old woman dressed in black; a young couple who couldn't stop touching each other; two women who might have been academics—they looked like they'd be at home in a library, he thought—and an old man with grizzled white stubble and intensely green eyes. He supported himself on a gnarled stick.

Finally the shabby tourist bus was almost full, and Lars stepped inside last of all, paying the return fare for the monastery visit. He placed his backpack carefully on the rack. It was heavier than last time, and he didn't want the canister inside it clanking against the metal of the rack.

The bus set off almost at once across the rock isthmus that, according to the guidebook, was built as a later addition to the monastery, when convenience overcame isolated seclusion on the monks' wish list.

He studied the tourists on the bus again. He needed to be sure that, unlike him, they were what they seemed. Most were apparently day trippers from the capital city, Podgorica, while others had come from abroad and wore backpacks, shorts, sandals, and caps against the intense heat. One or two of the older local people also wore an Orthodox cross around their necks.

He sat next to the old lady in black and nodded a greeting. She crossed herself, and he returned her pious gesture. He was praying too, in his way, but not for something that she would understand.

The bus crossed noisily between the perfectly calm stretches of turquoise water on either side of the isthmus, belching exhaust fumes into the clear air.

They disembarked on the far side, in the shade of the massive cypress tree. A few scrawny chickens pecked at the bare grass and the scraps of potato chips and snacks previous visitors had dropped. The air was still, dead. The tree above him could have been painted against the sky. The dark green, almost black cypress stood like a shadow against the shattering blue.

Lars took a drink from a plastic water bottle and waited for the others to shuffle towards the monastery in that soporific, almost dutiful way adopted by visitors to sacred places. He didn't follow them on the unguided tour but looked around, from time to time checking carefully where they'd stopped. Their first pause was at the tiny chapel to pay a preliminary homage to Saint Sava, and then on to the main attraction, the monastery itself.

He set off at an angle, away from them. Before he entered the monastery, he wanted to take a walk around the small island. He felt exposed here, at the end of the isthmus on a small outcrop of piled rocks. There was only one way out. He'd told them he wouldn't do the job if there was only one exit, and they'd had to make a complicated plan so that he could extricate himself if things went wrong.

He hoisted the backpack over his shoulders. It was heavy. It was not just the rifle this time, but a small air tank with five litres in it that would, he hoped, get him out of danger if that proved necessary. He'd almost decided to use it anyway.

He stood on the shore facing north first of all, balancing himself on a huge stone that was part of the breakwater of tumbled rocks scattered all around the island. Straight ahead of him, the coast curled round to the right, five miles away, before reaching another high cliff promontory where it presumably curved back northwards again.

To his left, at the head of the bay, was the small town and its tourist beach. The absence of any sand visible on the beach at this distance was explained by the inseparable mass of humanity that had camped on it for the day in rows of beach chairs.

Directly to the right, out to sea, were four or five large yachts, some of them more like ships. He passed his eyes over them, resting briefly on the one that interested him, the *Aurora*. She'd finally arrived. He'd been right, at least he was sure about that. The island was the only place to get a shot.

Then he walked around the island, which took only a few minutes, until he faced south. From there, the rocky cliff coastline to the left and ahead of him dodged in and out of bays and estuaries. On each promontory stood some human mark—a lookout post, a lighthouse, the religious motif of a cross or small chapel—each in its own way reaching out to the calm blue Adriatic Sea with a hand to welcome or repel, and an eye to observe.

Lars put down the pack and took out a small telescope. He looked across the southern waters, empty except for a few small yachts with their sails furled in the dead air. He studied the farthest visible promontory and read the distance; just over three and a half miles. It might take an hour and a half, he thought, depending on the currents. Too far for the small air tank. If he took that exit, he would have to come in to shore earlier than he'd have liked.

Then he carefully replaced the scope in the pack, strapped it up, and walked back to the cypresses, across the flagstones and past the church of Saint Sava, into the cool darkness of the monastery itself.

There were still some stragglers from his party, admiring the painting of the Virgin painted onto the old pink plaster.

He joined them and looked up at the crumbling, sad-eyed figure of the Madonna. She was a figure that expressed life, not the death he had come to give. He exchanged a curt nod with the two remaining tourists, the bulky American man and his frizzy-haired woman— foreigners like himself, visiting another country. He saw them watch him take out a sketchbook and begin to make some outlines. He was drawn to the eyes of the Virgin, big, dark, and almond-shaped, which seemed to contain a message of vulnerability and peace.

Lars felt the power of his anonymity amongst these tourists, but he didn't feel anonymous before the Virgin, and this unnerved him. He turned away, not wanting her gaze on him any longer.

He admired the paradoxical privacy of his own fame; he was concealed within his complete disconnection from the world around him. Soon—after this second hit perhaps, and with the invaluable help of the media—he would begin the transformation into myth. He was what myths were made of. That's what he believed. The myth of the assassin meant a lot to him. Even the word—*assassin*—was common to over fifty languages.

The man and the woman finally walked away from the painting, and he waited until they'd disappeared into a side room. He put the sketchbook away and, on the far side of the vaulted room, found the door to the steps that led up to the bell tower. It was locked, as it had been a month before. That was good. A newer piece of plastic tape explained in Montenegrin, Serbian, English, and French that the stairs were dangerous and undergoing repair work.

When he was sure that the last of his party had walked out of range and were looking at a collection of zinc cannonballs around the corner at the far end of the central chamber, he swiftly picked the ancient lock and entered the narrow stairway. The stairs began immediately inside the door, and with just enough room to turn with his backpack in the small space, he relocked the door and shot a bolt across from the inside to make sure.

Standing at the bottom of the narrow stairs, he looked up at a bright shaft of sunlight that came down in a diagonal stripe from the very top. It amused him for a moment that the monastery had once been engaged in the manufacture of cannonballs. War and the church had always been bedfellows.

Then he walked slowly up the winding stone staircase, until he reached the top, and through another door that led out into the bell tower.

The top of the tower was as far again above the roof of the monastery as the roof was above the ground. There was a fine, sweeping view, with a high balustrade for protection. The sea was blazing with the high light of the sun at midday, but the reflection wouldn't affect his aim from this height.

The target was on the yacht lying at anchor farthest out at sea, the *Aurora*, just beyond the rocky claws of the huge sweeping bay. The twin promontories of the bay enclosed it, nearly three miles apart. The yacht was right in the middle; a safe distance, one would have thought, if you didn't factor in the island with the monastery.

Lars undid the straps of the backpack and took out the barrel, casing, bipods, and lens. He fitted the barrel and screwed on the lens. The space in the bell tower was too small for lying flat. He would have to crouch, jacking up the rifle as far as the forward bipod would go and dispensing with the rear bipod altogether. It would be a sitting shot, knees drawn up, too much tension in the body, but that was all the space allowed. He kept below the balustrade all the time.

Now he looked again through the scope between the columns of the balustrade and towards the target, the lens in the shade of the tower's roof and away from the sun's glare.

The yacht *Aurora* was more like a ship, 235 feet long, rising 30 feet out of the water at the bow. Built in Sweden just the year before, it looked futuristic, something out of a science-fiction film. Its arrow-curved bow, indented halfway down with an aerodynamic wing, seemed to shoot the ship's lines of design around the sides to the stern, as if it were in motion even when at anchor. There was a bridge, with a sheer, almost flattened glass curve that extended above and around the foredeck, slightly forward of midships; a helicopter pad behind it, and behind that a swimming pool surrounded by umbrellas and deck chairs and a long, curved bar that stretched almost to each side of the ship. Uniformed waiters attended to several slim topless girls and fat topless men. The target himself was nowhere to be seen.

Lars checked his watch: 12:20 p.m. The target's visitor was late.

Then he checked the scene again through the rifle scope, which was more powerful, and read the distance: 2,401 yards—a greater distance than before, but still not the record.

He noted, however, that if he made this shot, he would have the two longest shots for a single sniper. Nobody would ever know it except him. But to Lars, this was like owning a stolen Picasso, kept hidden in the secret room of a collector's home. His knowledge of his own achievement alone would be enough for him.

He saw two members of the crew, wearing white uniforms with white caps, begin to descend the ladder to the starboard side of the ship and step onto a wooden motor launch that gleamed with bright varnish. They started the engines and immediately cast off, heading towards the beach.

Lars picked up the scope and trained it on the town. The road along the front, above the beach, was crowded with cars and buses as before. But there was a dark blue custom Bentley parked at the top of an old stone causeway now. He saw a short man wearing a cream seersucker jacket step out of the back seat of the Bentley, the door held open by a uniformed chauffeur. It was the American.

A few onlookers tried to get a closer look at who was in the car, but they were kept at bay. Nearly a dozen bodyguards were in evidence, as far as Lars could count. Someone tried to take a picture of the Bentley. They had their camera snatched by a bodyguard, smashed on the ground, and then returned with a wad of cash wrapped around it.

The short American put on a wide straw hat and pulled it over his eyes. In his attempt to dress in the understated fashion of the rich, he looked immediately noticeable.

Then the American walked down the causeway, flanked by four bodyguards, and onto some old stone steps, green with dried seaweed, at the bottom of which the launch had tied up. Two of the bodyguards came with the short man onto the launch; the rest returned to a pair of Hummers that were parked, Lars now saw, on the far side of the street from the Bentley. How these Russians flaunted their wealth in front of the American!

Turning his scope back to the launch, he watched it as it cut across the glassy bay to the yacht at a more sedate pace now that it had the visitor on board.

The five figures walked up the steps and onto the yacht. The short American was met by two other men who wore dark glasses and matching khaki shorts.

One of them shook the American's hand, the other guided him to a colourful striped armchair; there was a small debate on whether he wished to be in the sun or shade, and he chose the shade.

When the American took his hat off, Lars recognised the face. He had seen it before in pictures, a necessary part of his preparation, and he already knew the identity of the American visitor; Richard Rivera, PR guru, general fixer, and networker, with clearance from the CIA. He was one of three senior advisers to the Republican candidate in the American elections in just under three months' time.

The target didn't seem to be on deck.

Lars waited. The sun began its slow descent from the meridian. It was nearly an hour before the target appeared.

When he finally emerged and walked out into the sun, Slava the Russian, as he liked to be known, was dressed in a pair of faded jeans and a white T-shirt. Barefoot and unshaven, he stood on the deck, stretched, looked at the sky, then finally glanced down at his guest. It seemed to Lars that he wanted to demonstrate that he'd been sleeping. It bordered on disrespectful.

Rivera stood and shook hands with the Russian. Lars saw the words of greeting pass between them and then a joke, followed by a short laugh from Slava.

Levelling the rifle, Lars squatted with his back hard against the rear balustrade. It was uncomfortable, and he didn't want to hold the position for long. But by the time he had gotten comfortable and squinted down the rifle scope again, he saw that a party of bodyguards and crew were descending the steps again towards the launch. The target and Rivera were still on deck, but walking away into the door from which the target had just emerged.

Lars watched the launch take off. It did a couple of sweeps of the yacht and then seemed to be widening its area of observation. Two of the guards were training binoculars on the beach, on other boats, and towards the monastery itself. Lars pulled the inch or two of barrel that might be visible back inside the balustrade, making the shot impossible now. He was too cramped with the trigger up this close.

He withdrew the rifle completely and screwed on the silencer.

The launch widened its circle and finally came to rest a hundred yards away from the island, only a hundred and fifty yards from the bell tower. It sat there, rolling gently from its own motion rather than any great movement in the water.

Lars dared not use the scope while it was there. Its antireflective lens was no guarantee, and the sun was coming at more of an angle every twenty minutes or so.

Then the launch started its engine and made its way in loops back towards the yacht.

Lars turned the scope onto the deck of the yacht. The target and Rivera were standing at the top of the steps now. Two more launches had been lowered, or withdrawn from some internal dock at the stern. The deck seemed to be teeming with men in dark glasses, phones wired to their ears. There was activity all around Rivera and Slava the Russian, who stood there, apparently oblivious to the commotion around him, a man accustomed to being waited on by dozens of acolytes. Slava lit a cigar from a proffered humidor. Rivera declined his offer of another.

The three launches were gathered now at the foot of the steps. Slava ushered Rivera down the steps first, and then followed himself. They stepped into the first launch, which waited with idling engines for the guards to fill the other two. When all were aboard, the three launches set off.

Lars assumed they'd be going to the town—for a late lunch perhaps; a restaurant reserved outright by Slava, as was his custom. But
then he saw they were coming right towards him, straight at the island, directly into the sights of the rifle. Slava the target was dead
ahead. Lars's heart thumped against his chest. They were coming to
the monastery.

He broke into a sweat. He could stay where he was, wait and see.
Or he could pack up and join the others down below for the return
trip across the isthmus. If the Russians came, there was a risk that
they would insist on opening up the bell tower, no matter that it was
closed for repairs. They would donate some huge sum of money to
the monastery, just for the pleasure of going to the forbidden. That
was how these Russians were. Show them a forbidden entrance, and
that was the only place they wanted to go.

He could disappear in the tourist bus. Or he could shoot now.

Gently, he pushed the rifle through the gap in the stone balustrade and picked up the first launch through the scope. It was rising
and falling as the engines cut deeply into the water. It was a straight
shot, with the movement up and down only. He didn't think long.
He didn't have time. He zeroed again for the reducing distance and
fired.

Through the rifle scope, he saw the first launch suddenly fall from
its rearing advance down onto its bow, pushing the water ahead of it
as it lost way. The other two launches shot ahead, then saw what had
happened and swerved in towards each other in tight circles, returning fast to the first launch. Lars saw Slava the Russian, Slava the target. He seemed to have been punched in the chest, hit squarely by the
.50-calibre shell and knocked over the seat and into the stern.

Lars levelled the rifle again. He had the zero this time. Same distance. One boat was stopped in front of Slava's launch, idling its engine. Lars fired his second shot. It entered the engine of the boat,
shattering it.

The skipper of the third boat now jammed its throttle into forward gear. Its engine raced, and its prop churned the water. Lars's third shot hit the upper pins that clamped the outboard engine to the top of the transom. Held only by the pins at its lower edge, the wildly racing engine snapped back from its fixture; the propeller rammed upwards, screaming through the water and up into the wooden hull. Gouging easily through the hull, it shot up into the crowded boat.

There was chaos, blood flying, screams. The boat flew out of control.

He had two more shots left in the magazine. He fired one towards the engine of the target's launch, but it was still face on, the engine sheltered by the rest of the boat from where Lars was crouched. He decided to aim the last shot at the engine a second time, and prayed a second time.

The last of the scene he witnessed in the bay was a wild, scrambled pandemonium of bodies and arms. There were two men still intact enough to be making desperate phone calls. Lars didn't know any more than that, as he swiftly unscrewed the silencer, then the barrel, thrust the rest of the equipment into the pack, and headed back down the steps. The shadows had crept over the stone steps beneath his feet, changing their colour from honey to grey.

At the foot of the stairs, he gently pushed the bolt back and un-locked the door. The two Americans saw him exit. The woman with her pinched face stared at him; the man looked embarrassed, afraid even, as if he knew they had no business looking. Lars pinned the No Entry tape back over the door. There was a different group entering now, from another run of the bus across the isthmus. At least they hadn't seen him on the bus, as the American couple had. They stared at him, but he lowered his eyes and walked past them.

He crossed himself briefly in front of the Virgin's picture, avoid-ing Her eyes too, and walked out of the monastery's entrance into the blinding sunshine. He heard a distant sound: engines starting. Passing the small chapel of Saint Sava, under the cypress, where the chickens had a new sprinkling of food to pick at, he headed to the south shore.

On the pile of rocks that made up the southern breakwater of the island, he unslung his backpack, reached inside, and removed the small air bottle, then the micro aqualung and a pair of fins. The engine sound was growing. He looked back over his shoulder and saw that a helicopter had left the deck of the *Aurora* and was heading for the launches, which wallowed uselessly in the perfect sea.

Lars carefully descended through the tumbled rocks to the water, dragging the backpack with him. He picked out two of the smaller rocks under the water, broken off from the huge ones, and put them into the pack, then towed it and himself into the sea. He glanced back. He couldn't see the launches down here, but he saw the helicopter sweeping towards the island. Stumbling down the rocks, he slid under the water.

He swam heavily and clumsily with the pack in one hand down to the lowest of the piled rocks. He drew a waterproof packet out of the pack—his passport and money—and then shoved the pack under a rock until it was wedged fast. He rolled several other smaller rocks over it until it was invisible.

Then he set out beneath the sea.

Only now did he try to slow his panicked breathing, to conserve the precious air. He had only five litres, not enough for his liking. He wouldn't make the three and a half miles to the promontory, that was certain, not with all the exertion. He'd have to come in to land earlier.

$$9$$

A **NNA SAT ACROSS A** blue-painted wooden table in the Restaurant des Alpilles and took a sip from the glass of Sancerre Willy had ordered.

"Cheers," Willy said, and they drank together. "Happy birthday, my dear." He looked at her. It had been only three weeks since they'd last met, but he was always looking to make a compliment. "You're looking so French, Anna," he said, and smiled. "After just a year in the village. Like one of those women in the magazines. Chic, and as beautiful as ever. Happy birthday!" He raised his glass, and they drank.

"Thank you, Willy. You should see me normally," she replied. "Dungarees and grass in my hair."

"You look good whatever you wear," he insisted. "You look well too." He put his hand over hers on the table and squeezed it.

Willy was a good man. "A dependable Hungarian"—that was how Finn had described him before she and Willy had met, with a heavy emphasis on "dependable." And he was smart too. "You know what they say about the Hungarians, Anna," Finn had once said to her. "They come into the revolving door behind you and come out ahead of you."

She noticed that still, two years after Finn's death, she continued inwardly to refer to Finn's opinions.

She, Finn, and Willy had lived through a lot together. She didn't need Finn's opinion of Willy to know she could rely on him. He was the last thing left standing after the hurricane of Finn's death; a man rooted into her life, into the earth itself. In his seventy-two years, more than fifty of them in the West, he had developed a tanned leanness, with a fierce sparkle in his eyes that looked directly at her out of a face lined like a woodcut. He had supported her in the past two years, and before that too, before Finn died even. He had been an undemanding friend and father figure, always there for her if she called. Just as he'd always been there for Finn.

She tried to imagine him as the handsome youth of more than fifty years before, when he'd fled from Hungary after Russian tanks entered Budapest in '56. Back then, his country's brief leap for freedom was crushed. He had fought on the barricades, retreated, fought again until it was almost too late, survived, and escaped intact.

In the West, the British had eventually recruited him. He'd made more than twenty trips across the Iron Curtain, Finn had told her, but he swiftly became disillusioned. Willy had thought the West was fighting for Hungary's freedom, but, like other refugees from the East, he was to be disappointed. Hungary was just a walk-on part in the geopolitical game of the Cold War.

Willy was important to her, she realised, not for the first time. He wasn't just her last link to Finn; he was a mirror for her own survival as an exile.

"How's my godson?" Willy asked.

"He's loving life, Willy. Every minute of it. Maybe he's a little self-absorbed sometimes, but I consider that to be a good thing. He finds out things for himself."

"He needs a man in his life, Anna. He's surrounded by women. You, the school . . ."

She laughed. Willy was always trying to get her fixed up with various "safe" men under the guise of it being right for Little Finn. He had a straightforward view of the relationship between men and women, but without the arrogance she knew in many men from the East.

She and Willy had married shortly after Finn had died, but it was only for her security. He was more than thirty years older than her, after all. But she'd easily agreed that their friendship justified this arrangement. She was able to have a new name, a new identity, until she'd been able to broker the deal with the French and do it properly.

"I mean it. He needs a man," Willy repeated adamantly.

"But not any man," she stated.

His eyes narrowed. She knew the look. It preceded something artful.

"What about you, then? Get yourself a new man, why not?" Willy changed tack, his easy smile not quite concealing the old-fashioned attitude behind it. "You're young, you're beautiful, you shouldn't be alone all the time," he pressed her.

"Like . . . get a new sofa, you mean?" she said. "Or get a new car?"

"Well . . ." Willy wasn't sure this wasn't such a bad comparison.

"Look, Willy, I'm happy as things are. And if I weren't, why would a man be the antidote?"

"Are you angry with Finn? Is that it? Do you feel he betrayed you?"

"Finn never betrayed anyone but himself."

"And you and the boy were collateral damage."

She smiled at the aggressive chess game of his thoughts, always pushing the pieces out at her.

"Not necessarily, Willy," she replied. "It's all a matter of how you perceive it. Do I look damaged?"

"No. But you're tough, Anna. Maybe you're too tough sometimes for your own good. You can sit there and tell me, 'It's just a matter of how you perceive it.' What kind of thinking is that? It's not reality."

"Reality is exactly what it is. It's that kind of thinking, Willy."

"But romance . . . !" Willy protested. He was off again, a new tack, new methods of persuasion. "What about a little physical comfort? What's wrong with some fun? Eh?"

She laughed. "You're the old devil, Willy, not me."

"Romance never let me down," Willy insisted. "It's been like water in the desert."

"So it's some unalloyed good then, is it?" she replied. "No, Willy. There's good romance and bad romance, same as anything else. Read the poets. Anyway, maybe you should ask some of your exes how great their romances were. Or would it take too long?"

"You're cheeky and you are tough, *édesem*. Thank God I only have to be married to you."

She laughed. She liked it when he called her "sweetheart" in his own language.

"You'll frighten men away with that kind of talk," he insisted. "You want to be the Virgin Queen?"

"If the alternative is frightened men, yes. Finn was never frightened of anything."

"Ah, Finn." Willy shook his head, suddenly quiet, and made no attempt to hide his deep sadness from her. She liked that about him too, that he was honest with his feelings and didn't try to protect her from them. "Finn was a beautiful man," he said.

"And a fool in almost equal amounts," she added.

"I understand. You're not over him. I apologise."

She smiled and held his hand.

"You have nothing to apologise for, Willy. You've loved us both."

A waitress brought them a *pissaladière* and some salad and filled their glasses.

It was true. She wasn't over Finn; he was never far from her thoughts. How could she be over him? Finn was the reason she had left everything—Russia her home, her past, her roots, her people. Her Year Zero was 1999—the year she'd met Finn. She'd made the most of the men in her life up to then, but Finn was the only one she'd ever truly loved.

And Finn was never far away, even two years after his death. He had been a part of her life for just seven years, until they'd finally got to him. She and Finn had seven years of almost permanent tension, some of it bad, but most of it was good, the beautiful tension of being in constant awareness of each other.

They'd met in a setup, an arrangement between the KGB on her side and MI6 on his.

In 1999, he had been encouraged by his station head in Moscow to strike up an affair with her, while she in turn had been instructed by her SVR boss to do the same. Up to then, the KGB had failed at all their attempts to entrap Finn, and so she, the youngest female KGB colonel—a beauty in her own right, she was accustomed to hearing— had, much against her will, taken the job. She was no honey-trap, but a senior officer at the heart of the KGB's foreign operations. She had worked inside the SVR, and right at the heart of the SVR itself, in the highly secret Department S.

But after 2000, when Putin became president, she had been told why Finn had remained in Moscow for so long. There was a mole, a double agent—a traitor—close to power in Putin's circle, and Finn was believed to have sole access to him. Find the traitor—that was her patriotic assignment.

She recalled Finn's last conversation with Adrian, his recruiter in London; how Adrian had threatened and cajoled and finally issued an ultimatum to Finn to stop his investigations. But Finn had pursued his own line, and met with his death in Paris, after he was betrayed.

She looked across the table at Willy. It was Willy who had saved them, before Finn chose to take his final step. She and Finn had hidden out in a beach hut at Willy's driftwood restaurant on the most unwanted, unattractive stretch of sand near Marseille. Only the hippies and drifters went to Willy's beach, and even they had to be vetted by him.

Those were the happy days, hot in summer, cold in winter, in a windswept hut hidden behind the dunes, which themselves were hidden across miles of unwelcoming salt flats. Willy had kept them successfully away from prying eyes.

"What is worrying you, then, if your life is so good?" Willy said, interrupting her thoughts, bringing her back to the present.

She didn't reply, but looked into his eyes.

"Tell me," he said. "I see a cloud."

"Someone came to the house," she answered finally. "On Saturday. A neighbour saw him."

She saw Willy immediately become practical; no anxiety, no sympathy, just analysis.

"Not a caller, then?" he said.

"No. He just looked, came right up to the gate and looked through."

"Maybe noting your car?" Willy said.

"Possibly, yes."

"You have a description?"

"Not a useful one."

"And in the village? A car? How did he get there?"

"I haven't asked anyone, and the man who told me didn't know."

"Someone will likely have seen it," Willy said. "In these villages, that's what they do, look out for invaders. That's what they've been doing for a thousand years. It's in their blood."

"I only heard just before I came to see you," she said.

"You've told your French security?"

"No."

"You should have."

"There's nothing to say."

"Yes, there is. I'm coming back with you, staying there tonight. Maybe we can find out more."

"That will certainly set tongues wagging," she said, and laughed.

"Hell, we're married! I claim my rights!" he joked. "And I want to see my little godson. I have something for him. Just a small present."

They drove back after lunch, across the low, olive-rich hills of the Alpilles with their neat stone farmhouses and perfect villages.

They didn't talk much as she drove. Willy saw she was carrying the gun and simply nodded approvingly. Anna felt tense. She realised she was anxious being away from her son with the unsolved knowledge of this unwelcome visitor. Willy spoke once, when they were nearing the village. It was as if he'd been unwilling to raise the subject.

"Have you told them about Mikhail, Anna?"

"Them?"

"The French? Or anybody else?"

"No, Willy. Mikhail is all I have to keep me safe."

"And all you need to get you into deep shit too," he said.

She didn't reply.

She had told nobody about Mikhail. Mikhail . . . Finn's great source, who couldn't be discredited, no matter what they said in London. Mikhail was true.

And she had told nobody—not even Willy—that she alone knew who Mikhail really was. Alone in the world, she knew Mikhail's identity, and only Mikhail knew she knew it. That was trust, trust on a scale that dwarfed even her trust in Willy, and in Finn himself. Mikhail was so big, so important. He walked such a narrow tightrope at the heart of Putin's elite.

She'd wondered more than once why Mikhail hadn't killed her the one time they'd met, and she'd seen who he was. That was trust on a scale that was unimaginable to her.

Back in Germany, it was Mikhail who had found Finn, when she had been unable to. She had told nobody this. And she had told nobody that after Mikhail found Finn, he'd found her too, in the pink house in Germany, so that she could see Finn one last time before he died.

Finn had never told her Mikhail's true identity. It was for her own protection, he said. And then, on the night of his death, she saw Mikhail.

Mikhail was the gold seam for whoever found him; his enemies in Russia, or his so-called friends in the West. And when Mikhail had revealed himself to her, he had somehow known that she would never reveal his identity. He knew she could have had anything she wanted by revealing that, even her route back to Russia, if she'd wanted it.

That was a trust never to be broken, even with Willy.

When they reached the village, they saw the children playing in the sun-browned garden at the rear of the crèche. She saw her son, and her heart slowed. As they'd approached the village, she realised she'd become increasingly afraid, imagining everything.

But he was there, falling off a red plastic structure into the sand, over and over again, laughing more and more, and urging his friends to do the same. She recalled that he'd told her in complete serious-ness, three days before, that he was going to marry Amandine, aged three.

She and Willy took him from the teachers, who were reluctant to give him up. Willy hoisted him onto his shoulders, and he waved good-bye to the women. They loved him, Anna saw. Sometimes he was painfully like his father.

The three of them walked back up the lane to the house.

"Call them now," Willy said. "The first thing you do is call your security. You won't get rid of me until they're here."

"I'll do that," she said. But she was angry that after so many months of freedom from anxiety, it should all have washed back into her life—into their lives.

Willy had given Little Finn an ant house. While they played with it in the garden, she called her contact in Paris.

The man listened to her story. He didn't seem to feel any urgency.

That was how the French were, she thought. Unlike the British, who injected urgency into anything, the French sucked it out. She wasn't sure at first if he was taking her seriously, but she'd come to know the way they worked.

"When will you send a team down here?" she asked.

"A team? I don't know. But someone will come today—I promise you. We'll take care of everything."

She went out into the garden. Willy went inside to fetch a bottle of wine.

"So they don't know," Willy said, when he'd poured himself a glass. "Listen, Anna. If the French knew about Mikhail, they'd give you permanent security, not this excuse for it. Maybe you should tell them."

"I've already told you. No, Willy. They'll be all over me forever if I tell them about Mikhail."

The afternoon idled into evening. The air was completely motionless, the trees like statues. Movement became an effort.

"Even the weather is waiting for something," Willy complained.

He clumped off around the enclosed courtyard, inspecting everything for the third or fourth time. It was completely enclosed, with two-storey walls and high metal gates on three sides, and the house and high wrought iron railings where the palm tree stood on the fourth. Once again, he seemed satisfied.

He dozed off for an hour in the evening shade of the sycamore tree.

Anna went into the house and began to make supper. Willy appeared and began to make phone calls, until she asked him to stop. The French might be trying to reach her, she said, and there was no reliable mobile network in the village. Little Finn had gone back into the garden to play with his ant house. Anna heard him singing from time to time, and every so often she went outside, just to make sure he was there.

At seven thirty, Willy poured them both a glass of wine. She called

Little Finn in from the garden for supper. He didn't come at first, and she sent Willy out to get him. When he didn't return either, Anna went into the garden.

Willy was looking under an open shed, calling the boy's name. She felt a flutter of fear. She could see from the doorway that Little Finn wasn't in there, so why was Willy calling for him? When he turned around, she saw the look on Willy's face. And she saw that Little Finn had disappeared.

10

BURT MILLER WAS A large, ebullient man, full of loud self-confidence. This expressed itself in numerous ways, but could be summed up by an almost profligate attitude of general largesse. He doled out ladlefuls of life to all comers, and in equal proportion to the magnanimous bounty he habitually awarded himself.

"Life is about expansion," he once boomed to junior recruits at the CIA training centre in Virginia, otherwise known as the Farm. And then he would point out with his trademark guffaw that his physical size had kept pace with his expansive nature, as well as with his other, more worldly assets in the thirty years since the agency had first invited him to serve his country.

"I'm twice the man I once was," he would proudly, and accurately, proclaim.

Back in the 1960s, when he was a fit, agile sportsman adventurer at the age of twenty-two, he had entirely illegally entered Soviet-occupied Central Asia on foot, off his own bat. He proceeded to learn four of the local languages and cultivated local mafiosi, who twenty-five years later would become the foundation stones of Russia's new capitalism.

He and his then new wife, Martha, honeymooned for a year in the mountains of Afghanistan with his Pathan tribesmen friends, one of whom would, in maturity, come to control half the world's heroin trade. Under various noms de plume, he spent his spare time writing academically entertaining articles for *National Geographic*.

He swept through Central Asia like the Karaburan wind, befriending old-style Communist bosses, medieval mullahs, anti-Communist revolutionaries, criminals, royalty, fixers, taxi drivers, and spies with equal bonhomie.

His world, as he would put it to the wide-eared recruits at the Farm, was the world according to Burt.

And now, after forty years as the self-proclaimed King of the Stans, his Central Asian beat, he owned the Coca-Cola franchise for half the region, prime vineyards in the south of France, an island in the Caribbean, and a network of agents in Russia's former territories who were not only source material for his intelligence operations but also a lucrative business partnership for his numerous commercial activities, some of which failed, but most of which succeeded.

As he told his younger, more awestruck operatives after their graduation—when like a fairy-tale uncle he took them on clandestine CIA adventures—things usually worked out how he wanted them to; and if they didn't, it meant he had simply been mistaken about what he'd wanted.

"Self-belief is ninety percent of the battle in this game," he told them. "Same as in any game. But most important to remember is this—omniscience isn't part of the human condition," he added with another bellow of laughter.

And now, sitting in the plush varnished teak saloon of the yacht *Divinity*, which gently rolled, blacked out and brooding, off the coast of Marseille's industrial zone, Burt, like Socrates before his students, was regaling another team of his boys, new acolytes he'd tempted away from the agency to serve in his own private company. He was giving them the world according to Burt.

"God," he said jovially. "God is what happens. That's all you need to know. What happens is why we're here. The rest is nothing."

And what had happened with Logan's missive concerning the Russian colonel undoubtedly had this divine hand, perceived by Burt in any case, behind it.

"It's Burt's line to God that counts," he said, beaming, but with a large slice of self-mockery rather than any evangelical or otherwise religious connotation. "Remember that, boys," he instructed the three pumped-up young men in black combat fatigues that he had unsuccessfully tried to head them off from wearing. "Much time is wasted, many lives, and untold sums of money, on what might happen, or on what has happened. But all you need to devote your underdeveloped minds and overdeveloped bodies to is what happens. What happens is king, god, and all the philosophy you'll ever need."

As his words ricocheted around the confined space of the yacht's saloon like trapped birds, they were met with puzzlement, admiration, and a kind of wonderment at the meaning behind his arcane statements from the three young men, who suspected the teacher was good—great, even—but didn't really have a clue what he was talking about.

Larry, Joe, and Christoff were more at home on the assault course than in the library.

So Burt colonised God with the same broad-minded good humour with which he colonised a new recruit, a disaffected tribal chief, or a factory in Tajikistan that made anything from aluminium to ladies' hairpins. He was a clown with a brain, a trickster with unassailable cunning, and he cultivated an image of buffoonery you believed at your peril.

He offered the three young warriors accompanying him a glass of *premier cru* Château Laroque for the third time, and for the third time they refused.

The upper echelons of the CIA, with one or two crucial exceptions, regarded Burt's spiritual views as an aberration derived from some strange Eastern influence he had picked up on his travels. But even his detractors couldn't deny the evidence of his great effectiveness, both as an operative and an inspiring instructor to the latest talent, and now as the owner of one of America's big three private intelligence firms.

For his maverick and independent mind, as well as—it has to be said—his financial independence and impeccable contacts, he was a prized asset to the CIA, the NSA, and all the rest of America's government spy agencies. He was much needed, indeed loved, by the agency big shots, as much as they were wary and at times disapproving of his modus operandi and his general joie de vivre.

Burt had found himself on the wrong side of agency policy many times in recent years, but he had worked with it, lain low, waited for the policy to change—unlike his old Brit acquaintance, Finn, who had tried to change things and died for his trouble.

For one, Burt derided the abject worship of the electronic intelligence "that has taken over our intelligence community like a cargo cult landing from the skies on a Stone Age tribe." And he had the human intelligence from his own network of sources to reveal the weaknesses of this overreliance on technology. Burt claimed not to be able to use a computer, and every so often, as here now on the yacht, or in one of the numerous private clubs around the world to which he belonged, he would wave a huge Havana cigar at imaginary American satellites up in the heavens.

"They might be able to see what brand of cigar I'm smoking," he would say. "They might even be able to sniff its aroma, for all I know. But there is one thing they can't see—and which is all that really matters—and that is the intentions of the man who's smoking it."

He was now sixty-two years old, his athletically charged youth superseded thanks to doing exactly what he liked in the smoke, drink, and food department. Accentuated by an expensive light blue blazer and a pair of lurid yellow slacks that totally negated the camouflaged blackness of his team, his rotundity seemed to swell even beyond its natural limits to include the yacht, the sea, and the grey, all but invisible shore beyond, towards which he now looked keenly for a sign through a polished brass porthole.

But it was a cell phone on the blacked-out yacht that gave the signal. It was answered by Larry, the taller of the twenty-somethings.

"She's heading south," he informed Burt. "She's with the Hungarian. We have all three cars on them."

"You can bet Willy's seen at least one of them." Burt chuckled. "One of the best, Willy is."

"We think the French have at least two vehicles with them too. Unmarked. One of them's some kind of utility truck," Larry added, with one finger now pressed to the ear without the phone, just in case Burt made one of his louder exclamations.

"And the Russians?" Burt said. "Have we any Russians?"

Larry repeated this question into the phone and shook his head at Burt. "We don't know. Maybe. The autoroute's packed with vacationers, both sides, north and south."

"And then there's the Brits," Burt said. "We can be sure that Logan hasn't just invited us to the party." He beamed hugely. "It's like the Wacky Races out there."

"That's it," Larry said, and clicked the phone shut. "We're on."

With a final look of fond farewell at his glass of Laroque, Burt finished the wine in one friendly slurp.

"Internal shower," he declared, and smacked his lips.

The three others were already up on deck, champing at the bit, as he hauled himself off the bar stool.

"No dawdling now, boys," he barked, clambering up the steps some minute or two behind them. "Come on, it's time to play!"

They descended into a black twenty-six-foot rib with muffled engines.

It had taken Burt a considerable amount of power from his persuasive arsenal to scale down the operation they were about to put in play. The whole team now consisted of one yacht, the *Divinity*—with its twenty-six-foot rib—three cars with watchers, and a backup van of his own special forces just in case. But, at Burt's insistence, the latter were well to the rear.

Although his own company had paid the half million for knowledge of the Russian colonel's whereabouts, the special committee on Operation Mathilda—which is what they were calling Anna—also included the CIA chief from the Paris station. Burt considered that politic.

But then the CIA had tried to impose its own methods on the operation rather than Burt's. Burt, however, could more or less tell the CIA what to do. That was the way America's intelligence community had developed in the past few years; former senior men like Burt had set up their own operations, and now the agency was wholly dependent on them.

"Number one," Burt had stated at the one and only meeting of this committee so far, with a relaxed coolness that acknowledged no opposition. "We're on foreign soil. Number two. We don't want to scare the pants off the woman. She's our friend. We love her, and she is lovely. We've come to help her, and we will. We want to welcome her to the United States of America with gifts of kindness, not Halloween wraparound shades and sidearms. That will only remind her of what she escaped from in Russia. Number three. She has French protection. They are our allies, you may remember. We are their guests."

Burt had successfully laid out his stall. The only thing he wished to add to the operational inventory, after cutting out the small army that the committee's CIA chief, Bob Draco, was preparing, was a truckload of watermelons.

"Watermelons?" Draco had queried.

"Yes, they have to be watermelons. And a full truck," Burt insisted.

Burt knew he was making his demands, disguised as requests, from a position of strength. He had been picked for this delicate lift of the Russian colonel, not just because it was he whom Logan had contacted, but because he already had previous acquaintance with the target. He was in pole position over other companies like his own who wanted a piece of the action.

Back at the turn of the millennium, when his young friend Finn had gone "feral" and was pursuing his own investigations—against the explicit instructions of British intelligence—Burt had contacted Finn and offered him support, even though it could only be of a moral nature. After all, the Americans had been dissuaded of Mikhail's usefulness by their friends in British intelligence—Adrian leading the pack—whose false assessment concluded that Mikhail was a fraud.

But Burt, whether through his contact with God or not, had always believed in Finn, known he was right, in fact, and he consequently knew that Mikhail was truly the gold seam inside the Kremlin that Finn said he was. And this was not simply because Finn said it was so; it was because Mikhail had been this gold seam in the previous eight years, during which the CIA, and Burt through his friends there, had received a steady stream of Mikhail's intelligence from Finn, via MI6, thanks to the desire of the British to impress their American friends.

Burt had worked closely with Adrian through those days in the 1990s when Russia was struggling towards its short-lived democracy. But he had kept a Chinese wall between the working relationship with Adrian and his friendship with Finn. In fact, Adrian's treatment of Finn—and hence of Mikhail—had earned Adrian a very black mark in Burt's book.

Adrian had ignored what was happening, the cardinal sin in Burt's book. And Finn had taken the ultimate fall.

But most important of all his assets in Operation Mathilda, Burt had actually met the woman, the Russian KGB colonel, Anna. Finn had uniquely—if you discounted Willy, anyway—introduced her to him at Burt's London apartment in Mayfair. There they'd had a pri-

vate supper, just the three of them, Burt's butler hovering in the background. Anna had spoken to him that evening in confidence about
Finn, and had asked him if he could really help her man.

She and Burt had hit it off, just as Finn had said they would. Burt
mourned Finn's death, almost like a son's. He'd liked and admired
him, and that was good enough for Anna.

Finn had been Logan, Burt thought, but with his idiot conscience
still intact. And it was his conscience that had killed him.

And so Burt, apart from his own natural qualifications for the job,
was the obvious choice in the thirty-six hours since Logan's communication had been received. The money had been paid, Anna's
whereabouts communicated, the Russians were nowhere to be seen,
at least for now, and Burt had flown from New York into Marseille.

And then there were the British. They too would no doubt be
somewhere out there in the undergrowth. But so far Burt was fully
confident that he was ahead of the game.

The four men climbed down a wooden ladder into the twenty-
six-foot rib, which set off with silenced engines on the mile and a
quarter to the beach. The yacht, in total blackout on this moonless
night, had disappeared altogether by the time they were less than fifty
yards away.

One of Burt's dictums, which he had taught repeatedly at the
Farm, was that if you were after someone, rather than chase them up
hill and down dale, it was better to know where they were going in
the first place. Burt knew where Anna and Willy were going. It was
the only place they could go.

His entire plan for the night ahead was based on this—that Anna
and Willy would head for Willy's beach hut at the end of a three-mile
track across the inhospitable salt pans close to Marseille's industrial
area. It was where Willy had hidden Finn and Anna. Neither the
British nor the Russians knew of it. But Burt did. In a moment of revelation between them, Finn had told Burt that Willy's beach hut was
where they had stayed for a night or two when Anna had fled from

Russia. And back then, Burt saw that Finn was being only partially open. It was Finn's and Anna's hole-in-the-wall. Burt could tell that. Willy's beach hut was the perfect hiding place—if you didn't know about it.

The rib crunched gently onto the beach. Larry was on the phone again.

"They're going for exit seventeen," he said.

"What did I tell you, boys?" Burt said. "They're making for a spot eleven miles inland from this very beach. All the tails, all the vanloads of gun-toting CIA hoodlums like yourselves, all the watchers and all the satellites that clog up the pleasant skies above us, couldn't tell you where they were heading. It's Burt's line to God that counts. Give me that phone."

Burt placed the cell phone delicately in his large hand and spoke in clear, unmistakably authoritative tones.

"You don't follow them, right? You stay on the tramlines. All the way down to Marseille. No more tails. Lose them."

There was a brief pause as this settled in.

"The truck goes behind them," Burt said. "Then it drops its load right at the foot of the slip road. Let me hear it."

There was a lengthy pause.

Burt put his hand over the speaker and looked at the three jocks who stood on the sand as if they were about to set off on a hundred-metre dash. Burt was chuckling to himself, to them, to the universe.

"This is better than the bouncing bomb," he said. "Not that you'd know about that."

Finally, and with no more words from his end, Burt clipped the phone shut.

"It's an old French farmer's trick," he explained. "When they go on strike for greater subsidies in this beautiful country, they clog the main intersections with watermelons. Thousands and thousands of watermelons. Beautiful. Believe me, boys, this is God's own country," he said, and watched with amusement the shock of the youthful muscle that surrounded him, who thought that God was born and raised in the US of A.

But Burt was laughing. "Anyone following that blue Merc is fruit salad," he said.

He handed back the phone and took a long, slow piss in the dunes. When he returned, he spoke carefully, serious now.

"I want the two of you"—he indicated Joe and Christoff—"to walk with me down the beach. You will wait at intervals that I will show you. Anyone approaching from the west—in other words towards the beach hut—you politely stop. Though God knows how you can be polite in black spandex pants," he added. "Just try. If they aren't polite in return, you take them down, as silently as possible. We don't expect anyone, but just suppose the Russians or the British, or maybe some extraterrestrial group that's also interested in the woman, do know about this place, be prepared. Larry, you go over the back of the beach. Approach from the land side. Stay down in the dunes. Do not be visible at any time. When they're out of the car—the both of them—when they're out of sight, disable their vehicle. Okay. Me? When I drop you two off at your posts, I will go alone right along this beach to meet them."

Burt lit a cigar, against general blackout procedures, and waved Larry off into the darkness with its glowing tip.

11

ANNA SENSED HER MIND sliding with increasing speed down a black crevice. Its departure was taking her sanity with it. She was no longer aware that she was standing in a courtyard, her own garden; she no longer felt the clothes against her skin or the sun on her face.

She felt something violent at her shoulders, something that shook her so hard the fragments of thought that had scattered with her mind were jumbled up in twos and threes until some of them were thrown together in the violence and began to process signals in some kind of informational order. Something began to make a vague sort of sense.

It was Willy that was shaking her, that was her first clear impression. Her vision began to function dimly. She saw his face. Felt his big hands on her. He was staring at her intensely, but his eyes seemed pulled out sideways in a panic, as if they were on elastic bands. She felt his physical power. She had feeling. It was getting more real. His mouth was open. She began to hear the sounds, but not the words. Then her name. Anna! Anna!

She was suddenly overwhelmed by the aftershock from the trauma that had struck a single second before. Little Finn. Not in the garden. Not in the house. Disappeared.

A bolt of adrenaline-induced heat rose up through her core, and she broke away, rushing straight ahead at a closed shed door. She began to pull it frantically, but the catch was on, and it wouldn't budge. She didn't notice the catch that prevented her opening the dilapidated door. Only he must be inside. That was the answer. That was all there was, nothing else. The shed was the only place he could be.

Willy caught up with her and grabbed her firmly by the shoulders.

"Anna! Anna!"

He was clearer. Her dissolved senses began to coalesce into recognisable forms. The disappearance of her mind went into rapid reverse and her consciousness shot through her in one clear shattering image, like random streams of iron filings flying across the smooth surface of a table towards the point of a magnet.

They'd taken him. They'd taken her son.

"Get your phone! Be quick! I'll start the car." She heard him this time. She looked dully at the shed door. It was padlocked, she now saw. There was nobody inside.

Without thinking now, she ran into the house, picked her phone up off the table by the door, snatched up the gun, and heard the metal gates clanking open and the engine start. She ran out. They didn't close the house or the metal gates. Willy behind the wheel turned the blue Mercedes out onto the lane down the hill.

"We may catch them," he said. "They must be close."

"Stop!" she screamed at him. Her mind was now blinding white, absolutely clear. She was functioning like a machine, with a relentless, automated attention to detail.

Willy slammed on the brakes. They were by the wrought iron fence where the palm tree reached up past the roof of the house. She ran out of the car and picked up something off the road, a small green plastic object that was part of the ant house.

She ran into the car.

"Now we know," she said with unnatural loudness. "They took him through the railings. He was small enough to fit through the railings."

She cried out with an animal anguish and wrapped her hands around the top of her head.

"They took him through the fucking railings, Willy," she moaned through the blur of her arms. "Why didn't we think of that? He's so small, they could pull him through."

Willy put his foot down and slammed the car to the right, into the village square, past the barn with the weighbridge, onto the road down the hill. He began to throw the car into the corners in a screamingly low gear until, finally, they flattened out onto the straight road with the plane trees that led to the town.

She dialled the phone. It was answered immediately.

"They've taken my son," she said with icy calm now. The reversal was complete. "They've taken my son, where were you? Where was our protection?"

She listened.

"It's too late. You're too late."

There was silence again.

"That's where we're going now. We'll be there in a few minutes. But it's too late, isn't it."

Another silence.

"Ten minutes, then," she said, and clipped the phone shut.

It was Wednesday. The dusty car park that was full on Saturday market day was empty but for two unmarked cars. Four men seemed to be on four phones, but she saw that only two of them had phones in their hands as she and Willy drew up in a billow of dust.

Willy was out of the car first, shouting at them in Hungarian, then French, berating them with every obscenity he could come up with. Now it was she who put her hand on his shoulder.

"We have to think, Willy," she said, and he quietened under her hand as if he'd been given a dose of morphine.

On their way into the town, they'd looked in every car along the road, but there was nothing, nobody, who alerted any suspicions.

At one point as they sped from the flashes of light to shade, light to shade, under the spreading branches of the plane trees, Willy said: "It was the women at the bed and breakfast. The so-called Danish lesbians."

"Yes," she replied. "They sent women. Of course they sent women."

And now they were standing in the dusty car park with four French intelligence officers and no plan.

The elder of the four men broke away.

"We're putting up roadblocks on every road from the town, twenty miles out," he said. "We're checking any private air movements in the area this morning. Alerts are going out to air and sea ports. We'll find your son."

"Will you?" she said.

The officer didn't reply to the question.

"There'll be two men stationed at the house. You mustn't stay there, but we need to have a presence. They'll contact you via there."

She could see he was keeping himself under control. He understood. He had children of his own, perhaps. He knew what was happening to her. For the first time, she felt like weeping. There was someone else in the world, someone she didn't even know, who understood.

"One of us will come with you. In your car. The rest will go, one ahead, one behind, in these two cars. We'll be joined by others. Helicopters are being scrambled at Nîmes. We'll take you to a safe place."

A lot, a little too late, she thought. Anna's mind flitted across the possibilities like the eyes of a gambler at a roulette table. But they were all losing numbers. The banker always won.

The Foreign Legion headquarters was at Nîmes, she realised. There'd be men, equipment. But whoever had taken Little Finn would know the alert would be almost immediate. They would have a route out, roadblocks or no roadblocks. And nobody could begin to attempt a search of the summer traffic that sped bumper to bumper down the autoroute to the beaches.

Willy took her arm and pulled her aside.

"There's one place we can go that you know."

"I'd thought the same thing," she said.

They turned back to the officer.

"We'll have a house for you . . . ," he began.

"We know where we're going," Willy said. "We'll need all the backup you say you have. I have a place near Marseille. It's completely private. Believe me. Between you and me, even the immigration authorities know nothing about it."

The officer had his orders, but Anna and Willy were climbing into their car. He had no time to persuade them one way or the other, only to order his men into the two cars and follow.

"Head for the intersection of the autoroute, the first one south of Avignon," Willy shouted.

He started the car, and Anna saw men running to the two other cars. One pulled out ahead of them, one tucked in behind. She heard the sound of one of the men fitting a magazine into what was unmistakably a bolt-action rifle.

They drove with unreasoning speed, as if they were going to meet someone, rather than running away. At the intersection south of Avignon, a French electricity truck with an engine several grades above its usual requirements joined them to one side on the three-lane motorway, and a black Audi took the inside lane. They were boxed in neatly by their protectors.

At the next intersection beyond the meeting place, three police cars pulled onto the road, ensuring that the massed traffic slowed, giving the watchers more eyes and more time to search the flow.

There were tourists on their way to the sea this side of Marseille, all of Marseille's own commercial traffic, and yet another stream of commercial and tourist vehicles heading for Ventimiglia and the Italian border. There was no chance of finding anyone in this exodus.

"We'll find him," Willy said at one point. "We'll find him, Anna."

But Anna was already sitting on a hard chair in a bare interrogation room at the Forest east of Moscow, with Little Finn crying in a corner. It was her they wanted, and they would have her. All that remained to be decided now was how they would contact her, and when. The sooner the better, she thought.

From time to time, glancing in the mirrors, Willy would say, "Check the green Peugeot three cars behind our tail." Or "Watch that truck on the outside. I don't like it."

"Just drive, please, Willy. You can't do more than that."

"All eyes now are important," he'd say. "You cannot watch too much."

She let him do what he wanted. She knew she couldn't argue anymore. In her mind, they had won. They would put Little Finn in some filthy orphanage in Krasnoyarsk, or bring him up in an unkind KGB family for indoctrination.

All she had to defend him with was Mikhail. Would she sentence Mikhail to death to get her son back? Of course—of course she would.

The police cars dampened the lawless holiday elation of the tourists, and they crawled at a sedate pace within the speed limit like a presidential procession, three lanes wide.

She saw their exit looming ahead, three kilometres, two, there it was, the lane to the exit on the right and then up to the roundabout and onto the country roads.

Willy pulled into the exit lane and the electricity truck gave way and hung behind them. The Audi stayed out to the left and swung in at the last minute, to block anyone else with the same idea. The two cars of the intelligence team that had started out with them were in front and behind.

"Watch that truck. I tell you, watch that truck," Willy urged.

She looked behind them and saw a truck that had been with them for an hour now. It was pulling onto the exit road.

The sky was darkening in readiness for the night. A huge swath of pinks and purples fired the horizon to the west behind them. Ahead, the smokestacks of Marseille's industrial zone pumped white smoke up from half a dozen stacks, the smoke turning pink in the reflected night sky.

They reached the top of the exit lane. They had their protection car in front and one behind, but it and the black Audi had fallen back. The lights of the truck Willy had asked her to watch were right behind them.

It suddenly slowed as she watched in the mirror and Willy pulled up behind the car in front, at the roundabout. She saw the truck's bed tip up to the sky, and it squealed to a halt, sliding slightly on the hot tarmac. It had stopped. She didn't see what came out of the back of it, the thousands of watermelons that tipped and rolled down the slight incline of the exit road. But she saw that, now, nothing was following. There was only the car in front and the electricity truck that was with them. Their protection had been reduced to just these two.

Neither of them uttered a word. It was clear the game was in play. Was it a French game or a Russian game? She didn't know. She noted that the helicopters that had accompanied them and were going about their own tasks in the search had turned for home with the onset of darkness.

Night had fallen.

She saw Willy's tight face in the reflection of lights. She knew he was concerned only to save her. But either he didn't dare say, or he just refused to admit it. Her safety was irrelevant now, with Little Finn gone. She was as good as theirs. It was all over.

Willy talked on the phone to the car in front of them and gave instructions. They weaved through country roads, turning right and left with little logic. It was Willy's own devised maze, the way he'd always approached the salt pans when she and Finn had stayed there. Confuse and lose. But there was nothing behind them. It would take twenty minutes, probably, to clear the road by the exit.

Ahead, the night shadows of the smokestacks lightly bleached the darkness with their white smoke, as the Mercedes, the point car, and the electricity truck approached an old gravel pit to the right. They turned in and descended into the pit, along sand-covered tracks.

The car in front pulled up, and the elder officer stepped out. Willy swung round and halted behind them. The electricity truck followed suit. They were at the start of the hidden road across the salt pans, and completely concealed from view.

The officer stepped forward and indicated the electricity truck.

"They'll stay here and close the entrance, just in case," he said. Then he looked at Willy. "It seems a good place," he said. "What's down there?" He waved his head in the direction of the sea.

"There's a half-hour ride across a broken salt road," Willy said. "There's nothing on the way, just the pans running out to either side, for as far as you can see in daylight. At the end are just dunes. And beyond that, my hut. I came here in 'fifty-six," he said. "From Hungary."

"I know when you came," the officer said.

"There are a few hippies who'll be there," Willy said. "They pay me for campsites in the summer, go to India in the winter. Like the birds. But it's all concealed from the land side, and mostly from the sea. I make them keep their tents down in the dunes. No one else comes here. To the left along the beach, there's nothing until you reach the industrial zone; to the right, there's three miles to the first tourist beach. Too far for anyone to bother to walk. No roads lead to the beach on either side of the camp for three miles. It's a beautiful

beach," he added. "With a fine view of Marseille's factories and occasionally a filthy smell that comes from them too, when the wind's
in the wrong direction. It's no tourist trap. It's a place of exiles."

The officer walked across the dusty track to where the electricity
truck was waiting. He gave some instructions, and Anna watched as
the truck reversed and then drove back up the track to the top. The
men opened the rear doors and began to put out cones, and an exca-
vation vehicle was wheeled off a ramp.

The officer had returned.

"We'll come with you until we know you're okay," he said.

"Have they found him?" Anna said, knowing it would have been
the first thing she was told.

"Not yet," he replied. He looked at her with compassion. "Do not
give up hope," he said. "There is still hope, until long after we hear
from whoever took him."

Anna and Willy decided they would prefer that their protection be
concentrated at this end of the road. There was nothing and nobody
at the far end in the dunes, except the hippies. Reluctantly, the officer
agreed; he would come there personally at dawn unless there were
developments, he said, in which case he would come immediately.

It was a fine night as they drove across the slightly raised causeway,
with only the stars visible, more prominent without the moon. The
stars were so bright in this dead place, Willy had once said, they made
shadows.

In less than half an hour, they were approaching the dunes. There
were no lights.

Anna felt her heart constricting as they approached. It was the last
place she'd seen Finn, before his disappearance and death. From here,
against all operational necessity, he had gone to tie up one loose end,
as he'd put it. The next time she'd seen him was in the back of a car
in Germany, dying, while Mikhail drove them through another night
as dark as this one.

Willy pulled up the Mercedes behind a high dune, parking where they were invisible from both land and sea. He took her arm outside the car. They stared up at the stars, no words to say what they both were feeling.

And then they tramped over the dune and saw the little driftwood hut. Other similar cabins and tents dotted the sand, until they reached the sea. There was a fire burning, a guitar was playing somewhere inside the hippie encampment, and the smell of good hashish wafted across the beach.

12

BURT STOPPED AT THE sea's edge, a hundred yards from the hut. He could just make out the dull glow of a fire from this angle, flickering between the dunes. Taking a long pull on his cigar, he exhaled into the night sky, and walked on as if this were a postprandial stroll.

He saw the two figures before they saw him. They were standing back from the edge of the water, perhaps looking out to sea, perhaps staring into space. He began to approach until he judged he was both within earshot and far enough away not to threaten them. It was quiet; he could make out the distant chords of a guitar now, but otherwise there was no noise. The almost nonexistent waves made hardly any sound. When he was satisfied, he stopped again.

"Anna?" he called, just loudly enough without shouting. "Anna?"

He saw them both whip round and take a step away. Willy seemed to reach for something, but he evidently didn't have anything to reach for. Anna had a weapon in her hand, but he couldn't see what it was at this distance.

"Anna," Burt repeated. "I'm a friend. Take it easy."

"Who are you?" she said, and he saw her lift a long-barrelled pistol into the aiming position.

"Remember Burt?" he said. He hadn't moved. But once again, he took a long draw on the cigar.

She said nothing. The pistol remained pointed at his head.

"You, me, and Finn had dinner at my house in London," he said simply. "January twenty-eighth, 2004. I'm Burt. Burt from London. Burt from America. Burt, Finn's friend."

He still didn't move.

"What are you doing here? How did you get here?"

Burt watched her standing quite still and staring hard at him, but she didn't lower the gun. He saw Willy withdraw a little behind her. Maybe he was going to have a go at getting up the beach. Would he have a gun too? Probably. Knowing Willy, it would likely be something old-fashioned, a Browning 9mm, something like that, he guessed.

"May I approach?" he said.

She was silent.

"I'm not armed." Burt held his hands in the air.

"Keep your hands like that, then," she said at last. "Come up to ten yards, no more."

He didn't move immediately. "And ask your friend, please, to stay where he is," he asked politely. "And be visible."

He saw her turn and say something to Willy, who now moved into his vision again from behind her.

He began to walk on again at his own leisurely pace, his yellow slacks now glowing like a smallpox distress flag and his cigar waving in his hand above his head.

Anna and Willy stayed absolutely still. He walked until he was standing ten yards away, and then he stopped again.

"May I lower them?" he asked.

"Keep them in sight," she said.

When he was up this close in the darkness, he saw from her face that Anna recognised him. But she still kept the barrel of the pistol aimed steadily at his head.

"Why are you here?" Willy spoke at last.

Burt addressed her. "Anna, we've found your son. He's safe," he said.

A silent beat seemed to envelop them. And then she burst out, "Where? Where have you got him?" Fear, anger, and relief were mingled in her voice. "What have you done with him?"

"We've found him," Burt repeated. "Saved him at the last minute, as it happens. We were lucky, Anna. They almost had him back to Moscow."

She walked up to him now, taller than he was by a few inches. She held the gun loosely by her side.

"Where is he?"

"He's safe on a boat. Come with me. You too, Willy." He nodded. "He's close by, just out there." Burt waved his cigar in the general direction of the sea. "There's a yacht a mile or so out. You can't see it, it's blacked out. It was two women who abducted him," he said, keen now to keep the talk flowing. "They took him almost at the same moment as we found you. They beat us to it—just. But we found them. There's an old grass airstrip up in the Cévennes forest, just by a little ski area up there. That's where we got to them."

"How is he?" Anna said at last, daring for a moment to believe that she was listening to the truth.

"We've probably given him too much pizza and ice cream." Burt allowed himself to grin. "But otherwise he's fine. Well, I don't think he's aware of very much. But I think he's had enough of our company now. He's waiting for you."

"How?" she said.

"There's a boat to reach the yacht. Back up the beach a way. Keep the gun, by all means, but don't point it at me too much. I have some excitable young men in the dunes." He turned and whistled through two fingers. Larry came over from behind the dunes to the right.

"It's all right. He looks mean," Burt said. "But he's a real pussy-cat."

"If this is true . . . ," Anna began.

"Come and see for yourself," Burt said. "We shouldn't wait too long. There are others out there in the darkness tonight. Everyone wants you. But you have my protection, if you wish, from now on. American protection."

He approached her and rested his free hand on her shoulder, and Willy made a movement forward.

"It's all right, Willy," she said.

"Finn was a friend," Burt said. "And you'll need some better friends now than you've had so far. With the exception of you, of course," he added for Willy's benefit.

"Is it okay, sir?" Larry said, apparently eager for it not to be.

"All is perfect," Burt said. He turned back to Anna. "The boat, and your boy, are this way," he said.

They walked up the beach, at first in silence. Joe and Christoff appeared out of the dunes. It was Burt who broke the silence.

"You'll have to think what you need to do," he said to Anna at one point. "There aren't many options, as I see it. For your safety, and of course your usefulness to us, I recommend you get as far away from Europe as you can. You won't be safe here—either of you. I can guarantee your security. You'll have a house, schooling for your son, citizenship of course. We'll help you settle in America. It's not such a bad place to be. Most of the Americans who cause real trouble in my country, we've sent to other countries so they can cause trouble there instead." Burt laughed. He turned to Willy. "Haven't you ever thought of emigrating out of Europe?" he said.

"I'm happy here," Willy said.

"If we can find your place on the beach, others can too," Burt replied.

Anna looked at him, questioningly.

"It was Finn," Burt said. "Finn trusted me."

They reached the rib, and Joe pulled the anchor out of the sand. At last, Burt's muscle-bound company had something to do with their biceps. It was a heavy boat and, though only just grounded, hard to push away from the clinging sand.

Burt escorted Anna into the stern, and the others climbed in. The silent engines were started, and they headed into the darkness.

They reached the yacht in five minutes, and Anna saw Little Finn holding a woman's hand and looking over the side at the water, rather than at their approach. When he looked up as they drew alongside, he didn't seem in the least bit surprised to see her.

She felt a rush of grief and happiness that choked her. Burt sent her up the ladder first, and she took her child in her arms and held him closely. There were tears in her eyes, and she clung to him, noticing nothing else.

"Are you okay?" she said at last, and stroked the long hair away from his forehead.

"Look at that star," he said. His head was turned away from her, up towards the night sky. A shooting star was just completing its trajectory to the southwest.

"When are we going swimming?" he said.

PART
TWO

13

NEW YORK'S UNION CLUB at Sixty-ninth and Park is America's oldest gentleman's club. It was also Burt's idea of where to keep good company while visiting the city. In its 175 years, American presidents, newspaper magnates, railway and shipping tycoons, even the occasional writer or lyricist, have graced its three-hundred-foot dining room, played cards or backgammon in its purposefully designated salons, and fallen asleep in its sumptuous library.

For Burt, however, the historical continuum was more than simply glory by association. The club's longevity overarched fleeting fashions and outlived breakaway clubs that disagreed with the Union's founding principles. For Burt, the club itself was a gigantic clue to the skills of survival and prosperity.

Adrian Carew surveyed the roll call of its elite membership as Burt signed for the key to the smoking room—"with its matchless humidor," as he'd enlightened Adrian. Burt's name was written in gold leaf on a dark wood board. Club Secretary, Adrian read. Burt Miller, philanthropist and chairman of Cougar Intelligence Applications Corporation.

Burt's little joke, Adrian remembered now, to name his company CIA. It was said that the agency had been moved to insist he add the word *Corporation*.

They walked beneath the impressive domed ceiling of the entrance hall and turned right down a series of Alice in Wonderland corridors lined with portraits of the club's alumni.

Adrian searched his mind for a suitable put-down of the whole setup. *Excessive* occurred to him, *architecturally overflamboyant*, and the mostly dreadful portraits were a typically American weakness for the supremacy of the individual over the institution.

But even as he erected these mental defences, Adrian was painfully aware that it was he who was here on Burt's ground at Burt's bidding, not the other way around.

"The club's ethos," Burt was saying, "is prosperity by inclusiveness. If you're rich, you get in." He laughed loudly.

Adrian dutifully smiled.

"During the Civil War, we refused to disbar our friends the Confederate members," Burt said.

Genuine inclusiveness of a kind then, Adrian thought. And he wondered at Burt's own legendary ability to embrace all comers, friend and enemy alike. He also wondered which of these he was this evening.

They reached the door to the smoking room; Burt waved Adrian inside and then opened an external door to a small terrace that overlooked the club's service entrance.

"Our new smoking patio for the diehards," Burt said with a broad grin. "That's you and me, Adrian."

And now Adrian sat in a cold, uncomfortable metal chair on this tiny balcony. It was the first week of November. The temperature felt like it was below freezing. An unexpectedly early snow flurry had fluffed the dark alley below them as well as the balcony's para-pets with a white dusting blown through the tunnels of Manhattan's streets by a bitter wind. With amazed annoyance he noticed that his companion was apparently oblivious to the cold. Burt sat in a simi-larly uncomfortable wrought iron chair, puffing cigar smoke into the night and wearing his habitual good-humoured expression.

Grinding his teeth, Adrian sucked at a cigarette as if he might de-rive some thin warmth from the glowing end.

"When do I get to see the woman?" he said with a bluntness that came more from discomfort at another cap-in-hand mission than from the cold.

"All in good time, my friend," Burt said happily. "All in good time."

Adrian seethed. The fact that Burt, a private American intelli-gence contractor, albeit running a multibillion-dollar company and with a senior CIA background, could talk to him in such a way was at complete odds with his world.

Did the head of the British intelligence service now play second fiddle to private American intelligence contractors? He supposed so. The CIA's employees themselves were now ordered about by pri-vate companies like Burt's in many of America's embassies around the world, including Baghdad's. Private enterprise had its viselike grip around the country's traditionally government-run intelligence ops. The revolving door between government spy agencies and these pri-vate spy companies ensured that American government intelligence contracts were awarded by government officials who had previously directed the companies they were awarding them to. Adrian consid-ered it all to be way upside down.

The military industrial complex has now become the intelligence industrial complex, he thought, and Burt had carved himself and Cougar a strong niche at the very heart of it.

Adrian had thus known to approach Burt personally rather than go to his opposite number at the CIA, and he had come to Burt for a reason. Burt had kept Anna Resnikov to himself for three months now. It looked as if the agency was letting him keep her—at least for a period.

Soon—later this evening, in fact—he would see if Burt's apparently endless patience with the Russian colonel would survive what he had to tell him.

At last, after two years trying to get to the woman, Adrian felt he had something to work with, something that was going to put him back in the game. And he was looking forward to knocking the smile off Burt's face when he sprang it on him tonight.

It had been a difficult—not to say frustrating—few months. First, there'd been the unexpected arrival of her photograph. Adrian had gone at once to the Treasury committee to ask for the half million dollars the little thief who took the picture had been demanding. They had to pay up or lose her. She was what they'd all been waiting for, for over two years since Finn's death. Even Teddy Parkinson had come with him to the Treasury.

But the committee had delayed granting this ex officio payment, blustering; was MI6 the only place that hadn't heard of the financial crisis? Did they think that with institutions falling like flies, half a million dollars could be signed off just like that?

When Adrian pointed out to the five men and one woman on the committee that this kind of information didn't fall into their laps once in ten years, they had looked at him as if he were some kind of street-corner cardsharp.

And when, after the haggling and veiled threats were over, they finally granted him the money to pay for the information that went with the picture—the colonel's location—it was too late, far too late. The Americans had already grabbed her. Half a mil down the drain for nothing, and he knew he would end up carrying the can for that, thanks to the committee's procrastination.

Connected to his laying hands on the woman, there was also Grigory Bykov, Finn's killer. Some at the Secret Intelligence Service whispered that Adrian had become obsessed with killing Bykov, and that the woman's value was in gaining access to Mikhail, not in giving Adrian the green light to bump off the Russian. But the fact that the Yanks had got her had merely given the politicians back home an excuse to put Bykov's death sentence back on hold. Adrian had almost heard a sigh of relief in Teddy Parkinson's voice when he'd said, "Sorry you missed her, old boy. Bad luck. Not your fault. Those tightarses at the Treasury are the bane of all our lives, believe me."

It had enabled the politicians to delay indefinitely Bykov's moment of truth.

Apart from negotiating with the Americans—principally Burt—over access to Anna Resnikov, Adrian had also spent an inordinate amount of time on the assassinations of the two Russians. Helping the Russians, in other words. Why? It was beyond him. The British government seemed willing to break its back bending over for them. To Adrian, the victims were just a couple of billionaire hoods the world was better off without. Maybe by now the exceptionally skilled assassin had himself been bumped off. That was usually the way of these things.

And then, two weeks before he'd come to New York to try to persuade Burt to give him access to the woman, the Russians had started getting up to their old games. The Kremlin had threatened to move nuclear warheads into Kaliningrad. Just a day after the American elections! And the Russians had presumably made the threat to up the ante for the new president-elect.

But against all this damaging and inconclusive catalogue of events, Adrian at last had one card up his sleeve, and it was a killer card. He would wait, however, before he laid it on the table this evening. Let Burt have his moment to gloat over the woman's capture.

"What progress have you made with her?" Adrian enquired. "Has she given us Mikhail?"

"The process is only just beginning," Burt replied. "We're taking it gently. A lot of bureaucracy, as I'm sure you'll understand, Adrian."

The large man looked at him across the freezing patio. "Our debriefing of her is starting this week, as a matter of fact."

"You've had her for three months!" Adrian protested.

"Competing interests, Adrian, competing interests. Everyone wants a piece of her, and I've been covering my back. She's now, I'm happy to say, Cougar's asset and Cougar's alone."

"For how long?"

"We'll see. It depends on what she gives us, doesn't it."

"You're treating her as a very long game," Adrian said disapprovingly. "You may have less time than you think to find Mikhail."

Burt sucked on his cigar. He stood up and walked over to the edge of the balcony, where the light snow fell on his bare head. He seemed oblivious.

"Mikhail is the endgame, Adrian," he said at last. He turned round to face him. "You guys threw him away, now it's up to us to revive him. Anna may or may not know his identity. But having fought off the agency's desire to put the thumbscrews on her, I'm not going to hurry the process for the sake of the Brits who ditched Mikhail in the first place. She's a very clever and a very tough woman. If she knows the identity of Mikhail, I want her to tell me voluntarily. Any other way, and I believe we lose her, and lose Mikhail."

"She knows, all right. She's just concealing Mikhail," Adrian said angrily.

"We don't know that," Burt replied with infuriating equanimity. "Let's stick to what we know, shall we."

"Isn't it time you read her the riot act?" Adrian demanded. "If she doesn't give us Mikhail, you'll pack her and the boy back to Russia. That should sharpen her memory."

"She's our friend, Adrian," Burt protested. "You're missing the point."

Adrian seethed once again at this insulting implication. Burt added, "I'll tell you something. Finding Mikhail is just the first part of the process. It's the beginning of the endgame, if you like. If she supplies the information voluntarily, that's when she'll be most useful. If we force it out of her with threats or worse, she can mess up the operation at any time, and without us being aware she's doing it."

"The operation? What operation?" Adrian said, suddenly interested.

"Okay, let me include you in on this, Adrian." Burt leaned in generously. Adrian felt cigar breath on his face. "Once we know who Mikhail is, then it's two bits to a dollar she's the only person he'll speak to. That's her real value, don't you see. Actual contact with Mikhail is the beautiful result all of this. Mikhail has a clear connection to Anna, through Finn. But Mikhail's smart too. Very smart. He's evaded all of us for a long time. And he only ever spoke to Finn. So that's why we need her onside. Marching shoulder to shoulder with us, in fact. She's our only link, and therefore our only chance not just to find him but, crucially, to get to him."

"And if she doesn't give us Mikhail?"

Burt sat back, supremely self-satisfied, to Adrian's way of thinking.

"She'll give him to us," Burt said. "Eventually. Even if she really doesn't know who he is."

Adrian lit another cigarette. Whatever Burt meant by this arcane remark was beyond him.

A waiter appeared with a silver tray on which were two whisky and sodas. He brought them out to the balcony, and Burt tipped him handsomely.

"So what's your plan with her?" Adrian asked when he was gone. He spoke in a conciliatory way now, having reminded himself that access to Anna was now through Burt, not through government channels, the CIA, or anyone else.

"First we're going to give her a list," Burt said. "There's been a big increase in KGB activity in the United States over the past year. Big turnover of names—new names coming in, old ones going back to Russia. It'll be a process of identification. Who of this new pack of wolves she knows, and who she doesn't."

"For what purpose?" Adrian demanded.

"It's useful in itself," Burt answered. "But principally, it's a psychological thing. It's about letting her limber up. Getting her to focus. Allowing her to get used to helping us in the smaller things—then, when the big question comes up, she's already relaxed. In the flow."

To Adrian, it all sounded unnecessarily elaborate, and Burt saw his expression of disapproval.

"Like I said, we need her willingness, Adrian," he said. "Without that, there might be Mikhail, but there won't be the prospect of real contact with Mikhail. See?"

"If you say so," Adrian replied.

Adrian got to his feet, as Burt placed the empty tumbler on the table.

"Let's go have some supper," Burt said. "It's damn near freezing out here."

As they walked back inside, Adrian saw the water in the ashtray was frozen over.

They ate beef Wellington at a table beneath a middling good portrait of George Washington. Adrian decided that Burt the Anglophile was nevertheless demonstrating by his choice of table a rather crude independence from any British interference with the woman's debriefing. It reminded Adrian of Margaret Thatcher having paintings of the Battle of Waterloo hung on the walls at 10 Downing Street every time the French president paid a visit.

It was Burt who brought up the subject of Adrian's visit again. As usual, he liked to demonstrate he was in the driving seat.

"Wait until we've finished with her," he said. "Then she's all yours. Under our conditions and supervision, of course."

"I have a special relationship with her," Adrian protested. "We met on several occasions when Finn was alive."

"So I understand. Which is why it's unfortunate that you left on such bad terms with him," Burt said resolutely. "Face it, Adrian, you blew it."

Adrian was practically catatonic at the casual nature of the criticism.

"Finn and I were as close as you can get, for sixteen years," he said. "Officer to handler. You know that kind of relationship, Burt. Ultimately, it's unbreakable."

"If Finn were alive, I'm sure he'd forgive you. But he's not alive, and she is—and I don't think she's going to forgive you. In any case, to me it's not worth the risk of upsetting things as they are."

"She knows how close Finn and I were. And she knows I was just doing my job."

"Like all the concentration camp guards say." Burt chortled.

"I have the right to see her." Adrian put his knife and fork down with too much of a clatter.

Burt's face changed to a hard, cold-eyed flatness that was all the more shocking for its contrast with his usual bonhomie.

"This isn't about you, though," he said emphatically. "Or the British. Or even the Americans. It's about her. It's about getting what we can from her." His face relaxed. "Reasonably, Adrian, can you see any way I'd risk this delicate process by suddenly associating myself with a very bad memory for her? So far, we in America have a clean sheet with Anna. We've rescued her and her boy, goddammit. What do I get for letting the British in? Just the risk of alienating her."

At the end of dinner, Burt, mercifully as far as Adrian was concerned, didn't want to smoke another cigar. They drank coffee and cognacs in the library, and Adrian picked this moment to play the card he'd been waiting all evening to play.

Withdrawing a brown envelope from his pocket, he passed it across to Burt, who by now was sliding slowly but majestically down the overstuffed cushions of a dark green embroidered velvet sofa. He appeared to consider that their business was done.

But Burt hauled himself up and opened the envelope. He gave Adrian a sharp interrogatory look.

"What's this?" he said.

"A tape."

"A tape?"

"With a story on it," Adrian said.

"You have something to play it on?"

"You're not going to play it in here, are you?" Adrian said, shocked.

"This is the Union Club," Burt replied. "The library of the Union Club. Perhaps the most discreet six hundred square feet in America. And as you see, it's empty and probably will be for a week, knowing the members' reading habits. They come in here to sleep or not at all."

Adrian did have a recorder with him, in case there'd been an opportunity to play the tape somewhere. He pulled it out of his pocket and handed Burt some earphones.

14

AT SEVEN THOUSAND FEET, the custom Chevy Silverado began the slow climb up from the mesa. It cut through a narrow gap in high red cliffs into an equally narrow pass of switchback curves that trebled the real distance to the higher plateau above. The knife-edge existence of the mesa's dry sagebrush scrub finally gave way altogether to bare rock and to a thin orange sand that blew in the wind.

Only where an occasional stream tumbled into the valley were there signs of life—small clumps of aspen trees, the leaves of which were a shocking gold in colour, or turning to murky yellow before they fell away. It was the end of the first week in November. The sun was high in a savage blue sky, but there was the unmistakable chill of approaching winter.

Anna sat in the middle seat of an elongated version of one of Burt's company's fleet cars. It was a vast grey and gold, gadget-rich, bullet-proof truck that could withstand an explosion of a thousand pounds of TNT directly beneath it. For what purpose it was needed here—on American territory in the middle of New Mexico—she wasn't sure.

But by now she'd come to know Burt well enough to suspect it was just one of his toys—the military version of a vehicle adapted by his labyrinthine security corporation.

She studied the bleak, spectacular scenery through a blackout window. Little Finn's questions were growing less frequent, and he seemed awed by the sight of the rocks and bluffs that towered above them and by the yawning drop below.

As the vehicle climbed, Anna sat back into rich-smelling black leather. Over the previous nine and a half weeks, they had been housed in a comfortable shingled family home in pleasant woodland, near a place called Tysons Corner in Virginia.

As Burt told her in his deceptively guileless way, this was the location of the CIA's highly secret Counterterrorism Center and the Pentagon's Joint Terrorism Task Force. These units were housed in a huge underground complex designed for the purpose by the Walt Disney Imagineering Company, which Burt joked had taken time off from designing theme parks to bring reality to America's fight against terror.

Burt was naturally indiscreet. It was true he believed that his own secrecy business suffered from a vast overload of discretion. But in reality Anna knew that his indiscretion gave away nothing of real value. It was just one of the tools he used to slowly bind her to him. He was clever in this, she had to admit. The intimacy he fostered in their friendship, the inclusiveness he awarded her, a former KGB officer, was beguiling.

On a visit to Cougar's company headquarters close by to Tysons Corner, she'd felt she was being shown around her new working environment, like a fresh recruit.

"Why are we here?" she'd asked Burt on several occasions over the weeks at the shingled house. "What are we doing at the heart of counterterrorist ops?"

"If you want to get anything done in this country these days, you invoke the spectre of 'terrorism,'" Burt replied cheerfully. "It's the magic word; the open sesame to all things; the source of all gold. But don't worry, Anna," he added with a grin, "it's nothing personal, nothing to do with you."

The period at the shingled house in Virginia was, Burt told her, for the purpose of negotiations. These were just formalities, he said.

These negotiations were over her future. She was a commodity of value. She was wanted by several of the United States' sixteen state intelligence agencies, and also by many of Burt's competitors in the even darker world of private contract intelligence. Access to her was keenly contested in high places. Senators—especially those on the Senate Intelligence Committee—were being leaned on, and Burt was deploying all his own contacts in government to keep her for himself. In the private intelligence world, she realised, she meant money, government funding on a grand scale.

During this period at the safe house in Virginia, she preserved a relentless sangfroid with Burt and the half dozen intelligence officers from the Byzantine American intelligence community he invited to meet her. But inside her mind was the unasked question: When would they ask her about Mikhail?

Paraded initially at an apparently depthless reinforced concrete bunker near Liberty Crossing, the centre for the "secret of secrets," as Burt called it, America's Threat Matrix, she'd felt like Cleopatra being led through the streets of ancient Rome. Her status as the youngest female colonel in the KGB had first won their interest. Her personal charms as a woman increased it.

And there had been lengthy discussions at one stage about literally parading her, by exposing her "defection," as they were calling it, to the media. Bob Draco from the CIA station in Paris had accompanied them across the Atlantic, and he led this movement.

"It's time to snub the Russians," he said. "They need a direct hit. Or at least a shot across the bows. They're getting far too big for their boots, and they need to be taught a lesson." He backed up his argument with the examples of Russia's invasion of Georgia and its threat to move warheads into Kaliningrad.

But Burt steered these more hawkish members of the Black Committee, as they were calling it—and their friends on the Senate committee—away from such precipitous action.

As her captor, Burt held the floor in these sessions. America, he said grandly, could always make its announcements in the press later. Better to let her interrogation—or debriefing, as it was politely called—unfold before adding any stresses to the process. The last thing they needed now was the media snooping around. Exposing her at this moment would leave nothing in the locker for later.

Burt had protected her too from those who wanted to "shake her down" right away; to get the juice out of her while she was still rebounding from the low of losing her son to the high of being reunited with him. There were those who wanted her drugged for the information they were after.

Again, Burt's performance at least seemed like protection. She was to be led, not driven, he said. She would give—oh, yes, she would give—but only when she was ready to give.

All of Burt's stately pirouettes in these negotiations over her future had been deftly performed. To Anna, their deftness seemed almost too expert, however. That she was present at all in some of their secret discussions suggested to her that she was meant to see all the arguments concerning her fate. Burt's constant riding to her rescue and his protection of her against the apparently less subtle creatures in the American intelligence community—all of it added to Burt's elevation as her saviour.

Burt had thus slowly developed his role from being her rescuer, to her defender, her knight and aegis against not just the Russians but the Americans too. That was the drama that had played out over the previous weeks.

And she knew it was all done for her benefit, to bind her to him.

Over to the right of the vehicle, as it wound around the switchback curves, Little Finn was pointing at a herd of elk wandering through the dark, sunless depths of the canyon that fell away into a greyish area of trees far below. Anna told him they were a type of deer—she didn't know the English word *elk*. Burt provided the information from the front seat, and Little Finn squealed, "Elf, Elf, Elf," enjoying the word, until she touched him gently on the arm to distract him. He settled back in the leather seat, and she wedged a pillow against the door, so that finally he settled down.

That was the meaning of the drama of the previous months, she was sure of it. Since she was both audience and player, she was being led to draw a conclusion—that Burt was her only hope. She realised that she was being artfully "developed," in order for Burt to emerge as a defence between her and the snapping dogs at the CIA. She'd better give Burt what he wanted, or the dogs would take her. That was the clear message.

And now here she was, heading into the remotest wilderness of New Mexico in one of Burt's company trucks at the onset of winter. She was accompanied by Burt himself and by members of Burt's private army from his private intelligence company.

One evening, just before they'd left for the Southwest, he'd informed her quite casually that the Cougar Corporation received over one billion dollars of government money annually to perform intelligence work—and perhaps military functions too, she guessed.

As if to back up her guess, Burt fulsomely detailed the many activities Cougar involved itself in; the provision of "warfighters"—by which he meant private soldiers in Iraq and elsewhere; covert operations; electronic surveillance; overhead reconnaissance with UAVs, unmanned aerial vehicles; intelligence analysis; the development of intelligence software; private spy networks that were run out of American embassies all around the world; the interrogation of enemy suspects; communications interception.

He explained that his own private employees provided a significant percentage of those hired to run the Threat Matrix, the secret of secrets; that his company personnel, 18,000 of whom had the highest possible security clearance, were involved in programmes that could tap into every telephone call and every e-mail in or out of the United States; that even the landing points of undersea fibre-optic cables were now in the domain of private security companies, his and his competitors'. They could monitor communications not just on American soil but anywhere in the world that was connected to these fibre optics.

"America now contracts out nearly three-quarters of its intelligence budget to companies like Cougar," he said. "That makes a total of over fifty billion dollars a year."

She'd wondered then at the difference between this new America and the way the Kremlin's spy agencies plied their trade. In the new Russia, the KGB was itself the state. And yet it called itself the *kontori*—the company. It controlled all the financial and operational strings of the state's intelligence activities, as well as Russia's political will and most of its strategic industrial might. Was that really so different from the new America?

If nearly three-quarters of the American intelligence budget was handed out to private companies, how long would it be before the state and the private intelligence companies—the *kontori*—became one and the same thing, just as in Russia?

Sitting in the truck as it ground its way around yet another bend on the mountain, she recalled how she'd been feted, befriended, loved even, given chauffeurs and comfortable homes, teachers for Little Finn. But if the audition were a failure, she would find herself on the way to the airport in a locked, nameless van.

The real interrogation was about to begin. Nobody in all the preceding weeks had mentioned Mikhail. But without Mikhail, there would have been no rescue of her, no red carpet treatment, no Burt.

Burt was now listening to something on headphones in the front of the truck, while Bob, one of his "fitness freaks," drove, and Larry, the bodyguard from the beach, sat in the third row seat, "riding shotgun," as Burt had put it.

In the middle seat Anna and Little Finn continued to look out over the canyon that was fast dropping away beneath them. Sheer red rock bluffs towered over the pass they were going through, cutting out the sun, and way up above them, on a small outcrop at the top of the road, she could now see a few dilapidated brown adobe buildings.

Planted among them, and looking out over the huge stark landscape, was a wooden cross, twice the height of the houses, its white paint faded and peeling. It was dipping at a violent angle after two and a half centuries of sun and wind and ice, and maybe—Burt said when he took off the headphones—violent worship.

The higher mountains beyond the little village rose to thirteen thousand feet and were white with snow that capped their peaks like candle snuffers. An early snowfall down at the level where they were had left patches of white in the fields where the low winter sun hadn't reached, and there was a grey slush at the road's edge.

"Back over your shoulder," Burt enthused from the front, "you can see a light-coloured plateau, about thirty miles away. That's Los Alamos."

Anna turned and looked at the patch of light that was appearing as they headed higher towards the sky. The sun was illuminating a stretch of flat mesa, about halfway up another set of mountains, on which the weapons research station and the birthplace of the atomic bomb was bleached into the huge, empty land, its buildings invisible in the flat light.

As they came round the final bend and up to the edge of the village, she saw that the bare rock and infertile sand had gone. There were meadows up here, and a few scraggy horses and a herd of cattle were still finding something to eat in the winter pasture.

The first of the buildings they reached was crumbling sideways into the meadow, its brown adobe walls peeled back to reveal mud bricks. The whole imperfect structure leaned at an angle so extreme that the doorway had been distorted into a rhomboid.

A toothless old man with a weather-beaten face, wearing a beat-up Stetson and torn and faded denim overalls, shouted something at them as they passed the home and shook his fist.

Burt laughed.

"They can be pretty crazy up here," he said. "They don't get out much, if you know what I mean. They need to meet new people—not just the relatives," he joked. "But don't worry, you won't be staying in the village," he added.

He pointed at another long adobe hall structure, which came up beside them to the left of the truck. It had no windows, but a squat bell tower sat on its wavy roof.

"That's the *morada*," Burt said. "There's a Catholic sect run by the *hermanos*, the brotherhood. Call themselves the *pentitentes*. You see them out here on the mountain at Easter time, carrying crosses, flagellating. They used to have crucifixions up here. Not with nails, but even tied to a cross, they had the occasional death. It's cold around Easter time. Traditionally, a young man from the village was chosen by lottery to hang up there, and if he died, the *hermanos* would take care of his family and his obligations. They were excommunicated by Rome, for giving the church a bad name." Burt guffawed, as if this were a preposterous thought. "They say they still crucify people up here in the out-of-the-way spots," he added. "But they do it in secret now."

Anna wondered how much more out-of-the-way it could get than this dismal collection of mud houses at ten thousand feet.

The truck moved into the quiet, impoverished village and pulled up at a general store. They all climbed out and stood in the damp earth street, feeling the icy air coming down from the mountains ahead. There were just adobe buildings, she now saw, their mud walls in various states of decay. The rooftops were made of corrugated iron, rusted and torn.

Apart from the crosses everywhere, it could have been a village in the foothills of the Caucasus—Chechnya or Dagestan, Anna thought. But this was America.

"Founded in 1754," Burt said. "By the Spanish king. They came up that way"—he pointed south—"from Mexico. They first arrived in 1583, settled here, then got driven out by the Indians. Then they came back and stayed." He took her arm. "Let me show you something."

Anna took Little Finn's hand as they crossed the dirt road, and they followed Burt into what looked like an unkempt field. But when they were inside it, she saw it was an untended graveyard. Burt pointed at the second gravestone they came to. "Kilt by Indians," it read.

Anna shivered in the cold after the warmth of the car. Burt had promised her somewhere remote—that was all he'd said about their destination—but this was not the America she'd imagined.

Burt read her thoughts.

"Not what you expected huh?'

"No."

"It's like Siberia out here," he said. "It certainly has about as much respect for Washington as Siberia does for Moscow. The Hispanics have been arguing—sometimes fighting—for a hundred years to have their land back. They don't even speak English up here, many of them."

Anna wondered how much she was in this empty hole on the map for her protection and how much to encourage her to comply with greater alacrity.

"You won't be here long," he said, as if reading her thoughts again. "It all depends on how we judge your safety. And Little Finn's," he added. "And how other things come into play," he said vaguely. "We'll see."

Burt bought Little Finn a candy bar at the general store, which seemed, also like the remoter parts of Russia, to sell just a few oddments, whatever was available at the lowest end of the demand chain. Most of the shelves were empty; there were a few lightbulbs, their boxes dusty, a few boxes of screws, a chain saw, some jam. . . . Always tins of jam wherever you went, she thought. If there was nothing else, there were tins of jam. It was the same in Russia.

She wondered if Burt had brought them here deliberately, into this store. There was nothing here, except the message that there was nothing here.

And the place they were going to was thirty miles beyond the road's end, farther into the mountains from the village. True wilderness, Burt had said, as if he'd been a travel agent selling a high-end Outward Bound experience to wealthy metropolitan adventurers.

"In winter there's no way out of where we're going," he'd said. "Except by chopper."

They climbed back into the truck. Little Finn was silent. They drove out through the village, past a few homes with metal arches with names inscribed in wrought iron. The dirt road got rougher, almost impassable even without snow. They crossed a riverbed, and beyond that the track was hardly visible. They were now driving over rock.

"It's just a few more miles," Burt said after nearly an hour. "Deep in the forest. Few people even know of its existence. All this land is part of the land grant of the Spanish king back when. It's called Nuestra Senora del Rosario San Fernando y Santiago Land Grant." He guffawed. "They sure liked a long name. I'm the only Anglo who got to buy land up here. The others got their houses burned down." He chuckled at his own smartness. "It takes time, and luck, to be able to get a foot in up here. But they know me. I give to the church, fix the roof, buy their cattle in the winter, arrange their medical insurance. We've got a good relationship."

The road improved as they went deeper into the forest. Anna guessed that they kept it almost impassable at the beginning where it left the village, in order to dissuade the curious.

Finally, after a slow, bumpy thirty miles beyond the hill where the village stood, the truck came into a clearing about a quarter of a mile in diameter. There was a meadow with a stream running through it. Some horses grazed behind wooden fencing. The place was as still and silent as anywhere Anna had ever been. But she saw that, in springtime, this would be a good approximation of paradise.

Little Finn saw the horses first, and then the chickens that roamed around the field. Then, wide-eyed with excitement, he saw some goats and a pair of llamas. He tugged Anna's arm to go closer as they stepped out of the truck.

At the top of the meadow was a large log house.

"About as safe a safe house as you'll ever see," Burt said. "Welcome to your new home." He beamed happily.

15

IT WAS SIX O'CLOCK in the evening and Anna was putting Little Finn to bed when Burt, alone in the study of the log house, put the tape Adrian had given him into a machine for the second time.

Adrian had suddenly been supremely confident, he recalled. He'd clearly been waiting to spring this news on him from the moment they'd met in New York five days before.

Burt settled into a large leather armchair. There was a fire blazing in a grate in the corner of the room. But before pressing play, he went back over the background for what was on the tape, looking for inconsistencies. Adrian had given him the context of the information it contained, but he wanted to be sure.

"Picture this, Burt," Adrian had begun. "A man walks into our embassy in Kyrgyzstan three months ago. August sixteenth, to be exact. He's looking for a relative of his who's gone missing on a trip to western Europe. He wants our help."

"You're going to tell me who he is, presumably?" Burt asked.

"He's from the Federal Security Service Reserve, Burt, KGB to the core. This relative of his was on an assignment in Germany."

"For the KGB?"

"Yes."

"Why doesn't he go to his own people?" Burt queried. "Or the German embassy, come to that?"

"First of all he couldn't go to the Germans because this relative was doing something clandestine there, that's why. He knew he'd get no help from the Krauts in the circumstances."

"And his own people?"

"That's the juice," Adrian said. "He believes his relative, who is a brother, by the way, has been killed. But he's sure it's not by the Germans or any of our intelligence services. What he tells us is that it's his own side he believes has killed his brother. The Russians, he says, killed their own agent. He wants to find out if this is true, and either way, he wants to find out where his brother has got to. If he's still alive, even."

"Some risk he took," Burt replied.

"Oh, yes. A great risk. But he's angry. He's from one of the southern republics, and this is the last straw for him. Years of racism, years of Russian arrogance, years of Russia and the Russians walking all over his country, wrecking his women and his people and his land. That's how he sees it."

"Where's he working?"

"The Defence Ministry in Moscow."

"Very good," Burt said. "Very interesting. So what do you do to help him?" Burt raises an eyebrow in ironic deference to Adrian's great healing powers.

"We keep him talking until we've run a check on him. We find he's definitely a middle-ranking figure in the Defence Ministry in Moscow. So far, so good. And then we think, Why not? We drug him and hold him for eight hours until he tells us some very interesting things. Some of which are on that tape."

"Then you let him go?"

"Yes. We hold him for as long as we dare. We don't want anyone alerted that he's missing."

"And then you help find his brother." Burt guffawed at this unlikely scenario. It was a sound that was probably louder than the library at the Union Club had heard for several decades.

"We make enquiries, yes. But what we do in the main is contact him again and tell him how much he's compromised himself. We have him nailed. All on tape, photographed inside our embassy, full of stuff the Russians will recognise. We tell him we need more of his help. Then we'll see what happened to his brother.

"But we also tell him that if he doesn't help us, not only will his brother be gone forever, so will he. Once we hand over the material to the Defence Ministry, or the KGB, he's done for."

"What made you think he was worth it?"

"As I say, he's a middle-ranking figure, but during the few hours we held him we could tell he had access. Initially we thought we'd get some good insight into the regular running of the ministry, if nothing else. You know the kind of thing—what its current general aims are, who are the key figures with influence there, who is closest to the Kremlin. That sort of thing. Humdrum stuff, but all adding up to a bigger picture."

"But you got more than you bargained for."

"There was one thing he told us when he was drugged that made me think he might have more use than that."

"And it's about us."

"About America, yes. When he was drugged, he spoke in various tones of voice, various degrees of volume, he either sat completely still or thrashed about—you know how it is. There was one theme that he referred to twice. On both occasions, he almost shouted about it, waved his arms. It's a theme that concerns you very much, Burt. Defence secrets. American defence secrets. He said the KGB has an agent here in America, who communicates via a Russian official at the United Nations in New York. Someone who's employed inside one of your own defence establishments."

Adrian had sat back in his chair, and Burt saw a feeling of satisfaction wash over him.

"Or so this guy says," Burt replied. "Which one? Which defence establishment?"

"That's something we're still working on," Adrian purred, with the clear intention of implying he knew. "We think he doesn't know," he added disingenuously.

"Or you're holding out on me, Adrian."

"Not at all," Adrian said primly. But he hadn't finished yet.

"We've kept in contact with him, of course. Let's call him Rustam. First we held drops to communicate with him and pick up his material at Sokolniki, the Moscow metro station. Then we moved the drop to Sokolniki, the town, in Tula Oblast. After that, we kept to the theme, first time a metro station, then the town or place from which it gets its name. He's being very compliant. In fact, he's fucking terrified."

"You've turned him. Well done, Adrian."

Adrian soaked up the compliment, but his face was still hard, Burt saw.

"What about the brother?" Burt said at last. "Did you go after him?"

"We did."

"And what did you find?"

"It was very difficult. We wanted to do it without alerting the Germans. But we found him all right."

Adrian was not going to volunteer any further information. It was Burt's turn to insist now. Adrian had done enough special pleading for a lifetime.

"Well?" Burt prompted.

"He'd been murdered. Poisoned in Hamburg. The police didn't have any identity for him. We told them he was one of ours. They'd had him on ice in some super-closed-down facility for a month, against the possible spread of contamination. One of those places built since 9/11. It was a job to retrieve him, but we did, even though I don't think the Krauts believed us. But what could they do? They had nothing on him.

"Then we showed a picture of him to Rustam. Jackpot. It was his brother, just as we thought. The poison was identified as polonium-210. Same stuff they've used in western Europe before—the Russians, that is. So it looked pretty clear-cut that the Russians had murdered one of their own, an agent who was the brother of a KGB reservist and decent figure in the Defence Ministry who'd just been waiting for one more grudge to blow him over the edge. Now, Rustam is almost happy that we drugged him and got all his lovely secrets. He's going to be most helpful in finding this agent in America."

Burt sat without speaking. Eventually he looked up and fixed Adrian with a friendly stare.

"Why bring this to me? Why not go straight to Langley? You're the boss in London, you could talk to the head of the CIA here, direct."

"This is your operation, Burt."

"You mean Anna."

"Yes, the woman," Adrian said, and sat back.

"So," Burt said. "This is your way through to meeting with her."

"That's right." Adrian allowed himself to feel the warm glow of victory. "I didn't want to miss the opportunity to get that favour from you personally. If I go to Langley, there'll be all kinds of fingerprints over it. I don't want to foul your operation," he said with deliberate insincerity. "What I want—what we both want, Burt—is Mikhail. If I tell Langley I want to speak to the woman, they're going to trample all over your carefully laid plans for debriefing her. I don't want to damage your operation, Burt. I just want time with her. Deal?"

Although Burt saw this was an expert piece of blackmail, he didn't show it. But Adrian's threat hung over him in the library. If Burt didn't give him what he wanted, he'd go to Langley, and they would give him what he wanted. Which would mean, in turn, that Burt would lose control of Anna in the melee that was bound to happen.

"You've got me," Burt said. Then he grinned. "Well, I'll be damned, Adrian. You sat on this the whole damn evening."

"And you get to take this to Langley yourself," Adrian chimed in, pointing at the tape. "A feather in all our caps. But only once I've seen her."

"Okay . . . okay, then," Burt said slowly. "What gets me, though, is why you're so goddam keen to speak with her."

Adrian contemplated the benefits of openness or concealment, and decided on the former.

"I have some unfinished business," he said. "Finn's killer. We know who he is now. But my orders"—he said the word as if it were choking him—"were to get to the woman first. Without getting to her, I've been told, we can't terminate Finn's killer. This will put pressure on them back in London to concede. They've been pussy-footing over this for long enough, and there'll be no more excuses they can come up with."

Adrian fixed Burt in the eye. He knew now he was on a winning streak.

"So," he said. "You tell Langley that you've given me full access to her. I'll inform my political masters, and I'm sure it will filter through to London from Langley anyhow. Then I'll have what I want. I can wash my hands of Finn, we'll have done the right thing. Honour is done and seen to be done."

He drained his glass in a final punctuation of his triumph.

"In the meantime," he summed up, "you need Mikhail more than ever. You have a Russian agent in one of your top defence establishments, Burt. So we don't just have to find Mikhail for all the former reasons. We have to find him to know who this Russian agent is."

"Working together," Burt said.

"That's right." Adrian smiled thinly. "Working together."

Burt turned towards the window of his study at the log house. It was dark outside, but in the porch lights he saw it had started to snow.

Adrian had given him a week with Anna, that was all. Otherwise the threat to go straight to Langley, to disrupt Burt's debriefing of Anna, would become a reality. Adrian wanted in. It upset all of Burt's carefully laid plans for her far longer debriefing. Things were going to have to move a lot faster than he'd expected. Never mind. It was what was happening.

Burt switched on the tape. First he listened to Rustam talking in the drugged state, at the beginning. Then he picked up the transcripts of Rustam's later information, the further intelligence about this agent the Russians had in place in America.

Burt both did and didn't want to believe it. For one, it would be a huge coup for him to take this to Langley; a huge badge of honour for Cougar, and an increase in procurement budgets. But it was also information that Adrian held over him, to get access to Anna. And he didn't like that.

─────────── 16 ───────────

B URT WAS WAITING FOR Anna when she came out onto the porch the next morning. He seemed his usual self, at ease with the world, content with what happens. But she also detected a new urgency. After three months of waiting, she guessed he wanted to proceed quickly now to the main event.

He asked after Little Finn, how he liked the nanny and house-keeper he'd provided—questions that had an unusually perfunctory attitude behind them.

Little Finn was with the nanny now, she told him as they walked down the wooden steps into the meadow and he took her arm.

"There'll be ten of us here from now on," he said. "The Hispanic lady Frutoza looks after Little Finn and cooks the meals. I know, she sounds like a fizzy drink. Her family's lived in this valley for two hundred years, and she and her husband are like family. He's the one who keeps the house running. Then there's Larry, Christoff, and Joe. They're backup in case of trouble, but no one will get down here in winter. That makes five, plus you, me, and Little Finn. And you have two constant companions from now on. They arrived at four o'clock this morning. They're Logan and Marcie."

"Interrogators?" she asked.

"Yes. And they'll be with you every second of the day, whether there's formal debriefing in progress or not. One or other of them never leaves your side."

"They work for your company?" she asked.

"Marcie worked in conflict resolution down in the Balkans in the nineties. She's a tough lady, and she was smart enough to handle a roomful of bad men, not to mention NATO troops. She's a New Yorker, CIA background, now works for me. She's been to Interrogation School," he said, and smiled at her. "She went on to teach it at the Farm . . . at Langley."

"And Logan?"

"Logan. Ah, Logan." Burt walked on for a few paces before continuing. "He was a CIA officer, also in the Balkans in the nineties, who took a fall for someone else's mistake. But he was one of the best." He looked at her with a mixture of amusement and concern in his eyes. "I'm giving him another chance, Anna, let's call it that. He's complex. . . . Sometimes I feel he has similarities with Finn."

"In what way?"

"Led by his passions. A little . . . undisciplined, if you don't mind me saying so."

"Finn was disciplined in his lack of discipline, I'd say."

Burt chuckled. "In any case, I think you'll like him. Not that that's the point, of course," he added.

She thought about this strange, unnecessary addition to Logan's description.

"Both of them have been studying you for nearly two months," Burt said. "As well as Finn. And Mikhail. All under my supervision, of course. They'll be on top of their material."

It didn't sound like a threat, but Burt's method, she'd learned, was indirect.

"Then I'll try to be on top of my material too," she said.

Burt laughed and patted her on the back.

"And your role?" she asked him. "You're everywhere on the pitch, aren't you, Burt?"

"I'll be there," he said vaguely.

"And what are your expectations?" she asked him.

"Expectations are for dummies. You know that. And you know what we need now. Mikhail."

She didn't reply.

He stopped and separated from her, then turned to face her.

"We have a week, Anna. Then Adrian arrives."

She couldn't conceal her shock.

"Adrian! Why? I've nothing to say to Adrian. I thought this was your operation."

"I know," he said. "And it is. So far. But that's why it would be best for you to finish this up before he gets here. It's all about Mikhail, Anna. It's up to you."

"I don't know where Mikhail is, or who he is. Finn never told me. Mikhail was handled in a total vacuum by Finn."

Burt linked his arm in hers again.

"Let's just say you think you don't know him," he said mysteriously. "But he's out there somewhere. Very close to Putin. You know him, even if you don't know he's Mikhail."

She saw him looking at her intently, but she kept her face expressionless. One thing was true. Finn had never told her. It was Mikhail who had revealed himself to her.

"My future depends on finding Mikhail?" she asked.

"As do all our futures," Burt replied.

At ten o'clock Logan sauntered over from the guesthouse alone. He was elated. Employed by Burt in a senior position at the company, he was now going to meet the woman he'd been thinking of since he'd first looked properly at her picture in the days after he'd taken it.

He was wearing jeans, a cowboy shirt, and boots that crumpled over at the top. His hair was long and tangled from sleep. To his surprise and even shock, he saw she was already in the kitchen.

Nodding a shy hello to her, he poured himself a coffee. When he had drunk half the cup with a swiftness that clearly burned his mouth, he walked over to Anna and held out his hand.

"Logan," he said.

"I guessed you weren't Marcie."

He smiled and pressed her hand a little too long for her liking.

"I'm glad to meet you," he said.

"Well, that's good," she replied. To Anna, he seemed like someone relaxing on the first morning of his vacation. But she thought this impression wasn't cultivated for her benefit. It seemed genuine. Logan evidently wasn't someone who was concerned about making impressions.

"I think we only need to remember one thing, Anna," Logan said, sipping his coffee and watching her.

"What's that?"

"We're all on the same side."

"Thanks, Logan. I'll try to remember."

He smiled at her. "Friends," he said.

"We'll find that out, won't we?"

He was lazily charming, and, she saw, a watchful figure. His intense blue eyes, which he rarely offered for contact with hers, were striking. He was good-looking in an uncared-for kind of way. If he'd been a piece of furniture, she thought, she'd describe him as artfully distressed.

"I'm sorry," he said suddenly. "Can I get you some coffee?"

"I'm okay, thanks."

He smiled again.

She studied him for any signs of weakness. That was what would help her in the days ahead. He couldn't hold her gaze; that was interesting. Self-conscious? She thought so. Or was that an invention? Was this his default behaviour with a woman, or was it just with her? He was conscious of his own attraction, she observed, and maybe compensated for it by hiding behind an attitude of self-deprecation. That was how Finn had been.

Just then, Marcie entered the kitchen, and the atmosphere changed at once. Corkscrew hair tied back with multicoloured play-school ribbon, Marcie projected an extrovert vibrancy that contrasted with Logan's laid-back attitude. She wore a denim dress and scuffed black biker boots. Cheap and garish glass jewellery seemed to be hanging off her in various places. Striped socks rose above the boots. She had a hippieish air.

"Anna!" she said, with boisterous pleasure. "Marcie. I'm looking forward to us getting to know each other."

Anna smiled back.

"You've met Logan," she said, though it was obvious she had, and it was said just to make conversation.

"Yes."

"Be careful of him," Marcie warned. "He thinks he's God's gift," she added, lowering her voice, in the pretence of a private confession.

Logan just smiled and didn't protest.

The relationship between Logan and Marcie would surely be part of their tactics. To appear to create small splits between them invited her to develop intimacies with each of them separately. They were a team, and were also individuals. She would have to watch the moments when apparent conflict between them encouraged her to be confessional to one or other of them.

She decided for the time being that Marcie was the more dangerous of the two. She was superb at creating the deception of normality in the situation they were all in.

"I'll watch out for him," Anna said.

"You do that," Marcie replied.

Interrogation is a battle for control. To the uninitiated, it may seem one-sided. If the interrogator has domination over the life or death, pain or release from pain, of a subject, how can control be other than in the hands of the interrogator?

Anna knew that it was not so clear-cut, however. In many exhaustive training sessions at the Forest she had learned that the object of interrogation had ways of subtle manipulation.

At the KGB's main training centre in Yasenevo southwest of Moscow, known as the Forest, instructors were particularly focused on interrogation and resistance to interrogation. It had been a separate course alongside self-defence, hand-to-hand combat, the making of improvised explosive devices, weapons handling, escape and rescue, recruiting an agent, and all the others.

One vital lesson the Forest had taught her was that nobody would ever need to use interrogation—of any kind—unless ignorance and doubt were present. Principally, she'd been taught, even in situations where physical domination was overwhelming and completely one-sided, that there was still doubt over who controlled the outcome of an interrogation. Logan and Marcie had an obvious need of their subject. To begin with, they did not know what she knew. A low-level battle of wills would underlie all the ensuing days, Anna knew. It was true, of course, that no physical threat was hanging over her. There were no blazing lights twenty-four hours a day, permanently deafening noise, the threat of torture, fabricated sounds of torture, or actual torture itself. There was no coercion, let alone terror, in Logan's and Marcie's methods.

Burt meanwhile spent their sessions in the study, sitting on the sidelines, and only occasionally guiding the process to lower the temperature, or guide them over any impasses with a light, deft touch.

It was Logan who began, after the three of them had sat down on three sides of the large table in the study, while Burt took an armchair by the fire.

"If you knew who Mikhail was," Logan said, for once looking straight in her eyes, "what would prevent you from telling us?'

As an opening salvo, Anna saw it contained several traps.

"Mikhail's security," she replied.

"His security," Logan said slowly. "As a member of Russia's elite under Vladimir Putin?"

"That's right."

Logan's eyebrows raised. "You want to protect him from us?"

"His security in Russia is absolutely necessary," she said calmly, "or he's no good to the Americans."

Marcie put her hand on Anna's arm—another message intended, perhaps, to indicate the special relationship she planned to develop with her.

"You think that we might endanger Mikhail's security?" she said, and looked genuinely concerned.

"I can't know that," Anna replied. "But—on the hypothetical basis that I knew who Mikhail was—then I would have to accept that as a possibility. Endangering Mikhail's security not only risks his life, but also risks losing what you want from him."

"So you'd act on that possibility," Logan stated.

"Yes. The protection of a source or potential source is paramount."

"Yet they can't be a source unless there's some degree of danger to them," Logan replied.

Anna said nothing.

"Why do you think Mikhail only ever communicated through Finn and nobody else?" Marcie asked.

"Because that way he controlled contact. And of course he trusted Finn."

"We're assuming Mikhail is a man, then," Logan said. But Anna had prepared herself for this potential trap.

"If Mikhail is as close to Putin as we all believe he is, then he can only be a man," she said.

Logan smiled at her, in a way that suggested he was commending her method rather than the information she was providing.

But Anna ignored him and leaned her elbows on the table. She decided to take some small control, to disrupt the question-and-answer nature of the proceedings, if only for a moment or two.

"What we're attempting to do is to make contact with Mikhail," she said. "You have to understand that's completely different from what happened between Mikhail and Finn. It was Mikhail who made contact with Finn, not vice versa. It was Mikhail who dictated the terms. We're trying to reverse that. I'm not sure it can work."

"Why not?"

"Because Mikhail is the one who does the choosing," she replied. "That's his past form."

Logan searched in his jacket for a cigarette and finally found a crumpled box. Burt stood up and turned on the exhaust. Logan knocked out a cigarette and lit it. Marcie looked at him in disapproval.

"Okay. Let's look at Finn," he said. "But first of all, I'm sorry. This is bound to be difficult for you."

"Finn died two years ago," Anna said. She would give him no room to feel sorry for her, if that was his approach.

"Finn was found in the back seat of a Jeep Cherokee outside the British embassy in Berlin," Logan recapped. "He was respectfully delivered there. I think that's the right word. It was a friend then, or friends. Everything about the way he was found suggests that. But who? Who brought him there at considerable risk to themselves? We don't believe it was the killer, naturally."

Anna was there again, on the Autobahn on that dull, cloudy October night, with the car barrelling along at speed, the junction arc lamps flashing on her face and Finn's as she cradled him in her arms in those last hours of his life. It was Mikhail who was driving. It was Mikhail who had found Finn, and then in turn found her so she could say good-bye to Finn for the last time.

"You were in Germany then, Anna," Marcie said, breaking into her thoughts.

So they knew that much, she thought. "I was in the south," she said. "In Bavaria."

The past unravelled. She had found Finn's secret house in Tegernsee, down near the border with Switzerland. Finn had given Willy instructions to find it, if he ever disappeared, and Willy had given the instructions to her when Finn didn't return. There, in the small pink house that Finn had kept a secret even from her, she had read through all Finn's notes, found the microfiches that proved what the British intelligence service had denied. And Mikhail had found her there. He had taken her away, moments before the house had been encircled by security forces.

How did Burt, Marcie, and Logan know she'd been in Germany? It had been too risky to deny it. Perhaps it was a guess on their part, and now she'd provided the information.

"But you saw Finn?" Logan said gently. "Before he died," he added with uncompromising directness.

"No," she replied. "Finn was killed in Paris. I don't know how he got to Berlin. The last time I saw Finn was two weeks before he was killed in Paris."

"But he wasn't actually killed in Paris, was he?" Logan corrected her. "That was where the killer administered the nerve agent, yes. But Finn wasn't found in the rental car in the Paris car park where the nerve agent was discovered later. It didn't kill him in that car. He moved on after he'd been hit with it, sickening and, as we know now, dying. Somehow he ended up, after his death, in Berlin. In a different car." Logan leaned slightly towards her. "But there are three days between those two events. Forensics established that Finn died about four hours before his body was found outside the British embassy in Berlin. So that's three, nearly four days after he came into contact with the nerve agent. Four days of what? Who was with him? What did he do?"

"He didn't call me," she said. "That's why Willy gave me the instructions to find the house in Bavaria. We knew he must be in trouble, or he would have called. The instructions Finn left with Willy were only to be opened in an emergency."

"So," Marcie said in a funereal tone of sadness, "someone took his dying body to Germany."

"Unless he drove there himself," she said.

"Why would he drive to the British embassy in Berlin?" Logan said. "Surely he'd have gone to the embassy in Paris?"

"I don't know," Anna replied. "I'm as in the dark as you are."

"Let's say someone drove him to Berlin," Marcie said lightly, as if this were a sudden, bright idea. "Why? You were in Germany. Okay, you were in the south. But why would his helper take him to Germany—unless it was to reunite him with you?"

"You think it was Mikhail," Anna said.

"I'm as in the dark as you are," Marcie replied, and smiled at Anna.

"Let's say it was Mikhail who drove," Logan pressed her. "He would go to Germany to reunite Finn with you. Or let's say Finn drove himself to Germany for the same reason. You see, what I'm feeling is that Germany is not a coincidence. You were in Germany, and that's where Finn died. Maybe you drove him yourself to Berlin."

"Why wouldn't I say so if I had?"

"Because you were not alone," Marcie said. "It wasn't just you who took Finn to Berlin. You drove Finn to the embassy with Mikhail."

"And now," Logan concluded, "you want to protect Mikhail."

"It's a good story," Anna replied, "but it's not what happened."

"You were with him," Logan stated, and leaned in closely towards her. "You were with Mikhail the night Finn died."

She saw the keenness behind the blue eyes, the certainty, whether actual or contrived, she didn't know.

"It was both of you who delivered Finn's body," Logan said, quietly now. "That's the obvious conclusion. I'm right aren't I?"

"No, Logan, you're not right." She looked at him levelly until he looked away.

"What were you doing in that time?" Marcie said, changing tack. "In those four days?"

"I was in the house in Tegernsee. I was collecting Finn's research, trying to find a clue to where he might be. He'd disappeared two weeks before."

"But you weren't at the house in Tegernsee when German security forces broke into it," Logan said. "And that was around twelve hours before Finn's body arrived in Berlin. What were you doing in those twelve hours?"

So they'd known she was there; Anna was relieved she had told them the truth.

"I'd gone back to France. With all of Finn's evidence," she said.

"Where in France?"

"To the place where Burt found me three months ago. Willy's hut on the beach."

Logan sat in silence, so that her words refused to dissipate from the moment. There was a tense stillness in the room.

"Who do you think delivered Finn's body, then?" Logan finally asked her. He said it with an aghast expression in his voice that suggested outrage that anyone could doubt the obvious, let alone expect him to believe them.

"I don't know," she said.

"Who do you think? What do your instincts tell you?"

She didn't reply immediately. He waited again until she saw she would lose nothing by replying and much by stalling.

"Mikhail was the best source the British—the West—had in Russia," she said. "They squandered him in an attempt to be friends with Putin. But that doesn't make Mikhail any less important. Mikhail is evidently a great man of power in Moscow. So surely you can't think that Mikhail, who is this great man of power, and is no doubt watched by Putin's private security service, would do such a thing? Drive Finn's body half way across Germany? It's madness. And surely you can't think that Mikhail, who spent so much effort to avoid detection for nearly six years, would fetch up with Finn's body outside a well-guarded embassy in Berlin? Let me ask you something, Logan. Can you see that?"

And Logan admitted he couldn't. That behaviour didn't fit his idea of what any double agent, on any side, would do for a fellow human being. But then Logan withdrew a piece of paper from the pocket of his jacket and passed it over to her.

"If you weren't there that night, in the car with Finn," he said, "you won't have read this."

She read it. It was short. "You betrayed him in life," it said. "Honour him in death."

She felt herself drawing on her deepest reserves of calm. Her face was unchanged, her body relaxed, but her mind raced back to that night, back to Finn dying, and Mikhail laying the note on his corpse.

"Not your handwriting," Logan said. "Recognise it?"

She didn't.

"Was it addressed to anyone?" she asked Logan.

"Yes."

They looked at each other, neither willing to give an inch to the other.

But Logan eventually smiled, his own reserves of patience apparently infinite. "It was addressed to Adrian. You know Adrian, of course."

"I'm afraid so. Finn introduced us," Anna said. "He was Finn's recruiter, Finn's handler, Finn's father substitute—until he first let Finn down and then went on to threaten him and me."

"Finn is attacked with a nerve agent smeared on the steering wheel of his car. In Paris," Logan went on. "Nearly four days later he's found dead in Berlin, delivered by someone who is clearly a friend and is clearly angry at the way the British treated him. Angry at Adrian, perhaps, in particular. You must admit it, you fit the bill."

"So do a lot of people," she replied. She was calm now. "Look,

Logan, if you've done your research on Finn, you know that he had many, many friends. I don't know who he was with in Paris, or who he called when he knew he was in trouble. Dying," she added ruthlessly. "But he was popular—loved even—by many. There were plenty of people who would have done almost anything for him. I can give you a list if you like, but I don't know the answer. I don't know how his body got to Berlin, or who got it there."

At which point Marcie stood up. "Is Logan getting on your nerves?" she said.

Logan smiled tolerantly.

"There are many ways to say no," Anna said. "I guess he just needs to hear them all."

"It'll do him good," Marcie said. "My impression of Logan is that he gets his own way too much of the time."

With that, she left the room. On her way out, she called back. "If you want to have a walk at lunchtime," she said, "I'm all yours."

Burt looked up to the table for the first time now.

"Let's resume after lunch," he said.

17

ANNA AND MARCIE WALKED up through the meadow after lunch. It was a cold afternoon. The land was preparing for its long winter sleep.

"You and Logan have worked together before?" Anna asked her.

"No. I only met him two months ago, when we started working on you," Marcie replied.

"Burt says he was sacked. Something to do with the Balkan war. Weren't you out there too?"

"After the war, yes. I was working with the UN. Before that I was a teacher in New York, then I took a psychology degree. Then I studied conflict resolution at military academy. That's where I started this kind of work. Joined the CIA. Life progression," she laughed.

"And now you work for Burt's company," Anna said.

"For the moment. Burt's a good employer, I guess. He inspires."

"Yes," Anna said. "I can see that."

"But I'm not sure I'm going to get on too well with Logan," Marcie said.

"Why not?"

"We're sharing the guesthouse, you know? I guess it's his attitude to women. He's predatory, he has assumptions. He thinks he doesn't need to try."

"With women?" Anna said.

"Or anything else."

"Do you want him to try with you then, Marcie?"

"God, no!"

"Sounds like the perfect partnership, then," Anna joked. "A guy who doesn't like trying, and a woman who doesn't want him to." But again Anna didn't believe the rift Marcie seemed keen to project between herself and Logan. It was a trap Anna was intended to fall into. Marcie was developing her role as a safe place for divulging confidences—Marcie and Anna against Logan.

They walked on in silence for a few minutes, before Marcie spoke.

"Tell me about Finn," Marcie said.

And so Anna told someone else for the first time about her relationship with Finn. But she did it, not to unburden herself, only to play the same game of artful intimacy that Marcie had begun.

Back at the house, Logan greeted them both with a smile. Burt was nowhere to be seen. Marcie went up to the guesthouse, and Anna and Logan were left alone in the kitchen.

"Ready for another grilling?" he said.

"I don't think I'm doing anything else this afternoon," she replied.

They paused while Logan drank from a cup of coffee.

"East Coast," she said at last. "Private school, followed by Harvard, and then in the footsteps of your father into the agency."

"Eight out of ten," he replied with a grin. "My father was a banker, not a spook."

"Retired?"

"He died. In a car crash."

"That's bad luck."

Not "Sorry," Logan noted, just "Bad luck." She was a tough bitch. But he inclined his head in acknowledgement. "And you?" he said.

"What is there you don't know about me, Logan?" she replied.

"Not a lot from your own lips," he answered.

"What do you want to know?"

"Tell me about Finn."

"Everybody wants to know about Finn."

"I'd like to think this isn't all about sitting on different sides of the table," Logan said. "It looks like we're going to be spending a while together."

"Let's just stick to the script," she said. "We're just two people who happen to be working together."

"Whatever you say," he replied amiably. "I guess it's time to move anyway."

"Afternoons aren't my favourite time," she said. "I'm a lot better in the mornings."

"That's a shame." He grinned and looked at her directly for once. "I prefer the nights."

Burt was already sitting in the study when Marcie returned and the three of them walked in, Anna first, then Marcie, with Logan some way behind.

But it was Logan who began the questioning again. Burt hardly looked up.

Logan gave her a file first of all, which he asked her to open and read. She saw it contained a list of Russian names, but with no explanation of what or who they were.

"Recognise any of them?" he said casually.

She ran her eye down the list. There were twenty-seven names altogether. She read the list a second time, but this time it was to compose herself, to avoid making eye contact. All were KGB, in one form or other. But there were two names she recognised very well indeed. Near the top of the list was an old friend and former lover whom she'd known since school days. But three from the bottom of the list was the name that really shocked her. Vasily Dubkov. It was Mikhail's real name.

"Yes," she said with a touch of bored interest. "I recognise several. What's the significance?"

"Tell me first what you know about the ones you recognise," Logan said smoothly.

She knew twelve of the twenty-seven, some well, others remotely. Then there was Vladimir, her old school friend and lover. But at the bottom of the page, Mikhail's name seemed to burn a hole in her consciousness.

She outlined the details—background, rank, and experience—of each. She didn't do it in the order they were written on the page, but as she remembered or knew of them. That way, she could better conceal Mikhail rather than leave him until last, when she knew it would be more difficult. There were no names beneath his that she recognised.

But Marcie was interested in Vladimir.

"So how long have you known Vladimir?" she said. "Since you were children? How old were you? Did you stay in touch?"

What did they know about her and Vladimir? Anna saw no reason to conceal anything.

"Vladimir, like me, was from an SVR family. We were at school together from the age of ten. We trained together at Yasenevo, at the Forest, in the early nineties. Vladimir spoke out against the abuse of privileges by KGB officers. We were encouraged to voice our thoughts in those days. But he was the only one who fell for it. He was exiled to the KGB residency in the Cape Verde Islands for ten years. I met him again when I was assigned to watch Finn."

There was a silence in the room.

"Still friends?" Marcie said at last.

"We were always friends. My father wanted me to marry him." Anna laughed. "There was never any chance of that. My father wanted the union of two great SVR families. But I wanted a career—not to be married to a careerist."

"Like your mother was," Marcie said.

"Yes. My mother gave everything up for my father's career. They separated in the nineties when my father completed his posting in Damascus and went back to Moscow. My mother saw a way out eventually."

"This could be good," Burt said, stirring from the armchair. "Vladimir could be very good indeed."

But none of them explained why.

"What's the purpose of the list?" Anna asked a second time, but they weren't prepared to tell her yet.

They went through each name that she said she recognised. She filled in the details of whatever she knew. Then they went through the list from top to bottom, in order, in case she'd forgotten anything.

"All KGB?" Burt asked. "The ones you know?"

"That, or close to the Putin administration," she said.

"Good," Burt replied.

Then Logan began to fillet the twelve names she knew once more. He was interested in those who weren't simply KGB officers. Two of these were government officials. One of them worked in the Kremlin administration, and one of them was Mikhail. She knew she had to be extremely careful now, to be as open about him as she was about the others.

"This Vasily Dubkov," Logan said at last. "What about him?"

They'd left Mikhail last of all.

"He's a time-serving figure in the administration," she answered. "As I remember, he was the Russian deputy railways minister."

There he was in front of her on the page, with a low-key job that kept him away from the public eye. But unknown to all outside the highest echelons of the KGB elite, the deputy railways minister was also the SVR's secret controller of all Russia's foreign agents in Europe. Vasily Dubkov was there from the beginning, when Putin came to Petersburg from his KGB posting in East Germany. He was as close to Putin as it was possible to get. And he was Mikhail.

Anna kept her eyes fixed to the list and ran them down it twice more. Once she was confident her expression wouldn't betray her and her breathing was under control, she put the list on the desk. Then she looked Logan in the eye.

"So?" she said.

But it was Burt who answered.

"This is a list of appointments the Russians have made in the past year to their embassy in Washington, their New York consulate, and the UN in New York," he revealed.

Anna was aghast. Mikhail was in America. Vladimir, Burt went on to say, was part of the Russian delegation at the UN. But Burt believed he was running the KGB residency in New York.

"There's been a big turnover of personnel in the past year," Logan explained. "Both at the Russian embassy and at the Russian UN delegation. It's unusual. Very unusual, actually."

"We'd like you to take your time with the list," Marcie said. "You may remember other things."

For the rest of the day, they left her in the study, and she wrote down all she knew but the one vital piece of information. Mikhail's face came into her mind constantly and faded away again.

Over the next two days, Logan and Marcie were determined to seize control of the routine in small matters, the specific times they wanted formally to sit her down in the study, rather than walk in the forest, or ride the horses up to the ridge before the snow became too deep in December.

These small things were a ready-made battleground between Anna and her inquisitors. To disrupt their desired routine in minor ways was a tactic she used from the moment of their arrival. In the small ways, ways that weren't possible to identify, she could to some degree set her terms, her control, however minor it seemed.

But in the big ways, the control of information itself, she knew she held all the cards. And their weakness was that they didn't know she knew who Mikhail was.

Covering all the bases, she weighed up the effect of telling them about Mikhail—who he was, how to make contact with him, his background, his relationship to the Kremlin and to Putin, everything. It certainly occurred to her to tell them. But, she told herself in these opening days, Mikhail needed protection too. She owed him that, and she didn't trust her handlers, even the silk-gloved approach of Burt, not to blunder all over Mikhail, destroy his cover, and in the process destroy him.

He deserved to be the one to make the approach to the Americans, the British, whoever he wanted to. It wasn't for her to reveal his secret. She also knew that if she told them about Mikhail, she and Little Finn would be free.

Mikhail was also her talisman, her protective amulet. Mikhail was her wandering exile's deeply hidden stash of gold that could be used only once, and then only in the eventuality of extreme danger to herself and to Little Finn.

They sat in the study for longer and longer periods, broken up by walks, a horse ride with Logan, playing with Little Finn. Sometimes Logan and Marcie only seemed interested in the names on the list that she didn't know. At other times they wanted to extract anything further about the ones she did know. And then they'd return to the night Finn died.

"What about this guy?" Logan would ask. Or, "You must have come across this guy? Are you sure? Think again, Anna." They then showed her photographs of each of the men on the list, in turn, just in case the face had been given another name, and she might recognise that instead.

On the third day, they were sitting in the study in the early afternoon. She was tired, and felt her concentration was lower than usual. Logan suddenly brought the name of Vasily Dubkov into the room again. They'd been over it several times before, but the name had never been pulled out of the hat in as startling a way as it was now.

She had no expression on her face, no inflection in her voice. The deputy railways minister was, she had rehearsed to herself in bed at night, just one more name. She treated Mikhail the same way as she had treated the others.

"This guy Dubkov," Logan said. "He doesn't seem right."

"You say he's not KGB," Marcie said.

"I don't whether he is or not," she replied. "In all likelihood he is. But I don't know. I only know of him. He's a minor public figure, I suppose. I never met him."

"There's something odd about his appearance on the list," Logan said. He had his hand on his jaw and was apparently staring at his copy of the list.

Anna didn't respond.

"He was transferred to the Russians' Washington embassy—its cultural division actually—seven months ago. That's five months after Vladimir was assigned to the United Nations in New York and, we suspect, became head of the KGB residency there." He looked at her intently.

"What's odd about it?" she said.

"I can see why Vladimir's on the list," Logan replied. "He's KGB—not just verified by you, but by others. And the other names you've been able to identify as having various different backgrounds in domestic and foreign intelligence services. But why would the Kremlin transfer Dubkov to their cultural centre in Washington? He's a deputy railways minister. He's a nobody." Logan looked at her as if the answer, in its obviousness, barely needed stating.

"I guess because he's not just a deputy railways minister," Anna replied.

"Exactly. So who, or what, is he?"

"We can guess he's KGB," she said, "but look—I don't know for sure."

"Do you know what his background is?" Marcie asked. "Before he got the railways job, I mean?"

"That's another interesting thing about him," Logan interrupted. "He seems to have no background that we can trace."

"No, I don't. Where's he from?" Anna said.

"We're fairly sure Saint Petersburg," Logan replied. "We almost know that for a fact."

"When? What's the timing?"

"We don't know."

"If he's close to Putin, it's a sure thing he goes back to around 1990 or 1991," Anna said. "Back then Putin turned up in the city and became deputy mayor. Then Putin moved all his Petersburg friends to Moscow when he went there to take over the top job at the KGB in 1999, before he became president."

"Probably that's right, yes," Logan answered. "Maybe he and Putin knew each other back then, if not before then."

"Yes," she said. "Maybe."

Marcie looked up at Anna. "Maybe Dubkov goes back to when Putin was stationed in Dresden, East Germany, back in the eighties before the Wall fell," she said.

"It's possible," Anna agreed.

"But you don't know," Logan asked, and his question had a hard edge to it.

"No. I don't know."

"Nothing comes up on him," Marcie said. "No name, no photo match, nothing in the records at all about him."

"That's odd," Logan repeated. "He has no traces. Why would a deputy railways minister have no traces?"

Anna said nothing.

Logan looked at her hard. "There should be something, some backstory. He can't just turn up—even in an insignificant job with the railways—without some kind of background. And he certainly can't be posted to Washington without one."

She shrugged. "I would guess so."

"What else does your guesswork tell you?" Marcie said, and there was only innocence in her voice.

Anna paused to think. "It's possible he just did someone a favour back in Petersburg in the early nineties, some relatively small thing, and that got him the railways job. It was a small reward. Maybe he has no actual record. There are hundreds of thousands of KGB active reservists out there. They're all people waiting for the call. Most of them probably don't have any record that you could get your hands on."

"Except for one important difference between him and the hundreds of thousands," Logan said, with a slight acidity in his voice. "This guy is assigned to Washington. That's a big leap from nothing."

She had to agree.

He reached into his pocket and took out a stiff photo envelope.

"I want you to look at this picture again," he said and handed it to her.

She pulled the photo from the envelope and felt Logan watching her intently all the time. She moved neither slowly nor fast, the most difficult pretence of all—to be absolutely normal.

When she turned the photo the right way up to look at it, she saw Mikhail's face again. She studied it closely. It was the only picture they had of him. It had been taken in Washington the week before. There was only one picture of Mikhail in the public arena, even in Russia. And that wasn't conclusive unless you knew it was him.

Back in 2000 when Putin became president, a picture was taken at a very special religious service in the Kremlin's chapel. It was presided over by the Orthodox archbishop who had publicly proclaimed when Putin came to power, "God creates everything. And so he created the KGB to care for us. God bless the KGB."

At this service, the picture was intended to show only Putin, thus demonstrating that he cared for the people's religion. But in the pew behind him—a place of honour—was the left side of Mikhail's face,

Dubkov's face, hardly more than his ear and his jaw. It was unmistakable—if you knew it was him.

"Recognise it now?" Logan said.

At first she acted like she thought she might. But then she shook her head.

"No. I thought it was someone . . . someone who looks quite like him. But it isn't who I thought." She looked directly at Logan. "Sometimes you can try too hard to see what you want to see," she said.

"My perennial problem, apparently," he said.

18

O **N THE DAY BEFORE** Adrian was to arrive, Burt gave them all what he called a day off, though Logan was detailed to stay with Anna throughout the day. Marcie was going "into town," as she put it.

Anna and Logan decided to follow a herd of elk that Larry had seen up on the ridge, and maybe bring one down. Burt had a cupboard full of rifles at the house.

They walked off up the meadow at nine in the morning and onto a path into the forest. When they emerged on the far side through the trees, they were on top of the ridge. Logan looked through binoculars and then handed them to her.

"They're over a thousand yards away," he said.

The herd of elk, she saw, was moving slowly through trees on another ridge. There was snow everywhere up here, deep in places, and it would be slow, quiet work. Between them and the herd was a deep ravine, treeless, and they would have to go around somehow, find other cover, if they were going to get a shot.

Anna pointed down to the right, where some rocks afforded a

good place to remain unseen. From there, they could approach in the shadow of the far ridge where the herd was. If they didn't spook them, they would be able to get as close as 250 yards. She beckoned to Logan and began to crawl belly-down through the snow, over the top of the crest, and down towards the rocks.

It took half an hour of crawling, stopping to check their direction, or to lie completely still when one of the herd looked up. But they reached the rocks, and as they did so, he offered her a silver flask.

"Whisky and ginger wine," he said.

She drank and handed the flask back to Logan.

"You take the shot," she said, nodding in the direction of the herd.

"It's yours," he replied. "I want to see how good you are."

She wasn't going to argue.

When they began to get cold again, they crawled beyond the rocks, until they were in the shadow of the ridge, where they couldn't be seen. Then they stood and walked slowly up until they reached the far ridge she had spotted earlier. She'd been right—it was 250 yards or so from the herd. The elk were still there, in the shelter of the trees.

She took the rifle from her back and removed it from its cover. Then she put one shell up the barrel, the other five in her pocket. She looked back at Logan and, crouching down again, began to crawl to the rim of the ridge.

He watched her reach the top and bring the rifle round, lying flat in the snow, legs splayed, and then begin to take aim. He waited for nearly a minute of dead silence. Then he heard the crack of the shot, the echo that chased around the valley and up to the mountains, and the silence that returned deeper than before. He saw her standing and waving him up.

They walked together up to the edge of the forest. Thirty yards inside the trees they found the elk, killed immediately from a shot to the right of its foreleg and straight to the heart.

"Okay shot," Logan said. He grinned at her. "For a KGB colonel."

She knelt by the animal and carefully cut its belly with a thin-bladed knife; the stomach sac spilled out into the snow.

"How are we going to get it back to the house?" she said. "We'll never drag it up the ravine."

"Something for the boys to do," Logan replied. "They'll bring a mule. I think they'll be happy to have a job." She watched him scrape some snow from the forest floor until he'd made a bare patch. Then he walked farther into the trees and returned, carrying tinder for a fire.

When he'd got the fire going and they were sitting warming themselves, Logan retrieved some bacon and eggs and an old pan from his pack. He propped the pan up on some stones and put the bacon in first, for the fat, then broke the eggs and tipped them carefully in afterwards.

While the food was cooking and they'd been silent for some time, he asked her a question so casually that it put her on her guard once more. The freedom of the morning evaporated.

"You still miss Finn, Anna?"

"What difference is it to you, Logan?"

"Well, put it this way, it's not of national importance," he said, without rising to her response.

She didn't reply at first, and he poked the bacon over with a fork.

"So," she said finally, "it's not work, then?"

"On a beautiful day like this, it's all one as far as I'm concerned," he said.

"Why don't you tell me about you?" she said. "Why you were thrown out of the agency?"

"Who told you that?"

"It's true, then."

"Marcie?"

"Touchy about it?"

"The best people get thrown out of intelligence services," he said. "Finn included, I understand."

She sat back against a tree and took the bacon and egg sandwich he was offering.

"I don't think about Finn," she said, "or miss him—not as a lover or a husband, not anymore. Does that answer your question?"

"I find that hard to believe," he said.

"And you, Logan? Who do you think about? Tell me about the women you've betrayed," she joked.

He looked startled.

"No wife and kids when the job's over?"

"No longer a wife, and one daughter I never see," he replied.

"What's her name?"

"Angelica," Logan replied.

"Your wife made the wrong choice, or did you?" she asked.

"She did, since you ask. She left me about ten years ago. We were married in our early twenties, we were young, and we were still young when it was over. Then—" He didn't go on.

"Why did she leave?" Anna said.

"It wasn't what she'd expected, I guess. We began to fall out. Small things, bigger things. Neither of us seemed prepared to make the effort. And I was away a lot."

"The job was more important?"

"I lost the job. That was the end."

"So your wife left you, and after that—or maybe before that—it was one in every port," Anna said. "That was Marcie," she added and laughed.

"Oh, not just the ports," he replied, smiling in return.

When they'd finished, he refilled the pack. They descended into the ravine and up the far side to the ridge above the house.

"What's the best way of getting to know someone, do you think?" he asked suddenly.

The innocence of the question reminded her of something that Little Finn might have said. And then she realised it reminded her of Finn himself.

"Sitting in a study asking personal questions all day not enough for you?" she replied.

"I find I'm enjoying getting to know you," he replied.

"Better be careful then, Logan. There's a string of dead spies behind me."

He was shocked by her casual reference to Finn.

They walked out of the forest and into the meadow in front of the house. He stopped, took her arm, and faced her.

"I know you know who Mikhail is," he said suddenly. "So Burt must know too."

"Well, just don't tell anyone else, Logan," she said mockingly. And then she pulled away from him. She walked back to the house twenty or thirty yards in front.

When they reached the house, they found that Burt had left, and Marcie wasn't back.

"Marcie won't be back until the morning," Frutoza told Logan. "She and Mr. Miller left in a helicopter."

Frutoza cooked dinner for the two of them, and afterwards they settled into the sitting room to watch a movie. She didn't particularly want to watch the one Logan chose, but said nothing. What she wanted was to observe Logan with as few barriers between them as possible, to see what he was like when he was doing what he wanted to do.

Afterwards, she decided to have a whisky before they said good night. Not to her great surprise—she had grown used to it—he let his eyes linger a moment too long on her.

"Good night, Logan," she said, and walked to her bedroom at the back of the house.

When she'd switched the shower on and was about to undress, she was aware of someone and turned to find Logan in the doorway. He hadn't entered the room, but leaned against the jamb of the door. He was fiddling with an ornamental dagger she carried with her and had put on the table by the door. It was a gift from Mikhail. Finn had given it to him, and he had passed it to her the night that Finn died.

"What's this?" he said. "You used it on the mountain."

"It's a gift from a friend," she said.

"Where's it from?"

"It's Caucasian. From Chechnya. My grandmother gave it to me."

"It's a very beautiful thing."

"Was that it?" she said. "I'm going to bed."

He paused.

"Why not come over to the guesthouse?" he said.

She stopped and looked at him. He was smiling, relaxed.

"What for, Logan?" she said. "To play Scrabble?"

There was a moment of tense silence.

"Sure. Okay, sure. I'm sorry, Anna," he said.

"There's nothing to be sorry for, Logan. It's been a nice day."

19

ON THE FOLLOWING MORNING, Anna was reading on her own in the sitting room while Larry was showing Little Finn how to sit on a horse. Logan hadn't appeared. She heard the distant sound of an engine, and as it came closer, she saw it was the helicopter. She glanced up, but saw that Larry was removing Little Finn from the saddle. He'd heard it too.

She stood and looked out of the study window, watching it touch down on a pad at the bottom of the meadow. She could make out three figures descending before it took off again. Burt, Adrian, and Marcie moved up across the meadow, talking closely.

It had been four, maybe five, years since she'd seen Adrian. When Finn had first left the SIS, and she was living with him back in London, they saw Adrian from time to time. She was still watching Finn then—at least as far as her controllers in Moscow were concerned. The KGB believed that Finn's departure from MI6 was a decoy to fool them.

Adrian had been very attentive, she recalled. He'd been very complimentary about Finn's work in Moscow, but he was watching Finn too, she knew. Adrian wasn't convinced that Finn had bought the lie that Mikhail was a fraud.

On one occasion, she and Finn had even spent a weekend down at Adrian's country house, with his wife, Penny. Even in front of his wife, Adrian had practically pawed her.

But when two years later Adrian found that Finn had been disobeying his instructions to stay away from Mikhail, Adrian turned nasty. He'd finally issued a very ugly threat to Finn—as ugly as if it had come from her own side—and then he'd told Finn he'd wreck him, and destroy her too. It was for that reason that they'd disappeared and fetched up in France at Willy's place, where they'd stayed until Finn's murder.

After Finn had died, Adrian organised a memorial service for him in London. She hadn't gone to it. It wasn't worth the risk. And anyway, the hypocrisy of Adrian celebrating Finn in death when he'd threatened him in life disgusted her.

She watched Adrian approach the house now and felt a surge of anger.

When the three of them entered the house, she stayed in the sitting room. Finally Burt came in alone. She could see he was no more pleased to have Adrian here than she was.

Burt sat down opposite her. He made a halfhearted attempt to be good-humoured, but she wasn't buying it. The thought of Adrian in the house with her and her son made her sick.

"Adrian's presence here is a formality," Burt said, without preamble. "It's a gesture to our British friends."

She didn't believe that and made no attempt to hide her feelings. There was more to it.

"Certain events that have recently come to light have forced a change of pace," Burt continued. "We no longer have as much time as I'd hoped. In fact, everything has suddenly become very urgent, as I told you."

She'd never seen Burt like this, operating at a pace other than his own.

"Your cooperation is critical now. You don't have to say anything to Adrian—in fact, if you have anything to say, I want you to keep it between us. But Adrian has Langley's ear, or will have if he thinks you're not cooperating."

Burt looked her in the eye, and she saw an urgency in his face.

"Let me put it this way," he said. "If they take you up to Langley, if you're taken off my hands, you'll be drugged."

"Why would that yield anything different?" she said.

"Only you know that."

"I also know that drugs aren't reliable."

"That may not be what they think at Langley," he said. "I just want you to know the score, Anna."

So the men of power were at war, she thought. She paused and watched him.

"Thank you, Burt," she said, and meant it.

"I'll tell him you're in the study," Burt said.

Adrian made no attempt to greet her, or even to shake her hand. He stopped in the centre of the room and acknowledged her with a brief nod—almost embarrassed, she thought. He seemed to know he'd be unwelcome, and he had no way of dealing with this except brusqueness.

She stayed in her seat.

Adrian walked over to the study window and looked out of it sightlessly as he spoke to her behind him.

"You must realise, Anna, the time for silk gloves is over. It's time to move on to something stronger. Either we have your help, or you are of no help to us. In the latter case, it is merely a matter of our kindness—or not—whether we send you back to Russia. So this is the moment of truth. We need Mikhail."

"I've said everything I know about him," she replied.

"Which is nothing," Adrian said coldly, without turning round.

She didn't reply.

Adrian finally looked round to face her, but didn't step away from the window.

"What about your son?" he said.

"I don't think a two-year-old is going to be much help to you," she said.

"On the contrary," he replied. "It's his future we're talking about, just as much as yours."

"What do you mean by that, Adrian? Why don't you say what you've got to say and get out."

"What are the orphanages like these days in Russia?" Adrian said. "Any better than they were?"

She saw no reason to reply.

"So you're prepared to face being returned to Russia. With your son," Adrian added, grinding his teeth irritably at the necessity for such crude threats. "For whatever fate awaits you both," he added.

"My fate, as you call it, is not in my hands."

Adrian looked at her coldly from the window. She couldn't see his face with the brightness behind him.

"Fatalism is not a defence against events," Adrian said. "It simply encourages those events. You can make your history. Here—in America. I repeat, we need to know Mikhail. That is your choice, for yours and the boy's future."

"What do you have in mind to exchange me for?" she said. Adrian at last left the blindness of the window and walked over to the desk in front of where she was sitting. He perched himself on the front of it and crossed his feet on the floor a few inches from her—too close. She felt his breath and the smell of his clothes and saw the livid anger in his eyes.

"We're not planning to return you, my dear," he said, "if we have your cooperation."

"You want me to invent Mikhail, Adrian? Threats don't work if the person you're threatening has nothing to give up."

"So that's it." Adrian stood up abruptly. "I hope you're prepared for what happens."

"It's not in my hands," she said.

"Can you imagine what they'll do to you—and the boy—if we send you back?"

"There's nothing they'll give you for me," she said.

"It doesn't matter." Adrian looked even more furious. From the headmaster who'd leaned on the front of the desk to the street fighter who stood before her now, he looked ready to break her neck.

"We might just return you to Moscow to encourage a better quality of defector next time," he sneered.

"Not a strategy I'd rely on," she said.

"You're a tough bitch, aren't you," he snapped. "But I wonder how tough you'll be in a cell at the Lubyanka. With the boy," he added.

"So you've come to fuck up Burt's operation when it's hardly begun," she said, and saw, as she'd predicted, that Adrian liked to see a woman swear.

"We haven't got the name we want," was all he said, taking a seat behind the desk now. His attitude suddenly changed. He became less threatening—a new approach, she saw.

"If this is about Finn," he said, "you know the way it was."

"This isn't about Finn."

"Finn left MI6," Adrian said, ignoring her. "He disobeyed every agreement to stay out of the way. And tragically he died—as a result of getting in the way. Do you have any idea how sad that made me? Finn and I were close, Anna. For sixteen years. He was like a son."

"If this is about your absolution for Finn's death, you don't get to use me as a tool."

"Finn would have been more forgiving."

"I'm not Finn."

"No." Adrian paused, then leaned his elbows on the desk and clasped his hands together like a prayer. "But revenge for Finn's death, however, is within our grasp," he said.

She looked up at him, for the first time. There was no need to speak.

"We've found Finn's killer," he said. "The man who administered the nerve agent."

Her eyes flickered. For the first time since she could remember, the closeness to Finn's death was almost unbearable.

"How sure are you?"

"We know. And once we have Mikhail, my political masters will allow me to deal with him," Adrian said.

She looked at him. She didn't know what to say

"The two hang together, you see," he explained.

A silence descended on the room. Her thoughts were humming over what he'd said. She imagined the car park in Paris, two years before, Finn's rental car, and the man who had dealt death to him.

She pictured too the laboratory itself, a building she knew well in Moscow, where the KGB made its poisons. Right in the heart of a residential Moscow district, it was. That was typical of the regime she'd escaped from. They built their poison laboratories in the centre of the city.

"We will get our revenge," Adrian said grittily through the silence.

"Revenge for Finn? Or for you, Adrian?" she said. He looked at her, and she saw a weariness in his eyes. Adrian had aged noticeably in the years since they'd last met, she realised.

"For the future, Anna," he said, for the first time using her name. "To deter them from doing it again."

"You think they'll care? The killer's probably some common criminal they trained up for the purpose. Expendable. That's what they do. Killing someone like that won't deter them."

"But it must be done," Adrian said.

She didn't ask him who the killer was, though she saw in Adrian's eyes that he wanted her to. She knew he wouldn't tell her, and she wasn't going to give him the satisfaction of refusing.

And then Adrian reverted to his ruthless exposition of her position.

"Do you really think you can get your way?" he said to her. "Think hard before you decide you don't know Mikhail. It may be final. You're useful now, and maybe for a while longer, but eventually that will come to an end. You'll need to be a bit more accommodating if you want your freedom. You'll need friends. And in this game, friends are the people you help."

"If I need friends, are you offering?" she said.

He looked like he wanted to strike her. But then he calmed his face and regarded her with cold eyes.

"For the last time, who's Mikhail?"

"And for the last time, Adrian, I don't know."

"Burt can protect you for a while. But his time's running out too. I'll see to that," he said.

Adrian got up from his chair, but he didn't leave the room. She stayed seated, as she had been since he'd entered. He walked back over to the window, and once again his face was lost against the blinding white of the winter sun. Then he turned to her.

"All right. Suppose I believe you," he said. "Suppose I accept you don't know Mikhail. What would you do in my position?"

She said nothing.

"Time, safety, and all hope are running out for you," he said, and left.

20

ON THE DAY AFTER Adrian's visit, Burt suddenly announced that they would be decamping for New York on the following day. Adrian's visit seemed to have injected a new vigour into Burt's measured plans. Burt had made a decision and seemed happier with the prospect of action. In the study after breakfast there was an air of expectancy.

But Anna knew that Little Finn would have to stay. They were on an operational footing now, Burt told her, and it was unsafe for the boy to be moved around.

"Why New York?" Anna asked.

It was Marcie who answered her question. "You're going to make contact with Vladimir," she told her. "Vladimir is the new starting line for Mikhail."

At seven o'clock on the following morning, Anna, Burt, Logan, and Marcie left the log house. Little Finn seemed more concerned that the bodyguards were leaving. They'd played endlessly with him since Anna's arrival in America, and Burt promised him some more bodyguards to play with. "They're on the helicopter right now that's coming to pick us up," he said, and stroked Little Finn's head with affection.

By nine o'clock they were on a Cougar company jet to New York, and by afternoon the four of them, as well as Larry, Christoff, and Joe, moved into a set of three fifth-floor apartments on Twenty-third Street. More of Burt's property empire, Marcie informed Anna.

Inside, the apartments, except the bedrooms, were in chaos. There were a dozen Cougar employees setting up communications equipment, testing listening devices, and filling floors and tables with computers, empty boxes, and tangled skeins of wire.

They were tired from the journey, and there was nowhere inviting enough in the apartments to sit around just yet. Anna made her excuses and went to her room. To sleep, she said. But what she needed now was to plan for what lay ahead. And that meant the deception of Burt and all of them.

In the morning, the preparations—laying the ground for her approach to Vladimir—would begin.

At ten o'clock on the following day, Anna and Logan drank coffee in a kitchen piled with boxes of catering equipment. He was civil, but reserved, she noted. Her rebuff, perhaps? She'd voiced her concern to Marcie about Logan's discipline. Perhaps Logan had received a warning from Burt.

They all met after breakfast in Burt's control room, as the technical people who had rigged the place were calling it. It had four windows overlooking the street, fitted with blackout blinds.

Logan as usual opened the questioning.

"We're interested in your relationship with Vladimir," he said.

Outside the window, the New York sky hung low like a wet, grey blanket, and there was little cheer except in the eager faces in the room.

Burt had appeared only briefly, to explain to her that they would need to get right beneath the skin of her former attachment to

Vladimir, in order to establish a base for her contact with him. And the first task was to figure out all the options available for the approach.

"Tell me, what's the purpose of making contact?" she'd asked Burt.

"So that your presence here is known to the Russians."

"As bait for them?" she said

"No." Then: "Only in part," he corrected himself.

"I show myself to Vladimir. . . . What then?"

"If the Russians know you're here, then it'll become known to Mikhail."

"So you think he's here? In America?"

"He may be, he may not be. But if he is, I believe he'll contact you. Even if he's not here, there's a chance he will. And that way, Mikhail will tell us who he is."

"And you'll give him the opportunity to accept or refuse the Americans?" she asked.

"Everyone has a choice."

Anna saw an opportunity. If Mikhail came to her, then she was relieved of the burden. She would be his intermediary, as Finn had been. And it would solve the impasse between her and the Americans. It was, perhaps, a way out.

At that point, Burt left the room.

But now Logan was looking directly at her with his clear blue eyes, and he didn't let his gaze fall as he usually did.

"You and Vladimir go back a long way," Marcie said. "But we're most interested in the time when your relationship became an affair."

So they knew that too.

"It was just a week," Anna said.

"You've told us briefly about Vladimir," Marcie said. "We want you to fill it out a little."

Anna paused to decide on the best place to start.

"As soon as I was assigned by my controllers to join Finn in France," she began, "every eleven days I would compile a report for my chief in Moscow. The reports went to Nikolai Patrushev, the FSB chief. He and Putin were old comrades from Petersburg, and Putin was taking an interest in Finn. Because of Mikhail, of course. Finn and I would compile the report together, to make sure I was able to give them genuinely useful information. Finn, I know, gave away certain secrets of the British—minor ones—in order to establish my usefulness. We both knew that unless I was seen to be useful, I would be recalled to Russia, perhaps for good. And that would be the end of us. Already I was writing my reports for the sole purpose of staying with Finn.

"On my first recall to Russia, which was routine after over two years with Finn, I was debriefed at the Lubyanka in Moscow and then at the Forest. There were two schools of thought, I came to realise. The first one was that my mission as Finn's lover was wasting valuable time and resources without getting the crucial information that would lead to the discovery and arrest of Mikhail. The second was that it was a long process, and that victory would come only with patience."

She looked up at Marcie. "Nothing changes, does it, Marcie, whichever side you're on?"

Marcie gave a smile of sympathy and encouragement.

"Anyway, I was aware that certain factions around Patrushev were snapping at my heels and that I needed to redouble my efforts, not only to be reassigned to Finn after my recall, but also for my own survival. There was deep suspicion in certain quarters that I was already on the outside.

"Vladimir and I were sent together to the Forest for ten days of physical retraining, the establishment of new code work, and so on. Vladimir was by now working as the liaison between me and the chief, Patrushev. We'd always been close friends, and that was the reason for his new position on my case with Finn.

"It was an exhausting ten days—I'm sure you know what these

things are like. And I was increasingly anxious that my involvement with Finn was going to be shut down. If I was taken off the case, I wouldn't be allowed to leave Russia. I realised then that I couldn't— or more accurately didn't want to—live without Finn. To get back to him, I had to establish to my own side that I was totally loyal as well as being able to make progress on my assignment. I believed I needed to establish my loyalty, in particular, in as many ways as I could.

"Vladimir was fond of me—keen on me, yes. He always had been since school days. One night at the dacha where we were both staying out at the Forest, he made one more attempt to seduce me. I'd laughed him off, in the manner of the old friends we were, on several occasions already. I don't know whether the cynical plan was already formed in my head, or whether that came later, but anyway we went to bed. He thought I'd finally given in—as he probably saw it, anyway. We spent the next week working fourteen hours a day, making love, talking about old times, teasing each other—it was a good week. I told Vladimir I loved him. He asked me to marry him, and I accepted.

"It was then that I was fully conscious of what was happening. I wanted to be with Finn, yet I had told Vladimir I would marry him. I was using him to establish in the minds of my superiors, and particularly Patrushev, that if my loyalty to the Kremlin was doubted in some quarters, I had the strongest personal ties to Russia. When all this is over, I told Vladimir, we'll be married. I then realised how much I dreaded them calling off the assignment, and finding that all I had left was my agreement to marry Vladimir. Much as I liked him, I was now devoted to Finn."

"Did you feel any . . . guilt about that?" Logan said.

Marcie looked at him sharply. "That isn't relevant," she said.

"I justified my actions towards Vladimir," she replied, "because I knew he was to be trusted no more than I was. He was a KGB officer. That was his task, no doubt, to bind me in. And therefore his proposal of marriage to me was as cynical as my acceptance—"

She stopped.

"But it wasn't?" Marcie prompted.

"No. Vladimir was sincere. But I wasn't to find that out until a year later. To my relief, after the retraining programme with Vladimir, I was reassigned to join Finn in France. We both felt—Finn and I—that this might be our last chance to stay together. He asked me then and there to leave Russia. He told me he would stop the dangerous work he was doing behind the back of the British intelligence service and that we'd settle down in the West, have children . . . raise pigs, I think he said, though I'm not sure whether he meant actual pigs or was referring to the children.

"But I still couldn't make that leap. Leave Russia, leave everything I knew, for the hazard of life with Finn. I thought I could play it out just a little bit longer.

"I was recalled a second time, around a year later, and against my better instincts—and I guess Finn's, though he put no pressure on me—I did return to Moscow. Once more I was debriefed, and this time the faction in the KGB that was angry with the lack of progress on Mikhail was getting the upper hand. At four o'clock one morning at the dacha where I stayed with my grandmother, we were woken by the kind of loud knocking that heralds only one thing in the annals of the KGB—arrest. But it was Vladimir at the door. Alone. He told me they wanted me at the Lubyanka, the KGB's headquarters in Moscow. Just for further questioning, he said. But we both knew.

"We drove from the Forest into Moscow. At his insistence, we stopped at his apartment for a fortifying drink and breakfast, as he told me." She looked up at Logan and Marcie. "The rest you know," she said. "Vladimir smuggled me into Finland."

"He loved you very much," Marcie said.

Anna didn't reply directly. Instead she said, "Later, Finn would say that I owed Vladimir my life and my freedom," she said. "Finn said that Vladimir had loved me so much that he had delivered me to another man, the man I loved. Finn said it was the most selfless act he'd ever seen."

She sipped from a glass of water, but it was only to pause and reflect on that moment five years before.

"Everything Finn said about Vladimir only confirmed what I knew, but hadn't dared to admit to myself—that he was genuine all along, and that I had used him mercilessly. Vladimir risked his own life to allow me to be with Finn."

Anna fell silent. She was lost for a moment in the deliberate cruelty of her own behaviour.

Marcie was respectfully silent. Logan was making notes, or pretending to.

The second session of their questions about Vladimir was more brisk, less reflective. This time, Burt was present throughout. How should Anna make her approach to him? Should it be an "accidental" meeting? Or should she make herself known to Vladimir deliberately, so that he couldn't mistake it? Her behaviour towards Vladimir would clearly be different in either scenario.

"Will Vladimir believe it's accidental?" Logan said. "It's too much of a coincidence."

"I don't agree," Marcie said. Marcie now seemed to Anna to be entrenched in an antagonistic position towards Logan. "Coincidence is seductive."

"Not to intelligence officers on foreign territory," Logan objected.

"It depends how much Vladimir wants to believe in the chance of running into Anna," Marcie cut in. "It depends on the story Vladimir tells to himself. But if he thinks it's a coincidence, then it's the better method. Anything he knows is planned will have a sour feeling to it, which will take a lot of time and effort to dispel."

Anna said nothing in response to either thought. She was trying to think herself into Vladimir's mind.

Burt looked at her, watching her thinking.

"What if Vladimir sees you, not the other way around?" he said.

She looked up at him, nodding slightly. "That would be the most intriguing from his point of view," she said. "He would have to make the move."

"What if he doesn't make the move?" Logan said.

"Then Anna can always see him at a later stage," Burt says. "It doesn't negate that possibility."

"It has more chance of seeming a coincidence," Marcie agreed.

"What do you think, Anna?" Burt asked her.

"It's always better for a false seduction to begin from the other side," she said.

"Is that where your strength is?" Logan asked. "False seductions?"

Marcie shot him a look.

"Just one of my strengths, Logan," Anna answered him coolly, and Marcie laughed.

When they'd tentatively agreed that it should be Vladimir who made the move, they moved on to what Anna's story should be. Should she be relieved to see him? Would he be her rescuer again? She—a remorseful and forlorn figure who was disillusioned with the West, homesick for Mother Russia. He—the hero, the rescuer? It was Anna who finally put a firm rejection on this proposal.

"I don't regret the past," she said. "I don't regret that I left Russia for Finn, and that Finn finally left us in death. I'm not a person who feels regret for what cannot be changed. Vladimir knows that."

Burt nodded in agreement.

"You really have no regrets?" Logan said.

"None."

Burt nodded his head in understanding.

"Vladimir loved you," Marcie said. "He will want to see the woman he loved. If he still harbours affection for you, let alone a dream, he will want you as he remembers you. To him, I think, you're stronger than he is—more wilful and independent, almost careless about the future. I think we need to massage those emotional muscles of Vladimir's, to enhance—exaggerate even—those qualities you have, and maybe he would like to have, as well as admiring them in you."

"Yes—good, Marcie," Burt drawled. "Anna, you need to present yourself as entirely confident in whatever the future holds, here in America or back in Russia. It doesn't matter to you. You will be— you are—who you are despite your circumstances. Quintessentially you. That is your strength. Let's play always to the truth.

"Firstly," he continued, "Vladimir gets no choice about meeting you, no time to plan, no time to rehearse a reaction. We'll work on the details. Maybe he has to follow you, that would be best. But you'll meet him cold, no previous contact. It could be that you walk into one of the cafés he goes to. Either he'll approach you, or he'll stay back, watch you, then follow you. He'll be wary, sure—he'll be looking out for tails. He won't believe entirely in the coincidence, but he'll want to believe."

"He'll be afraid too," Logan said. "He smuggled you out of Russia."

"And if he no longer has those feelings for me that he had?" Anna asked. "Maybe he's thought for years now that our affair was just fiction from my point of view. Maybe he'll be angry. Maybe he'll have learned to hate me."

"Is he a resentful man?" Marcie asked.

Anna thought for a moment. "No, he isn't resentful," Anna replied. "I think the key to Vladimir, apart from his feelings for me in the past, is that he has seen the way our system operates. Don't forget, he was banished for ten years at the beginning of the nineties to the Cape Verde Islands. He knows the viciousness of our masters, and their essential stupidity. In some ways, if Vladimir had had the incentives I had—a lover in the West, in other words—I'm not sure he wouldn't have seen that as a way out of his past too."

"But does he have the courage?" Marcie said.

"Where we're getting to, I think," Burt said, "is that rather than you suggesting you want to return to Russia, the role you play is tempting him to come the other way. To us. Principally to you, of course. But like Marcie says, does he have the balls?"

Anna stayed silent.

"There are some things we can't know until you both meet," Logan said. "And even then, Vladimir isn't just going to throw his hands in the air and defect, just because he loves you."

"There are two things the first meeting needs to achieve," Burt summed up. "The first thing is a second meeting. The second is the most accurate assessment you can make of his feelings towards you."

"Vladimir's not like one of the mindless apparatchiks who fill my old organisation," Anna said.

"And yet he's got the top spot at the UN in New York and, we believe, is the KGB's resident here," Logan said. "He must be trusted a great deal."

"Let's play to his known differences with the KGB," Burt said.

"Appeal to his personal courage," Marcie said.

"What do you think, Logan?" Anna said. For a reason she didn't fully understand, she wanted his reaction.

"You fooled him once with your pretence of love," Logan said. "Maybe you can do it again."

Anna looked at him questioningly, and saw a broad smile break across his handsome face.

"Only joking."

Anna found herself smiling back at him, as if they had some implicit secret.

"You should be wired, of course," Logan said adamantly.

"Why?" Marcie, once again contradicting Logan at every turn.

Anna decided to wait while the others had their say.

"It's too much," Marcie said. "We'll know from Anna what takes place."

"Certainly we will," Burt said supportively.

So she was to be trusted to convey what took place between her and Vladimir.

"What about you, Anna?" Marcie said.

"In my opinion it's unnecessary," Anna replied. "Besides, I want to be able to demonstrate to Vladimir that I'm not wired. There are ways I can show him fairly conclusively that I'm not. He can search me if he likes. He'll do what he has to do. But if he even thinks I might be wired, we lose everything with him."

"You?" Burt shot a look at Logan.

"Okay," he said.

But Anna saw that he didn't agree.

"That's four of us then," Burt said.

Outside the control room, Burt took Marcie aside. They withdrew into one of the smaller rooms in the labyrinthine apartments, and Burt shut the door.

"What's with Logan?" he asked without preamble.

"I think he's getting too involved with Anna."

"He's behaving badly. Is she getting to him?"

"I think so. She doesn't take him as seriously as he wants her to take him."

"He'll need watching," said Burt. "I don't want him fucking things up over some juvenile infatuation."

The meeting between Anna and Vladimir had now been sanctioned by four National Security committees. There had even been a special note in the morning White House intelligence briefing.

Marcie and Logan returned with files on Vladimir's activities, his known contacts and preferred New York hangouts—all the minutiae of his life since his arrival in America a year before.

A round-the-clock spot team was put on to Vladimir, provided by the CIA but reporting to Burt's headquarters. "We're working together," Burt said grimly. Vladimir was photographed wherever he went outside the UN and the Russian compound. Logan and Marcie returned with recorded conversations, tapped phone calls, even satellite images of Vladimir's movements, as well as the surveillance on the ground.

The vast array of American technology had been brought to bear. The WorldView-1 military satellite that invisibly circled the earth on a daily basis was tasked to pay special attention to Vladimir and anyone he came into contact with. The satellite was capable of mapping 300,000 square miles a day, with definition that could read a car licence plate anywhere in the day's field of view.

This overkill, as Burt called it, was, he believed, running the risk of itself being spotted by the Russians. But it was justified at the CIA by the fact that the entire state intelligence community now needed Mikhail more than ever. It was firmly accepted that the first step in drawing Mikhail out into the open—if indeed he proved to be in America at all—was for Anna to present herself at the heart of the KGB's presence.

The Russian agent the British had detected through their source in Moscow's defence ministry was now given critical status. And finding Mikhail had become more important than ever.

As a piece of valuable bait, Anna discovered that those around her had become more courteous than ever. She was now a most prized piece of meat, the lure without which the endgame could not be reached, let alone won. And she accepted her role, not just because there was no choice, but also because in her mind she was personally curious to see if Mikhail would contact her. It would lift the burden of the previous months, of the two years since Finn's death. Mikhail's anticipated approach to her would be the real beginning of the end—a new life.

All of these preparations took weeks of grinding slowness to approach the moment of contact itself, and it was now just a few days before Christmas. Burt insisted they all take some time off—Anna to reunite with Little Finn, and Marcie to stay with her. They were all invited to Burt's ranch for Christmas itself. It consisted of half a million acres of New Mexico wilderness, and Burt took Little Finn on tours to find the herds of bison and elk. They even spotted a mountain lion on the day after Christmas. "A cougar," Burt proudly said, and smiled.

But for the three days of the vacation Anna was loaded with boxes of photographs of Vladimir and transcripts of conversations covertly obtained. Recordings of Vladimir's voice were also included, as well as several lists of his favourite New York shops and cafés. She memorised them all, the cafés, bars, shops, parks—and anywhere else he liked to spend his free time.

Finally, details of the routes he habitually took to and from the Russian compound and the UN building were marked with refinements, detours, and inconsistencies, all updated daily.

21

O **N THE THIRD DAY** after they returned to New York, Burt took a call from the leader of his team of watchers in the city. The Russians at the UN had celebrated their Russian New Year on the night before, in a Russian restaurant on Sixty-third Street. They were expected to return to their offices at the UN building in two days' time.

On the morning of January 8, Burt, Anna, Marcie, and Logan, as well as four members of Burt's company staff, listened to a running commentary from the spot teams on the ground.

That morning, as every morning on Vladimir's working days, they picked him out leaving his apartment block on the west side of Central Park, which the Russian diplomatic mission had colonised in the previous ten years, and saw him step out into the cold, snow-driven street to a waiting car.

On some mornings, he took the subway downtown, out of choice, it was assumed, but this morning the weather clearly drove him into the ease and warmth of one of the pool cars the Russians used. It gave them less chance, Logan observed. If the weather didn't improve, Vladimir would go straight back the same way without stopping at any of his usual haunts.

But the skies cleared at lunchtime, the snow disappearing to the north, and at 2:37 in the afternoon the team, alerted by other watchers inside the UN building, reported Vladimir now leaving on foot and turning towards midtown. He finally took a taxi on Fortieth Street.

Burt placed Anna in one of three yellow New York cabs that seemed to be part of his own inventory, and she and the stubbornly sullen driver waited for instructions.

A report came through that Vladimir had got out of the cab on Broadway near Washington Square and walked a few yards up the street into a Barnes and Noble bookstore. Anna's taxi drove downtown for six streets and waited again, a block away from the store.

"He's looking at books," a watcher said unenthusiastically.

Then they heard that he had exited the store and was walking back two blocks towards a secondhand bookstore off Washington Square itself. Over the car's speaker phone, she heard he had walked inside.

"He's browsing," another watcher announced over the car's speaker phone. "He looks like he'll be some time."

Burt came on the line. "Could be the opportunity," he said.

"He used to spend hours in bookstores in Moscow," Anna agreed.

"Let's go," Burt said.

She could tell from his voice that he was nervous now that control was slipping from him to her.

She didn't need to look at the map she had with her. Stepping out of the cab, she walked briskly for one block, until she saw the huge store on the corner of the square. She crossed the street and walked to the right, towards the entrance.

Inside, she tried to catch sight of where he was, but the store was too big. Racks of books stretched away into the back and spilled out over the sidewalk on a side street. She walked in with her head slightly lowered, but keeping it facing straight ahead. But she took in as much of the store as she could without breaking pace.

Stopping and browsing with unseeing eyes, she tried to cover the whole store without turning her head away from the racks. Above all, it was important not to catch his eye first.

Eventually she saw him and breathed a sigh of relief. He was right at the back. If she stayed near the front of the store, he would pass near her on his way towards the exit. She picked up one or two books, not letting her eyes leave him now.

At the apartment, Burt and Logan were silent, listening tensely to the commentary of the team.

"He's picking up a book with a yellow cover," one lookout who had followed Anna into the store reported.

"We think it's *The Interrogation* by Le Clézio," came through a moment later.

Burt sucked his teeth and temporarily switched off the speaker going out. "Training gone out of control," he hissed at Logan. "They should be looking out for anyone tailing him, not at the damn book titles! Tell them."

Logan sent out the order. Then he and Burt left the apartment for a waiting car.

At just after three thirty, the street team jabbered over the lines that Vladimir was heading towards the exit of the store. They fixed Anna's position at a rack in the centre aisle of three, one of which he would have to take.

"He's heading for the left-hand aisle," a voice said. "He hasn't seen anyone."

"Nobody tailing him from their side," another voice came through.

Anna saw him from the corner of her eye coming from the gloomy recesses at the back of the store into the better-lit front area and then stopping again at a rack about twenty yards away from her. He thumbed through several books, eventually picked a fourth, and, without looking inside the covers, turned to the left and headed for the pay counter.

There was a queue of three people in front of him, a man and two women. He waited in line. She watched him looking around as he waited. He didn't look at the book. It was a book he knew he wanted. His gaze followed the counter up to the right, then left. Was he watching? she wondered. No, just bored, just filling time. She was too far behind him for his gaze to light on her without turning.

Finally, he reached the front of the queue, took out an old leather wallet, and paid the young assistant, who put the book in a brown bag, handed it back to him, and spoke some cheerfully perfunctory words. Then he turned and tried to fit the book into the pocket of his coat, but it wouldn't quite go. He took some gloves from his pocket.

"He's intending to leave the store," came through on Burt's car speaker. "He's putting his gloves on."

"Where is she?" Burt said.

"Right by the door. But it's a broad exit. He won't necessarily walk by her."

Anna watched the gloves go on. Vladimir took the book in his right hand and walked back into the centre of the shop to the rack where he'd found the book, then turned right towards the exit. He was coming down the central aisle, where she was standing.

She didn't turn, but made sure her profile was clearly visible as she looked down at a copy of something by Stendhal—she had no idea of the title. She was holding two other books underneath it, as though she'd decided on buying them.

He was just yards away now, closing and glancing to the left and right, walking slowly but not stopping. He seemed in no hurry despite his intention to leave. At that point she stopped looking at him and became engrossed in the book in her hand. She didn't want to be tempted at the last moment to be the one to make the discovery.

In a few seconds, when she realised she was holding her breath, she became aware of a presence next to her. She didn't look up, but saw his feet about two yards away. He'd stopped. She turned away from him slightly, as if she were annoyed that someone was looking at her. Then she felt a hand on her arm and looked up.

When she saw his face, the first of several expressions that crossed it in rapid succession was fear.

She stared back at him, her own face empty of everything except complete shock.

Then she looked around, in apparent fear herself, hunting for anyone with him. She looked back at him and took a step away from him, removing his hand from her arm. "Vladimir! What are you doing here!" she breathed.

He looked at her steadily. The fear was still in his eyes, but now alternated with uncertainty.

"It is you," he said.

"Why are you here?" She sounded frightened even to herself.

"I'm alone," he said. "It's all right, I'm alone."

"Why are you here?" she repeated. "Why are you following me?"

"I'm not following you," he said, and she saw the uncertainty in his eyes recede and a sense of calm take over for a moment.

She didn't reply, but glanced around the store anxiously, looking for anyone else who might be with him.

"I'm alone," he repeated. "Anna, I'm alone."

She focused her eyes back on him. "You're looking for me," she said. "They're looking for me. Please, Vladimir. I have a small son."

He seemed stung by the remark, but recovered quickly. Then he spoke very fast. "There's a café on Third Street. West of Park Avenue. If you want to see me, I'll be there. The café's called Mendoza." He turned away from her and walked to the exit and left.

"What's happening?" Burt asked harshly from the car.

"He saw her," came back over the speaker. "They talked. Briefly. He's left the store."

"What's she doing?"

"She's standing there."

"Which way's he headed?"

"He's turned left out of the store and is walking fast. Now he's stopped. He's looking for a cab."

"Anyone with him? Any tails?"

"None. Almost sure of that."

"Be sure. Watch if anything follows his cab. Watch if he's on a phone."

Anna stepped out of the store onto the sidewalk and turned to the right. She walked twenty yards north of the store as they'd agreed, stopped, then recrossed the street when the pedestrian sign came up. The cab was waiting for her on the corner of the street, closer to the store than where it had dropped her. She stepped in.

"Where to?" the driver said with complete lack of urgency. It occurred to her he was playing his role too well, and she almost laughed out loud.

"Third Street," she said. "On Park. A café called Mendoza. Drive past it and drop me about a hundreds yards farther on."

"Hear that?" the driver said into the speaker.

"Check." It was Burt's voice.

There was silence.

The cab pulled out and waited for the light, then turned right as soon as it was green.

"What's up, Anna?" Burt said through the speaker.

"We're meeting."

"Anything else?"

"He seemed as close to being convinced as we can expect."

"Good. You okay?"

"Fine."

"I hear you looked completely terrified," Burt said and chuckled. "You got the part."

"And a raise, I hope," she replied.

She heard Burt's laugh, but he said nothing.

As the cab took her steadily downtown, the speaker blared again. One of the watchers.

"He's been in a cab for five blocks. Seems to be heading for the venue."

"Give him time to get inside before getting close," Burt ordered.

Anna's driver usefully lost time by turning right instead of left and doing three sides of a square around two blocks, away from Park Avenue. Then they heard he had entered the café.

"Follow," Burt said.

The cab took her across the street again where it had picked her up and headed fast towards Third Street. They passed the Café Mendoza. There were traffic lights fifty yards beyond.

"Before the lights?" the driver asked.

"Take me just beyond them," she replied. She wanted a good walk in.

"The target has entered the café," the speaker droned.

There was a pause of two or three minutes as the cab waited at the red lights.

"The café's about half full," the speaker reported. "Mostly students from the university."

"I don't want any comms in there," she heard Burt say. "Get out of there and stay clear from now on."

Anna walked the two blocks from the east of the Café Mendoza. She suddenly felt a feeling of freedom, unexplained. Perhaps it was because it was the first time she'd been free for nearly six months. Just this short walk, alone, raised her spirits. And Vladimir had been compliant.

She thought what it might be like one day to walk down a street like this, without the catalogue of aims and secrets, the needs of others, in just the freedom of her own mind.

It was a busy street, lined with tourist stalls and cheap restaurants and cafés. Pedestrians wrapped against the cold stopped only briefly or dashed inside, more for warmth than with any intention of buying anything. There were chestnuts roasting in a metal barrel. The vendor was stamping his feet and warming his gloved hands over the heat. He was wrapped in layers of clothing and a balaclava so that she could just make out a black face and a pair of eyes.

A few yards before the café, she stopped and looked at a stand that was selling postcards and scarves. She collected her thoughts, and made a check around her. She didn't trust Burt's teams to spot anyone following Vladimir. She could do it better.

Then she walked the few steps and turned right into the doorway of the café. She saw Vladimir immediately sitting with his back to her at the far end. He was in the process of ordering something from a waitress who stood, pen poised over her pad.

Anna walked to the counter, where there were bar stools, sat on one, and ordered a coffee. She adjusted her hearing to the low hub-bub, not looking towards the rear of the café. She paid for the coffee and took a magazine from the pocket of her coat.

She then turned to watch as a waitress cleared the table next to Vladimir's. Before anyone else could take it, she walked to the back of the café and told the waitress loaded with armfuls of screwed-up paper mats and dirty crockery that she'd like a menu.

She put the cup and the magazine on the table, took off her coat, and sat down in the chair that faced outwards. She sipped her coffee, watching from the corner of her eye as Vladimir saw her again from the next table.

It happened almost in slow motion. Vladimir glanced up from a copy of the *New York Times* and was interrupted by the waitress bringing a glass of water. He removed some utensils from a paper napkin, then apparently remembered from some previous existence that he'd looked up at her, seen her, but not registered what he'd seen with his eyes, and he looked up again. She was looking straight at him.

In her eyes, he saw alarm, the same alarm that she'd seen in the bookstore. They were like a mirror, but her face was invented for him, while he just couldn't believe what his eyes were telling him.

"It's really you" he said.

"And I guess it's really you, Vladimir," she said. She saw what she thought was a kind of loss or longing in his face, or it might have been grief.

A look of worry immediately replaced it. He looked startled now, his eyes flickering beyond her to another table. Then he carefully took in the whole café, turning slowly, pretending to be looking for a waitress. Then he looked back, and they both started the same sentence.

"What are you doing—" They both recognised the humour, and she laughed first. Then he laughed too, but it was a nervous response to hers.

"I'm living here," she said.

"In New York?"

"Yes. And you too?"

"Yes."

There was another pause, more awkward this time, neither wishing to ask a question that might seem too inquisitive.

"Anna," he said. "I must ask you. Are you alone?"

She didn't know immediately whether he meant alone as a former lover, or alone, with no watchers.

She smiled freely. "At this moment, yes," she said. "I'm alone in every way."

"And you have a boy."

"Finn's son, yes."

"I'm happy for you."

"And you?"

She saw him watch her to see if the question was disingenuous, to look for signs that she knew.

"I'm the same," he said. But he didn't wish to talk about himself. "I'm with the Russian mission here," he said in a slightly clipped voice, as if it were something to be ashamed of.

"Shall I join you?" It was the most normal remark in the world. Then she laughed. "At the table, I mean."

He looked flustered. Every word seemed a mine of possibilities. Then, bringing his thoughts together, he looked at the empty chair at his table, as though someone might be in it. Then he nodded, leaned over and picked his coat off the back of the chair, and hung it on his own without turning around, not wanting to take his eyes away.

He was looking good, Anna thought. Not just prosperous, but fit, healthy. His black hair, which grew thick around the temples, was swept across his forehead in a way that would have suited New York in the 1950s. His hands were manicured; his face, apart from the intensity in his eyes, was calm. He looked lean, with slightly dark Caucasian skin, as if he had a suntan. She remembered how handsome he'd looked in uniform twenty years before. He hadn't changed much—there was still strength in his jaw, and the skin around his neck was taut, not flabby. His eyes in their fright were as intense and dark as ever.

She crossed over to his table and put her coat on the back of the chair where he'd removed his.

His food arrived—pasta, she saw.

"Don't wait," she said. "Eat. It'll get cold."

He looked at the pasta, but his appetite was gone.

"Are you going to eat?" he said.

"I'll eat yours if you don't hurry up," she said. But he made no move to eat.

"Why are you here?" he said suddenly, and all the promise of his slight relaxation a moment before vanished.

"I live not far from here." It was not an answer to his question.

"Where?"

"You want my address?" She gave him a smile that indicated the unlikelihood of receiving it.

"I'm sorry," he said, and looked momentarily defeated.

"I've never been in here," she said.

"The food's okay."

She picked up the menu.

"I'll have chocolate cake," she said. "I won't eat it all."

They were silent. She saw he was not yet willing to accept this as a chance encounter.

A waitress came to the table, and she ordered chocolate cake.

When she'd gone, they both began to speak at once again, and each stopped for the other.

"You first," he said.

"As far as I know, I'm alone," she said. "They stopped following me months ago. I've been debriefed for longer than I thought possible. I'm clear."

"Good," he said. "I hope you're right."

They were silent, neither appearing able or willing to come up with an appropriate remark.

"You want to see me?" he said.

"I'm seeing you now."

He looked hurt, confused.

"I'm sorry, Volodya," she said. "But how can we see each other?"

"We can make another accidental meeting," he said.

She saw he was desperate that this not be the last time.

He stretched his hand across the table towards hers and then stopped, unable to commit himself.

"I'm sorry about . . ." He didn't finish. There seemed perhaps too many things to be sorry about.

"I'm sorry too, Volodya."

He didn't want to approach the subject of them too closely. Not yet.

"Your grandmother," he said. "You know she died last year."

"I know."

Anna thought of the night at her grandmother's five years earlier, when Vladimir had woken them at five in the morning to take her away.

"I owe you, Vladimir," she said. "Thanks to you, Nana and I were able to say good-bye to each other before she died. But she was ready to go. You gave her a great gift, as well as me. I know she died happy, knowing I was safe. Eighty-five years of life, and at last one of her family breaks free, escapes their fate. It was what she always wanted for me. So thank you from her too."

"I've seen your mother," he said. "Once or twice."

"That's kind of you."

"And him?" Vladimir said. "Your father?"

"I'll never speak to him again," she said.

"He's gotten old," Vladimir told her. "He's in a care home for the Paradise Group," he said.

Anna couldn't imagine her father, the great SVR officer and tyrant, sitting in a care home. But the Paradise Group would look after him, whatever he wanted. They were the most senior retirees from the heart of the KGB. She didn't reply. The thought of her father disgusted her. Her chocolate cake arrived, and she urged him to eat once again. They both ate without noticing the food.

She finished half the cake and pushed the plate across the table to him.

"Coffee?" she said.

"Are you?" He'd hardly touched the pasta.

"Yes. Two coffees," she said to the waitress. "And another fork for my friend, please."

The coffees arrived, and he heaped sugar into his. Conversation had ground to a halt. There was nothing to say that wasn't charged with meaning, either dangerous or intimate. She was prepared for him to backtrack on his request to meet again, and had her response ready when he did.

"How many of them are there outside?" he said. "Or in here?"

"Volodya, there's no one. Or not that I know."

She wrote something on the bill the waitress had left, as if she was paying. Then she pushed it under his newspaper, a distance of a few inches. She was sure it would be unnoticed by anyone but the two of them.

"And you? Are you usually watched?" she said.

"No. Not usually."

"Then if you wish, we could meet again," she said, and lowered her eyes to the bill under the newspaper. "On Tuesdays I go to a gym. There's a café behind the gym. I can usually be sure to be alone for an hour. I'll go there. There's a fire escape at the back. I'll come straight out of the back and be in the café. Three o'clock."

He didn't reply.

"But if you don't wish to meet me," she said, "then I'm glad I've had the chance to thank you for what you did. You didn't just save my life, you saved my love of life." She paused, as if uncertain she was saying the right thing to her former lover. "Finn always wanted to thank you too," she added finally. "It amazed him."

A look of anxiety crossed his face.

"They killed him," he said.

He looked down at the table. He had saved her. But the organisation he worked for had killed the man he had saved her life for.

"I know," she said, in a way that understood his remorse. "But don't worry, you're safe. Your secret will be buried with me. I'm not here to threaten you. Ever."

He didn't reply at first.

"I'm sorry," he said at last. "I'm so sorry about Finn."

"It's not your fault. But thank you, Volodya." She gave him a big, happy smile that was the first genuine expression she'd worn since they'd met. "And I'm happy to see you. Really I am."

She took out a purse from her coat.

"I'll get this. Pasta, salad, coffees, and half a chocolate cake. Fair exchange for saving my life?"

He smiled for the first time. "Fair exchange. We're even."

Then he fractionally extended his hand across the table again. It was such a small gesture, she might have missed it if she hadn't been in a state of heightened awareness of his every reaction. She laid her own hand on top of his for the briefest moment.

"I'm happy to see you too," he said. "It was something I never dared to dream."

She left some dollar bills on the table, and stood up.

"Maybe I'll see you again," she said.

"Maybe."

She felt him watching her leave the café and knew he'd be alert for any movement behind her out on the street, anything to indicate it had been a setup. She hoped Burt's team and anyone else from the American side were far away.

But Burt's decision to be spontaneous, to cut out the teams of watchers from the café, had been the right one. Even as she stepped back out onto the cold sidewalk, she saw nothing.

22

ANNA SAT AT THE end of the long wooden table at the Twenty-third Street apartments, her chin rested in one hand. Logan sat slightly slumped next to her on the right, with his elbows on the table, while Marcie was bolt upright on the other side of her, a position she always adopted when Burt was present.

At the far end of the table, flanking Burt, sat Bob Dupont, Burt's silver-haired head of internal security, and next to him was a man in his thirties with jet-black hair and dark eyes whom Anna hadn't seen before but whom she learned in passing, though without an introduction, was called Salvador.

On chairs around the walls outside the door and prowling the corridors outside the door were the ubiquitous bodyguards, with Larry, as ever, in charge. The bodyguards had been doubled, and then doubled again like some rampant algae, until a small army of them had grown up, as if to suck the air from any opposition to Burt's plans.

It was now just under an hour since Anna had returned, and Burt had insisted they should meet immediately. He said this with even more than his usual sense for drama.

Anna was listening to Burt as he wound up his appraisal of her encounter with Vladimir. They all were, in their different guises of concentration—Logan, Marcie, Dupont, Salvador.

Outside the windows, which Burt commanded should be left without the blinds pulled down—against nearly everyone's advice—the early winter New York night had descended over the city, and snow had begun to fall.

She was tired, she realised. Her mind raced back again over her recent conversation with Vladimir, as it had done repeatedly since she'd left him in the café. She was recalling each word, each expression in his face, looking for anything she might have missed—some nuance in his voice, perhaps, some hint in his eyes, or in the gestures of his hands. Was there something hidden in the silences and pauses between them? All might be indications of something that Vladimir hadn't actually said, or of which even he himself was ignorant.

She knew the meeting with him had taken the strength out of her for the moment, and that alone shocked her. Meeting with Vladimir at all, let alone meeting him again after all these years, had been a strange experience. It had brought back the past—Finn too, as well as Vladimir himself—and most vitally, it had brought back her intimacy with both of them.

And the meeting with Vladimir had also brought her face-to-face with memories of Russia and the stark danger her old country represented to her and Little Finn. Vladimir in New York was an uncomfortable proximity to that.

But while Logan and Marcie and the others were hanging on to Burt's detailed exposition, with its customary flattering flourishes of praise in her direction, her mind was working along parallel lines at the same time. She was weighing the fateful decision to deceive Burt.

To meet again with Vladimir, in secret from Burt's teams of observers, at the café behind the gym was to take a dangerous step. It risked her whole, albeit tenuous, security and that of Little Finn, painstakingly won over the past months.

Nevertheless, she was already beginning to run her own storyline of her planned breakout from the twenty-four-hour-a-day scrutiny she had lived with for so long. She felt her power increase, both from her own decision to meet Vladimir in secret and as the crucial figure in Burt's plans.

She looked up at Burt now and felt a change in his own demeanour too. Behind the natural ebullience, she detected a new unfamiliar anxiety, however faint, and she wondered if it had anything to do with the presence of Salvador.

"So we have a narrowed field of possibilities," Burt was saying, while five floors below an ambulance screamed its siren into every corner of the city streets. " . . . but it's not constricting. It helps us, in fact. What Anna has done is to reduce the sauce nicely." He beamed at her. "She has left Vladimir with just two options; either to meet her again or to refuse contact. Whichever course he takes will tell us something."

Logan looked up sharply. There was a frown on his face.

"What about the option of simply informing his boss at the KGB residency here?" he said, with unusual bluntness. "That's what he'll do, surely? And then the Russians will most likely set up a counter-operation."

"I don't consider that in the frame," Burt replied abruptly, to the surprise of everyone.

There was an awkward silence in the room.

"Why not, Burt?" Marcie asked eventually.

"It is an option. We must consider it," Logan persisted. "If anything, it's the closest to a certainty we have."

"And we'll leave it out of our considerations," Burt said, once more with the clear intention of closing this avenue of discussion altogether.

Logan took his elbows off the table and straightened in his chair, putting one hand on the arm as if intending to get up. His eyes flashed with anger, or just incomprehension. Anna read the faces around the table and saw confusion and consternation in all but Salvador's. He seemed entirely impassive.

Burt let his gaze rest on Logan for a moment, and paused to indicate the importance of what he was he going to say.

"Listen again, Logan. All of you," he said. He swept his gaze now around the table. "If we include that as a possibility, if Vladimir brings in the Russians, their activity will be visible on the streets. Yes? And that will draw others in, from our own side. So we'll have the agency and God knows who else crawling all over this. We need to keep it tight. Just us. Just Cougar. This must be deeply personal. It's about a relationship, a once cruelly intimate relationship between Anna and Vladimir."

He looked at her without expression. This was not how Burt had ever behaved with her. It was not like Burt to be anything but strenuously sensitive in the matters of her past. But now his tone of voice was almost crude, as if he wanted to sting her.

Where is he leading with this? she thought. What is the purpose?

"It's between Anna and Vladimir now," Burt repeated. "Under our protection, of course. That way it's controllable. Savvy?"

He looked at Logan in particular. Logan nodded without agreement, but Burt wasn't finished. "Once we let this operation out of our own control, we lose our momentum," he said. "It's vital we all understand this now. We don't just lose our grasp on the operation, which is a company matter—Cougar's. We will also most likely lose Mikhail. Why? They're all waiting out there to pounce on Mikhail. To be blunt, Mikhail represents a huge victory for whoever gets him, and victory means money, government contracts, expansion, Cougar's expansion. Mikhail is the bottom line—he is on the profit side in the profit-and-loss account. Mikhail means power. I intend Mikhail to be Cougar's asset and Cougar's alone. We're the biggest game in town right now, and all the rest of them want a place at the high table."

There was a stunned silence around the room. Mikhail had suddenly been presented as a balance sheet item, rather than a figure of national importance to America's security.

It was Dupont who broke the silence. He spoke in the soft, rumbling tone of voice he used in matters of urgency.

"Because we don't want Vladimir to bring in his own people by informing the Russian intelligence services here," he said carefully, "and because we don't want the agency responding to their subsequent presence on the streets, that doesn't mean it's not an option for Vladimir."

Anna sensed for the first time that what Burt wanted was interfering with the facts. She was reminded, chillingly, of Adrian. When people got in Adrian's way, Finn had once said, he ignored them, as if they and what they represented didn't exist. But there was something else too in Burt's behaviour that she couldn't detect, which sent off an alarm in her mind. Burt wasn't like Adrian. Be wary, an inner voice told her. Be wary of the man who behaves out of character.

In the deeper recesses of her mind, she sensed that Burt was weaving some landscape of deceit, against which the truth, when it came, would be starkly illuminated. There was some purpose behind Burt's almost nonsensical denial of his cohort's objections.

But she thrust her instincts away, unable to comprehend them, whether through tiredness, from the intrusive presence of others in the meeting, or simply from the need to think in the present rather than listen to her inner voices. In her logical mind, she analysed and understood the competitiveness that Burt was trying to inspire in his team. But it was an unfamiliar form of competition to her. It was more of a competitive hunger engendered against the rival powers of Cougar within America's own intelligence community, than against Russia. How many fronts was Burt fighting on?

"And if that happens," Burt continued, ignoring Dupont's considered interjection, "if other firms like Cougar get in on this, then they'll interfere. And that will simply have the effect of putting more distance between us and Mikhail than ever. We don't want Mikhail developing into some common asset. The more competing interests there are on the ground, the greater the risk of blowing the whole thing. And then, like as not, nobody will win the prize. It is therefore a matter of national security to keep it to ourselves."

It was Logan who volubly refused to accept Burt's thesis.

"But that doesn't mean it won't happen," Logan insisted again, his voice betraying exasperation that now bordered on incredulity. "We have to plan for Vladimir informing the Russians that he's met Anna, even if he doesn't. It's madness not to!" He was looking aghast at Burt, as if unable to comprehend that Burt didn't see, or was ignoring, this simple fact.

There was now visible confusion fluttering around the table at Burt's wilful disregard of the most likely outcome of Anna's meeting with Vladimir. And once again she heard the voices inside. *Confusion is the aim.* But for a second time, she ignored her better instincts.

Burt was now looking amiably around the long table. Marcie was staring down at her hands to avoid meeting his eye in this confrontation; Anna flickered her eyes in acknowledgement of nothing. Bob Dupont was silently fidgeting with a pencil. For a moment the scene reminded Anna of a set of courtiers in the presence of an omnipotent but mad king.

Only the dark-eyed Salvador remained still, contained in himself and apparently unaffected by Burt's disruption of clear thinking. Whoever he was, Anna thought, he was either too far on the inside to be troubled by Burt's curious and illogical insistence on his point, or he was observing Burt from a different position than the rest of them, a position that derived from knowledge.

As Burt rested his gaze on Logan once again, Anna felt she saw a challenge.

"Logan?"

"Burt," Logan said, giving no ground.

There was a tense silence as Burt seemed to be gauging Logan's opposition. But then Burt relaxed again, allowing a broad grin to spread across his face.

"Anna," he said, and glanced down the table at her as if she were the last resort of sanity in the room. "Why don't you give your opinion. You are the mind and heart of the operation in so many ways. Will Vladimir go to his chief? Will he really reveal that he's met you—at this stage? Tell us what you think."

She thought for a moment, but only in order to appear to be giving Burt some vestige of support through her opposition to him.

"Not out of personal choice—no, he won't," she said carefully. "You're right about that, Burt." But that was all the meat she could throw Burt in the circumstances. "Vladimir would rather keep it to himself, I'm sure. But don't forget, he'll be afraid as well. So I think we can assume he will make a report, formally or not," she said.

"Why?"

"Because it's less of a risk for him than concealing it," she said. "He'll weigh it up, see the risk attached to concealment, and then go to his boss. That's my opinion, and it's based on knowing a little about the way his mind works, as well as what any intelligence officer would do in the circumstances. He'll be uncertain whether the meeting between us was under surveillance by his own people. So he won't take the risk."

Burt's grin faded, and Anna saw the showman that was Burt by its very absence. She saw the ruthless core of him, the powerful ambition that had propelled him through life in the guise of good humour. Burt, like Adrian, hated to be denied. But Burt was not Adrian.

He continued to look at her, willing her on, his face an open invitation to her to spread enlightenment. She felt she had said enough, that her words were already excessive. But she nevertheless felt driven onwards, unable to listen to the voices that were telling her to stop now, to wait, not to be led by Burt. For one thing was certain. He was leading her—them?—somewhere that was too obscure for her to see clearly.

"I don't quite understand the premise of this argument of yours any-way, Burt," she said, buying a little time from her instinct to cease.

"Oh? Why not?" he replied, even though to all of them it was obvious.

"Surely the idea of my meeting Vladimir in the first place was precisely so that he would inform his superiors here. The only way Mikhail will know I'm here is if Vladimir does reveal it. Mikhail will pick it up very quickly. So we actually need Vladimir to inform his superiors. It's not an option, it's a necessity."

There was silence in the room. Anna saw only Salvador move, a small movement, but he looked up at her for the first time, and then he looked at Burt.

Burt's gaze hadn't moved away from her.

"Let's take a break," he said suddenly and stood up. "All of you. Take a walk, have a coffee, whatever you like. All of you except you, Anna." He turned to fix her with a neutral stare. "You'll stay here with me, please."

There was surprise, but all except Logan got to their feet. Logan was only just pushing back his chair as Marcie, Salvador, and Dupont were leaving the room.

"Logan?" Burt said.

"I'd like to stay," he said.

"You'll see Anna later. Don't worry, I'm not going to strangle her," Burt said without mirth.

Logan looked back at her as he left, and she saw something in his face she hadn't seen before; an intensity, passion perhaps. Then he slowly turned and left the room.

She and Burt were left alone in silence.

Burt stayed standing and went to a sideboard, where he extracted a bottle of brandy and two glasses. He poured the liquor into them both without asking her and handed her one, while keeping the other cradled in his pudgy hand. He remained standing at the far end of the room and took a sip from the glass.

"So. Let's proceed," he said. "As you have just said with such admirable clarity, if Vladimir informs his chief here, Mikhail will pick it up?" He spoke smoothly. "Is that right?" He looked at her and beamed. "Or did you mean *would* pick it up? If he were in America, that is?"

She saw her mistake, remembered the voices calling her to stop, and she believed she could recover from it while knowing it was too late. Her only defence was in the semantics.

"Of course, I meant Mikhail would pick it up, if Mikhail is here," she replied.

Burt let her explanation hang in the room, so that it became thin and then dissipated like smoke to reveal the landscape behind it.

"I think you were right in the first place," he said. "You are careful with words, Anna. So—Mikhail won't know unless Vladimir reveals the meeting with you to his superiors. Will he."

It was a statement, not a question. Burt's tone of voice was closing around her like a trap.

Anna withdrew into her thoughts but found no solace, no way out. She knew now what was coming. Burt's artful, confusing pretence had done its work. In her effort to correct his apparent misconception about Vladimir's options, she had overstepped her own watchfulness, the watchfulness that had safeguarded her knowledge of Mikhail.

She found she had nothing to say.

"Because Mikhail is in America, isn't he," Burt stated remorselessly. "So 'will' was the right word, not 'would.' That's true, isn't it?"

She waited for the blow.

"You know Mikhail is here, don't you, Anna," Burt said, leaning over the table with one hand supporting him. "You've known for a while. He's on our list, isn't he." He pounced.

"Right then. How were you going to make contact with Mikhail?" he asked her. "Through Vladimir? Or was it in some other way?"

She felt the ground sliding from under her. "That was the way," she said. "Exactly as Logan and myself and others were saying. By Vladimir informing his chief here, yes."

"Oh, yes?" The apparent curiosity in Burt's tone was flayed completely, to reveal the utter disbelief that lay beneath it. "Okay. Let's try this, then," he said. "Vladimir wasn't going to inform his head of station here or anyone else, was he?"

"As I said, I'm sure he will."

Burt stood up from his angled pose of leaning on the table. He looked at her with triumph in his eyes.

"In which case, why did you arrange to meet Vladimir, in secret, without my knowledge, at a café behind a gym? "

She heard a sharp, involuntary intake of breath and realised it was hers. But she neither acknowledged Burt's statement nor denied it.

Burt left the silence hanging once again.

"And if you and Vladimir were to meet in secret from me, then it was also in secret from Vladimir's own people, wasn't it? Both of you wanted to meet without surveillance. Which means that Vladimir wasn't going to inform anyone he'd met you. And that means there was no way Mikhail would know you were trying to contact him. Correct?"

Her silence was the answer he was looking for.

"Your health," he said, and raised his glass until she lifted hers. Then he drank greedily.

"You said no wires—," she said.

Burt grinned at her, his bonhomie apparently returned in full. As ever, he was supremely pleased by his own cleverness, which was far more important to him than her attempts to deceive him. In fact, she felt that his cleverness needed her deceit in order to be exercised to the full.

"That's what we said, yes," he agreed, and gave his friendly chuckle. "No wires. But we had that café—and all his other regular haunts—wired so good you could hear the lettuce screaming."

More sirens rose from outside the window—the only true voices of the city—and filled the pause like a dissonant musical interlude.

"Next stage," Burt said, moving on now into the mopping-up operation. "Were you even intending to contact Mikhail at all? Or has this whole operation with Vladimir just been a farce from start to finish? I'd like to know that, please, Anna."

"Yes. Yes, I was."

"But not my way?" Burt said.

"No, not your way, not through Vladimir."

Burt sat down.

"Okay. Good. I like this. Let's say I believe you," he said with flamboyant generosity. "Why not? Why weren't you going to contact Mikhail through Vladimir?"

She didn't answer.

"Come on, Anna. Tell me why you wanted to contact him your way?"

She collected her thoughts now at last. "Because Mikhail is too smart to be lured into making contact with me on the basis of his own side having knowledge of my whereabouts. He wouldn't trust that. If my meeting with Vladimir reached him through Vladimir and then the KGB networks here, he wouldn't take the risk."

"Good, that's very good, that's very smart of you," Burt said, and there was genuine admiration in his voice. "Your intuition is, as always, invaluable. So why not say that to me earlier, though? To me, Anna?" he said, as if he were hurt that his friendship and discretion were not above scrutiny. "That way, we could make a different plan. So in my way of thinking, there's another reason for you planning to do it your way, isn't there."

"Yes. Yes, there is." She looked up at him and met his eyes unwaveringly. She had found her strength, no matter what was to come.

"It's personal," she said. "Just how you like it, Burt. I wanted to give Mikhail the choice. Whether to work for the Americans or not. Can you understand that, Burt? I wanted that to be his decision, not something forced on him by you, the Russians, me, or anyone else."

"Ah, choices. Choices are the chief source of confusion in the world," Burt replied.

"No. That's not true. Choices are freedom."

"Then freedom is confusion," Burt said.

"Maybe. But that's as cynical as anything I ever heard in the KGB," she said.

"Well, touché. But to win, you must adopt your opponent's methods," Burt said. "And then you must make their methods, no matter how terrible, twice as bad as they make them."

"If you believe that, that's where you and I fundamentally differ," she said.

Burt smiled at her, as if he were enjoying a game.

"All right. Let's say that Mikhail has a choice, then," he said. "Why should I give him this choice?"

"Several reasons. For one thing, he deserves it. He's earned it a million times. But more importantly than that, as a willing accomplice, he's worth infinitely more to you than if he were forced. The reason Mikhail worked for the British before was that he would only work through Finn. No one else. Because he knew he could trust Finn and only Finn."

"We think along exactly the same lines, you and I, Anna," Burt said, in one of his customary volte-faces. "As I treat you, you treat Mikhail. We both understand that without willingness, there's very little worth the gamble. With yours—and Mikhail's—willingness, we can achieve everything."

"That's also what Finn believed," she said.

Burt didn't reply immediately. Then: "And will he trust you? Mikhail?" he said at last.

"I believe so. But it's the only route anyway, as far as I'm concerned."

"That's as I've always thought."

He came around the table and took the seat next to her.

"You're right in everything," he said, "and everything is right."

"What happens—" she said.

"—is always right," he completed. "Sometimes, through distrust comes greater trust," he said. "And that's what has happened here. All this has been necessary. Thank you, Anna. You're as good it gets."

"So where do we go from here?" she said.

Burt smiled, and she found she was smiling back at him.

"Before you tell me who Mikhail is," he said, "what was your plan for contacting him?"

She felt free again. The truth had released her.

"I was going to play along with Vladimir as we arranged," she said. "Improvise with him for as long as it took. Then I was going to send something by courier to Mikhail at the Russian delegation in Washington. As soon as I could make myself some time alone."

"Perhaps after your secret meeting with Vladimir?"

"Most likely."

"Something he would recognise?" Burt asked, "but that no one else would?"

"Yes."

"What?"

"It was a *kidjal*, a Caucasian dagger. It was something Mikhail gave to me on the night that Finn died, the only time I met Mikhail. Finn had given it to him."

"The dagger you said was your grandmother's—an heirloom, I believe?" Burt asked her.

"Yes."

There was dead silence. Burt's face gave nothing away. And then he broke the moment by smiling at her again.

"Then that's what we'll do," he said at last. "We'll send him this dagger."

She looked at him, half believing it was going to be this easy.

"You were right, Burt," she said. "Mikhail was on the list."

"I guessed so," Burt replied. "But I had to be sure."

"He's Vasily Dubkov. At the Russian cultural centre in Washington, D.C.," she said.

"So you'll send him this dagger as a cultural artefact to be identified perhaps?"

"Yes."

"Just one thing, before we move on," he said, and put his hand on her arm. "Mikhail's identity is to remain just between the two of us. For the time being. This goes no further than you and me."

She nodded her assent.

Then he stood up and looked down at her.

"And now, thank Christ, I can dispense with the services of Salvador," he said. Behind the triumph in his face, she saw a kind of relief, even compassion for her. "I'm not sorry to do that," he said. "Salvador is very effective at extracting information."

"Your chief company enforcer?" she said.

"And a very good one too," he replied. "Though we don't call them that these days."

"Strange name for an enforcer—Salvador," she said.

"Saviour? Yes, it is, isn't it. But it makes a kind of sense." He smiled at her again. "In this upside-down world, at any rate."

PART
THREE

23

ALONE IN A RENTED apartment, in a foreign city, Vladimir slumped in a scruffy armchair he had bought for forty dollars from a refugee Somali at a flea market in the underground car park around the corner on West Eighty-eighth Street.

After his meeting with Anna, he felt cut off from his own side now, as well as from the Americans. She had driven a wedge of anxiety into his routine.

As the deputy chief of the KGB residency in New York, he had position, if less actual influence than some of his junior officers. The most ambitious of them had linked their positions in the intelligence service to the ministries and the big state energy giants, all now overseen by the KGB back home. But he had missed out, or, as he more truthfully acknowledged, had felt less motivation for the fruits of greed and power than some of his subordinates. He was still trying to work for Russia.

He reflected that while he had never had the political will—or maybe it was lust—to extend his power beyond the job, at least he was good at his job.

His own department was called Line X by Moscow Centre. Line X had produced the best, most prolific, and most profitable information in the past two years from its agents in America, outstripping all the other KGB operations. The Main Adversary, as America was still known at Moscow Centre, continued to produce a regular flow of greedy, or dysfunctional, or merely bored agents who possessed the highest security clearances—Flash and even Critical, as the Americans called them. They were sources who were happy to take the Russian dollar in exchange for, mostly technological, secrets. Line X was the KGB department responsible for technological espionage.

These Russian dollars came from the Kremlin-controlled energy companies; companies that provided a quarter of the world's natural gas and had the world's largest oil reserves. Control over them had made the KGB far more powerful than it had ever been during the Cold War. Russia itself might be little changed, but under Vladimir Putin, the KGB was no longer a state within a state. It had become the state, and consequently commanded the state's money. At the KGB's New York residency, and at the KGB residency in Washington, D.C., money was almost no object when there was a potential American agent to acquire.

The foreign service of the KGB, the SVR, to which Vladimir was attached, was the elite of the country's intelligence power. SVR officers were paid far better than they had been in the Cold War, when the most a successful officer stationed abroad could expect were a few foreign-denominated goods to take back home at the end of his service. Now, under Putin's regime, the intelligence services were awash with cash, siphoned off as they liked from the state energy companies, all of which were now run either by Putin's KGB cronies or by businessmen who took their orders from the Kremlin.

Corruption had increased proportionately, of course, and Vladimir rued that. Corruption was inefficiency. The favoured officers at the KGB residence in New York, he knew, now creamed off fat percentages from their company backers in the motherland, in return for under-the-counter favours on American soil that only an intelligence officer could perform.

In person and as a spy station, the employees and the residency itself now had far more money than had ever been available. In the new cold war against the Main Adversary, operations against America's political, industrial, and intelligence institutions were now at full throttle on the Russian side, and he, Vladimir, had been highly commended for his recruitment of American agents in the past year.

But still, as he sat now on the scruffy armchair in the darkness, at this moment he had other things on his mind. He realised he wanted to stay sitting in the chair and drink away his dissatisfaction with the present. He sat without seeing, and as so often in the past, he tried to concoct in his imagination a better future. And he bleakly wondered if that had been his mistake all along.

Walking in darkness over to the cupboard that was screwed badly to the wall and getting looser, he rummaged blindly for the bottle of vodka that was normally there. He found it, shook it in the darkness next to his ear, and heard the splash that told him there was little more than a mouthful left.

He replaced it, picked up his coat and hat from the hook on the inside of the door, and, still without switching on the light, went to the window and surveyed the street four floors below. It was lit in bands where the streetlamps traced by the angled fall of the snow washed their glow onto the wet tarmac.

On a freezing night like this, any watcher would be in a car—he was confident about that. But there were none idling their engines anywhere within his field of vision.

He left the apartment for the walk down the four flights of stairs to the street. The lift was broken again. But he didn't mind the walk. It suited his mood to be slow.

The two questions since his meeting with Anna were continually playing across his mind. Had she been sent—assigned—to meet him by the Americans? Or was their meeting in the bookshop a genuine coincidence?

Either way, he was wishing it had never happened. He felt himself drawn towards her once again. The embers of his feelings towards her, that stretched back to school days and which he had long assumed were cold ashes, had sprung to life almost immediately.

His mind told him one thing about their meeting, and his heart another. His mind told him—loudly and clearly—that the meeting had been a setup.

But what he desperately wanted in his loneliness and loss was to believe the demands of his heart. And his need for that was stronger than his logical mind. He realised he was caught in a trap, knowing one thing and believing entirely the opposite.

He turned to the left out of the apartment block and saw the desultory Christmas lights still strung around the entrance to the seedy hotel next door. He noted the tramp with the tatty coat and blackened hands, like a burn victim, he thought, and who seemed to suck the intermittent heat from the hotel lobby whenever the automatic doors hissed open. He observed the various aimless or purposeful passersby who came at him through the snow that now fell with increasing force.

In truth, nothing was any different than it had been before the meeting. Nothing, essentially, was any different anywhere, he thought. New York, Moscow—there seemed to him suddenly no difference between the two, except perhaps in the details of their veneer. And in the past twenty years, since the Soviet Union had collapsed, Moscow had caught up a lot even in that respect.

He looked up and back again along both sides of the street, but he realised he didn't know who he was looking for—his own side or theirs. Maybe they were just the same too.

He took a taxi uptown through Manhattan, via the Henry Hudson, and then had it drop him half a mile from the KGB residency in

Riverdale. He walked a long, roundabout route, which he varied each time he came here, but stopped spontaneously at a bar on Mosholu Avenue, where he ordered a coffee, not vodka. He observed who entered and left with his usual, artful disinterest and talked to a couple of women in their thirties who were sitting at the bar, finally buying them cocktails and a frozen vodka for himself. They were single, and he was tempted to drown himself in them for the evening.

But after an hour he said his good-byes, took a phone number from the more persistent of the two, and left. He walked the remaining eight blocks, careful to note that he was alone, and entered the building with his January key.

There were two night staff there, who watched television, he noted, when they should have been checking the SIGINT machines, but otherwise the place was his own. Everyone, it seemed, was away until January 13, apart from essential staff. He walked up some stairs and entered his cramped office.

There were piles of papers and notes from before the Russian New Year, when he had last been there—reports of private conversations at the UN, suggestions from eager officers looking for promotion, complaints.

As deputy director, his own and his chief's wider family consisted of over two hundred people, including the diplomatic representatives as well as actual intelligence staff. The Russian delegation at the UN was several hundred strong, of whom seventy-three individuals were from the various branches of the Russian intelligence services.

It was of these seventy-three that Vladimir was the clandestine deputy chief. His diplomatic status with the Russian UN delegation concealed his real job as chief of Line X, the intelligence arm of S&T, the KGB Science and Technology Department.

Line X was not just historically by far the most successful department. He had continued and expanded its role. Each year since 2000, American technological secrets stolen by Line X through its American agents had contributed over five billion roubles to the Russian economy. Secrets obtained from Russian operatives and their American agents right across the territory of the Main Adversary now accounted for just under half of all Russian weapons systems, which were adapted from this theft.

None of these great technological leaps, however, had been filtered by his political masters in Moscow through to the civilian economy. Russia was an intelligence state, not a country with its citizens at heart.

And since Putin had come to power in the year 2000, Line X funding had increased dramatically. In the past two years alone, right up to this moment when the world hovered on the brink of economic crisis, funding had increased sixfold. Putin's orders, transmitted by him personally as president the year before to all intelligence department heads at the Washington embassy, had been that "all efforts are to be directed at recruitment, in the defence establishments, in the space exploration centres, in the defence-related technical companies and in the private intelligence companies."

The latter, these private intelligence outfits, had blossomed across America's intelligence since 9/11.

Recruitment of American agents, Putin had demanded, was to have no limits, financial or otherwise. Russia's newfound wealth was to be the source of a greater intelligence assault on the Main Adversary than the KGB had ever dreamed of in Soviet times.

Vladimir picked up a dirty coffee cup at the back of his desk and, turning it upside down, read the week's encryption keys that were disguised as a circular manufacturer's stamp on the base. Then he entered his computer.

He picked out five code names—simple words buried in a long report about a meeting with the delegation from Equatorial Guinea at the UN in the week before Christmas—and wrote down the names as they appeared for January, in capital letters: SOIL, RAINFALL, METAL, EROSION, and ZERO. Of these, he guessed only one could help him in his current task, but he was prepared to contact two or three in case he needed to widen the net.

"Erosion" was a thirty-seven-year-old Columbia University graduate and addictive gambler who sat on the Intelligence Procurement Committee in Washington—one of several that handed out contracts to private intelligence companies—albeit in one of the lowlier positions. He was Vladimir's most prized possession.

He encoded a message for Erosion, requesting an immediate meeting, in the next twenty-four hours it would be understood, and then he sent it by text on a cell phone registered to an electrical store in Annapolis owned by a third-generation Russian and long-term "illegal" by the name of Stan Riker.

The other two code names he had chosen out of the five, along with their contact information, Vladimir kept with him, against regulations, as he left the residency and walked towards the river.

The taxi he found eventually dropped him on the far side of the river, and he walked from there to Fourth Street, where there was another bar, other single, lonely people. It was a bar he'd never visited, and he didn't waste time. He went through to the back and found a pay phone.

With a black-market telephone card obtained by the geeks in Communications, he called a contact, a friend, a KGB officer stationed in Geneva—one of the few people on his own side he believed he could trust. What he asked for, using the old code name for her that he hoped still worked, was a back bearing on Anna—any recent sightings, hearsay, and rumour—anything that might help him make his judgement before they met again in a week's time.

24

ON THE MORNING AFTER the revelation of Mikhail's identity, Burt and Anna alone discussed the details of her plan to contact him. It was straightforward, and beautiful, Burt said, in its simplicity.

The dagger would be sent to the Russian cultural centre in Washington, D.C., purporting to come from an elderly émigré who wished to know its provenance and value. There was a box number to reply to, and a peremptory request to return the dagger, whether the cultural centre could be of any help or not.

If Burt was surprised by Anna's easy agreement to continue with her original plan, with his and his watchers' oversight, he didn't show it. For herself, Anna understood Burt's adoption of her idea completely. It was the best way, that was all, maybe the only way to take the step into Mikhail's awareness.

Burt had his people in the capital run a routine check on all the staff at the cultural centre, in the course of which it was established that Mikhail was actually in residence, and not on vacation or travelling for work.

When that information was nailed down, Burt and Anna sat alone, working on the message to accompany the dagger. At Burt's insistence she wrote it in her own hand, to be typed later. She chose an awkward and old form of Russian to couch her request, in the make-believe that this émigré was an older person who had been in the West for many decades. At Burt's direction, the address she gave to Mikhail for his reply was mailbox no. 3079 at a mail office on Fifty-fifth Street.

On one of his occasional trips from the apartment, Burt had set up the arrangement, and she realised that this was the element Burt loved most, to be an operative himself again, on the streets, as he had been in his youth.

Burt then asked one of the bewildered guards to find a typewriter—secondhand from a flea market, he insisted, but make sure it worked—and in the interests of the security around Mikhail, he personally typed her words and personally handed it to the fake UPS driver to make the delivery. Finally, the dagger itself had been bound in cardboard and bubble wrap.

"I'm having the mailbox watched," Burt informed her. "But it's not anyone from here—someone who's out of the whole Mikhail loop."

She wondered why he didn't trust even the closest of his employees with the information, but she sensed he was right. Like her, Burt wanted nothing to impede the smooth reception of Mikhail's contact with her.

"Why watch it at all?" she said. "Either he leaves something, or he doesn't. Watching won't change that."

"It's just to ensure that nobody opens that box apart from us," he said. "By accident or not," he added.

And she saw the sense in that too.

"And then what?" she asked him. "If he makes a drop?"

"Don't worry, my dear. I'll bring whatever he leaves straight here. Nothing happens without you."

But maybe something can happen without you, she thought.

After lunch, Burt had checked that the package had safely arrived, accepted and signed for by a receptionist at the cultural centre, and he was in an even more jovial mood than usual, though none of his staff at the apartment knew the reason for his elation.

For them, it was a time of waiting, as they believed, for Anna's meeting with Vladimir. Anna retired to her room to rest. But once there, she began to work out her own mission, her plan that, once again, had to be unknown to Burt.

In the evening, they all ate supper—Burt, Anna, Marcie, and Logan—and there was the desultory feeling of nothing happening among all of them but Burt.

After supper Logan suddenly suggested, in front of them all, that he and Anna go to the movies. There was nothing going on, he reasoned. With the usual security, surely a visit to the movie theatre was a good way to relax. But he didn't suggest that Marcie accompany them.

It was completely unexpected and, Burt said, all the more welcome for that reason. They could go to see a matinee in the next few days, he said, but only if she wished to.

It was the first moment of near freedom she would have had since the last day with Little Finn at the house in France, back in August.

"Let's see," she said. "Sometime in the next few days I'd love to, Logan. Maybe a walk would be better, though, rather than sitting in the theatre."

And so, the next morning, Logan, Anna, and six watchers walked "for miles in the damn cold," as Larry complained afterwards. She and Logan stopped and drank coffee and watched the watchers as they stamped their feet outside the café, trying to look like normal people who happened to be standing in subzero temperatures in a New York street in January.

Meanwhile, inside the café, Anna found she was more relaxed than she'd been for a long time.

Deemed a success by Burt, the exercise was repeated the following day, to the consternation of the watchers, and then on the third day after the dagger had been sent, she agreed this time to accompany Logan to the movies.

Logan had asked her this time in a way that carried a suggestion of something more than just time spent in her company. She had consulted Burt about this developing relationship and about the wisdom of accompanying Logan on what looked remarkably like a date.

Burt took her alone into one of the many small ops rooms in the apartment that was vacant.

"If you're all right about Logan, I want to ask you something," he said.

"So I have the right to turn you down?" She smiled.

"Oh, yes. Nothing's changed. I want you to know that. You are highly respected here, and always will be by me. More so than before, if anything. No. This is a request, Anna. I'd like you to be friendly to Logan."

"Friendly?"

"Yes." He looked at her and grinned. "Be sweet with him. Can you do that?"

"Sweet with him? That seems to be a role I can't escape," she said.

Burt paused and seemed to be deciding what to say. Then:

"It's something about Logan," he said eventually. "I don't live with my mistakes. But I'm going to have to live with this one a little longer. If it is a mistake."

"Is Logan a mistake? Is he unreliable?"

"Logan was one of the best officers I ever had at the agency. Maybe the best."

"And now?"

"Let's say I'm giving him a chance—a reward too—with this assignment in the past months. I'm not certain how he's responding to the opportunity. But I know he'll respond to you, Anna. People do. As an SVR colonel or as a beautiful woman, I couldn't say." He smiled conspiratorially as he turned to her. "This isn't something I'd ask you, Anna, unless I thought it was important."

"I can be friendly to Logan," she agreed. "Is that it? Or am I watching him?"

Burt walked away from her in the windowless room and sat in a swivel chair that was too small for him. He looked as if he'd been forcibly squeezed into it.

"I'm going to tell you a story," he said. "It might help you understand Logan a little." His rotund body fit the chair like a cushion. "Logan ran agents in the Balkans in the nineties," Burt began. "He was involved in an operation at the heart of the Milosevic government. Running an agent inside the Tigers, you know, the organisation led by the notorious paramilitary Arkan. As I'm sure you know also, Arkan was responsible for the murder of at least twenty thousand Bosnians. He was a killer, politician, warlord, bank robber. . . . Logan got very close to him through one of his female agents. So the agency decided to bring Arkan down."

Burt paused, as if unwilling to divulge what he was going to say.

"But then the CIA station in Vienna made a mistake. They confused two communications sent out from our embassy there. One of these communications was intended for Arkan himself. It was a warning, a threat. We were going to get him, and he had nowhere deep enough to hide. The warning was intended to panic him into making the mistake that would allow us to follow through with his assassination.

"The other, second message was a detailed account of Arkan's internal operations that could only have come from his inner circle. This communication was intended for our station head in Sarajevo. The two messages got mixed up, would you believe—they were sent the wrong way round. Arkan received the CIA assessment of his own operations, clearly aided by inside sources, and our station head in

Sarajevo received the threat to Arkan. Incredible, isn't it?" he said, looking at her.

"It happens," she replied. "I'm sure I could match you for any mistake of the CIA's with mistakes from the Russian side. Even mistakes as crass as that."

"There are mistakes, and there are spectacular mistakes," Burt said. "Arkan learned everything we knew about him, and he soon found the source of this information inside his own circle." He paused. "She was tortured to death."

"I see."

"Do you?"

Burt paused, discomfited, it seemed to her, by this unaccustomed departure from his regular world of relentless optimism.

"And it was a 'she,' " Anna added.

"Yes. Logan's agent was also Logan's woman," Burt continued. "And as if that weren't enough, Logan was made the fall guy for the whole mistake, to save someone else's skin at the station."

Anna said nothing, but was thinking what Burt said next as he was saying it.

"Logan became what you might call a compromised, angry, washed-up piece of emotional wreckage," Burt said.

"Who you've hired again," she said. "Not the best material for an intelligence officer. So why? Why wasn't he pensioned off? Why is Logan working for you?"

He looked at her.

"Two reasons. The first is a personal loyalty to him. If this doesn't bring him back," Burt said, "I fear he'll be lost for good. And by 'bring him back,' I don't mean bring him back to this world of ours necessarily, the world of secrets, but bring him back to any kind of life at all."

"That's taking a big risk," she said. "Surely your heart isn't that big, Burt. It's a charming thought, but not much use in our operation now."

"The second reason may seem odd to you. But it's important to what we're doing. Naturally Logan hates the CIA. To me, that's a valuable asset. In this business of private intelligence companies, the revolving door between the CIA and us contractors is constantly spinning. It's mostly one way, CIA people coming over to our side. They can earn twice, even three times, what they earn with the government. Department heads and even heads of the CIA come into the private sector, bringing their knowledge and government contacts with them." Burt paused. "That's all good, or nearly all good. But we're in a situation of concealing something from the CIA, and the revolving door can in theory go both ways. I have to be careful that former CIA employees now at Cougar aren't talking to their old colleagues. That's why Logan hating the CIA makes him trustworthy— at least in that."

"It's still a risk in other ways," she said, "if Logan's unstable."

"As I say, Logan was the best, and he was allowed to take the fall for someone else. In the end everything is and everything isn't a risk," he said, and he grinned once again, now he'd made his way through the uncomfortable story to the other side. Then he went on. "He doesn't have any woman close to him. He keeps his various women at a long arm's length. For obvious reasons, I guess."

"So you want me to look after him."

"Just be sweet. And only if it fits for you," Burt said. "Only if it seems to work in the context of the assignment. And nothing too intimate, unless that works for you too."

She was silent.

"That's fine, then."

The next morning Anna postponed her date with Logan at the movies to another day. It would be the fourth day since the contact with Mikhail. She needed time, but the reason she gave was that she felt unwell.

In the course of that day, after her discussion with Burt, she began to make her preparations. Everything was going to have to be alarmingly spontaneous, but it was all she could do. Improvisation was familiar to her. Any trained intelligence officer could follow instructions, but only the best improvised successfully.

In the course of the day, she collected what she could find in the apartment, away from prying eyes; a large wedge-shaped doorstop made of wood that was used in the conference room, and then another one she found lying unused in one of the smaller rooms; a small hammer that was in a kitchen drawer. There wasn't much.

After some discussion between Burt and Bob Dupont the following morning—details that related to her security outside the apartment walls—it was agreed that she and Logan could go to the movies, accompanied by the usual swarm of minders.

With the boyish enthusiasm of a teenager on a date, Logan bought tickets and popcorn and they watched the new Clint Eastwood film at a theatre on Broadway. From time to time he used a whispered comment on the film as an excuse to put his hand briefly on her knee, as if it were merely to get her attention. Anna was amused by his sudden eagerness to be physically intimate, but she didn't respond, and he didn't press her. He seemed pleased just to be in her company, and she found, to her surprise, that she was similarly enjoying the experience. But her mind, when it wasn't focused on the movie, was elsewhere.

They emerged from the movie theatre at just before five p.m. onto Broadway, where the half a dozen watchers were spread out on either side along the sidewalk.

It was well below freezing, even this early in the evening. But Logan suddenly declared he didn't want to go back to the apartment, despite the instruction that it was a movie, then back "home."

Anna could see Larry standing on the sidewalk outside the movie theatre, clapping his hands together from the cold, but also out of impatience to get going. The other watchers were invisible, but out of some professional habit or merely for her own amusement, she began to pick them out—one standing looking at a paper, two others waiting by the street as if for a taxi, another over to the right, beyond

Larry, and the sixth idling by a newsstand on the sidewalk to the left. All were ahead of her and Logan or to the side, she noted.

Behind them, in the movie theatre itself, there was no one, and what had been running through her mind in the course of watching the movie now came to dominate her next step.

"Better go," she said to dampen Logan's enthusiasm, and as she'd expected, she just increased it.

Logan hesitated without moving towards the waiting car.

"Why not walk for a bit?" he said.

"We should go back," she replied. "Won't they cut our privileges if we disobey?" she added in a tone of mockery.

"Let's go somewhere," he said, slowly revealing intentions that were beginning to be insistent.

She returned his open gaze. "Look, Logan, if you want to sleep with me," she said, "why don't you just say so?"

"Yes," he said. "That's about it. I do."

"Only it isn't very convenient, is it. Not right now."

"That's a not a no, then," he said, and gave her a broad smile.

"It isn't a yes either."

She put her arm through his, and from the corner of her eye watched as Larry scowled at them.

"But if it ever did happen," she said carefully, "I'd rather we had a situation that was a bit more relaxed than this, don't you think?" She laughed.

She felt him squeeze her arm in his. The warmth of the movie theatre was fading fast out here on the sidewalk.

She looked around casually at the watchers. "I've no doubt I could evade all of them," she said easily. "But could you, Logan? Burt says you're the best. But are you really that good?" She smiled up at him with the challenge, and he laughed, the tension easing between them.

"Are you kidding?" he said.

"The Mercer Hotel in half an hour. Make your own way. Alone, or you've blown it. And I bet I beat you."

"How much?"

She looked him in the eyes. "You never know your luck."

Then suddenly she was gone, not onto the street, but straight back into the movie theatre. She didn't look back.

She knew she only had a few seconds. Six pairs of eyes were on her. But she crossed the foyer at a brisk walk, and when she turned, she saw that the watchers were only just moving towards the doors outside.

She pushed through the doors to the interior. The auditorium was lit only by dull wall lights high up. There was nobody there, no staff or stragglers from the movie still left behind. When she was through the door, she snatched a fire extinguisher from the wall on the inside, fed the hose through the two handles of the doors so that it gripped them shut, and placed the end of the hose behind the lever, so that when the doors were pushed, it would set off the extinguisher.

She ran now—down the side aisle, through a fire door to the right of the screen, slamming the door shut behind her. She looked down the dimly lit concrete corridor, took one of the wooden doorstops from the inside pocket of her coat, and beat it into the foot of the door with the hammer. Once it was jammed as far it would go, she ran down the corridor. It might give her a few extra seconds, perhaps, longer than the task had taken at any rate, but those might be the seconds that counted.

She came to another fire door. Pushing it gently, she saw the street. She had come out at the side of the theatre.

She looked to the left and exited in front of a group of three men who were passing. She didn't look back, but walked in front of the men, letting them screen her. In another long few seconds she reached the end of the block, half walked, half ran straight across the street, dodging hooting cars, and kept running.

Outside the theatre, by the waiting car, Larry saw Anna turn almost as she did so and watched her begin to walk back inside. He hesitated, then walked fast towards Logan.

"Where's she going?"

"Ladies' room," Logan said.

Larry whistled, and the two watchers on either side of the theatre came up fast towards him.

"She's gone back inside. Ladies' room—so he says," Larry added, and scowled at Logan. "Stay with her." He looked at Logan. "You. Get in the car."

"Sure." Logan walked to the car and looked from the sidewalk in through the front passenger window at the driver. He tapped on it.

"We're almost there. Just waiting for her," Logan said through the fractionally opened glass. The driver didn't acknowledge he cared either way.

Logan walked around the trunk at the back of the car and made for the door to the back seat on the street side. He opened the door. When he saw a bus coming fast and pulling out to pass their stationary car, he stepped in front of it and ducked through, feeling the rush of air as it passed behind him. There was a loud blast of its horn.

He dodged a car into the next lane with inches to spare. Then he ran across the three remaining lanes, inviting angry blasts from half a dozen cars, and reached the sidewalk on the far side.

Larry was watching him like a hawk. He saw him approach the car, speak to the driver, inexplicably walk around the rear instead of getting in from the sidewalk, and then open the door. He saw the sudden jerking movement as he leaped across the path of the bus, and knew that things were falling apart. He shouted to one of the three remaining watchers to get inside the theatre.

"She's making a break! Get her!"

They ran inside and found their colleagues waiting in the lobby, uncertain what to do. But it seemed it was dawning on them that something was going wrong.

"She's making a goddamn run!" one of the new arrivals shouted.

All three ran for the interior doors. They came up against the crude obstruction of the thick rubber hose jammed through the handles on the other side, and smashed their way through them, to be met by a flailing fire extinguisher that was shooting violently from side to side in the corridor and firing streams of foam.

Fifty pounds of reinforced steel spinning at high speed caught the edge of the wall, whirled away at higher speed still, and smashed into the ankle of the man in front. He collapsed howling, then fell to the floor clutching his ankle and shouting obscenities.

The other three didn't stop, but ran on two sides down the aisles of the auditorium, two on one side, one on the other, and came up against the fire doors that flanked the screen.

"Jesus. What's she got on the other side of this?" one shouted.

On the sidewalk, Larry shouted at the remaining two watchers, one to cross the street to the far side and hunt down Logan, the other to head in the opposite direction, up to the left of the theatre.

He himself stepped straight off the sidewalk in front of the waiting car and ran across the four lanes of the street, dodging cars, slipping once almost to his death in front of a truck that refused to brake, until he reached the far side. He would kill Logan if he found him now.

Anna caught her breath after running for three blocks. She saw a cab rank on the far side of the road, crossed the street quickly, and stepped into the darkness of the rear seat.

"The mail office on Fifty-fifth and Broadway," she said, and the cab pulled out and headed uptown.

Her mind raced back over the years to her training at the Forest. Three or eleven, those were the Moscow Rules. When you had a dead drop, a number, you added either three or eleven to the number, and if neither of those came right, you began to count up from three towards eleven.

The box number Burt had chosen was 3079. Therefore Mikhail would place anything for her in 3090 or, in the event of that being incorrect, in 3082. He would work on Moscow Rules. He would know that's how she would work.

If neither of those numbers were true, she would have to begin from 3083 and work upwards.

The cab reached the mail office in less than ten minutes. She gave the driver the fare and a twenty-dollar bill on top, and told him there'd be a hundred dollars if he waited for her. Before stepping out of the cab, she wrapped a scarf over her head and carried her coat rather than wearing it. Then she opened the door and, leaving the car behind her, walked into the mail office.

They would only have one watcher here, and not one of Burt's regulars. Whoever it was would be watching 3079.

She stepped down a broad, brightly lit corridor, not looking ahead, only noting the numbers on the boxes at the sides. She began to slow when the numbers descended below 4000. Then she stopped purposefully by 3090 and rummaged in a pocket for a key. What she brought out was a small lock pick she'd made the day before in the apartment.

Fitting the bent piece of metal into the keyhole, she agitated it from side to side. It was just large enough, but not as good as it should be. She'd had to guess at the size of the locks. The box opened after nearly thirty seconds, too long, and she rummaged inside with her other hand, finding some mail, three letters. She looked at them, saw a name, the logo of the New York Electrical Company on the envelope, and pushed them back. The box was in use.

She locked the box and stepped over to 3082. Anyone watching her would probably make his move now. It might be seen as suspect to be opening two boxes.

She fitted the key again. It seemed to take an interminable length of time. She expected at any moment a shout, a hand on the shoulder, the click of a readied weapon. But the door finally opened unwillingly, and she reached inside to find a single sheet. She looked at it and knew it was from him. She wrote an X on the floor of the box and shut the door. Then she locked it again carefully.

Larry saw Logan weaving down a street that ran perpendicular to the four lanes they had crossed. He called into the radio to two of the others and gave them the location, ordering them to turn off Broadway and head west.

They would keep Logan flanked on either side, while he would stay on the target. Logan was around fifty yards ahead of him, moving fast, not looking back, only to the sides when he reached a street. He was running fast, and Larry ran after him in fury.

Then he saw Logan descend some subway steps into the subterranean depths of the Twenty-third Street station. Larry ran forward, simultaneously ordering the two watchers to pick up a cab each and wait for him for instructions. As he descended the steps two at a time, there was a call from the three watchers at the theatre.

"She's away," was all the man said.

"Fucking find her!" Larry shouted.

He saw Logan running now, towards the corridor that led to the downtown trains. He hurled himself after him, jumping the stile, and as he did so, he ordered the men in the two cabs somewhere above him to head downtown and wait at the exits from the Fourteenth and Eighth Street stations for further instructions.

Anna stepped back into the cab and gave the Mercer Hotel as her destination. She opened the folded paper again and read. There were four lines, each a place, a time, and a date. All were places she had never heard of, somewhere in New York—one main venue to aim for and three fallback meetings.

She memorised the information, and screwed the paper up in one hand as the cab turned into Mercer Street, where the hotel jutted out onto the sidewalk.

"Drive past it, please," she instructed the driver. A hundred yards beyond the hotel, she told him to pull up. She gave him the fare and added a hundred-dollar bill.

Outside the cab, she watched the hotel entrance in the distance, then bent down and dropped the paper into a drain. She stood up and walked towards the hotel.

On the platform at Twenty-third Street, Larry caught sight of Logan at the far end as he stepped onto the train. He just had time himself to force a set of doors open to let him in.

If he's getting in at the bottom of the train, he thought, then the station he's disembarking from must have an exit at that end of the train. But it seemed unlikely that Logan would know that, unless this whole exercise had been planned long in advance—and it seemed improvised.

He began to make his way down the train. It was crowded, and he moved slowly. He'd travelled three, four cars by the time the train pulled in to the next station. He waited in the train, and when the door was clear of people getting out, he risked a look. Logan was just twenty yards away, walking down the platform. Larry withdrew.

"He's getting out on Fourteenth Street," he barked into the radio. "You have two minutes."

Then he sat down with his back to the platform and almost felt Logan walking by behind him. Without glancing for more than a few seconds through the window, Larry watched the stairs at the end of the platform as the train pulled out. Logan was nowhere in the stream of people walking along or turning for the exit. Somewhere, he thought, Logan had moved back onto the train, and it must be within a few cars of where he was sitting.

He radioed again with orders to both watchers to move on to the next station, if Logan didn't emerge.

At the Spring Street station, he saw Logan again, stepping out a second time, from two cars away, and heading with his back to Larry towards an exit. Larry stepped out. He was sure now.

"He's coming out on Spring," he said. "Hit him hard."

He would stay behind Logan in case he made a run back.

Anna walked into the lobby and looked around her. She checked her watch. She'd taken thirty-five minutes, but she couldn't see Logan. She walked over to a sitting area and checked the bar. He had not arrived. Not that it mattered now. She would sit and wait in the most prominent part of the lobby and see who showed up.

It was Larry who walked in. He looked the wrong way, then turned in her direction. She was looking straight at him, and she saw that his face was set with infuriated calm. So they'd found Logan. She stood up and walked over to him.

"Sorry, Larry," she said.

"Are you coming quietly?"

"Oh, yes," she replied.

25

VLADIMIR STOOD IN FRONT of Villamil's painting *The Bullfight* in Washington's National Gallery and admired the chaotic scene of capes that swirled like smoke, men hidden beneath them, and the tall wooden pole that drew the viewer's eyes into the centre of the painting and down to the scene below.

It was more like a battle scene, he thought, than the formal execution of the corrida.

He was aware of the man who had stepped up to another picture three to the right of him, a Goya. The man was slightly closer to the picture and seemed equally absorbed.

Neither of them glanced in the other's direction, but Vladimir knew just from his field of vision when he took his attention away from the painting that it was the man he had come to meet. He was on time as always, eager to give, pulsing almost visibly with some need to divulge classified information that would have put him in prison for the rest of his life if he were caught.

Why? Vladimir wondered, as he always did. But Erosion was his best source. He gave to Vladimir what he gave for reasons the Russian didn't really understand.

Erosion sat on a special committee, which was privy to information of high value to the Russians. He was paid well by the American government, he had a pleasant house in the suburb of Chevy Chase, a wife he seemed to appreciate, two kids in decent schools. It couldn't be the money, Vladimir thought, as he often did when he was trying to comprehend the motives of his agents.

Thanks to Vladimir, Erosion also had a healthy and growing bank account in Mexico City. But all this cash in return for secrets was money the man dared not openly reveal. To spend it on luxuries, to be richer than his perfectly respectable salary permitted, would ultimately have drawn the attention of the CIA or one of the other government intelligence agencies who might take an interest in individuals like Erosion. He held valuable secrets of state, and could ultimately draw down all the wrath in the world. What was the money for?

The SVR paid its American agents well, but Vladimir found it hard to believe that a man with so much could hazard it all for a few hundred thousand dollars he was afraid to use. It was more like the illusion of money than money itself. Was it greed, then? Money for money's sake? No, he thought, greed did not fully explain the phenomenon, not just of Erosion but of his other American agents. He detected a hoarding mentality. Sometimes he thought it wouldn't really matter what the Russians gave in return for these secrets—acres of land, tons of coffee beans stored in a warehouse, artworks—because the disease seemed to be about possession. It was the hoarder's faulty mental state they were feeding. The man was an empty shell, and maybe he sought exterior things to fill the hole in himself. Money just happened to be the commodity that was most familiar to the hoarder's imagination.

From the corner of his eye Vladimir saw the man take a final look at the painting and move slowly away, pausing at the next briefly, another Goya, then looking at his watch. A decision was made, and he walked purposefully towards the gallery's cafeteria.

Vladimir waited until he was out of sight before looking down at his programme, studying the room's other offerings and walking past the next two pictures, until he paused at the third, the one Erosion had been studying. But this time, he looked sightlessly at the picture, the countess of something or other, and instead began with imperceptible precision to make a sweep of the gallery's large hall.

There was a man at the far end who hadn't taken his hat off; a couple, probably retired; two girls who looked like students; and two uniformed staff members who guarded the doors at either end as well as the pictures between them. He decided he would watch the man with the hat a while longer, to make sure he recognised him if he appeared again, in the café, without his coat and hat.

Temporarily satisfied, Vladimir made his own way into the café.

Erosion had just reached the front of the queue at the self-service counter and was paying for his lunch; soup, bread, cheese, and something sweet in a wrapper. Vladimir joined the end of the queue. When he had paid, he carried his tray to the nearest available table, without looking up to find where Erosion was seated. He put the tray down, took off his coat, and placed it over a second chair. Then he sat down.

The café was half full; it was easy to observe without seeming to observe. He found Erosion sitting at a table in the corner where he sat for their meetings when he had some material. So he had received the drop Vladimir had left for him the night before. His presence meant the presence of information, the table where he sat a sign for a delivery.

The drop would be made here in the cafeteria, and the pickup would follow. They never need look in each other's eyes.

Vladimir saw the man in the hat enter the café. He had removed it, along with his coat, as Vladimir had expected. It meant nothing in itself; anyone who had entered the museum would have entered it wrapped up against the cold outside, and then slowly unwrapped in the warmth inside.

But despite the perfectly normal behaviour of the man, Vladimir decided to follow through the pickup without the man still present in the café. That would mean a wait until he had gone. Vladimir's tradecraft had taught him that no pickup was better than a messy one. If it meant returning to the museum later, when the man had gone, that's what he would have to do.

Vladimir read the morning's newspaper, the meal taking second place in his attention. He ate slowly, until he finally observed the man with the hat take his tray to the trolley by the door and exit from the café. A civilian, he thought, just a casual visitor.

He glanced up and saw that Erosion had also finished his meal and was piling up the plates and wrappers onto the tray and then carrying the tray to a trolley and leaving. No glance, no word exchanged between them. It was a simple drop-off. The signal to indicate the need for a face-to-face meeting had not been made. It was routine. Vladimir continued reading and idly left the remains of his plate of pasta. It was two thirty in the afternoon.

He watched the busboys in the kitchen behind the serving counter and took his tray to the trolley, where he slid his hand beneath the tray Erosion had left and withdrew a screwed-up napkin at the same moment as he slid his tray onto the trolley. He didn't put the paper in his pocket, not yet, but concealed it in his hand until he was clear of the café and he'd had the chance to check the first exhibition room for the man in the hat. But as he entered it for the second time, he saw it was empty, just the two staff members who sat by the doors like statues.

He slipped the paper into his pocket and left the room, into the next hall, consulting his programme to see the history of the painting he'd chosen to stop and observe. When he was calmly in a state of almost believing his own interest in the painting, he left the gallery and took a cab to the airport.

On the way, he read the coded words Erosion had left him on the napkin.

There had been a Russian intelligence officer at Langley, around four months previously. It isn't known what was the purpose of her visit, it read. There was considerable excitement about her presence among the various echelons of government,

Erosion was eager to please, as always. Was that it, he wondered, simply a desire to please? Was that the motivation of the lost people on the American side who aided his, the Russian, cause? But deep inside himself, he knew with bitterness that he possessed the desire to please in equal measure.

So it was a "her." Vladimir tucked the screwed-up napkin in the pocket of his coat to dispose of later. Anna—there was almost no doubt it was her—had been at Langley. But was she working for them, or were they just debriefing her? Either way, she bore the marks of a defector, as far as the Forest was concerned. Back in Moscow, they had erected shooting targets bearing her image, for trainee officers to practice on down on the rifle ranges at Yasenevo.

Where did that leave him? With the knowledge of her likely affiliations, certainly—and then his prospective meeting with her. He knew he would not pass on the information to his superiors, not yet in any case. Anna was his—one way or the other.

The plane touched down at LaGuardia at half past six in the evening. He took another cab, through the Midtown Tunnel to Manhattan. Then he switched cabs for the ride along the East River, and disembarked once again several blocks from the residence in Riverdale.

He walked without stopping at any bar this time. There was an urgency about him, the fresh blood of pursuit in his nostrils. He wanted clarity. He wanted to know, absolutely, if such a thing were possible.

He entered the residency as the evening shift was coming on and went upstairs to the cramped room, tapped the codes into the computer on his desk, and looked at what came up. He saw that his friend, the SVR resident in Geneva, had made contact. He scrawled down the message on a piece of paper, marked with the stain of a coffee cup, reached for the china cup with the month's codes stamped on the bottom, and began to decipher the message.

"She was offered to our head of station in Montenegro in August last year. For a high price. It was agreed. The interlocutor was an American called Logan Halloran, formerly with the Main Adversary's station in the Balkans, now believed to be operating alone. A freelancer. Money paid to him, but no exchange. Shit everywhere. Believed the MA got her."

Vladimir sat back in the chair and swung gently from side to side. The blinds were pulled down as they usually were; there was just the desk lamp for light. He felt himself cocooned.

So this man Halloran had sold her to all of them, perhaps. Who else? To the British too, as well as the Americans and the Russians? She was more a hostage than a defector, he thought. The Americans had bought her like a sack of corn.

And the Montenegro resident would no doubt have had a lot of explaining to do. Moscow wanted the female Russian colonel very badly, and he'd slipped up. A demotion in rank? Or would they put him right out in the cold, like they'd done to him, Vladimir, all those years ago with his posting to the Cape Verde Islands? Or would it be even worse for him than that?

Vladimir sat in the darkness, having pushed himself away from the pool of light on the desk. He surveyed his options. The longer he held on to the knowledge of her without informing his superiors, the worse it would be for him. If they ever found out.

26

BURT PAUSED BEFORE A nineteenth-century clapboard house that stood about three hundred yards above the beach. A bitterly cold wind blew onshore from the direction of Greenland, and the icy waves nodded their heads onto the raked pebbles with a lethargy that, in a human being, would have been the final stage before freezing to death. A few gulls circled above their heads, screeching faintly into the wind.

He turned to Anna. Without removing his hands from the pockets of his coat, he simply nodded towards the house.

"That belonged to my grandfather," he said. "From my mother's side of the family."

"So you didn't start with nothing, Burt," she said.

He guffawed hugely. "No. I had a great deal. A great deal. But I could have frittered it away." He paused, as if reflecting on the possibilities of simply spending the family fortune. "He was in steel," he added. "Out in Pittsburgh. But they all bought their summer homes in Long Island and built their country clubs in Pennsylvania for weekends."

He walked on, and she kept in step with him, the wet stones crunching softly beneath her feet. She couldn't see them, but she knew his scouts were out, ahead and behind them somewhere. Larry had been pacified. He'd wanted to break parts of Logan, in the wilful belief that it had been him who had led her astray.

Logan was now at the apartment with Dupont and Marcie, while Burt had brought her up here alone. They were to be questioned apart, her and Logan.

For his part, everything that had happened twenty-four hours before confirmed to Burt that he had been right. She knew what she was doing, particularly when it came to Mikhail. And since he hadn't let her run free himself, she had devised a way of doing so. The escapade to the Mercer Hotel was brilliantly done, and he still hadn't asked her why, what was the purpose of it. Yet he knew that it had been something to do with her and Mikhail, and nothing connected to Logan. Logan was just the wrench that opened the door.

Burt glanced sideways at her as they walked. She seemed to read him perfectly, he thought, just as she'd read Logan. How he admired her for that. Her genius for the long game lay in her bet that she could expect his, Burt's, admiration even when—no, particularly when— she sabotaged his plans. She'd played him along for weeks, and now he was about to find out why.

Something told him now, and had told him right back at the start, that even with her vulnerable child as a pawn and an execution squad and worse waiting for her back in Russia, she would have still hardened herself to threat like tempered steel.

"You reached the hotel a few minutes before Logan," he said conversationally. "That's some feat. All he had to do was get there. But you did something else too, didn't you."

"Mikhail made contact," she said simply. There was no reason to lie.

He didn't ask her how Mikhail had made contact. He didn't regret that he personally had kept her in the loop about the exact arrangements whereby Mikhail was to make contact. She was spontaneous, she worked with whatever material she had available. It wasn't his own devious thinking or even instinct that had led him to allow her to know the mail office and box number. So it must have been, he thought with amusement, his direct line to God. He'd acted entirely without thought.

"When?" he said. "When did he make a meeting?"

"The day after I meet with Vladimir."

"The day after tomorrow."

"Yes."

"And you and you alone want to be the one who asks him what he wants."

"Yes, Burt. That's the only way it's going to work. With his willingness. Neither you, nor your organisation, nor all the organisations or the full force of the American government can change that."

"I understand."

"I know," she said.

He chuckled to himself. And I know you know I know, he thought. She was a gift from God, this girl.

"You want to leave the apartment alone?" he said. "Go solo. You want to meet him with no surveillance whatsoever?"

"That's the only way this is going to work. He hasn't survived this long inside the Kremlin, all around Europe, and now over here by being blind. He'll know. That's my opinion."

"Mine too," he said, and thought briefly that this, perhaps, was one good thing that could come out of the privacy of an intelligence operation being conducted through a contract company. If the CIA had their hands on this, they'd just lie to her. There was no way that Langley would let her off the leash on her own, not with Mikhail as the prize.

But most likely, even in the context of the private intelligence companies, he believed that only he, Burt, would have had the foresight to consider it, let alone act on it.

They walked on for a hundred yards or so. His face where the scarf didn't quite cover it was burned from the cold.

"And you'll trust me in this," he said. "In letting you go solo."

"Completely," she lied.

It was perfect, he thought. He was taking advice, orders almost, from his own captive. For that, in truth, was what she'd been all along. The perfection of this turning of the tables filled him with a sense of contentment that was only partly due to his knowledge that she was right about Mikhail. He knew they only had one chance with Mikhail, and that was her. If she couldn't get through to him, nobody and nobody's legions could.

He asked her if she wanted to find somewhere warm, have a drink perhaps? But she preferred to walk, and he was happy to be outside. The more the weather threw at them, the more he enjoyed it.

"You were lucky you didn't break my man's leg with that damn fire extinguisher," he said.

"Yes," she said. "I'm glad I didn't."

"He's got an ankle the size of a football, though," Burt said with some mirth.

"I'll apologise."

"And Logan?" he asked her, after they'd tramped along the beach about a quarter of a mile from his grandfather's old house.

"None of this was his doing," she said.

"I'm angry with him. For you, it was about something important, for him it was a whim. He could have jeopardised everything we've spent months working on. I had half a mind to turn him over to Larry." Burt chuckled. "People don't cross me unless it's for a good reason."

"I'll remember, Burt."

"You had a good reason." He laughed. She talks to me like we're equals, partners, he marvelled. And I guess we are, in some way. She apologises for nothing, except the guy's damn leg. She justifies nothing. And that was another reason he had to trust her now.

"Logan's not going to be pleased with you," Burt said.

"I'll have to make it up to him."

He looked at her, but her face gave nothing away.

"Would you have gone to a room with him?" he said. "If we hadn't got to him?"

"That's what I said," she replied. "It's the least I could have done."

He caught himself feeling protective of her, like a father. He didn't like it that she was so casual with herself.

"It's not the way I'd like to think of you giving yourself to men," he said, and heard the awkwardness in his voice.

She laughed out loud and put her hand on his back.

"I don't give myself to men," she said. "That's a very sweet, old-fashioned thought."

"You'd do it for yourself, then?" he asked. "Sleep with him?"

"Oh, yes," she said. "I like Logan, and I'd like to go to bed with him. He's done me that favour, he's broken the spell of Finn. He's cleared the way, and I'm grateful."

A rare cloud crossed Burt's mind as he thought of Logan's part in her entrapment.

"You'd sleep with him?" he asked and felt suddenly like an awkward father with a sixteen-year-old daughter. It was deeply unfamiliar territory.

"As a friend, yes," she said. "Why not?"

They turned away from the sea and made for a car park at the edge of the beach dusted with wind-blown sand.

As they arrived, the car drew in, followed by another of Burt's war vehicles, as Logan called them. Somewhere the watchers had seen Burt's movements—and even his intentions.

They drove back to the city, and Anna slept most of the way. Despite the coming events, she felt more calm than she had done for many weeks. Her ultimate goal might be different from Burt's, but they both shared the same methods to reach where they each wanted to go. They also shared a wish to find Mikhail in order to reach their goals.

That evening, she and Logan went out to dinner, at Burt's suggestion. It was a reconciliation, he said.

Larry was furious, the muscles in his face twitching with barely repressed frustration. There were the usual watchers with them, and they followed them along the street afterwards as they headed for another apartment to which the keys were magically provided.

"See you in the morning," Burt had said to her quietly, and away from everybody, before they'd left. "Ten o'clock. We have work to do."

For Burt, the whole arrangement had a surreal quality to it. But he realised there was no ulterior motive, either his own or from the two of them, and that the seemingly forced nature of the assignation had more to do with natural circumstances than he liked to admit.

If she had been a man relaxing on the eve of an assignment, he realised, he wouldn't have given it a second thought.

In the restaurant, Anna and Logan skirted around the events of the day before, he because he didn't want to bring up his own failure, she for more philosophical reasons; the events of the past were not in her mind to use as a bludgeon for the present.

But as they entered the apartment after dinner, she looked at Logan and said, "So I won the bet. You got caught."

He saw the mischief in her eyes.

"Yes. You did."

"But I'm quite generous," she said.

"I appreciate that."

"Maybe you'll be better in the bedroom than on the street," she said with a laugh. "You couldn't be any worse."

He looked at her supremely confident eyes and felt his nerves and his skin and his flesh reaching out towards her touch. But she just stood and looked straight back at him, in neither a challenge nor a retreat.

Still facing each other, they took off their coats and hung them on a stand by the door. They both looked around at the service apartment; a sitting room with a huge window thirty-four floors above the street, the elegant digits of Manhattan's skyline lit around their edges like constellations.

Behind the sitting room, a door was open to a bedroom and another large picture window. The apartment, he thought inconsequentially, had no kitchen.

He flicked the lock on the door behind them and kissed her. They kissed for a long time, standing four feet inside the room. She unbuttoned his shirt, and they kicked their shoes away. Then she took his hand and walked to the sofa.

"There's a bedroom through there," he said.

"Maybe later."

She let go of the confusion of passions and motives that tried to insinuate themselves into her mind. She wanted sex, that was all. If he was looking for something more, that was his lookout. He was what she wanted right now.

But when they made love, she didn't have her eyes open, as she had always done with Finn.

For security reasons left unexplained, but which Burt described as "normal procedure," they decamped from the apartment on Twenty-third Street the morning after her night with Logan. Her meeting with Vladimir would take place the next day.

At ten o'clock, when they both arrived at the apartment—and Larry grimaced in the background, unable to meet her eyes—Burt, Logan, Marcie, and Anna left in a car for the Downtown Manhattan Heliport, where a helicopter took them away from New York to another property in Burt's apparently inexhaustible empire. It was a farmhouse this time, in the New Hampshire countryside.

By midday the four of them were sitting around a hickory table in the kitchen, while a new security team patrolled the perimeters. Larry, it appeared, was being given a rest.

Burt wasted no time. "The immediate requirement for both your meeting with Vladimir and then your meeting with Mikhail concerns a piece of intelligence gleaned from our British friends," he said.

Marcie and Logan both looked up in surprise, while Anna, Burt noted, remained focused on a point somewhere in the middle distance beyond the sliding glass doors in the kitchen, which looked out onto snow-covered gardens. But Logan and Marcie both saw that Burt was in no mood for interruptions.

"The reason for meeting Vladimir a second time at all might have seemed vague to you," he said, looking at Logan and Marcie. "The possibility of turning the deputy head of the KGB presence in New York, while worth pursuing, is as we all know a long-term strategy, however unlikely its outcome. That element of Anna's assignment is a secondary reason at this stage. The principal focus is this British fragment of intelligence, highly classified, restricted to just us in this room. And that is just for Mikhail."

"What meeting with Mikhail, Burt?" Marcie said, unable to contain her curiosity any longer.

"That's something I'll brief you and Logan on separately," he replied.

He looked up at Marcie and Logan and received surprised expressions from both of them. Anna turned from her sightless view of the vista outside and looked at Burt.

"This British intelligence originates from a reliable British operation in Russia itself," Burt continued. "It comes from a source in the Russian defence establishment. The British source has provided convincing information that the Russians have an agent called Icarus in the United States. Icarus is an American who is working in a highly sensitive government defence programme somewhere on our territory."

Burt paused and sipped from a glass of water.

"It may be that Vladimir knows of Icarus, of course. He may even run him or her. That's possible. But Icarus may also not be his source. He—or she—may be a source and an operation that's being run out of their embassy in Washington." He looked around the table. "As you know, relations between the Russian embassy in D.C. and the KGB in America have always been competitive, to say the least. If their embassy is running Icarus—if Icarus is an embassy source—it's quite possible Vladimir will have no knowledge of him. But Mikhail will have the access to such information. Of that I'm certain."

Burt paused again, but this time to allow questions, without actually inviting any. It was Marcie who spoke.

"If Vladimir runs Icarus," she said, "will he necessarily know who Icarus is?"

"No. Good question. Icarus may be run remotely, at the end of a chain, via another American agent of the Russians. That's the way they've done it in the past. Like us in Russia, when they're operating on enemy territory they know that some sources, in the main those who are closest to high-grade material, won't risk having any direct contact with a Russian intelligence officer. Most likely, in fact, as Icarus is believed to be a very important agent to them, he or she will communicate via another American agent who they've recruited over here in the past, maybe a long way back in the past. That agent would be someone whose only role is just that—to be a go-between for Icarus. High-profile double agents of the Russians in the United States want whatever security they can get. My belief is that Icarus—if not high profile in terms of actual name recognition—is extremely high profile in his or her field."

He looked at Anna now.

"So tomorrow's meeting with Vladimir is strictly personal. A further getting-to-know session. I want you to establish whatever trust can be built between you, based on your past relationship with him. Vladimir is a long game, as I said. It's Mikhail who is the only recipient of our questions about Icarus. I want you to ask Mikhail directly and only Mikhail. Mikhail is our best chance with Icarus. And in everything."

Anna wondered who else inside Cougar, or anywhere else, would know of her meeting with Mikhail. Bob Dupont? The thought crossed her mind that Burt was going right out on a limb with her, taking a huge risk. It seemed to her impossible, but Burt was full of surprises. Maybe she, Burt, and Mikhail were the only people in the world who knew Mikhail's identity. That would be typical of Burt.

Logan fidgeted with a brand-new, highly sharpened pencil from a pile of similar ones in the centre of the table. Lying beside them was another pile of pristine, unused notebooks. Nobody, it seemed, ever made notes in here. They were almost like a discreet decoration that said simply "conference room."

"Icarus," Logan said. "What's the need-to-know situation with Icarus, Burt? Who's in the select club apart from us?"

"Icarus goes nowhere outside of this room. Icarus is to be as tightly guarded as Mikhail."

With the meeting apparently over, Anna and Marcie decided to walk outside. Logan and Burt started making toasted sandwiches from the contents of a fully stocked fridge. Burt seemed to have at his constant disposal not just the portfolio of Cougar properties but a kind of parallel world of fully operational lives that he could dip into whenever he felt like it.

Outside, Marcie and Anna walked silently towards some stables, where the noses of four horses were searching out over the half door. Marcie stroked them all in turn, dutifully being fair, while Anna took a fondness for one with a broad white blaze.

"Who looks after all this stuff?" she said. "And why? Who even uses it?"

"Abundance is an explanation for Burt's life," Marcie said. "They say when he was a young man, among all the other adventures he enjoyed, he spent six months in an ashram in India."

Anna burst out laughing. "Burt in an ashram! Presumably he was the Buddha."

Marcie laughed with her. "I guess. The Buddha Incarnate is not a bad way to describe Burt's opinion of himself. Now he even looks like him. You've seen the way the fat in his face has made his eyes look kind of Eastern?"

They both grinned.

"Anyway, so they say," Marcie went on, "in this ashram the guru offered him peace, wisdom, or abundance. He chose abundance. But I guess he and the guru didn't necessarily have the same idea of what it was. Burt thinks abundance is endless replications of material wealth. Wherever he is in the world, there's always a full fridge, a clean bed, a box of Havanas, and a decent wine cellar."

They walked on beyond the stable block. As usual during these interludes after a meeting, the unspoken rule was that they never talked about anything that had taken place. But when the silence between them had settled into a comfortable mist, Marcie approached the subject Anna knew was on her mind.

"So. Last night, Anna. Who was being led to the slaughter, you or Logan?"

"Neither of us." Anna laughed. "It was just a bit of fun. Forgetfulness."

"As far as you know. Burt wouldn't have let it happen for no reason."

"I'm sure you're right there. Burt will have his reasons."

"It doesn't bother you?"

"I don't think about it, no."

"Are you starting some affair, or what?"

"Oh, Marcie, come on."

"Well, I can't help asking."

"And I can't help not being concerned."

"Just be careful. This isn't some holiday romance. Logan's not exactly a gentleman, let me tell you."

"Logan's nice. But I appreciate it, Marcie, thank you."

"You're smart, Anna. But maybe not so smart in this."

"I'll bear it in mind."

She looked at Marcie's stern face and laughed. "I will," she said. "Don't worry about me."

"Enough's happening to you without getting fucked over by Logan."

"Okay, okay. And now I'm going to phone Little Finn."

She squeezed Marcie's arm and walked slowly back across the garden to the front door.

When she entered the house she heard, above loud reggae music, Burt shouting from the kitchen, "Come and have toasted sandwiches."

She walked into the kitchen and found Burt and Logan laying out a dozen sandwich fillings on the counter.

"Where are the servants?" she said.

"Right here." Burt guffawed. "I'm the chef. This is the sous-chef. What would you like?"

"I'm going to call Little Finn first."

"Go right ahead. Find some quiet room."

She spoke to Little Finn for a few minutes, which was all he could manage. He sounded completely at ease. Is he like me, or like Finn? she wondered. Nothing much seemed to perturb him.

When she came back, Logan was absent, and she accepted a sandwich from Burt with just melted cheese and tomatoes. She wanted to ask Burt a question that had come to her in the meeting, but it was the unwritten law with Burt that nothing was discussed outside the formal times for discussion.

"Can I ask you something?" she said.

"Anything," he said expansively.

"Is Icarus known outside your company? And to the British, of course?"

"You mean, does the CIA know?"

"I guess so, yes."

"That's a very personal question," he said.

"Then don't answer it."

Burt laughed. "I'll tell you. And just you," he said. "The answer's no. Not yet. They know only about a possible Russian agent, that's it."

"A national security risk, and you haven't told the government?"

"Not yet, as I say. But I will. It's all about the revolving door. If I tell the agency before I've got it sewn up, the chances are that someone outside the agency will hear about it."

"A competitor?"

"That's it." He turned to face her fully. "Yes, it's a risk. I have a deal with Adrian. When that's played out, then I'll let the government in. By that time Cougar will be indispensable." He rubbed his thumb against his forefinger and grinned at her. "More money," he said, but she knew he was joking, at least in part.

"Does the deal with Adrian involve Mikhail?"

"Yes."

She thought for a moment.

"Why are you so free in telling me that?"

"So you have something to give Vladimir," he said.

She was silent, wrong-footed by Burt.

"Is all this just the thrill of risk for you, Burt?" she said at last.

"Isn't it for all of us?" he said. "Why else would we do it?"

27

ON THE FOLLOWING MORNING, the helicopter took all four of them back into the city. Anna was dropped at the airport to make her own way to the gym for her meeting with Vladimir, and it was arranged that she would return to the apartment as soon as she was finished.

The last thing Burt said to her was, "You're unprotected. I know you're close to him, or were, but be careful of what you eat, drink, and touch. I want you alive this afternoon."

It was a warning that revived her memory of Finn's last night.

She took a cab and felt once more the sense of freedom from oversight, a freedom that she expected to win in its fullness soon now. Whatever was to happen, her usefulness would be over in the unwinding of Vladimir and the cooperation, or not, of Mikhail. She felt that all outcomes were for her the beginning of a new life.

She entered the gym at just after midday. She did a workout and then showered and had an hour of massage. Then she dressed and found the exit at the rear of the club. It was nearly three o'clock.

She turned left out onto the street and walked the few yards to the café.

When she entered, she saw Vladimir hadn't yet arrived. She took a table at the far end, looking out, where she could survey the scenes in the street and memorise the faces of anyone who didn't just pass along. But she was confident that, at this stage, Vladimir would not have alerted the KGB bureau. He would want to meet her alone, at least one more time.

He entered the café eight minutes after she'd sat down and made his way to her table without looking to the right or left. He was wearing the same coat, no hat this time, his thick head of black hair seemingly always set in a neat mop. She looked at his hands as he took off the coat and, to her alarm, remembered them on her body five years before.

"You came," he said.

"Of course."

"Are you hungry, or shall I order coffees?"

"I'm going to eat. I'm starving," she said.

"Then I'll join you."

She ordered an omelette and a coffee, and he pasta, the same as he'd eaten when they'd met before.

"Are you living on pasta, Vladimir?" she asked.

"On my salary? Yes."

"Why aren't you making money on the side, like all the other officers in our new democratic Russia?"

He didn't answer. She knew that Vladimir was probably one of the best officers they had, if for no other reason than he was entirely immune from corruption. But he would only be suspected for that, of course, in the paranoia of the upside-down world of Russian intelligence.

Neither of them spoke for a minute, as if each knew that what was said next would throw them over an edge from which there was no return. It was Anna who finally broke the silence.

"So have you checked me out?" she said.

"Yes," he replied.

"And what have you found?"

"More or less what I expected." He wasn't going to reveal what he knew about her apparent status with the Americans. That would only be information that was potentially useful to them.

"But you came anyway," she said. "So what you believe to be true isn't an obstacle."

"Not yet."

The coffees arrived, and he heaped spoons of sugar into his.

"You know how they blew Litvinenko's murder," he said casually.

"What do you mean, 'they,' Vladimir? Aren't you part of them? Besides, they didn't blow it—he's dead, isn't he?"

It was a little over two years since the KGB had murdered one of their own former officers in London by slipping the poison polonium-210 into his tea at a sushi restaurant in Piccadilly.

"And is it 'they' who murdered Finn, too?" she said. "Are you part of them or not?"

"I am, and I'm not, Anna." He sighed. "You remember what that's like?"

"Yes," she said quietly. "Yes, I guess I do. But I remember what I said to you back in 2000, out in Yasenevo, when I hadn't seen you for nearly ten years. 'Aren't you better than this?' But you're still there, hanging in with the thieves who stole our country and doing their dirty work."

"And you?" he countered. "Whose dirty work are you doing?"

"Everything I do, I do for my eventual freedom," she said. "You want to know what I'm doing here today? I'm here to persuade you, Vladimir. But aside from that, I would like it if you too did what you needed to do for your own freedom. Finn never quite made it. He was sidetracked by one more loose end he wanted to tie up. And they—or is it you, too?—got him. Can you do that? Can you act entirely for yourself?"

He didn't reply. But she was satisfied she had made her initial move.

"The reason they blew Litvinenko's murder," he said, deliberately avoiding answering her, "is that they didn't want it to be known, and it was. They didn't want it to be traced back to Russia, back to the KGB and the Forest. There was a lot of talk at the time that they'd done it as an act that blatantly showed the ruthlessness of their power and their willingness to use it. That's not the case. When they slipped the polonium into his tea that afternoon, he didn't drink from it immediately. In fact he didn't drink for so long that the tea went cold. When he finally picked it up and sipped it, that was all he did. He didn't want cold tea. That sip was enough to kill him, but not for days. And in that time the British were able to trace the polonium in his body and build their case. A fairly watertight case, I admit. But if he'd drunk the whole cup, he'd have been dead that afternoon, and the British would never have found the poison in the autopsy. It's extremely difficult to trace unless you've got a dying man to examine for days on end."

"And what's the purpose of this macabre story as I sit here drinking coffee with you? Wait for it to get cold and then don't drink it?"

"It's about whether you and I, Anna, can deal with each other on the personal or only the political and intelligence level. It's about whether any trust can exist between us as who we are to each other, not who we are as far as my people—once your people, remember—and the Americans are concerned. Can we eliminate all considerations outside each other?"

"Then it's the almost same as what I was saying," she replied. "Are we ultimately working for ourselves, or are we working for others? I've told you what I'm doing. Everything, including making an invitation to you on their behalf, is for my benefit. That's my endgame, not entrapping you or any other Russian spy. The fact that I believe your freedom can't lie in Russia—not with your background—and it might lie here is incidental to my own interests. By coming here, I'm fulfilling a task that will result, someday, in my freedom from it all."

"So you believe."

"With the cards that I have, yes."

"So you're here to make me an offer?"

"Yes. But as I say, whether you accept it, or even consider it, is not important to me. I'll have done what I was asked to do, discharged my responsibilities to them. If you refuse, I'm a stone. They can't extract water from me. At some point my usefulness to them will be at an end."

"I hope you're right," he said. "Really, Anna, I do. You know, I care for you as much as I ever did."

"You'll always be my true friend. That's what I believe."

"And more than that?"

"I can't see the future. But if you accept this invitation, don't do it for anything other than your own welfare. Then you won't be disappointed."

He smiled and went to put his hand on hers, but withdrew it before they touched.

"One thing I've always loved about you is that you're impossible to disbelieve. You never gave me any hope. I love you for that."

"I never found that hope gave me very much, other than anxiety and disappointment."

"That sounds cynical."

"It isn't. It's what makes me free."

"I'll think about that."

She leaned across the table and looked him in the eyes. She did put her hand on his, where he'd been too afraid to do so.

"Finn died because he didn't act in his own interests. He thought he could put something right. He was guilty about a boy who'd been killed, again by your people, in Luxembourg. He blamed himself. It was one of his contacts who had given the KGB the information that was the boy's death warrant. Finn wanted to absolve himself of this guilt. He couldn't be selfish—in the best sense of the word. He wanted to change the things and people outside himself. That's what doomed him. He never asked himself the question, 'Is this guilt in my best interest?' He went instead to look for absolution, and they killed him."

She left the palm of her hand flattened against the back of his.

"You really think you can be free, darling Anna?"

"I can only act freely."

"And that's what you're doing now—with this invitation."

"Yes. Do whatever's right for you, Vladimir, and you'll always be my true friend. You can come over to the Americans or stay where you are, it's the same to me."

He glanced sideways at the plates the waitress had left some time before, and Anna withdrew her hand.

"The food's cold," he said, and they both laughed.

He called the waitress and asked her for two more meals, the same again.

"Is your son like you?" he asked suddenly.

"You know," she replied, "I can't work it out. Sometimes he seems more like Finn. But he's only two years old."

The omelette and the pasta arrived, and this time they ate immediately. The conversation had lifted the heavy weight of expectation from them both, and had restored their appetite.

When they'd finished, and Vladimir had ordered more coffee, he looked at her, and she saw concern in his face.

"How much do you know about how you were found in France?" he said.

"Why?"

"Haven't you ever thought about it?" he said, and she saw he was deliberately not answering her question.

"Yes. But I've had no real information. Anyway, the outcome was the best it could have been in the circumstances."

"Tell me what happened."

"Moscow found us. My son was kidnapped. They nearly had me back there. I'd have had to go back. I knew that, of course."

"For your son's sake."

"Yes."

"Even though it wouldn't have been in your best interests. You'd have been shot."

"Touché," she said smiling. "But then the Americans arrived just in time and got my son away from them."

"The cavalry riding to the rescue," he said, and smiled thinly.

She didn't see the point he was making.

"And that information, of course, comes from your American saviours," he continued.

"Yes. They were watching me at the same time. They saw what happened. They intercepted my son before he could be taken out of France. And then they found me."

"Heroes."

"What are you getting at? Trying to undermine my relationship with them? Come on, Vladimir, things were going nicely."

"I'm trying to help you."

She saw the depth of his concern for her this time, and she laid down her objections.

"What have you got to say?"

"When I was checking you out in the past week," he said, "I spoke to an old contact. In Geneva. I was asking him about the last sighting of you in Europe. He told me this story. Our resident in Montenegro received a communication from a man he'd known in the Balkans in the nineties. As a result, our resident came into possession of photographs of you, taken last summer in France."

"So that's how they found me."

"That's how they would have found you . . . if they had."

"What do you mean?" Suddenly she was alert only to what he was saying.

"Our resident paid half a million dollars for the location that would fit the pictures of you. Your address in a village in the south of France, yes? Of course, he received all the necessary permissions to pay the money, from the highest in the land, so they say. He wanted to cover his back with such a large sum involved, and with you being the object of their obsessive vindictiveness in Moscow. But when they turned up, you'd gone, you and your son. There was nothing but a dead trail. Needless to say, our Montenegro resident was dragged over the flames in Moscow for losing the money and losing you. It's probably set back his career twenty years. But you know what they're like, of course. They'd have taken the credit at the Forest if they'd got you, but failure is always someone else's."

She looked into his eyes. What she was looking for was some sign of triumph, something that told her he was feeding her doubt and disinformation. But what she saw was the same concern, the same Vladimir who had never done anything to her before that wasn't in her best interests.

She was silent. Neither believing nor disbelieving. He filled in the answers to some of her questions before she could ask them.

"I didn't take it at face value," he said. "You know how it is. It was second-, even thirdhand, source information, and maybe even it was planted for some reason of their own. But the more I've thought about it, the more I sense there's at least some truth in it. There are material facts that can be established, for example; the fate of the Montenegro resident, for one. It was checkable, at least in part. So I've come to believe there is some truth in it, in any case."

"Have you checked it out?" she said.

"I haven't had the time."

"Half a million dollars."

"Yes. Hard currency, same as always."

"They really want me that badly."

"Worse. It's small change to them."

He looked away for a moment, as if afraid they were being observed. But the café was a third full, with nobody who attracted his interest in particular. Then he looked back at her.

"So I asked who had offered the photographs in the first place; who had profited, with no merchandise in exchange," Vladimir said. "It was an American who had worked for the CIA in the Balkans in the nineties—which was how he knew our Montenegro resident. He seems to have been acting independently, judging from how he made his approach. His name's Logan Halloran."

28

ANNA'S SENSES FELL AWAY. She heard nothing of the buzz in the café. She gazed sightlessly at her hands, now clasped tightly on the plastic table in front of her. She felt nothing in their touch. It was only the smell of fried food that slowly brought her back to some approximation of full consciousness and then reassembled her other senses. She was shattered, and what emerged from the wreckage first was cold analysis. Anger, perhaps rage, was a luxury that might return later.

"Is that all?" she said without looking up.

"It's all I know."

She looked up and saw him staring intensely at her.

"I need your help, Vladimir."

"What do you need?"

"Money."

"I have around five hundred dollars with me."

He reached for the inside pocket of his jacket and withdrew a worn leather wallet. She recognised it from the days in Moscow that now seemed permanently unreal to her, and from the bookshop. He withdrew all the notes and carefully pushed them into her hands, shielding the movement from anyone not at the table.

"That's all I have. What else do you need? A place?"

"I do. But not from you. It's something else I'll have to think about."

"I understand."

"I want you to do one thing. I'm leaving out of the back of the café."

"Are there watchers?"

"A team of five, as far as I know. They're probably all out at the front. I want you to stay for fifteen minutes after I've gone, then leave exactly as you would have done."

"Okay."

"We need a place of contact."

"There's a café on Ninth and Broadway," he said at once. "The Ganymede. It has a library. On the third shelf from the top there's a copy of Daniel Defoe's *Robinson Crusoe*. Page two sixty-seven."

She registered the information, and her mind immediately translated it into the Rule of Three, the Rule of Eleven.

"That's it, then." She smiled at him. "And you can let me know too if you accept the invitation. Who knows, it may be more important than I thought."

He didn't smile back. "Be careful, Anna."

She pushed her hat into a bag and got up from her seat. She left her coat on the back of the seat and walked into the interior of the café, towards the kitchen and bathrooms.

There was a small kitchen with three or four chefs and washers, where grease hung on the walls like translucent skin. Someone eventually noticed her, a small Chinese man in a stained white chef's coat.

"Bathroom there," he barked at her.

She didn't move but leaned on and simultaneously held the doorjamb as if she were feeling unwell.

"Bathroom there!" the Chinese man snapped again.

An older white man looked round from a skillet on the stove.

"What's up?" he said.

"I'm feeling unwell," she said. "Is there somewhere I could lie down for a few minutes?"

He wasn't going to refuse her.

"Take her to the back room," he said to the Chinese. "I'll look in later."

"Thank you."

"You okay?"

"I'm all right. Just a bit faint."

The Chinese man led her through to a room at the rear of the café, with a bare cement floor, a desk and chair, and a couple of old, stained armchairs.

"Here," he said.

"Thank you," she replied, but he had gone.

She quickly took in a metal door that led to the outside. She opened it and stepped out into a tiny concrete courtyard, covered with snow that had iced over on the surface. She surveyed the mildewed walls and saw a fire escape that led down from a building abutting the rear of the yard. But for her it led upwards.

She waited. Finally, the older chef opened the door, looking for her when he hadn't found her in the room.

"I just need some air, I think. I'll only be a few minutes. Please."

He looked at her and seemed easily to overcome his suspicion. "Mind how you go," he said. "I gotta get back."

He shut the door behind him, and she waited a couple more minutes until she knew he'd gone. Then she climbed the iron fire escape, which zigzagged several floors until, on the third floor, she saw an open-plan office that had maps of the world on the walls—maybe some kind of trading company, she thought.

There was no one sitting at the nearest desk, which had a view of the fire escape door. Outside the door, cigarette butts were scattered in the snow. It was a door in use. She opened it, stepped inside, and walked briskly into the centre of the room. A secretary looked up abruptly.

"I thought I'd left my coat," Anna said, "but it isn't here."

It wasn't much of a reason, but saying it got her past the secretary, and she sailed through to a far door that led onto a corridor with an elevator and stairs that ran beside it. She took the stairs. In a few minutes she found herself in a dead-end street, with the noise of traffic on Broadway at the far end. She guessed it was a block, maybe more, from the entrance to the gym she had entered earlier.

She looked left, down towards the entrance. Burt would have someone outside the gym, no doubt. The crowd on the sidewalk was sparse in the icy weather as she turned out onto Broadway and away from the gym to the right. She began to walk steadily, without a coat but with her hat now pulled over her ears.

Larry watched from the inside of a clothing store directly across the street from the café. His point men were, variously, in one of Burt's yellow cabs, another stamping his feet and blowing on his hands at a bus stop, a third on the other side of the café just inside the doorway of a stationery shop and apparently making a phone call.

There were two others out there at a greater distance, who he couldn't see from this angle.

He looked back at the café and watched as Vladimir exited, hands thrust deep in the pockets of a herringbone coat, just as he'd arrived nearly an hour before.

"We're almost through," he breathed into a mike on his coat. "Solomon is leaving," he explained, using the code name for Vladimir.

She's decided to let him leave first, he thought, and after trying to find any significance attached to that, dismissed it as one of those unnecessary complexities that plague an operative and fog an otherwise transparent situation.

He put his weight on the other foot and waited.

After nearly ten minutes he began to be agitated and radioed to the point man at the bus stop to get himself inside the café.

There was another wait.

Finally the words came through. "She must be in the bathroom," the point man said. "Her coat's here."

But it was the words "must be" that alerted Larry's senses to a complexity that, this time, might be worth taking notice of.

"I'm coming over."

He entered the café, saw the coat, and immediately sensed something missing other than her.

"Where's her hat?" he said.

"Her hat?"

"Yes, where's her fucking hat?" He checked the pockets of her coat and found nothing. Without waiting for an answer, he pushed his way past and into the corridor towards the kitchen and bathrooms. He found the ladies' bathroom and roughly pushed open the door, to find it empty. He immediately radioed the operative outside the gym.

"Get up north on Broadway. Fast. She'll be on the sidewalk. No coat, just a hat and whatever she was wearing underneath." He realised he couldn't remember.

He then radioed the man in the taxi, ordered him to get out four streets up and come back down Broadway in the other direction, and gave the same description.

Larry went past the bathrooms, opened a door into a back room, and saw the metal door on the far side. He yanked it open and saw footsteps in the crystalline snow, leading to a fire escape.

He ignored the man who seemed to be asking what the hell he thought he was doing and ran across the yard and up the stairs two at a time until he found where the steps entered an office.

29

BURT SAT AT A desk in one of the anterooms at the apartment. He was mystified and—for the first time—troubled now by Anna's behaviour. There seemed no reason for her disappearance. He'd given her everything she asked for.

He was surrounded by activity, but deep in thought. Electronic surveillance monitors were up and running within half an hour of her disappearance. Young men in T-shirts and with headphones over long, unkempt, and in some cases dirty hair pored over data that crept in multicoloured lines, like cracks in a rock, across half a dozen screens.

Burt himself was a river of apparent calm among the choppiness of his many tributaries. He sat puffing on a cigar that choked up his immediate surroundings, and if anyone objected, you couldn't tell. Working for Burt Miller was an honour his employees equated with working for one of the more public legends of the American dream. He didn't demand anything from these men and women except an almost holy dedication, but for them, it was also a secret pleasure to belong to Burt.

"Anything?" he barked across the room in a voice that travelled right through the apartment.

"We think we have her cell phone," a voice came from the room next door.

Burt hauled himself out of the chair and walked next door, cigar clamped between his teeth and his jacket swinging as if he had a cosh in the pocket.

"Where?" Burt demanded.

The young man in green combat pants and yellow T-shirt with "Animal Lighthouse" written on it replied without taking his eyes away from the screen, even though the information was coming through headphones.

"It seems she dropped it down a drain when she came out on Broadway," he said.

Good girl, Burt thought, and damned her gently in the same thought.

"Do you want it retrieved? is the message, sir."

"Not now. It won't tell us anything. I want everyone on standby, on every block from Ninth down," Burt said.

Bob Dupont came up behind Burt.

"Have we got more resources?" Burt asked him.

"We'll have over two hundred men on the streets before night-fall," he said. "And then more as the night goes on."

Burt didn't answer.

"Why this area, Burt?" Dupont said.

"She'll have to stay somewhere," Burt replied. "Even though she's Russian, she doesn't seem the type who sleeps on the streets. Any-where north of here, there'll be nowhere that'll take anything but a credit card. We have to narrow it down to the ethnic districts, the places where being American doesn't mean much more than wearing a baseball cap and flak pants. And where they'll take her cash, no ques-tions asked, unless they think they can earn more by turning her in."

"It's a long shot."

"Of course it's a long shot, Bob. But they're always the big prize bets." Burt grinned at his security chief, who, not for the first time, found his boss's eternal enthusiasm and optimism something he would never understand.

"You think she'll meet Mikhail?" This time Dupont whispered in Burt's ear.

As he had done several times that afternoon, Burt erupted with laughter, but he didn't say it was because a whisper in a room full of detection devices, albeit aimed out there, was what amused him.

"She will," he said loudly.

"Why?"

"Because she needs me as much as I need her."

"The kid," Dupont said in agreement.

"If you wish to be so indelicate," Burt replied.

At just after five thirty that afternoon, when darkness had descended over the city—"She'll wait for the darkness," Burt had prophesied—a call was picked up from a monitor in one of the smaller rooms. A twenty-two-year-old female graduate from Columbia, wearing an impossibly short skirt, called it through. It was relayed at once to the ops room.

But before Burt answered, he walked the corridor, exhorting his troops to work like they'd never even dreamed of working.

"Find the location, children," he said. "Think 'bonus,' the size of which is beyond your wildest dreams."

When he returned to the ops room, she'd been on the line for nearly a minute. Burt took a pair of phones. A coin box, Burt thought, not three miles from here I'll bet.

"I'll do the talking," she said.

"Sure," Burt answered.

"We've a minute less thanks to your delay. I know about Logan and the photographs. I know of your deception in France. I know the Russians never had my boy. So from here we have a shared aim. I'll follow through with Mikhail tomorrow, and then we make a deal."

One of the kids from the corridor room ran in with a slip of paper, which was a zeroed map with a large "X." Burt thrust it at Dupont, who ran from the room, all sixty-three years of him rejuvenated into a silver-haired sophomore athlete.

Burt remained silent.

"The deal is that whatever Mikhail says goes to the CIA," she said. "Immediately."

"Mistake," Burt said, but she had already gone.

"Coin box on Ninth, right next to the subway," Dupont breathed. "They all have it. All of them out there."

"Jesus," Burt said. "She's stayed right on top of her exit point, just as we fanned away from it."

They identified the subway station. Burt looked at the single line that ran north to south.

"That's where she'll head," he said. "Somewhere down that line." His finger followed the subway line downtown. "She's going there. She's picked a route with only a north and south, one line. No exit route to Brooklyn, just Manhattan. I guess she doesn't know the New York subway."

"We don't know that," Dupont said. "Maybe she's been studying it for months."

"I don't think so, Bob. She's improvising."

"That's the worst," Dupont replied.

Then everyone in the room fell silent at Burt's raised arm command, and in everyone's mind, there was a picture of teams descending towards the Ninth Street subway from all directions.

They waited. Dupont had left the room. He was setting teams at the stations to the south and north, three to the north and every single one to the south, as Burt had ordered.

Eleven men on foot and three cars arrived at the subway almost simultaneously. They began to fan down the blocks in four directions. Others arrived and hurled themselves down the stairs under the street. She'd picked the commuter hour, and the platforms were five deep.

Larry was the sole figure who entered the phone box. He didn't expect to find anything and was surprised to see, among the cards and phone numbers of hookers, a new one written in bold handwriting that just said, "Logan, watch your back. That is where I'll be."

Larry grinned, for the first time in days. He flipped the card into the pocket of his coat; a souvenir of her for now, and one he would take great pleasure in delivering to Logan personally.

Anna stepped into the waiting cab. She knew she had a minute or so, maybe less. She told the driver to take her east, and then after several blocks to chase uptown along Park, all the way to midtown and beyond, until they reached the Carlyle Hotel.

They would look for her back there, at the downtown end of Manhattan, in the poor areas near where she'd telephoned. She could have easily found a place for the night back there, and she trusted they'd fall for that.

A doorman opened the back door of the cab, and she stepped out, giving him a tip the way she'd seen Logan do at the apartment two nights before when they were met by the porter. She walked up to the main door and tipped the uniformed flunkey, who smiled and spoke a welcome.

Once inside, she made her way across the lobby to the bathrooms, where she spent twenty minutes ironing out the afternoon's activities from her dishevelled appearance. Then she walked across the marble lobby to the long bar, looking at nobody, until she reached a suitable table, as she saw it, where she took a seat and ordered a glass of champagne.

The bar was more than half full at this hour, and it was a large area. She looked around, without stopping on any of the faces.

Don't look at any of them, she thought. Wait for the one that comes to you.

By six thirty she had turned down two offers and had then been invited to join a table of three businessmen away from the bar.

She was, she told them, a beautician from Paris, on her first visit to New York, who had always wanted to see the Carlyle. Two of the men insisted they all have dinner, and she declined. She wanted just a quiet evening. She had an early start next day.

But when the pecking order of her preference from among the three of them had been silently and subtly established, the other two left and the lucky winner, unable to believe his good fortune, suggested they dine alone. After a lengthy preamble, he finally suggested his room, a dinner for two, another bottle of whatever she wanted. Russian men would have taken half the time to get there, she thought.

"Are you married?" she said, having already seen the ring.

"Does it matter?" the man said.

"I don't want this unless you're attached," she said. "I'm not the committed type."

Ten minutes later she was in his room, with his key, while he picked up another from the concierge.

Ten minutes after that, he was lying on the floor, bound and gagged with the cord that tied back the drapes. She just had time to drag him into the bathroom and switch on the shower when the dinner he'd ordered downstairs arrived.

She ate from both plates, drank a bottle of water, and had the trays removed before dragging him back into the room. She checked his breathing, put a pillow under his head, and told him that if he moved from the floor in the night she'd kill him.

Then she slept for nine hours.

30

THE SUN CAUGHT THE half-sunken pier on Seventieth Street, and the flat dawn light whited out the glass of the high-rises across the Hudson River.

Water dripped with a steady, pulsating monotony from the concrete pillars that supported the highway above her, and she jogged slowly in the damp, pillared arcade, observing with a steady eye the other, infrequent figures along the path: a couple of vagrants, another jogger, a man taking pictures in the dawn light who at first alerted her suspicions but was clearly on some project that didn't include her. She knew she was alone, as much as it was possible to know.

The river walk to her right was punctuated with steel benches, four seats to a bench, and a few ferries and harbour vessels plied the river beyond.

She wore jogging pants and shoes and a hat and earmuffs she'd bought the day before with Vladimir's money—less than a hundred dollars from a closeout sale on the Bowery for the whole ensemble— and, having jogged for a mile now, she was warm enough in the frozen morning that was breaking over New York City.

She was where she needed to be—and where no one else but Mikhail would find her. But she would jog for another half mile and then return to the fourth bench beyond the pier, which she'd passed a few minutes earlier. That way she could see the signs of anything untoward.

On the way back, vigilant to both changes and similarities in the faces and behaviour of the few people she observed, she was satisfied that she could make her approach. The fourth bench was just visible about a hundred yards away. She could see nobody anywhere near it. She checked her watch. It was time.

She jogged up to the bench and continued to jog on the spot, as she took a water bottle from her belt and drank. She then sat on the second seat from the left for a minute or so. The metal seat was icy through her jogging pants. After a few minutes had passed, she got up and moved to the seat on the far right. That was the signal.

She began to wait, looking out across the river, her back to the highway and the arcade beneath it. The steam of her breath puffed in clouds around her in the still-freezing air. Before her body temperature dropped, she took a fleece jacket that had hung around her waist and put it on.

After just over four and a half minutes, a man sat down on the seat at the far end. She saw him only in her peripheral vision, caught sight of a man's coat, a man's hands emerging from the pockets and being placed on his knees.

"It's not a morning for sitting still," he said. She recognised the voice.

"I have to keep walking," she replied.

The exchange was as arranged. She immediately got up from the seat and half walked, half jogged away from the view of the river and back into the concrete pillared arcade. Once there, she turned left and walked at a steady pace.

There was the small workman's hut Mikhail had told her about in his message. It was built of composite wood and ply, and the padlock on the door dangled open. He must have already been there before he sat down on the bench. He'd said the hut was unused at present, but if not, there was another fallback position farther along the river walk.

She slipped the padlock out of the catch and went inside. It was hardly less cold inside the hut, but she knew he was right. Nobody would stand around chatting outside at dawn on a January morning at the Seventieth Street pier, not without attracting attention.

She sat on an upturned bucket and looked at the tools that hung on the walls, a jacket with fluorescent yellow shoulders, and a couple of orange plastic helmets. He joined her a moment later.

He wasted no time. "What is it you want, Anna?"

It was two years since they'd met, for the only time, and then they'd been delivering Finn's corpse to the British embassy.

"The Americans want to know about Icarus," she said. "A British source in Russia has given them information that there's an agent code-named Icarus in a leading U.S. defence establishment and passing secrets to Russia. They don't know if Icarus is an individual, or if it's a collective code name for more than one individual. They're giving it the highest priority. That's all I know."

He didn't reply at once.

She looked at him. Now he'd removed his hat, she saw that he had aged since the only other time they'd met. She remembered the thick black hair, and saw now that it was greying and thinned.

"That's it?" he said.

"They want you reactivated, as they call it."

He grunted. "You and me? Like with Finn? Is that what they think?"

"I know that's the most you'd consider," she answered him. "I told them that."

"You're right. But do you really think they'd trust you to be the sole intermediary? The Americans are great meddlers."

"Mikhail, I don't know." She looked at him directly. "The only promise I made either to them or myself was to ask you."

"My position is precarious. Even more precarious than it was when Finn and I worked together. I may be close to Putin, but these days such familiarity is a cause more for suspicion than for innocence. Putin is become like all dictators or men of power. Those closest to him are the most watched, the most fragile. The certain is what's most uncertain, the close most distant, the friend the most likely enemy. They will not rest until they find Mikhail."

"What shall I tell them?"

He didn't answer her directly, but put his hand on hers.

"You too are on moving ground. I see it behind your face, Anna. What is your fragility?"

"They have my son. Finn's son."

"A hostage?"

"No. Not explicitly. But perhaps I can buy his freedom at least."

"I see."

They sat in silence. Then he broke the silence.

"What is he like?" Mikhail said.

"I think you would see Finn in him."

"Ah, Finn. He was a beautiful man."

"Yes," she said. "He was."

He looked at her, but didn't touch her this time.

"As you know, Anna, you are the only person in the world who knows my identity."

She nearly choked as she spoke. "There's another now. An American. Burt Miller."

He looked at her sharply, but she saw no hostility or even alarm in his eyes.

"The head of Cougar."

"Yes."

"They must have great pressure exerted on you for you to have told him that," he said. "Is it just him? Him alone?"

"I believe that."

"I see," he said again. "The knot tightens."

"He's acting outside the CIA, according to him. Just his own intelligence company. He wants Cougar to have you, and Cougar alone."

"Very wise of him. I don't want the CIA."

She was surprised. He was echoing Burt's own position.

"I believe Miller has at least a chance of controlling a source," Mikhail said. "But for how long?"

"I told him the deal, as far as I was concerned, was that all information should go to the CIA from now on."

"Not a good idea. Including my name?"

"No. Excluding that."

"What makes you think the CIA will go along with that? The failure in the Iraq War was due to secondary sources. That's where the false information came from. Secondary sources of the British and Americans who had been reliable up to that point, but were wrong in their assessment of Iraq's capabilities. The current directive at MI6 and, I believe, also at the CIA is that no more decisive information will be accepted from secondary sources." He looked at her. "In this, you would be the secondary source, as far they're concerned. They'll want direct access to me."

She didn't answer.

"So no CIA," he said.

"They'll try to blackmail you if you don't agree to work with them," she said. "If they ever find your identity."

"Maybe Burt Miller too. They will threaten *kompromat* against me, threaten to reveal my identity to the Kremlin. Of course they will have their threats. But I'm sure I will also convince the Kremlin that it is so much black propaganda, an attempt to sow seeds of suspicion on the Russian side. Their threats will not have any solidity. In the world of paranoia, paranoia itself can be your friend as well as your enemy."

He sighed.

"One day I would like to see your son, Anna," he said.

"I hope so," she replied.

"So." He clapped his hands on his knees and stood up from the pile of tarpaulins he'd been sitting on. He dusted the back of his coat with his hands.

"I'll look for Icarus," he said. "We'll see how we do. The future will take care of itself." He withdrew a piece of paper from the pocket of his coat, wrote something down, and gave it to her.

"Our next meeting," he said.

They kissed each other on the cheeks in the Russian way. She was taken aback.

"Unlike me, you are ageing quite well." He smiled at her. Then he held out an arm towards the door. "Until the next time," he said.

She looked through two small grilles at either end of the hut, and when she was assured there was nobody to see her, she left too. She jogged for a few hundred yards, memorising the details he had given her. Then she screwed the paper into a ball and hurled it into the river.

31

SHE DECIDED TO JOG. She was dressed for it; the hat and earmuffs covered enough of her face to make her sufficiently anonymous, and she guessed they would not be looking for a jogger, even if they should happen to be aware of her passing figure. And it was only fifty blocks.

She set off downtown, keeping under the West Side Highway in the protection of the concrete pillars, then cut back out to run along the river path to check in front and behind her. After ten blocks she cut in towards Eleventh Avenue and, turning right, continued in the same direction towards Chelsea. It took her less than half an hour to reach Twenty-third Street, and she paused at the end of the street and stood in the shadow of a newsstand to take in the block ahead of her to her left.

Then she ran on, pausing a block at a time, until she reached the block where the apartments were.

She checked the phone box and saw it was empty. Wherever they were, she didn't expect there to be a heavy presence right under their own noses.

She entered the box, called the number, and imagined the flurry of activity in the rooms that stretched eight windows along the fourth floor. From the box she could see them on the far side of the street.

A boy took the call. She asked for Burt, and there was another pause so they could again gain time to zero on her location. Finally Burt came on the line.

"Well, good morning," he said. "I hope you slept well."

"I did. Are you going to let me in?"

"Where are you?"

"Looking at your window."

She heard Burt chuckle. "I'll send Larry down. He hasn't had much sleep, I'm afraid, so be nice to him."

She put the phone down and jogged across the street, up past the underground garage, and saw the door open and Larry standing there.

"Hello, Larry."

"Hi, Anna."

"I'm starving."

"You'd better come in, then."

They stepped into the elevator, Larry opening his arm to usher her inside.

On the way up she said, "I'm sorry for the trouble, Larry."

He grinned at her, but she saw exhaustion in his eyes.

"I'll tell you, we turned half of downtown over last night. I saw places I never dreamed existed."

"Is Logan up there?"

Larry grinned again. "I saw your note. What are you planning to do to him?"

"What do you think I should do?"

"I don't know what your gripe is."

"The biggest."

"I'll break the little creep's arms any time you say."

"I'm sure I can manage that myself, thanks, Larry."

"I'm sure you can." He nodded.

Burt was waiting personally for them at the elevator. He took her alone to an empty room at the far end of the corridor, where there was no surveillance equipment, just two chairs. Dupont arrived then with a third chair and shut the door behind him.

"France . . . ," Burt began.

"Never mind that," she replied. "It's the past."

He looked at her with the admiration of someone meeting a true genius for the first time.

"I met with Mikhail," she said.

"Good," Burt answered, back to the present. "What's the score?"

"We have another meeting. He will tell me then about Icarus."

"Good. And Vladimir?"

"Work in progress. He knows what you want. I passed on the message."

"And further contact?"

"Yes," she said. She didn't elaborate, and he didn't press her to.

Burt's phone rang.

"Five minutes," he said, and clicked it off. He looked at her. "Adrian's arrived," he said. "Another jackal in for the kill."

"What does he want?"

"Same as everyone—Mikhail. But we have Mikhail, don't we, Anna? Just us."

"Maybe," she said. "He committed to nothing beyond looking for Icarus."

"Then the door is ajar."

"Maybe," she said again. "But I wouldn't get your hopes up."

Burt laughed, enjoying himself.

"Like I say, expectations are for dummies," he said. "You'll want to take a shower," he said expansively. "Marcie has your clothes. How did you spend the night? Comfortably, I hope."

"Very."

Burt laughed hugely.

"I hope this is the beginning of a long friendship between us," he said.

"Be careful, Burt, that's a hope," she replied. Then: "A shower would be good. I've had a long run. And I'd like to call Little Finn. I didn't manage it yesterday."

"Of course," he said. "You'll be seeing him very soon too."

"And Logan?" she said. "I don't trust myself if I see him."

"I told him it was better he didn't show up this morning," Burt said. "It seems we all have a lot of thinking to do."

She stood up. Nothing else seemed to be immediately required. Burt was completely relaxed. He would want to examine her story later, no doubt, but with Burt it was business as usual, which meant, apparently, watching things unfold as they did so, and things always seemed to unfold to his satisfaction.

"You caused me great distress by kidnapping my son," she said. "In the circumstances, I'll forgive for you that. But I won't forgive Logan."

"I understand," he said.

She left Burt and Dupont in the room and walked down the corridor. Marcie was waiting for her at the far end. She saw Adrian standing by the window of the conference room, looking out onto the street below, but he didn't turn, and she didn't acknowledge him.

She and Marcie went along to the far end of the apartments, where the bedrooms and bathrooms were, and Marcie gave her a towel and an armful of clothes.

"You ran rings around them for twenty-four hours," Marcie said. "Congratulations."

Then they both laughed, and Anna disappeared into the bathroom.

In the room that she had just left, Dupont remained silent.

"We're on a home run, Bob," Burt said. "You seem anxious."

"What's the deal with the British?" Dupont said.

"We share with them."

"Mikhail?"

"Mikhail's information. Once we have Icarus, Mikhail will prove to be a long-running bestseller. Take it from me, Bob, only Anna can achieve that. She's the key to Mikhail, and Mikhail is the key to a very profitable chamber of secrets. Mikhail is going to be the jewel in my crown, Bob—the jewel in our crown. We'll be the biggest game in town for a long time to come. Nobody will ever have made such profits simply by helping their country."

"You trust Adrian?"

"Of course not." Burt chuckled. "But I know he knows he has more chance of making a deal with me than if he blows this open and has to deal with Langley. You think Langley cares what the British want? I can carve a nice exchange with Adrian out of this."

Dupont was silent.

"Cheer up, Bob," Burt said. "It's always been a game of chess. We finesse Langley out of this one, keep them away from Mikhail. There's still work to do, but it's loose ends, just loose ends now."

"You know Logan ate with Adrian last night," Dupont said suddenly.

"You don't say!" Burt replied.

"It's damn cheeky, if you ask me. What are the Brits doing talking to our operatives?"

"It's a free world," Burt said casually. But behind his insouciance, he was wondering, not why Adrian would wish to dine with Logan, but why Logan would want to dine with Adrian.

"Listen, Bob," he said. "The only important thing in this is Mikhail. Only two people in the world know who Mikhail is. Me. And Anna. And if anything happened to me, you're next on the list. That's arranged under lock and key."

"It's need-to-know at a crazy level," Dupont burst out.

"If the CIA know Mikhail, what do you think the security clearance will be? Five . . . six people, maybe more? More than three times the risk, in other words. The fewer the better, you know that's right."

Dupont was silent, but he assented with a small nod of the head.

"Let things ride, Bob, we'll get there in the end," Burt said.

32

WHEN LOGAN RECEIVED BURT'S call at just after nine o'clock that morning, he was about to leave the service apartment. Burt's instructions not to come in afforded him a wave of relief. He would need no excuses now.

How long did this hiatus in Burt's requirements give him? Twenty-four hours if he were lucky. Time enough to get out of the country, in any case, and be well clear by the time the hue and cry began.

He had a plan, ill-formed but becoming clearer through the sleepless hours of the passing night.

When a triumphant Larry had shown him Anna's note the day before, and Burt had explained that she knew, it had almost broken him. What he wanted most of all was to speak with her. But he knew also that it was impossible now. His mind raged with grief, with guilt, and with a desperation to see her and to explain. But he knew it would be useless. And so the plan had formed. It was all that came to him in the night, and its clarity was what he hung on to. In the turmoil of his rage at himself, it was the only thing he could do. It was his road to absolution.

He didn't pack much, even in the small bag he had; he took a very expensive suit, that was all. Otherwise he took roubles that were still part of his emergency pack. Anything else, he could buy where he was going.

He put the thing he would most need in the pocket of his jacket— the spare, unused passport in the false name that would guarantee his anonymity for long enough.

Then he left the functional service apartment with its soulless air of other anonymous people like himself, other empty lives like his own who had passed through.

He walked to Pennsylvania Station and took the train northwards that linked to Toronto. There would be no record of his departure from American soil. From Canada, he could be in Moscow almost before they even knew he'd disappeared.

As he sat on the train that ground its way northwards, he made notes, to be destroyed later certainly, but for now a guide through his mind, befuddled from sleeplessness and despair.

It was the unexpected invitation from Adrian the evening before that had opened the door to his plan. Over dinner at a chic Italian restaurant uptown, Adrian—supremely confident, arrogant in his expectations—had not so gently pumped him for anything that might be useful concerning Burt's operation. Logan had demurred on the issues that were classified, but in the course of the evening Adrian revealed to Logan the name of a man.

He was a man Adrian was after himself, it seemed, and now he was the man Logan would hunt. Adrian had given Logan the man's current occupation—or at least one of his no doubt many occupations.

It never occurred to Logan that Adrian had deliberately given him the name of the man, for his own reasons.

And then, back at his apartment, Logan had obsessively pursued his own enquiries, while New York slept and it was daytime in the East. In Logan's fourth phone call of four, made at just after five o'clock that morning, he had finally located an old source of his, a Russian now residing in Cyprus. This man had filled in the yawning gaps left after Adrian's artfully imprecise description.

Logan's target turned out to be an MP in the Russian parliament, but that was more like an honorary title than an elective post in the modern Russia. That was his reward from the Kremlin, it seemed. In truth he was no politician; he had no history at the barricades of Putinism. He was a small-time nobody, a petty crook from Prazshkaya, south of Moscow. Those, at any rate, were his origins, and they were origins from which he'd never strayed very far.

Through graft and old-fashioned violence he had made his way into more serious, organised crime. He had been inducted into the Ismailovo gang, the Mafia organisation that controlled Moscow south. Bodyguard, hit man, bagman, and finally close lieutenant to the boss, he had been entrusted with the gang's bigger secrets—the drug runs from the southern republics and, beyond them, Afghanistan.

For ten years, when the Ismailovo mob and the KGB fought, made truces, fought again, and finally ended up as partners in crime, he had survived the hits and counter-hits. The KGB under Putin had eventually exerted its control over the Ismailovo, that was true, but it was the control of a monarch over a distant province, controllable only with the acquiescence of his subject.

The Ismailovo had made a deal. It was a black deal of coexistence and mutual profit between a Mafia mob and the country's domestic intelligence service, the FSB.

And all that had taken place with the imprimatur of the man who had mattered most in the previous nine years since 2000, Vladimir Putin, himself former head of the FSB, then president, now an eminence grise waiting in the wings for what everyone believed would be a third, fourth, and who knew, indefinite presidential term.

And of the many deals the KGB and the Ismailovo mob struck in this unholy alliance of organised crime and state intelligence agency, the most common was an exchange of personnel, on a job-by-job basis. KGB officers would guarantee the guarding of shipments of drugs from the south, and in return, the Ismailovo would provide the KGB, when asked, with an assassin for the KGB's own business, in order to keep the intelligence service's own hands notionally clean. And so the square of mob violence fitted the circle of the Russian state's needs.

Such a man was Grigory Byko, an Ismailovo mobster who had purchased a law degree, a killer first for the gang and finally for the state. Bykov, Adrian had told Logan, was Finn's murderer.

On the train northward, Logan surveyed his options. Moscow was the only possibility. Bykov never left Moscow if he could help it. His membership of parliament might protect him and ring-fence his deeds throughout Russia, but he was still, essentially, a small-time city crook at heart. The trip to Paris to end Finn's life had been the only time he'd ever ventured abroad.

Logan had learned from his Cyprus contact that nowadays Bykov owned a chauffeur business with armoured cars and bodyguards that dovetailed exorbitant rides for the rich with favours for his friends in the mob and in the Kremlin. He also owned a stake in a gold mine out east, somewhere in the Yakutsk region, Logan's source had thought. But it was a stake bought with the threat of violence or death, not money.

And, most presciently, Bykov owned a nightclub in the Patriarshiye Ponds, a plush area in downtown Moscow, to which the rich and famous flocked for its fashion and its beautiful whores. The club was called the Venus Apollo.

That was where he would have his best chance, Logan decided, if he had any chance at all. It was either that, or meet his own death—and his absolution lay in either outcome.

In Toronto he withdrew $100,000 in cash from an operational account. Then, on the flight to London and again on the three-hour trip to Kiev, he slept. He needed rest after the night before and before the task that lay ahead.

There was no visa requirement to enter Ukraine, and no fingerprint analysis in either stopover. Logan exulted in his plan. And God bless the Europeans.

He took a short internal flight from Kiev to the small Ukrainian town of Sumy up in the northeast of the country, bordering Russia. It was empty land, with fewer people and police than the border areas farther south, in the Donetsk.

In a cheap clothes shop in a backstreet of Sumy, he bought a set of workman's overalls, boots, and a cap, as well as a fur hat and a thick coat. From Sumy he took a bus in the direction of L'gov on the Russian side, but disembarked a few miles from the border. When night had fallen, around five in the afternoon, he began to walk. With every step he took towards the enemy, he was both a freer and a more marked man.

As he crossed the dark, flat, snow-covered fields, he never thought for a moment whether he would ever retrace these steps. The deed was enough; the deed was the reward. But if he made it back again, then he knew he would be a very lucky man indeed.

Where he walked was bare farmland, bird-watcher's country—and smuggler's country too. The FSB's Russian border checkpoints were strung at longer intervals on this stretch of less important borderland, but the border police, now firmly under the control of the KGB once again, could strike anywhere. What they were looking for was obvious smuggling, however, on a scale that required vehicles. Illegal trade across these borders consisted, in theory, of anything from pork fat to nuclear material. But it was always closer to the former, just petty stuff. The incentives of bribes for the guards along this stretch were not so great.

It was a long and lonely border, and it didn't suffer from the nervousness of Russia's borders with the Islamic republics. The villagers on the Ukrainian side were in many cases Russians like the border guards themselves. In Soviet times, Russia's historic desire for control of Ukraine had resulted in the movement of Russian people west, into Ukrainian lands. Out here, on the eastern borders of Ukraine, it was as much Russian as Ukrainian.

And so the guards were more than content to stay in the warmth of their guardhouses on a freezing winter's night. They didn't need much excuse to remain at their fixed posts, rather than roaming the fields on the bleak chance of arresting some poor Ukrainian villagers engaged in petty smuggling who didn't have any worthwhile bribe money.

Alone, at night, in an icy January fog that descended over the steppe, Logan guessed he stood a good enough chance. He wasn't sure how far on the Russian side the border zone extended; that was his main concern. It varied from stretch to stretch. He might have to walk a few hundred yards or five miles or more once he was through, in order to be clear.

Under the thick fog he never knew the exact moment when he'd crossed the border into Russia. The fields within his impaired vision were flat and ghostly white. There was no visible moon, no features on the landscape.

Once, he thought he saw a light or lights in the distance, but he didn't know if his eyes were playing tricks. But in case it was a checkpoint, he skirted away over the rough, frozen, snow-covered fields.

Whatever there was out there he couldn't see; he knew there was nothing much apart from small, quiet villages, the inhabitants of which had long since retired for the night.

Later he thought he heard the sound of a car, and where the fog had drifted, he made out a copse of skeletal trees to the north of his route. He had no idea of time, or even, in the dark grey fog, of space. In his recklessness he felt immortal.

By the time the sky showed the faintest sign of change from night to day, the fog had begun to thin and he saw the dawn attempt to make an appearance through heavy cloud. By then he knew he was through. And as the dawn came up, a light snow began to fall, which thickened and blanked out the skyline, as well as the footsteps he'd left behind him.

He trudged along the edge of a field behind a high hedge and slowly began to make out the features of the landscape ahead where he could glimpse it through now thicker flakes of tumbling snow. There were a few trees, but it was mainly snow-covered tilled earth, and the new snow was already beginning to cover the frozen crystals of earlier falls.

In the distance, he saw a village, and he felt a soaring belief that nothing could touch him.

As he approached the edge of the village, he saw a farmer spreading seed for some chickens under a low, hay-filled barn. He was still too close to the border, Logan thought. He didn't trust his accent not to sound foreign.

Skirting the farm, he came up into the village by a small church, its plaster walls crumbling beneath a snow-capped bell tower. There was nobody about. He looked at his watch. It was just after eight in the morning.

He walked on for three hours, until he'd passed two more villages, and at the fourth, slightly larger than the others, he entered by a small road that came into a square. He crossed the square, walked two hundred yards to the route out towards the east, and waited for a car.

Within half an hour he'd picked up a lift and negotiated a price to Voronezh. The driver was about his age and wasn't going to Voronezh, but for two hundred roubles he'd take him.

Logan spoke in a thin, rasping voice, barely audible, and told the man he was on the way to hospital for an operation on his throat.

They didn't talk on the road.

Time drifted slowly. They stopped for fuel, and Logan paid. The day never really dawned, but just hung with a mind half made up in a shallow, flat wanness that enfeebled the flat country around them. They made slow progress in the snow until it eased and were in Voronezh by the afternoon.

Logan offered to buy the driver a meal. He was starving, but he also needed one more thing from the man before he left. While they ate in silence, the man drank a few beers. When he went to the toilet at the back of the café, Logan removed the man's wallet from a jacket hung over the back of his chair and slipped out his identity card, pocketing it. He replaced the wallet and, paying for the meal, thanked the man and told him he was going to look for a hotel.

He walked to the railway station by back routes, in the unlikely event the man would check his wallet and come looking for him. When he bought a ticket to Moscow, the ticket collector barely looked at his new card. He waited for an hour before the train pulled in.

In his exhaustion, he was elated. He felt the light-headedness of supreme, unreal optimism. He knew he would succeed.

33

ON THE SECOND DAY of Logan's disappearance, Burt knew what Logan was going to do. Concealed beneath his usual jovial good humour, Anna detected, if not self-criticism, then a sense of sorrow that a protégé was on the course of self-destruction. Burt had tried with his great energy and expansiveness to guide Logan away from rash, impulsive behaviour, but it seemed that even his powers had not been enough.

"Logan is a loser," he pronounced with unusual cruelty and, as usual with Burt, brought his focus to bear on what was possible; Mikhail and, most vitally, Icarus.

Marcie, despite her months of increasing conflict with Logan, was anxious, while Larry's only reaction seemed to be a sense of frustration that it wasn't going to be him who dealt Logan some physical harm.

"It's the last we see of him," he'd said to Anna with a mixture of satisfaction and irritation.

For herself, Anna was surprised at her reaction to Logan's disappearance, and Logan would have been pleased if he'd known. Untroubled by her night of physical intimacy with him, she felt once more a fragile link between Logan and Finn. While Finn would never have sold anyone down the river as Logan had done, let alone a small child, what seemed about to become Logan's final act on this earth had the heroic madness that had characterised Finn's own end.

It was Adrian who, under questioning from Burt, had given Burt the information that led to his conclusion about Logan's aim. When Adrian, recounting their discussion on the night before Logan disappeared, told Burt that he had given Logan the identity of Finn's killer, Burt picked out this element of their conversation alone for analysis.

Adrian was a shit, he thought privately. He'd known just what he was doing when he gave Logan the name. He had found a shattered man and driven a stake right through the defenceless cracks of Logan's mind.

But despite his fury with Adrian, Burt dismissed Logan now, and any further discussion about him. They—everybody—was to get on with the matter in hand, and with no further distractions.

The first task was for Anna to check the dead drop that she had arranged with Vladimir. With his arms opened expansively wide in what looked like an impersonation of a variety club performer, Burt fulsomely agreed that she should leave the apartment alone to make this contact.

The drop was only a few streets away from the apartment, and he wished her to know that in this, she was free. But behind this munificence, and as always with Burt, strategy was everything. His purpose was to reassure her that in the forthcoming meeting with Mikhail—the crucial meeting—she would be equally her own master. Burt wished to set a precedent.

She arrived at the café called Ganymede late one morning when the sun was making a brief appearance through heavy clouds, which looked like they were going to win the day. The café was a student hangout, and she bought a coffee in a queue of sleepy-eyed youths carrying jute shoulder bags and with woolly hats pulled half down over their pale faces. Then she perused the rows of books in stacks by the window at the front, overlooking the street. She found the copy of Defoe, looked at the page they'd agreed, moved eleven pages on, and found a note on the page. On the back was written in pencil, "I like your invitation." Then there was a time and a date. Vladimir's proposal was to meet again, a week from now, and with three days added, that made ten days.

Perhaps he needed time to collect material for his initial offering to the Americans. Or maybe, she thought, it was a period for him to say good-bye to everything he knew.

Leaving the café, she returned to the apartments. There was a general air of jubilation that Vladimir, albeit the second string of their operations, was yielding fruit. Burt was particularly pleased. He seemed to take it as sign that everything else he'd planned was going to fall into place.

Mikhail had insisted that Anna meet him for the second time in Washington, D.C. It was assumed that another trip to New York was too high a risk for him.

Once again, the team was to decamp, to be flown down to another of Burt's safe houses in the capital.

It was two days before the inauguration of Barack Obama, and Mikhail had chosen the day of the inauguration itself for their meeting.

Burt, with Dupont alone now included in the knowledge of the meeting, professed himself to be in two minds about the choice. On the one hand, the million or more people who were expected to arrive at the capital and greet the new era was cover of a kind that might well provide enough confusion for a meeting. On the other side there were hundreds of thousands of law enforcement officers stacked in a ring around the central procession and presidential celebrations.

But he accepted that the meeting was set in stone, and he trusted Mikhail's instincts.

All Anna would say was, "The focus of everyone will be inwards—the law, the FBI, the CIA, everybody."

From this Burt guessed that the meeting would not be in the centre of the city itself, but outside the perimeter of events. Everyone, both literally and metaphorically, would be looking the other way.

The wooden house in the chic Washington neighbourhood of Georgetown was another tour de force in Burt's collection of classic American properties. To Anna, they now seemed almost like a separate project of Burt's, a one-man preservation society of Americana, with state-by-state attention to the detail of local nuances.

"I'm an American." Burt laughed when she displayed her astonishment at the house's beauty and authenticity. "I'm not a Virginian or a Texan or a Californian. I love the whole damn country in all its quirky mess."

On the day before the meeting, just before they all sat down to lunch, Burt took her aside into another study with another fire blazing like a picture in a holiday catalogue. He wanted to run over some details that had occurred to him on the trip down from New York.

He was particularly attentive to her every need, as if she were an athlete before a race.

"I don't like you going in unprotected," he said.

"We've discussed it," she said. "Nobody but me. Mikhail's a fox. Any sign that what he trusts will happen has changed, and he won't make an appearance."

"I know, I know," Burt agreed. "I agree with you."

He seemed unusually nervous. Maybe it was because this was the culmination of all his plans since the end of the previous summer.

"In that case, you personally could be better protected," he said. "What about a weapon?"

"Why? Against what? " she asked surprised.

"I don't know. But we're reaching the apex of the pyramid now, and any trouble will occur around this moment."

Was he being his usual prescient self, she wondered, or was it just nerves?

"If you're going unprotected by my watchers, as we all agree you should, I'd like you to be armed, that's all," he said. "Let me have that, Anna."

He was behaving like a father on his daughter's wedding day, she thought. Giving her away to Mikhail.

"It's not a great day to be armed," she said. "On a presidential inauguration."

"Well, you tell me. Are you going to be anywhere near the main event?" he said. "What are the chances of a routine search?"

"No," she admitted. "I want to be dropped out of the city, away from everything. Around Arlington."

"Across the river?" Burt said. "In Virginia?"

"Yes."

He didn't reply, but she could see his mind trying to follow Mikhail's logic, and that it finally approved.

"So what kind of weapon would you like?" he said.

"Are you sure, Burt? This ups the risks in all kinds of ways."

"Not so much. And I'd be happier. If there's any trouble from regular law enforcement, you'd have clearance after the event."

"Then I'll take a Thompson Contender," she said, believing that this might deter him.

Burt smiled.

"Not the carbine, I trust."

"No. The pistol. I can still shoot a man at two hundred yards."

"Then that's what you'll have. And the rounds?"

"Standard NATO issue. Point two two three. Two dozen."

"Okay."

And there it was, by the end of the day, delivered personally to her by Burt.

At six o'clock the next morning, Burt, Anna, Larry, and two

guards drove the few miles from Georgetown across the Potomac to Arlington Cemetery.

"Kind of a grim place to start the day," was Burt's comment.

It was dark as they left, but the day seemed to be dawning without rain or snow for the new president.

At her direction, they halted the Humvee—another in Burt's stable of outsized American vehicles—about half a mile from the main gates of the cemetery. Burt laid his hand on her arm and told her they would be in the vicinity whenever she called.

He'd insisted she take a cell phone, which she didn't trust, but she acquiesced in the knowledge that she could check it for bugs before she went anywhere near the rendezvous.

Then she began the long walk away from the vehicle, feeling the eyes of all four of them boring into her back, like dogs left behind on a promised walk.

After a few minutes she disappeared around a bend in the road.

She was carrying a small backpack over her shoulders and wore a long coat, boots, and a felt hat. The pistol was wrapped in clothing inside the pack.

When she'd walked for a mile, past the main entrance to the cemetery, she found the kind of place she was looking for. Everything now had to be improvised until she reached the rendezvous.

It was a small, neat mall, which would be closed for the national holiday. She skirted across the front of it and made her way around to the rear, watching for cameras, until she was out of sight from the road.

Behind the mall there was a delivery yard, and behind that, a high wall against theft.

She kept to the outside of the wall, where the dulled winter grey of grass offered a slice of neat wasteland, until she found a niche where the wall doglegged to the left; from here there was no view apart from straight out.

Checking that there was nobody on this piece of ground, she then dismantled the phone, examined it for a positioning device, and, when she was satisfied there was none, reassembled it. As long as she left it switched off, she'd be untraceable.

She then stripped off her coat, trousers, boots, and jacket until she stood in just her jogging clothes. She took jogging shoes from the pack and then unwrapped the gun from a fleece jacket and removed the firing pin for safety. She slung it under her armpit with a sling they'd concocted the night before that gave it an easy draw, and strapped it again around her body. She wore the baggy fleece over the top.

Then she turned the backpack inside out, so that it became the orange colour of the inside, instead of grey. She refilled it with the clothes she'd removed, put it on her back again, and pulled a woollen hat over her head, tucking her hair away completely. When she was satisfied that she was a different person from the one who had stepped out of the car, she checked the ground ahead from the niche in the wall. Content that she was alone, she began to run, away from the rear of the mall, across a small park, and into a residential street that ended in a cul de sac on the far side of the wasteland.

She checked her watch as she ran and saw that it was coming up to seven in the morning. It was about two miles to the rendezvous, she reckoned. She'd be there with plenty of time to spare, but it was necessary to obscure the time of her meeting with Mikhail from Burt and the others as much as possible.

She ran along neat streets in the grey morning and guessed that the people in cars, mostly families, were driving into the capital early to get the best view of the new president and settle in for a long wait. The presidential procession wasn't taking place until after lunch.

And the further she ran away from the great events of the day, the more she appreciated Mikhail's rendezvous. Everyone who wasn't in front of their television sets was heading away from here, in the opposite direction, towards the city.

The Glencarlyn Park was an area of clumps of trees and broad lawns of about a hundred acres. There was a one-storey stone replica building at the north side of the park, which had pillars along the front of it, in some kind of antebellum style. It was the type of folly you might find in the grounds of an English stately home. The gardens, grey and brown in the colourless January light, were laid out in a piece of gentle landscaping that spoke of informality. Couples might stroll here on summer evenings, families sit on the grass and picnic. It was a small, unnoticed place, close enough to the city without having to make an expedition.

She stopped at a wooden sign that spelled out the park's rules, but without really seeing them. Her eyes were alert to the area around her—movements, any figures who appeared, then reappeared. But she saw nobody. Even the joggers were taking it easy this early in the morning on a national holiday.

She ran once around the park, checking on the position of the pillared stone building and leaving it well to the north of her path. Then she exited at the eastern entrance and sat on a bench in the street, seeing the cars that passed without looking at them, noting their number plates and colours and brands.

She held a good two dozen of them in her mind before she got up and walked into a small coffee shop on the far side of the street that had decided to remain open for the day.

After buying a coffee, she picked up a daily paper from a shelf and leafed through it, glancing up from time to time at the television high up in the corner of the wall, where CNN was already beginning its coverage of the day, and already trying to string out information that would be repeated a dozen times. Sipping the coffee, Anna watched the street and checked her watch for the final time.

In the bathroom, she fixed the firing pin of the pistol into its position, checked the ease of draw, and zipped the baggy fleece jacket over it once again. She put the pack back on her shoulders and left the café, deciding to walk now. She saw her breath in the cold air and felt the damp on her skin, but it was going to be a day without rain.

When she entered the park again, she took a circuitous route, approaching the stone building from the rear.

The building where they were to meet was U-shaped, with straight sides that formed an enclosed patio at the rear. There were a few wooden tables concreted into the ground here, just as Mikhail had said. A figure was sitting at the middle table, and she knew it was Mikhail. He wore a long brown coat and a Russian fur hat, and she noticed the smallest detail even at this distance; the mud on the edges of his shoes, the wisp of greyish black hair at the back of his neck, a plaster wrapped around the middle finger of his left hand. It was the plaster that told her for certain it was Mikhail.

She surveyed the route behind her from which she'd come, and swept her gaze around the park. A man was pushing a bike along a path in the distance. She watched him from the corner of her eye. Another man walked his dog a few hundred yards in the other direction. She trusted Mikhail knew his job as well as she knew hers.

Then she walked towards the stone building, indirectly, along a path that bent around solely for aesthetic effect, but which led to the rear of the building. She sat down on a cold wooden bench, attached to the table next to the one where Mikhail sat. They were sheltered on three sides by the U shape of the building.

He didn't look up.

"There's something wrong," he said at last. No agreed greeting, no greeting of any kind.

She was taken aback, uncertain what he meant, speechless.

"With what?" she said finally. She'd expected the formal procedure at least, some preamble.

"There is no such thing as Icarus," he said. "Icarus doesn't exist."

34

LARS POSITIONED THE BEER bottle on the red plastic table with the precision he brought to everything. The TV screen in the bar was showing the early preparations for the day ahead, but that didn't interest him.

He was in Washington, D.C., and was unconcerned with events around the inauguration of the new president, but they still penetrated his consciousness.

The city was full of visitors, but there was one in particular that he—or his controllers, in any case—were interested in.

Two months before this day he'd been training for over three weeks for this one shot. He'd made camp in a lake area of Louisiana, where his controllers assured him he would be alone and uninterrupted. Did they have some kind of control over this huge area of wetland? Did they even own the whole dead place themselves, perhaps? He didn't know, and he didn't ask, but he was beginning to suspect the type of Americans his controllers were.

He picked a suitable lake out of the several hundred in the permitted area and set up the tools of his trade. He would need a lot of practice for such a shot, which lobbed in an arc and still struck its target.

He didn't like the area. Even when it was winter in the north of the country, here it was always hot enough for the mosquitoes to aggravate every waking second of the day down by the lake. At night he slept in a wooden cabin, with screens against the insects, but he still heard sounds. He didn't like this place or its unearthly noises; he didn't understand what was out there. It was unfamiliar country.

But in the first few days he'd set up a solid concrete and metal platform on a small hillock by the lake, on which he bolted the machine gun, a replica for the actual place where the shot would be made.

He'd demanded they provide him with only "green spot" ammunition, from the first five thousand rounds that come off the production line. Green spot was the beginning of the batch. It was all that interested him. It had that feather edge of perfection over other ammunition.

But what he used for practice was ex-NATO ammunition, the GMPG, or Gimpy in the parlance. The rounds were large, .762—or 308, as they called them in America—and he was going to need a thousand of them for the hit itself.

But for now, what concerned him was the pattern they formed on the lake, and his task in nearly three weeks of practice had been to tighten the pattern each day until he was sure he had the tightest area of drop to hit the target without causing too much damage over a wider area.

He had no idea of the identity of the target, and he didn't ask. They would tell him when he needed to know, and perhaps they would not tell him who the target was at all. It didn't matter to him either way. He was specialist, and his fan club, as he imagined it, was growing with every hit he made.

Besides, at half a million a job, who needed to ask questions?

But even before the practice in this infested hellhole down in Louisiana, he'd needed to inspect the actual location for the shot, and that was up in the capital. For he wouldn't be aiming the machine gun himself on this job. It would all be done remotely. He needed an exact map of the target area, with contours and a horizon measurement. It was all information that an Ordnance Survey map, or U.S. Geological Survey, as they called it here, as well as a theodolite that measured horizontal and vertical angles, could provide.

He'd done this preparation in the capital, on the roof of the six-storey building from which the furious blast of fire was planned to emanate. The blast would leave the roof of the building, arc over a second, higher building, and descend perfectly on the target.

The building was well away from the centre of the city. If he wondered why it was all to happen from this obscure building so far from the main action, and why it was on the date of the new president's inauguration, so many miles away—way beyond the range of his weapon—he didn't ask, even to himself. At any rate, it was nothing to do with the president himself.

Out on the hillock by the lake, he set up the barrel, bolting it to the solid platform just as it would be on the roof for the shot itself.

With each day, the pattern improved, but it was still not good enough even after two weeks, still too widespread, and he gave himself the extra days he needed. The testing was exhaustive, but eventually it came into the tight circle he knew he required.

He changed the barrel on the gun twice when it became shot out with practice, and finally, when he had the pattern that worked, he set up the barrel he would use, inserted some of the green spot ammunition in a belt, and fired off a few rounds, just enough to see the pattern and not to damage the barrel. It was the perfect circle.

And now, sitting in this bar in the northern Washington, D.C., suburb of Bethesda and watching the preliminary preparations for the inauguration, all he needed was an order. The gun was bolted to the roof, the theodolite was bolted to the gun instead of a normal gun sight, and a solenoid was fixed in place, between the trigger and the guard, with a cell phone attached beside it.

All it would take now was for him to dial the number, and a thousand rounds of ammunition would be discharged automatically, with their instant and inevitably destructive force that would destroy the target and everyone within twenty-five yards—and finally destroy even the barrel itself.

Even now, sitting in the bar, minutes perhaps before the action, he didn't question who the target was. The target was apparently unconnected to the inauguration itself. Maybe it was a figure who had come to Washington just for that day, like so many other big hitters; some businessman who wished to be near the action. The inauguration was, perhaps, simply cover his controllers were using for their own reasons.

On the television, the anchorman was rambling about some minor aspect of the presidential procession later that afternoon, and so it would go on as the day unravelled. He sipped his beer carefully, and waited.

When the call came, it was not what he'd expected. He was told to wait. It was not the order to fire. His contact would be with him shortly, the voice said.

Lars clicked the phone shut. The shot might be postponed, or it might be cancelled. Not unusual. Sometimes a target didn't follow the agenda he'd planned to follow. The accuracy of the timing for the shot was absolute, and there might be new arrangements.

He didn't like it, however. He'd done his work with impeccable care; why couldn't others do the same? He didn't like it either that here, in America, his controllers were always hovering nearby, ever-present in the background. He preferred to work alone and far from interference.

But it was their commission, and theirs to proceed with or not. Either way, he'd pick up payment. That's what they always told him. So he sat tight and drank now more freely from the bottle.

In a little under five minutes—a very short time, he thought dimly—two men entered the bar, one of whom he recognised as his contact, a tall, thin-faced man with a loose flapping coat and big shoes. Lars had met the American three times before, twice in Europe and once over here.

The other man he barely noticed.

They approached his table, sat down, and ordered a beer for each of them and a second one for him.

His contact took the phone from which the trigger call was to be made away from him. "Just to be safe," the man said. "If we have to abort, we'll have to dismantle the whole thing fast."

Lars agreed, without knowing exactly what he was agreeing to. But he knew better than to allow his frustration to distort his mood. There were setbacks, even on a job as precise as this one.

"We'll drink the beers and then go see the boss," the thin man said. "Further instructions," he explained.

Lars finished the first bottle and caught up with them on his second. The TV droned on without release. He was hearing what he'd already heard for the second or third time.

They left the bar after half an hour and headed away from the centre of the capital, into the suburbs, and then joined the Beltway towards the west. There were just the three of them, in a black Mercedes truck that Lars observed was bulletproofed, a special and expensive order. His controllers were, he knew, rich. They'd paid him a million and a half already.

They left the Beltway just before it crossed the Potomac and turned to the right along the riverbank. The waters swirled around a wide bend ahead of them. They pulled off the road again and down a paved road that turned to a track. There was another car parked ahead of them, black also but more like a limousine. Lars saw two figures sitting in the back seat, a chauffeur upfront.

"We may have to get you out of the country," the thin man said reassuringly. "That's what we'll find out."

But Lars didn't feel reassured.

They stopped the Mercedes thirty yards from the other car, and the three of them got out and began to walk the intervening distance.

Lars saw the thin man and his colleague walk some way to either side of him, and he began to realise his vulnerability as the space around him widened. By the time the misgivings that had dipped in and out of his consciousness since the job was interrupted had finally surged to the front of his mind, he felt the sharp, stabbing pain below his left shoulder and saw himself, as if separated from his body, falling sideways into the mud at the side of the track.

Maybe he heard the small fizz of air from the silenced gun, or maybe it was his last breath escaping from his lungs, but that was the last thought he may or may not have had.

The thin man bent down and tested Lars's pulse.

"That's it," he said to the two figures approaching from the limousine.

Then he and his colleague turned the body over, searched the pockets, and, finding nothing incriminating, slipped an identity card into Lars's wallet. It had a Russian name and Russian embassy clearance.

The thin man took the phone he had earlier taken from Lars and slipped that too back into the pocket of Lars's brown leather jacket.

As he did so, one of the men from the limousine made a call on his cell phone.

"We've found him," he said. "And just in time, by the look of it. It seems he had another terrorist attack planned. We got him at last."

The man receiving the call sat alone in an office at Langley. The agency was unusually depleted of staff today.

"Good work," he said. "The nation will be grateful to you and your company."

There was a pause as he listened to the directions the caller gave him to find the location by the river.

"Is he alive?" he said.

"No," the caller said. "Terminated. He pulled on my guys. They didn't have a choice."

"Pity."

"We've searched him," the caller said. "The evidence seems clear. It looks like it was the Russians behind him after all."

"Then it's a great feather in your cap, and your company will no doubt see the benefits."

35

MIKHAIL GOT UP FROM his seat at the next picnic table and crossed the few feet to where Anna was sitting. He sat opposite her and looked into her eyes.

"Icarus was disinformation," he said. "What the CIA calls a canary trap."

"How can you be sure?" she said, and felt her pulse quickening as the implications began to flood in.

"I'm sure," he said.

"Then why did you come, Mikhail? Why not use a dead drop?"

But she knew the answer to the question before she asked it.

"The trap springs," he replied, "as soon as someone mentions Icarus. That was the whole purpose of Icarus. A fake operation set up solely to catch the enquirer."

"Then why haven't they arrested you?" she said.

"Simple greed," he replied. "They want you too, Anna."

She let the implications of this swirl in her brain and then took out the cell phone from her pack and switched it on.

"Make the call," Mikhail said. "I can't go back now. That's why I didn't use a drop. I'm coming over." Mikhail looked up over her shoulder. "Icarus was all about finding me. It's the end," he said.

She followed his gaze and recognised, standing in the trees two hundred yards away, the biker she had seen earlier. There he was, a yellow helmet, black Lycra pants, the same cycling sweater . . . but there was no bicycle anymore.

She swivelled her gaze across the sixty degrees or so of her vision from the small portalled sanctuary of the stone building. There were two more men. She recognised the man who she'd seen earlier walking the dog. But there was no dog. The other man she hadn't seen before.

"We don't know what's behind us," he said. "Behind the building. But there'll be more. They've been waiting for nearly ten years for this. Make the call now. This is what they've wanted since Finn was first revealed in Moscow, to have the source Mikhail."

She began to dial Burt's number.

"How did you let yourself be followed?" she said to Mikhail.

"I took every precaution. But once they knew it was me, they've had all the time in the world."

The biker moved out of the cover of the trees towards them. The two other men were already walking towards them. And there'd be more, as Mikhail said, behind the building.

"Glencarlyn Park," she said into the phone. "You're two miles away. We're in a stone building to the north of the park. Be fast. We're under attack."

One of the two men was talking into a radio. All three men were quickening their pace. They'd seen her use the phone.

She withdrew the Thompson pistol from inside her arm and slotted a rifle round into the single shot chamber.

She and Mikhail withdrew behind the thin cover of the pillars. They were trapped here. It was better to stay in cover than to break around the side of the building.

She saw one of the men, the one she'd seen earlier with the dog, draw a weapon from his coat. She'd take him first, the armed man, take as many of them as she could before any more came at them from the back. She aimed the pistol from a hundred and fifty yards, and the man dropped like snow sliding from a roof.

She reloaded and saw the other two men fan away to the side, weapons drawn now. Then she saw a fourth man, right on the edge of her peripheral vision. He was close up to the right corner wall of the building, where the U extended, and using it as cover. He was only twenty yards from where they stood. The other two men began to run, moving targets, dodging at angles across the park but in the general direction of the cover to the side of the building.

Then a fifth figure appeared just at the corner of the other wall, twenty yards to the left this time.

She aimed at his left shoulder, all that was visible, as the first bullet from his revolver hit the pillar behind which she stood. The pillars were too thin to get right behind.

She thought her shot had grazed the edge of his shoulder, and he spun away, but it might have been just his reaction to her shot, rather than a hit. She reloaded fast. They'd know now she only had a single-shot weapon, and there were five of them, at least. It was just a matter of time—and of which of them was prepared to put himself in the line of fire.

A half-dozen shots rang out against the pillars, and she ducked back away from them. They would bombard her, and under that cover one of them, maybe two, would make a rush.

She glanced at Mikhail, standing six feet away from her behind the next pillar. Why was he unarmed? If he knew the dangers, why had he come without protection?

She fired again. She didn't see whether the shot had made its target or not.

"Shoot for the man to the left," Mikhail ordered her.

It was the man she thought she'd hit in the shoulder. She saw the edge of a coat flapping around the wall, and she ran to the right, from pillar to pillar, until she reached the far right edge of the yard, from where she could get a better view of the left wall, and where anyone firing from the right would have to come out and expose themselves in order to get a clear shot.

This time she knew she'd got the man to the left and saw the body fall away from behind the wall, surprised by her new angle of fire. Another volley came from the right-hand wall, as a gun was pointed around the wall and fired blindly.

"They'll want me, at least, alive," Mikhail shouted down the row of pillars.

At that moment, as the man to the left fell, she saw that Mikhail was running across the yard towards the left wall, away from the thin protection they enjoyed and into the open. He was taking the chance that there was nobody else to the left, but at the same time he left himself wide open from the right.

And they wanted him alive. That was his gamble, to make time for her.

She simultaneously heard the high-pitched roar of an engine and saw the Humvee swerving across the lawns beyond the trees.

Then she saw Mikhail fall. He was down. In quick succession and under heavy covering fire in her direction, she saw another man run to the fallen body of Mikhail.

It was Vladimir.

The Humvee thumped across a shallow ditch and along the edge of the trees, three or four hundred yards away, its tyres kicking up gouts of wet earth and lawn as it swivelled at them, its engine roaring.

She saw Vladimir look up as he dragged the body of Mikhail by the shoulders towards a van that had pulled up behind him, its back doors flung open. She saw his eyes and felt the ricocheting bullets fly around her head as the men to the right gave him cover while he sought to drag Mikhail's body, alive or dead.

She saw in his eyes the Vladimir she'd hoped never to see. It wasn't the Vladimir who had saved her life five years before, nor the Vladimir who had questioned their superiors many years before that, and been sentenced to the Cape Verde Islands for his pains. It wasn't the Vladimir she'd known since she was ten years old, at School No. 47 on Leninskaya Street, the Vladimir who had loved her from that moment on.

This was a new Vladimir, the one who had chosen, she now saw, to set his career and his life on being the one to track down Mikhail. It was the Vladimir who wanted to be KGB General Vladimir, who had made his final choice; to be inside the regime in Russia Finn had so fatally hated, and the Russia from which she'd escaped.

Careless of exposing herself now to the wild firing from farther up the same wall where she was crouched behind the pillar, she shot this Vladimir between the eyes.

Then she slumped to the ground, aware only that all the shooting had stopped, and she was sinking into her own blood.

36

LOGAN WALKED INTO THE Venus Apollo nightclub for the third night in a row. The only difference a casual observer would notice in his appearance from the previous two visits was that he now walked with a pair of crutches.

He was frisked at the door by two dark-coated, scowling bouncers, one of whom had a knife scar on the left side of his face.

Passing their scrutiny, he limped to the hole in the wall inside the club where the girl took the customers' coats. He checked his crutches too, with the coat and hat. He then limped unaided into the green velvet-draped lobby, where he was frisked again. This time, there was the flicker of recognition, even of welcome, in the otherwise expressionless face. For two nights, Logan had been making his presence known.

He was finally allowed, with the minimum of civility, to proceed unmolested into the huge kitsch cave of faux stars twinkling from the ceiling, beneath which a long curving aluminium bar set into a mock rock wall snaked into the semidarkness.

He walked with effort along the length of the bar, nodding a friendly greeting to the fashion-model hookers who, he knew from previous conversations, studied in the daytime at Moscow's universities for their psychology degrees or veterinary diplomas. And as he had done for the past two nights, he declined their offers of a private room, two-at-a-time, anything-you-like sex and found a quiet place to sit.

He chose a seat on a curved red velvet banquette that half-encircled an unoccupied table at the far end of the long, high room. Stars glittered above him against the indistinguishable surface, and for the third night in a row, he ordered vintage Dom Perignon at $2,500 a bottle.

The girls saw an opportunity to strike up conversation about his injury. One or two came to the table, made noises of sympathy, asked him what he had done, but they didn't stay. They were wary of him now. On his previous two nights, he had turned all of them away one by one and, as he had done so, paid them $500 each to leave him alone, with the promise of another five hundred if they stayed away. The strangely behaving American was making a name for himself at the Venus Apollo.

When he'd arrived in Moscow three days before, he'd rented an apartment in the Kitai district, where the older houses hadn't yet been levelled by developers in the previous decade of Moscow's smash-and-grab property boom. For $10,000 a week in cash, paid on a weekly basis, he'd taken the apartment for a month, on the reasonable assumption that the owner wouldn't turn him in until the final payment had been made. But by that time, he'd be long gone, whichever way his mission went.

There were great advantages to be had in times of economic meltdown, he thought, if you had cash. Moscow's high-end rental market had crashed, its nightclubs were emptied of high-rolling foreigners, and even the rich Russians who'd watched their paper assets descend into negative numbers were curbing their more outrageous displays of wealth.

He guessed that the girls at the Venus Apollo had earned more from him in the past two nights than in the previous month, and for doing nothing.

Nobody but Logan was drinking the club's most expensive champagne, and nobody came alone unless they were looking for a girl, let alone paying the women to stay away.

The bar manager brought him the bottle in an ice bucket and swivelled the cork free. He poured a glass and asked him, as he was bound to do, what other services the club could provide—by which he meant company.

"Nothing. This is all," Logan said.

He sat back in the gloom, sipped the champagne, and waited.

Grigory Bykov entered the club at just after midnight, the same as he had done on the previous two nights. It was a routine, Logan thought. He probably did a tour of his other business and entertainment interests before coming here. As on the two nights past, he was accompanied by four burly men in suits; big hands, big angry faces, big thighs, they swung their weight through the bar like wrestlers before a crowd at the start of a fight.

Bykov talked to the manager as he had done before—numbers, Logan assumed—and then settled into a table with the guards and a flock of girls. Later, on the basis of his behaviour so far, Bykov would go upstairs to the VIP room.

Logan drank another glass and watched the desultory scene in the club. There were few customers, fewer still who were paying anything that Bykov would call a living wage. Moscow had changed from the Babylon it had been.

The music beat against the walls and his ears, and beyond the bar, there was a dance area with flashing lights, empty but for a girl who thrust herself around a pole.

He was suddenly aware that one of the four men who had entered with Bykov was standing over him. He'd expected it, if not tonight then the next night or the one after. He looked up and saw another blank, expressionless face.

"Mr. Bykov, the owner, wants you to join him," the man said.

"Thank him," Logan replied. "I'm fine where I am."

The man didn't respond, or move.

"It's an invitation," he said, but his tone of voice was anything other than inviting.

"Then I'll join him," Logan said.

The man snapped his fingers to a barman, who swiftly appeared at the table and picked up the bucket with the half-full bottle and waited for Logan to get painfully to his feet, before following them to Bykov's table.

Bykov didn't get up when Logan appeared, and Logan was shown to a spare chair next to him. After some business manoeuvring his leg, he struggled into it satisfactorily.

"No dancing tonight," Bykov said, and laughed at him.

Logan looked up and into the face of Finn's murderer, the Russian MP with his years of Mafia experience and not much else. He saw a short man—Logan could tell, even though they were all sitting down. Bykov's face had the marks of smallpox scars, and one eyebrow seemed to have been severed in two, giving his face a lopsided expression. His eyes were small—aggressive and defensive at the same time. His expensive suit he somehow made to appear like a sheet thrown over an unwanted sculpture.

It was a mark of wealth he wore with utter disdain for the civilised world of tailors and designers of fashion, a world he seemed metaphorically to spit on. The hands that rested on Bykov's chair were thick and shapeless, the blunt tools of a killer.

"No." Logan smiled back. "No dancing. I had an accident on the ice."

Bykov wasn't a man who smiled or laughed unless it was at somebody else's discomfort.

"Safer inside," Bykov said. "Inside here."

Drinks were ordered, including another bottle of Dom Perignon, which Logan guessed accurately would find its way onto his bill later, and they all went upstairs in a lift to Bykov's private VIP area.

"Less noise," Bykov explained on their way up.

More girls arrived when they were seated in a wide circle of expensive sofas. It was like the setup in a Kazakh tent, Logan thought, and wondered if Bykov's deeper origins were in Central Asia. But this time, Logan had let two girls sit on the sofa on either side of him.

"You don't like my girls," Bykov said bluntly.

"I like them very much," Logan replied.

"You a blue boy or something?" Bykov said, meaning a homosexual. "You pay them to go away. Why?"

"No, not a blue boy. Just a connoisseur," Logan said.

"You won't find better girls than this in the whole of Moscow. In the whole world," Bykov said, and stroked the hair of the blonde beauty next to him as if she were a dog.

"Maybe later in the week," Logan said. "If I haven't found somewhere else to spend my evenings."

"How long are you in Moscow?"

"A month . . . maybe more. It depends."

"Come to my club every night. We'll give you a discount. Better than any you'll find in Moscow."

"Thank you," Logan answered. "I may do that."

The drinks arrived, and a new barman opened the bottle of champagne. Bykov's guards drank beer or vodka.

"American," Bykov stated, when they'd toasted each other.

"That's right," Logan said.

"What are you doing in Moscow?"

"I'm an investor."

Bykov laughed harshly. "Funny time to invest," he said.

"The best time," Logan replied. "Everything's falling. If you have cash, you can make good deals."

"You have cash."

"A great deal of cash," Logan said.

"What's your business?"

"Luxury yachts, an agency for sports players, entertainment—anything in that line that grabs my interest."

"You have a card?"

Logan took out his wallet and removed a card with his and his company's name.

Bykov flipped it to one of his men, who disappeared through a door at the end of the room.

"Good," Bykov said. "Maybe we do business."

"Maybe," Logan said. "I'm looking for soccer players on this trip, but I'm open to other things."

Bykov's eyes seemed to weigh the possibilities with a kind of ignorant cunning.

The man returned to the room and gave Bykov Logan's card, neither with nor without a nod of approval.

Logan explained at Bykov's prompting that the L.A. Galaxy team was searching for Russian players, to supplement their harvest of European talent. Soccer, he told Bykov, is going to be big business in America someday.

Bykov, it turned out, was a soccer fan. Logan hadn't known that. They discussed the merits of various Russian players; the Spanish, Italian, and English leagues, the gambling possibilities, and other underlying opportunities that Bykov seemed equally interested in.

Finally, at half past one, Logan said he had to go. Food and then sleep, he said. Bykov insisted that they have dinner. He would take Logan to the best all-night restaurant in Moscow, open only to members and their women.

"Maybe you take home a couple of my women," Bykov said. "Tonight, it's on the house."

Bykov was bored, Logan thought. There was nothing anymore

that was extreme enough to excite his years of blunted senses. Well, that was just fine.

But he didn't go along with the Russian immediately.

"Maybe I'll do that," Logan agreed, and after protesting that he was tired and needed a decent night's sleep, and Bykov insisting that he would provide many things to keep Logan awake, Logan acquiesced with a display of reluctance to go to dinner.

There was a stretch Mercedes outside the club and two Porsche four-by-fours, one in front, one behind. All were black with tinted windows, and the Mercedes was custom-made, Logan noted, bulletproofed in its entirety, underneath too, against bombs.

There were four bodyguards in the Porsche in front of the Mercedes and three guards in the Porsche behind. The fourth guard who had entered the club with Bykov stepped into the front of the Mercedes, next to the driver.

They drove in convoy down towards Pushkinskaya and across the square.

The stretch limousine had windows between the nearly eight-foot interior where he and Bykov sat and the driver's area. There were curtains, opened now, but which Logan assumed were there for when Bykov wanted to molest some female in the back seat. There was a television and a bar, a phone and fax machine, an office in fact. Bykov enjoyed showing off to Logan the communications systems, which included some kind of advanced satellite imaging system.

Bykov switched on the TV and flicked through DVDs of extreme pornography, children's cartoons, the Australian Tennis Open, and then on to a video link with his clubs and properties. He finally chose a soccer match played the previous weekend between Spartak Moscow and Lokomotiv.

Logan sat with the crutches on his left side, away from Bykov, and slowly unscrewed the bolt that connected the two halves of the one closest to him.

They had travelled a mile from Patriarshiye when Logan made a suggestion.

"Why don't I show you my company's prospectus?" he said. "Then we can discuss exactly what I'm looking for."

"Why not?" Bykov said, sounding bored. Perhaps *prospectus* was a word that didn't figure in his usual way of business.

"I can pick it up from the hotel," Logan said.

"Which hotel?"

The game on the TV flowed up to the goal Spartak were defending, and there was a roar from the crowd as a shot hit the bar. Bykov was only half listening to Logan.

"The Kempinsky," Logan said.

Bykov grunted. He didn't like others to make plans. Then, as if it had been his own idea, he switched on an intercom that connected them to the driver. "Kempinskya," he ordered irritably. Then he flicked the switch to off.

He turned to Logan. "It's on the way, why not?" he said.

The driver looked in the mirror, acknowledging the order, and turned to the bodyguard, who radioed the two vehicles in front and behind them with the new instructions.

As the driver indicated a right turn into Okhotnyy, Bykov sat back in his seat. He fiddled with the volume control, and as he did so, Logan cut his windpipe with the Damascus steel blade gripped in his left hand. Then he withdrew it and drove it in under Bykov's ribs and up into his heart.

There was little sound, except for the noise of the soccer match. But there was going to be a lot of blood.

With his other hand Logan pressed the button that closed the curtain to the front. He turned up the TV's volume as Bykov gurgled, pumping pints of blood, and finally slumped sideways.

Logan saw that his hand and lower arm were covered in Bykov's blood. He slipped into his coat in preparation for getting out of the limousine. Then he propped Bykov up in the seat next to him, as they crossed the bridge over the Moskva River. The Kempinsky was just on the other side.

Logan's last act inside the limousine was to rifle through Bykov's pockets, careful to avoid the blood, until he found a photo ID, which he put in his coat pocket.

The limousine drew up under the arced, porticoed entrance to the Kempinsky Hotel. Logan stepped out with his crutches at the same time as the bodyguard stepped out from the front seat. The two Porsches were up ahead and behind him as he shut the car door and hobbled away inside the lobby.

Just inside the lobby, he laid the crutches against a wall and headed, as fast as he thought was unremarkable to any observer, out to the left and towards the restaurant.

Within thirty seconds he heard shouting behind him, and he ran blindly now, across the restaurant's wide carpeted floor and out of the exit onto a street that was part of the hotel and joined it to a complex set of under- and overpasses that connected it to the bridge.

He ran to the right, away from the bridge and the majority of cars, and he didn't stop running. He'd never run so fast. But it was the slowest half hour of his life.

37

ON A CLEAR BLUE morning in late May, Anna walked back down from the high mesa towards the log house. From time to time she held Little Finn's hand and, when he was tired, hoisted him up onto her good shoulder.

Snow still lay in drifts in the shadow of the forest above the house, and it would cover the high mountains that circled the valley until July. But as they descended to the cabin, spring was evident. Yellow sego lilies, red Indian paintbrush, and mauve lupins dotted the pasture, and, to Little Finn's delight, the horses were back.

Larry walked up towards them, picked up Little Finn, and put him on his shoulders.

"See any bears?" he said.

"Lots," the boy said.

Anna laughed and shook her head at Larry out of sight of her son. They walked in silence down through the pasture and into the house.

"Burt called," Larry said when they'd removed their coats and Little Finn had run into the kitchen.

She didn't reply.

"He's coming down this evening. Wants us all to go to the ranch. It's Friday, remember."

She didn't remember. The days of the week had become irrelevant up here in the mountains.

"Can't he come here?" she said.

After two operations on her shoulder in Washington and three months recuperating up here at the cabin, Anna realised she'd become comfortably—even lethargically—tied to the place. She'd watched winter change to spring with precise slowness. She'd spent most of every day with her son, and the rest of the time she'd read books, slept, and done the exercises needed to restore the muscles in her shoulder. She didn't want to go to the nearest village, let alone to Burt's ranch, fifty miles away.

"Okay," she said, when Larry didn't reply. "I suppose we'd better go."

"We'll leave in a couple of hours," he said.

Anna went up to her room and lay down. It was a long time since she'd been released from the events that ended in her wounding at the park. First, because of her injury, she'd been excused from attending the Senate Intelligence Committee's hearing. Then her presence was not required anyway. Either Burt had got her off the hook, or she was disbarred from attending for security reasons.

But Burt was still in the thick of it, up in Washington, parrying the questions of the committee day after day.

She fell asleep and dreamed of Finn.

In a high-backed leather armchair at the Senate Office Building on Capitol Hill, Burt faced the committee for the eleventh day running. Today being Friday, they were going to break early, with just one session after lunch. They were on the home lap before the weekend.

The number of committee members and cross-examiners had shrunk this afternoon to just seven; the chairman, three senators from the Intelligence Committee itself, an attorney representing the director of the CIA, another attorney for the director of the FBI, and a director of the National Intelligence Agency.

On Burt's side of the table were Bob Dupont and Cougar's senior attorney.

Burt, as usual comfortable in any surroundings, fielded questions from friend and foe alike with equanimity. He was enjoying himself, "even in there," as Bob Dupont would say later.

"We can now turn to the representative for the director of the CIA," the chairman said. "Mr. Ronald Sabroso."

"Thank you, Mr. Chairman," Sabroso replied and looked across the expansive table at Burt. "I'd like to pick up on a couple of points from your testimony of May twentieth," he said, addressing Burt. "The Russian known as 'Mikhail' made an approach to you on what date exactly?"

"He didn't make an approach to us," Burt said smoothly. "He made an approach to one of my employees, the former KGB colonel Anna Resnikov."

"Who should have been a national asset," Sabroso said acidly, "not an employee of your company."

"The former directors of the CIA and the NSA are now both working for private intelligence companies," Burt said. "Ask them where their loyalties lie today."

"Can we get back to the question, please?" the chairman interjected.

Sabroso sucked his teeth. "Given the national security risk 'Mikhail' represented, why did you or your company not inform the Central Intelligence Agency about him?"

"Firstly, Mikhail was not a security risk to the United States of America," Burt said. "He was a security risk to his own country, on our behalf. He was—or would have been—a highly valuable asset."

"Would have been?" the chairman interjected.

"Mikhail is still in intensive care, Mr. Chairman," Burt replied.

"It's not known if he'll regain consciousness and, if he does, whether he'll be of any use."

"And secondly?" Sabroso said.

"Secondly," Burt replied, "Mikhail made clear that he would only speak to former colonel Resnikov. He stipulated that anyone else, the CIA included, would result in a complete breakoff of contact on his part."

"Which resulted in a shoot-out in a park a stone's throw from where we sit," Sabroso said. "And the probable loss of Mikhail as useful source at all."

"The reason for the events in Glencarlyn Park, as I stated in my testimony, was that Mikhail had made a sudden decision to defect that morning, at that meeting. He was effectively on the run. Colonel Resnikov was meeting him at his request in the belief that she was simply making a first contact."

"They'd never made contact before?" Sabroso asked.

"Only once. In Germany. Back in 2007."

Burt stared straight back at Sabroso, daring him to challenge the statement. But Sabroso was unaware of anything concerning Mikhail outside what Burt admitted to. And Burt knew he could be confident too about Adrian keeping his mouth shut. The whole affair—Icarus, and then the blowback in the park—was principally the fault of the British. Their source, their mistake—though Burt was also sanguine enough to admit to himself that he'd fallen for Icarus too.

"If the CIA had been given knowledge of this meeting. And the FBI," Sabroso said, nodding in the direction of his fellow attorney, "then proper backup would have been provided at the park."

The senator for Wisconsin, an ally of Burt's and lobbyist for Cougar, broke in. "I think Mr. Miller has already stated that the CIA's involvement in any way would have ensured that there was no possibility at all of gaining access to Mikhail," he said. "At least, thanks to the operation of Mr. Miller's, we still have that possibility."

"And three people dead," Sabroso said. "And a behind-the-scenes row with Russia's government."

"The three dead provoked the incident in the first place," another of Burt's supporters said.

The mood of the committee, even when it was fully attended, was clearly on Burt's side. He, unlike the CIA or FBI, had taken great care to nurture its members, in particular the senators themselves. That was normal business. "Casting the lens backwards," as one of the senators had said at an earlier session, "we have to be very careful how much we can trust the CIA."

That had infuriated Sabroso and, when he was informed, the director of the CIA himself.

After the session broke up at just after three o'clock, Burt took two of the senators aside before he headed for the airport and his private jet to the south.

They walked away from the committee room and out of the building, onto the warm May lawns on Capitol Hill.

"It's pretty much there," one of them said to Burt. "You'll be found clean."

"We'll get the all-clear soon, then," Burt said.

"Yes, I'm sure. It's this other business that's really taking up their anger. This terrorist assassin debacle is causing great problems on the Hill. One of our own intelligence companies hiring an assassin to do his business on American territory! That overshadows just about everything. The Intelligence Committee are only going through the motions with you. They're saving their wrath for your rival."

"I agree with you," Burt said. "But we must go through the motions." He lit a cigar and puffed contentedly across the green expanse. "And we need to be as transparent as we can be," he added, and paused. "For future good relations with Procurement."

"There'll be no problem with that," the senator replied. "These days the government knows they have to use you guys. They don't have a choice. Next year it's predicted more than seventy percent of all intelligence work carried out by the United States will be contracted out to private companies. The state just isn't capable anymore."

"And the bad boys from the company that hired this assassin?" Burt asked. "What's going to happen to them?"

"Jail for certain, and for a very long time. It's pretty much established that they hired this assassin. Two murders in Europe, just to establish a threat. He was a Serbian, apparently, not a Russian as they claimed. And it's pretty much established that they hired him for the sole purpose of creating mayhem and then supposedly 'catching' him."

"What they did," Burt said, "was all about a smallish intelligence contract company that wanted to get big in a hurry. They were creating a threat. An artificial threat from Russia. And they did it in order to be the first in line for funding when they 'uncovered' it."

"It may cause problems all around," the senator agreed.

"I always said intelligence contracting would lead to the false creation of a threat," Burt said. "It was inevitable."

The senator looked taken aback. "So how does that square with your company?" he said.

"With Cougar?" Burt said. "If private contracting exists, then I won't just be there, I'll aim to be the biggest. But once the state has a dependency on companies like mine, it will attract every kind of cowboy. The money's too good."

Burt sighed and drew on his cigar before turning and asking the senator, "So now, because this threat was artificial, what does the committee think? Does it consequently believe there's no threat from Russia?"

"That, unfortunately, is the knock-on effect," the senator replied. "They think that if a threat needed to be created, there can't be much of a threat in the first place."

"Just as I feared," Burt said. He looked at the senator. "Then may Mikhail revive," he said. "Because Mikhail's the real thing. He knows."

The gathering at Burt's ranch five hours later was the first time Burt had seen Anna since he'd debriefed her in the hospital room. To her surprise, he flung his arms around her, the only time he'd done so since they'd met on the beach in the south of France.

As ever, he took her aside before dinner for a private talk. They went into his study.

"Last fire of the winter," Burt said as he threw more wood into the blaze. "Even the nights are getting warmer."

He poured her a glass of wine and a whisky for himself, then sat down on a chair on the opposite side of the fire.

"Cheers," he said, and they both drank. "How's the shoulder?"

"Nearly okay," she said.

"Good." They were silent for a while. Then he looked at her directly. "I have someone who wants to see you," he said. "But only if you agree to see him."

She didn't reply.

"It's Logan," he said. "He has something to say to you. He's staying in one of my guest houses, but he's not a guest. Not tonight, in any case."

Anna put down the glass carefully.

"I didn't know he'd made it."

"No. I've been keeping it away from you while you recover. But as I told you, he's one of the best I ever had."

"What does he want?"

"That, you'll have to ask him," Burt said. "But you don't have to see him at all."

But she knew she had to see Logan, to settle the matter once and for all. She followed Burt out into the darkness, and he pointed at a light in a cabin beyond the paddock at the back of the house.

"Follow the lights along the path," Burt said. "They'll take you there." He turned to go inside and left her on the path.

Anna walked up the winding path and entered the small cabin without knocking. Logan was standing at the far end of the room, texting on his phone. He looked up in surprise.

"You've got some nerve, Logan," she said. "I could feed you to the rats."

He put the phone down and walked to the centre of the room, where he stopped.

"Will you listen?" he said. "Will you sit down and listen. Just for a minute."

She hesitated. Then she moved towards the fireplace and took a chair away from the light.

Logan sat down opposite her, underneath the arc of a lamp so strong it whited out his features. He was the interrogated now.

"You don't need to tell me why you sold pictures of me and my son to the Russians and everyone else," she said. "The reason's clear. It's the same reason that another man, a Russian, killed Finn. For money, prestige, power. How does it feel to win it that way, Logan?"

"It feels shit," he said.

"That's it? You want my forgiveness?"

"Yes. That's what I most want in the world."

Anna remained silent and looked at Logan. It was easy to forgive someone for whom you'd lost respect, she thought. It meant nothing.

"So what happened?" she said. "In Russia? I didn't expect to see you again."

Logan got up out of his chair and went to the table where he'd been standing when she arrived. He picked up something and re-turned. Hovering on the edge of the light from the lamp, he threw it gently at her feet.

She saw it was an identity card, on what looked like a gold chain. She picked it up and saw the photo, the name. It was the man Burt had told her about, the member of Russia's parliament and Finn's killer.

"He's dead? You got him?"

"Yes."

"And this?" She put the card down on the floor again. "Is this a gift for me? Like something the cat brought in."

"It's just the evidence. I wanted you to know Finn's killer is dead."

"It's what they do in Russia, Logan. The KGB kills Putin's enemies on his birthday. It's not a great tradition."

"It's all I had," he said.

"Well, I don't need it," she said, and stood up. "It's sad, isn't it. When Finn goes out to get redemption, he dies. When you go, you come back. But it's true what Burt says about you, Logan. You are very good. I'm impressed by that, at least."

"I want you, Anna," he said, looking up at her from the chair. "I want to start again. You're the only woman I've ever wanted."

She looked at him, her face softened, but it was no good.

"Thank you."

"Is there a chance? Any chance for us?"

"I'm sorry, Logan," she said. "Maybe in some other life. Just like all the others."

She stayed on the porch until she saw the taillights of his car disappear across the flat mesa to the south.